1.13.16

To Edie —

The Boundary Stone

GAIL AVERY HALVERSON

With Love,

Gail

* FIRST RUN

The Boundary Stone

GAIL AVERY HALVERSON

The Boundary Stone

Cover Design by Cathi Stevenson

ISBN 13 978-0-9969057-4-9

Printed on acid free paper

www.gailhalv.com

For my parents, my sister and nephews, and most of all, my beautiful husband and son

ACKNOWLEDGEMENTS

I could not have written this book without the incredible encouragement and enthusiasm of my sister, Cindy Hardy, my nephews, Ronnie and Robert Rast, and my very dear friends, Lisa Genereux, Lisa Chizmar, Patricia McMahon, Anne McMurray, Katie Roubanis, Sarah Smernes Edson, Beth Byers, Christine Walsh, Dawn Byers, Laurie Gregg, M.D., Christina Woollgar, and so many, many more. I am most grateful for the love and endless support of my parents, George and Sherry (Abbott) Avery, my husband, Rex and my son, Brett Halverson. I love you all.

Mark but this flea, and mark in this,
How little that which thou deniest me is;
It sucked me first, and now sucks thee,
And in this flea our two bloods mingled be;
Thou know'st that this cannot be said
A sin, nor shame, nor loss of maidenhead,
Yet this enjoys before it woo,
And pampered swells with one blood made of two,
And this, alas, is more than we would do.
Oh stay, three lives in one flea spare,
Where we almost, nay more than married are.
This flea is you and I, and this
Our mariage bed, and marriage temple is;
Though parents grudge, and you, w'are met,
And cloistered in these living walls of jet.
Though use make you apt to kill me,
Let not to that, self-murder added be,
And sacrilege, three sins in killing three.
Cruel and sudden, hast thou since
Purpled thy nail, in blood of innocence?
Wherein could this flea guilty be,
Except in that drop which it sucked from thee?
Yet thou triumph'st, and say'st that thou
Find'st not thy self, nor me the weaker now;
'Tis true; then learn how false, fears be:
Just so much honor, when thou yield'st to me,
Will waste, as this flea's death took life from thee.
-John Donne, 1663

PROLOGUE

"WE SHOULD NEVER ALLOW OURSELVES TO BE PERSUADED
EXCEPT BY THE EVIDENCE OF OUR REASON"
-RENE DESCARTES

Village of Stockbridge
Buckinghamshire, England
25 August 1660

Catherine Abbott stole quietly through a half-timbered hallway toward the wide staircase of the family quarters, carefully feeling her way in the cloaking darkness. A single curl fell from under her sleep bonnet and bounced in front of her eyes, obscuring her path. She shoved the wayward lock back into her lace nightcap and then turned to make her way down the staircase. She paused for a moment on the landing. Looking through the tall casement window, beyond the Abbey gardens that were as familiar to her as the back of her own hand, the ghostly stone chimney pots of Houghton Hall were outlined by the glow of a full moon. The sight of the imposing manor unexpectedly brought thoughts of her childhood friend to mind. A loyal, rambunctious, even reckless childhood conspirator, she'd known Miles all of her fifteen years. She smiled softly at the memories of long summer days spent running wild through the wheat fields with Miles and her younger brother, Charles, delicious memories of archery competitions and games of quiots with ropes and rocks in the cool, dark forest behind the Abbey. As she stared out over the hunting grounds toward Houghton Hall, Catherine wondered if Miles would be much changed when at last he returned from his university studies in Paris. The thought of him now, in the quiet moonlight, sent a shiver through her that she did not quite understand.

Catherine shook her head abruptly to clear her mind and tiptoed down the staircase. The sturdy wooden planks of English oak were warm to her bare feet as she descended to the floor below, but when she touched the black and white marble squares of the entrance hall, she felt a sudden chill. She wondered why the two floorings should feel so different when outside the late summer air was soft and warm. She often wondered why things were the way they were.

Catherine quietly unlatched the iron joinery on the heavily carved door of Abbottsford Abbey and slipped out into the still gardens that stretched in the moonlight toward the rolling, forested hills that surrounded the magnificent estate. She breathed deeply of the fresh, fragrant night air and untied the laces of her robe and bonnet, letting her curls tumble around her nearly bare shoulders. A slight breeze blew gently across her skin, briefly billowing the cotton ruff of her nightdress. She glanced back at the sleeping house, and then quickly crossed the courtyard toward Houghton Hall. Though she knew it hadn't rained in Stockbridge for nearly a fortnight, the dew beneath her feet was wet and cool. Again, she wondered why.

Climbing barefoot over a low, moss-covered fieldstone wall, Catherine made her way across the greensward into a luminous field of barley in full flower. Tipping her face to the heavens where millions of glittering stars sparked, she searched for something across the infinite blackness. Her gaze dropped down to an ancient oak tree at the end of the hedgerow, an ethereal sentinel in the silver light. Above the tree's crown, her gaze once again traveled upward, sweeping across the vast midnight sky. She was looking for a singular collection of stars that to her eyes looked very much like the ladle that Gussie used to serve the midday broth. At length, she found what she'd been seeking. *Ursa Major.*

Catherine reached into a small leather pouch and pulled out a charcoal stub and a piece of linen parchment paper. Working quickly, she began to sketch the position of the stars in relation to the topmost branch of the massive oak tree. Night sounds surrounded her as she laid charcoal to paper. Scores of deep-throated bullfrogs and crickets echoed by the moonlit pond where as children, the three friends scudded small boats carved from the fallen limbs they'd found in the surrounding woodlands. A hooting owl echoed softly in a nearby orchard, as she put the last few lines to her work.

When she finished, Catherine carefully folded her sketch and placed the parchment into the leather pouch, then made her way back across the grounds of the Abbey and up to the sleeping quarters. In the room next to hers, Aunt Viola softly snuffled and groaned in her sleep. Catherine quietly latched her door, and crossed over the soft tapestry rug that warmed her cozy chamber in winter. At the foot of the bed, Catherine lifted the lid of a hammered-copper trunk that her father had brought from the ancient bazaars of Bombay. She pulled a bundle of sketches from the trunk and untied the slender silk ribbon that kept them together. In a wide shaft of moonlight shining through the leaded glass windowpanes, she spread the drawings across the rug, four and twenty in number, and then laid them neatly in a row, adding her newly drawn rendering to the collection. She could hardly wait until the morning to share the drawings with her father, for with a growing sense of excitement, Catherine realized that just exactly as she had read in a book from her father's library, over the course of the summer the constellation had indeed moved from right to left over the top of the ancient oak tree. As she stared through the windowpane at the endless, star-filled sky, Catherine did not know how, but she avowed that one day she would understand the mysteries of this world.

CHAPTER 1

Smithfield, Aldgate Parish
London, England
24 December 1664

Heavy Christmas snows were falling on the small chapel of St. Michael's Church, a medieval stone parsonage just outside the boundaries of London proper. Swirling flakes and mid-winter fog were creating an eerie silence in the fields around the ancient sanctuary. Frozen ice crystals cracked beneath the hooves of the mare that was harnessed to a creaking cart. The cart pulled up short on a little-used path that led to a field just beyond the churchyard. Lashing the horse to a barren tree dripping with icy shards, two heavily cloaked men pulled shovels from the bay and made their way slowly toward a lonely corner of a snow-swept cemetery, leaning hard into a gusting wind.

"Ere," said the smaller of the two, as they stopped near a rough mound covered with new-fallen snow. He pointed toward a newly covered patch of earth.

"Dig," he grunted.

The two men began to steadily carve into the frozen heath. Just over a foot down, the rusty shovel of Ezekiel Angus Dodd hit solid pine with a heavy thud. His partner, Flynt Pollard, gazed down nervously, as Dodd stood upright, stretched his twisted spine, then leaned on his shovel and winked.

"Aye, thas it, nae," he said, glinting a crooked half-smile.

A sudden, electric shock charged through every last nerve ending of Pollard, a disreputable thief with an immoderate and largely inaccurate habit of cockfight bets. Though he knew exactly why he was here on this of all nights, hiding a small lantern in the folds of his cloak and glancing furtively across the desolate field toward the clergy-house of St. Michael's to be sure the priests were deep into their sacramental wine-fueled slumbers, he wished for all the world that he weren't. Graveyards gave him the fits.

"Bring ye' lantern closer, nae," barked Dodd.

Pollard could see that heaving the sodden weight of snow and wet dirt off a newly buried coffin was hurting Dodd's twisted back, for the little man was in a very foul mood, indeed. Pollard lowered his head and thrust his spade into the earth once more and wondered how the devil he had ever fallen in with the scheming caretaker of St. Michael's.

Pollard knew that the little caretaker was paid scant wages to polish the pews, the floors and the very large egos of the parish vicars. He also knew that Dodd was bankrupt. Slipping out of the house on Christmas Eve to dig up what he had planted mattered not a whit to the caretaker who had dragged him in on the scheme that very day over a tankard of ale. *Guineas are bloody hard to come by*, wheedled Dodd, a man with seven ravenous mouths to feed and one more on the way, and *aye, God, Pollard, we've got to take 'em where we can get 'em.* Dodd had tossed another coin on the barrelhead, tempting him mightily with another ale. That he was dead broke was more to the point, thought Pollard, grimly throwing another spade full of dirt on the snow.

"Nae, grab tha' end," whispered Dodd, his gravelly Scottish burr low and urgent.

Pollard thought for a moment about the small fortune he could make in just two days time. He also thought he might just bolt for the horse and abandon Dodd to this strange and ungodly business. Pollard stood in the knee-deep snow and cast a fearful glance at the craggy stone cairns in the little cemetery listing in the snow; melancholy markers of husbands, wives and countless children lost to the ages. The shadowy apparitions they made on the icy drifts were deeply chilling to a man of his considerable imaginations. But then he thought about the two menacing cutthroats who stood each night outside his dingy room above the brawling Ratcliff Alehouse, their twitchy fingers ceaselessly caressing well-worn sword handles, their leers and insults at the steady stream of harlots parading through the narrow, twisted hallway; and their mounting impatience for payment on the last unfortunate wager he'd made downstairs at the riotous dockside inn. He also thought about signing onto the first galleon headed for France. Mostly, though, he thought about Flossie. Uproarious, voluptuous, magnificent and truly expensive, Flossie. Two silver guineas would indeed go a very long way toward solving his most vexing problems.

Pollard sighed. "Aye."

He dropped to his knees and reached a trembling hand deep into the trenching. He took hold of a rope handle at the top end of the pine coffin that housed the remains of an unknown beggar who had just the day before passed from this world into the next, inhaled deeply, and gave a mighty jerk.

"Jaysus, the bloke's heavy enough!" muttered Pollard, heaving the coffin northward from its final resting place.

"Quiet!" Dodd hissed. "We're not being paid to measure the man, just to 'aul 'im back up."

With the beggar's coffin dragged halfway out of the muddy hole, Pollard looked up and froze. Dodd jerked his head around, his myopic eyes squinting toward the rectory.

"Damnation!" Dodd cursed, as he dropped his shovel into the snow.

A soft glimmer of candlelight appeared through a small leaded glass window above the narthex. Pollard quickly snuffed the flame of his lantern, held his breath and watched. Long seconds ticked by. The shadow of a stooped and shuffling old man crossed slowly past the windowpanes. The two men waited anxiously, as a frigid gust of wind billowed through their cloaks and swirled the snowflakes around them. Pollard shivered and pulled his woolens tighter. Dodd raised a finger to his lips.

"Shhhh," he whispered. "Don't move, nae."

Pollard nodded slightly and stood, shifting from foot to foot to keep warm. "Aye."

At length, the candle was extinguished, and once again, darkness fell over the rectory. Pollard exhaled in relief. The two men returned to their charge, struggling under a leaden moon to pull the coffin from the earth and jockey the cumbersome pine box into the bay of the waiting cart. When they'd finished, Pollard took a shovel and tossed the scattered dirt and ice back into the hole that was quickly covered by the drifting snows. *They'd be back in just twenty-four hours time, and by God's good graces, no one would be the wiser.* Pollard clambered up to the bench of the cart and reached for the reins. Dodd threw a blanket over the coffin and sat in the back.

"Giddup," hissed Pollard, more than anxious to abandon this God-forsaken snowy field.

With a quick flick, the snorting horse carried the men and their plunder back down the frozen path toward town as the faint light of dawn began to wash over the horizon.

Just outside the walls of London, the small hamlet of Smithfield was a bustling little village. In the quiet interlude before the break of day, however, the muddy lanes of Smithfield were deserted. Only the sleepy inhabitants of the local whorehouse, the fishmongers and the peasants who rose early to display their wares for the morning's market were rustling about at that particular hour of the morning. Scant attention was paid to the cart and its cumbersome cargo; the villagers had troubles enough of their own.

Pollard yanked on the reins and drew the creaking cart up short to a small, thatched roof cottage on Hawthorne Lane. He dismounted and gave a soft knock on the low, lime-washed door. From inside, the latch was unbolted and the door swung wide. Pollard was sorely troubled that they'd been in the cottage many a time over the last few months and he took a deep, apprehensive breath as they dragged a pine box from the cart once more. The two men hauled the coffin inside, banging it off the walls through a narrow hallway and past a single room sparsely furnished with a wide desk, a high-backed chair and a tidy bedstead. Pollard saw that the desk was covered with open books, stacks of papers, inkwells, quill pens and countless wooden candlestick holders, the candles burnt to the quick with heavy waxen layers dripping down the sides as though the occupant worked through many a long night. He wondered who would spend that many hours with their nose in a book.

Pollard banged into a low, timbered doorway that led into a small, windowless back room that was illuminated by several forged iron lanterns. "Mind yer 'ead," whispered Dodd. Pollard snarled and rubbed at the growing lump on the top of his skull.

Flickering candlelight cast macabre shadows upon the rough, plastered walls. With nary a word spoken, they pried the top off of the coffin and set the lid down on a freshly swept stone floor. The two men grunted as they heaved the lifeless body of the beggar up and onto a bare wooden table. Pollard literally shook in his shoes as he dared to glance around the cluttered chamber that was overflowing with journals and curious sketchings tacked with crude nails upon the earthen walls. He was truly spooked and more than ready to hie from this strange dwelling. Dodd was handed a small leather pouch. He took a quick glance inside. Two silver coins glittered in the candlelight.

"Two more on the morrow," came a quiet voice from the shadows.

"Aye. An' happy Christmas to ye, sir," said Dodd, briefly tipping the brim of his hat as he and Pollard backed nervously down the narrow hall.

Outside, Dodd dropped one coin into Pollard's trembling hands, and quickly pocketed the other, thinking of the Christmas feast he could now afford for his burgeoning family.

Then the two men, having completed their midnight labors, headed into the early light of dawn, satisfied with their wages and very well satisfied to have this ungodly night over. They left the small cottage as the sun began to rise above the pastoral hamlet. The door was latched quietly behind them.

In the windowless back room of the tidy thatch roofed cottage, a pearl-handled knife blade glittered in the light of a flickering candle, suspended over the now shirtless body of the beggar. Outside, the muted footfalls and low murmurings of the village waking to a Christmas morning could be heard. Somewhere in the cottage, a small clock softly chimed the early hour. A heartfelt prayer of forgiveness on this, the holiest of days, was whispered. Then, the razor-sharp bladepoint of a pearl-handled knife met the soft, yielding flesh of a man at once unknown and uncared about in this world, with a very practiced hand.

CHAPTER 2

Abbottsford Abbey
Stockbridge, Buckinghamshire
25 December 1664

The ferocious Christmas Eve storm that blasted through the county of Buckinghamshire during the night had finally subsided during the early hours of the morning. Raging snows had turned into the soft crystalized flakes that were now floating to earth, creating a magical mid-winter backdrop to the excitement that was about to take place inside the Abbey. In the cookery belowstairs, excitement of a different sort was unfolding.

"Mind ye, lass! The dried cherries go in tha' batter over there," cried Gussie Crawdor, to Annie, a heavily pregnant, dim-witted scullery maid.

Gussie pointed to an earthenware pipkin on the wooden sideboard of the Abbey's kitchen as the startled young girl jumped, dropping the wooden spoon she held.

"Great Gods!" cursed the exasperated cook to no one in particular. "I'll do it, m'self." She grabbed the spoon up off the floor. "Get along with ye', dearie," she sighed.

The cook tossed the spoon into the wash bucket as Annie clutched at her side and lumbered for the safety of the larder.

Gussie Crawdor ran her kitchen with an excitable temper that matched the frizzled russet hair that was constantly threatening to spring in all directions from the rough cloth that was tied around her head and she was in no mood to suffer a fool, no matter how befuddled or delicate her condition.

Pre-dawn preparations for the Abbey's Christmas feast had begun well before the household arose, and Gussie was responsible for it all. She took up the wooden vessel Annie had abandoned, rested it on her hip, and stirred the velvety cherry trifle batter with a well-seasoned stroke.

Gussie leaned back against the sideboard and contemplated tonight's guests who would include, to her everlasting vexations, Lord Mayor Hardewicke of the neighboring town of Wells, who sat with Lord Abbott on the board of the British East India Company. Lord Mayor Hardwicke, a lusty ne'er-wed whose outsized girth matched his outsized opinion of himself, could be quite the rouser. Gussie always thought he had an eye for Lady Viola, but then again, the Lord Mayor had a barker's eye for any lass in a skirt. *Aye, he was a cracking twaddler*, she chuckled, mentally ticking through the rest of the guest list. There would be the families of the neighboring estates, including the aristocratic inhabitants of Houghton Hall, and the well-to-do villagers from the little hamlets of both Stockbridge and Wells. *Thank heaven that the good Reverend Jessup sent his regrets,* she thought; *he was always quite the prig with his dour Puritan preachings. Aye, the feast would not nearly be as riotous if he turned up.* She sighed. *So much to do.*

Another thought struck the feisty cook. *The engagement of her lambkins to the spirited and spoiled Houghton lad.* Though Gussie was not entirely sure she approved of the match, for she thought the lad far too cocksure for her taste, she thanked God once again that it was not for her to gainsay the curious ways of the wealthy. Gussie gave the batter one final stir, and then thrust the bowl into the hands of a passing kitchen maid.

"Into the oven, one hour," she instructed briskly, and went searching for her husband.

"Archie!' she yelled, as he tended to the coals in the cove of the massive kitchen hearth, "bring three cases of Bordeaux up from the cellarage." "Put 'em in the larder!"

"Aye, lovey," said Archie, cheerfully swinging down a heavy sack full of kindling for the fire from his broad shoulders.

With everyone attending to their duties, a momentary hush

fell over the kitchen. Gussie worked through the evening's events, crossing off the tasks as soon as they were completed. Lord Abbott would make an announcement of the betrothal tonight and wine for toasting the young couple would have to be at the ready. She watched as Archie finished stoking the grate, then laughed out loud as he blew her a kiss on his way to the cellar.

The massive wooden worktable anchoring the center of the downstairs cookery overflowed with a profusion of batters, puddings, and pastries. Wooden staves laden with freshly slaughtered beef and lamb from the fields surrounding the estate were stacked off to one side. On the planked sideboards, several maids were polishing all manner of silver candlesticks and chargers, and laying out pewter table settings for the evening's feast.

The thick stone and plaster hearth that dominated a small coved chamber at the far end of the kitchen burned hotly with pungent oak timbers under a rotating iron rod that was coupled by chains to an ingenious roasting contraption. Charles and Catherine had invented the device when Gussie complained that her cooking pots were not big enough to roast more than two chickens. Gussie often marveled at the cleverness of her young charges. She had never seen such resourcefulness in ones so young. Especially from a wealthy family where spoiled children were routinely banished to their playrooms, only to be raised by hard-working servants to potter away their frivolous little lives with the foolish offspring of other wealthy families. Thank the good Lord that her lambs had been raised more sensibly. *Aye,* thought Gussie, slamming the cook stove door on a roasting pan full of turnips and onions, *if they had, to those two could make their way in the world just fine.*

Looking over at the massive stone hearth, Gussie was delighted to see that the long iron rod gigamaree they'd invented now held ten fragrant, golden brown chickens roasting evenly over the fire. A solemn-faced little girl with wispy yellow hair plaited down her back sat on a three-legged milking stool and slowly cranked the gear with a wooden handle. Sizzling, fragrant juices from the hens dripped into heavy copper pots nestled deep into the coals that would later be made into gravies. The chickens were the first of more than threescore that would be slaughtered by several young field boys throughout the long day.

Glowing with perspiration, Gussie took a moment to lean against a counter and wipe her damp brow with the threadbare linen apron she wore on heavy workdays. She took hold of the hem and flicked at a long-legged spider crawling its way across a pine storage cabinet, then gathering her thoughts, crossed the well-worn black and white marble squares of the warm, comfortable cookery, and shouted briskly to a small army of help borrowed for the occasion from the neighboring estates.

"Look sharp, nae! Bridget, Sarah, and Alice; yer' on the desserts down there," she called out, pointing to a counter at the far end of the cooking hall.

She looked over to the Lord Mayor's cook, Eliza, borrowed for the day to lend her sharp wit and considerable organizational skills to the preparations.

"Eliza! You'll oversee the girls?"

"Aye, Gussie," she called cheerfully. Gussie watched as, grinning, Eliza turned to the three maids and clapped her hands. "Get on with ye' girlies, do as she says!"

Under Eliza's direction, the three startled young maids quickly clattered to the end of the worktable and began to measure and mix ingredients into several large pattypans, stirring the velvety batters with large wooden paddles.

"McTavish, Johnny and me own Mr. Crawdor; yer' on the meats—and mind ye', don't be stingy with th' carvin'," yelled Gussie.

Archie Crawdor laughed as he passed by and gave his ample wife a lusty smack on her broad behind. Gussie swatted his hand away.

"Nae, d'ye think I've time fer yer tomfoolery this mornin', Mr. Crawdor? Get th' wine from the pantry, then toss another log on the fire, ye' daft man!"

Collecting the hand-forged pewter forks and knives in the larder, the pregnant maid, Annie, felt a searing stab of pain across her midsection. She inhaled sharply and clutched at her side, then fell to her knees with a second agonizing wave. The utensils clattered loudly back down into the pine thirkenbox they were stored in. She quickly glanced toward the chaos in the kitchen and closed her eyes, desperate to will the pain away. Hearing the commotion, Gussie poked her head in the pantry.

"Are ye all right, Annie?"

"Aye, ma'am," she said, grabbing the silverware, terrified that the baby was coming early and she would be sent home. She hated to miss a fancy party.

Gussie narrowed her eyes at the ungainly scullery maid. "Is yer' time near?" she asked.

"No, ma'am," she breathed." "Not for at least a fortnight, perhaps longer, I'm told."

"Are ye sure?"

The girl nodded, wide-eyed. A skeptical Gussie was nonetheless satisfied with the answer; for she needed every last pair of willing hands she could get this day.

"Aye, then back to it, m'lass," said Gussie, cheerfully steering Annie toward the wash buckets.

The intense, cracking pains slowly eased off. Annie breathed a heavy sigh of relief and reached for the soapy wash bucket. Gussie turned her attention back to the chaos of the kitchen and shook her head at the days work that lay ahead of them all.

CHAPTER 3

Blissfully unaware of the drama unfolding belowstairs, Catherine snuggled deep into the goose down feather mattress that lay upon her elaborately hand-carved tester bed. She savored the delicious warmth of the thick eiderdown coverlet that enveloped her and thought of the days and years that lay ahead.

"Betrothed." She dared to breathe the word aloud.

Catherine drew the crisp, finely woven Holland sheets up to her chin and absently bit her thumbnail, a habit from childhood that she fell to when deep in thought. Aunt Viola had tried many a time to make her stop; first wrapping her thumb in strips of rough cloth, then slapping her hand out of her mouth, and then finally, dipping her thumb into a vile-tasting poultice made of vinegar and ground mustard seeds. When her efforts failed to break Catherine of the habit, her aunt fell into an endless series of tiresome lectures, often chiding that no man would marry a lady with the hands of a field boy.

Catherine almost laughed aloud at the thought of her high-strung, maiden aunt giving marriage advice. She rolled over and leaned her head back upon her hands and wondered how much life would change from being a schoolgirl in the pretty herringbone brick and timbered abbey, her every move watched over by governesses, tutors and her over-bearing aunt, to becoming the mistress of the massive stone pile that was Houghton Hall.

It was, she knew, an arranged marriage. She bore no silly, girlish illusions about love and romance, being made fully aware from birth of the expectations of wealthy men's daughters. Aunt Viola had quite seen to that. Though Catherine, by most measures, considered her title to be a bother, Viola nearly always swooned at the thought of her niece becoming the future Countess

Houghton. Catherine supposed that Miles carried the full weight of his peerage as well, being the only Houghton heir. Nonetheless, she thought, Miles seemed to far more easily delight in the considerable privileges that accompanied his title than she.

Lord Abbott and the Earl of Houghton had long agreed that she and Miles would be married, though Charles would by law inherit the Abbey, their marriage was to be a ceremonial union of the two estates. A masterful stroke of commerce and ceremony to be sure, yet since she'd known Miles the full measure of her life, she did not entirely disapprove. Father would make the announcement at the banquet tonight. She wondered what the other young ladies of the village would say, their petty jealousies always on the tip of their sharp tongues.

Catherine smiled, knowing the excitement that her marriage would bring to Stockbridge. The little village and it's neighbor, Wells, were tiny, peaceful hamlets nestled together like two spoons in a gentle, forested glen nearly a full days carriage ride to the southwest of London. Had she lived through Charles's birth, the beautiful Lady Tamesine Abbott would have journeyed with Catherine to London during one of Lord Abbott's business trips where they would have shopped for weeks, assembling an elaborate marriage wardrobe of sturdy riding habits, sensible day gowns, shooting and walking gowns, elaborate court-gowns, sheer petticoats, corsets, nightgowns and delicate chemises, as well as fur cloaks and heavy woolen doublets.

Catherine looked up at the brilliant colors in the tapestry tester hanging above her bed and thought wistfully of the glorious adventure she and her mother would have had while she was fitted and fussed over for her marriage gown by the finest of London dressmakers. She sighed. There was only Aunt Viola to oversee the ceremony now, and she would not be nearly as much fun shopping for such fripperies. Talented with the needle, her beloved French tutor, Lisette Chanon from the village, would craft her wedding costume.

Catherine shivered under the covers. She'd thrown her heavily burnished tapestry curtains wide overnight so that she could see the winter snowfall, but by the morning a deep chill had set into her sleeping chamber. Pulling the bedclothes high over her head, she lay still and dreaded setting her feet to the cold floor. A soft knock at the door announced the arrival of her young chambermaid, Jane, who quietly entered to light the morning fire. Catherine groaned. Soon, a crackling warmth began to fill the room.

"Christmas services in twenty minutes time, Miss." said Jane, selecting a fur-trimmed gown and deep green woolen over-cloak from a massive English oak armoire.

Catherine gazed over at a heavily carved wooden cross that hung next to her bed. She bit her thumbnail once again, contemplating the dreadfully long church service that lay ahead. She looked over to the slight handmaid as Jane lifted the woolen gown from a hanging peg and began to freshen it with a few quick strokes of a small straw brush.

"Do you believe in God, Jane?"

Catherine watched as Jane nearly dropped the gown in shock. It was clear that no one ever had ever asked the young maid her thoughts on such subjects.

"Aye, I do, Miss," she breathed. "Do ye not?"

Catherine thought for a moment.

"I don't know, Jane," Catherine said softly. "I'm not entirely sure. I think I believe in only what I can see."

Catherine reached for a journal entitled "Philosophical Transactions," by the Royal Society of London that was lying next to several burned down candlesticks on the small table beside her bedstead. She read the cover aloud.

"The Royal Society, Jane." Jane looked sorely confused. "In London." Catherine tried to explain. "The Royal Society is the repository of all the known scientific knowledge in the world, can you imagine that? All the known scientific knowledge!"

"No, Mi'Lady," said Jane, turning back to her task.

Catherine opened the cover, running her fingers over its thick, hand-pressed parchment pages and then looked up, questioning.

"Have you ever heard of Copernicus, Jane?" she asked.

Jane looked up again and stared blankly as Catherine held the journal up for Jane to see. She tapped on the slim volume.

"No, Miss," replied Jane, warily. Catherine opened the book and pointed to a printed passage.

"Copernicus says that the earth revolves around the sun. But you see, Jane, the priests would have us believe that only *we* are in God's favor. That everything revolves around the earth, and not the other ways 'round."

Catherine lay back on her lace-edged pillows and stared up at the cross once more.

"No, Jane," she said, contemplating the carving. "I believe in God, but I don't know that I entirely believe everything the Church says."

"What about the after life? Are ye' not afraid of damnation?" asked an astonished Jane.

"I suppose I'll have to see when I get there," mused Catherine, slowly leafing through the crisp, tantalizing pages of the scientific journal.

"Aye'n wouldn't the priests have something to say about that!" said Jane. "Why, wouldn't me own father 'ave taken the strap to me for such thoughts!"

Catherine slapped the journal shut and sat straight up in bed with indignation, her chills vanishing with a fire that began to rise inside.

"The priests, indeed!" she exclaimed. "Aren't they the fine ones for telling us what to do and what to think and how to behave while doing the very opposite themselves, and all the time grandly lining their pockets with many a gold sovereign?"

The maid stopped in her tracks, wide-eyed. "I've never known anyone who wasn't afraid of the priests. Does yer' aunt know ye hold such thoughts?" Jane took a deep breath. "Aye," she whistled. "An' won't she be the buggars, then?"

"Nobody knows, Jane, nobody except Charles—and Master Howell, of course." She played with the edge of the coverlet. "He was engaged because he was the only tutor who agreed with Father that girls should be educated. If only Aunt Viola would allow me to sit with them more than once a day."

Near the top of her coverlet, Catherine picked idly at a loose thread from a thin, ice blue stripe about as wide as her quill pen woven through the flaxen fibers. She briefly wondered why anyone would weave such an unusual color into the exquisite, cream-colored sheets, then quickly abandoned the thought and turned her attention back to Jane.

"I hear them, you know. I hear them debating God and science while I am made to sit for hours in the conservatory with Aunt Viola staring over my shoulder, counting my every stitch for the May Day Fair tapestries. It's maddening."

Catherine threw back the covers and set her bare feet to the floor. She stood and stretched.

"Aye, an' yer' needlework is beautiful, Mi'Lady. And sellin' yer' work at the May Day fair does such good for th' village."

Catherine yawned. "Jane, I have no patience for embroidery."

"Nor do I, Miss," confessed Jane, helping Catherine into her gown. Catherine struggled into the sleeves, pulling impatiently at the fur trimmings.

"When Charles is finished, he lends me the scientific journals that Master Howell borrows from Gresham College in London. Father is truly interested in our thoughts and my opinions."

"Science, is it?" Jane looked terribly confused.

"Master Howell says that science is the basis of all life on this earth, and that scientific discoveries about the world are being made every day."

Catherine turned and faced her handmaid.

"Jane, I think I believe in what I can actually see, and not nursery tales for the weak and easily led," said a defiant Catherine. Speaking the words aloud for the first time, she realized that she sounded far braver than she actually felt.

Jane drew a quick breath at the thought. "Coo-ee, are ye' not frightened of the heresy? Are ye' not frightened of yer' aunt?"

Catherine smiled, instantly softening at the young girl's innocence. "If I am late to Christmas services? I am, indeed."

At that, Catherine laughed and quickly dressed in the pale morning light. Minutes later, she hurried down an icy path that cut through the barren garden to the estate's parsonage and joined her family just as the Christmas services began. Aunt Viola turned and arched a disapproving eyebrow as Catherine quietly entered the church. Her aunt absently motioned for her to join the family pew. Catherine slid in next to Charles. He gave her a slight nudge.

"*...And the shepherds in the field heard glad tidings of joy,*" intoned Father Jessup, austere and foreboding in his magnificent crimson robes behind the lectern of the small stone and timbered baptistery.

Catherine leaned back against the hard oak pew until her aunt caught her eye and motioned her to sit up straight. She sighed and sat forward, resting her hands in her lap. *Father Jessup could go on for hours*, she thought impatiently. Thank heaven for Lord Abbott's gentle, but pointed request that the good priest not stray too far from the customary canon. To her complete dismay, however, Father Jessup seemed to be warming to his biblical charge. Still waking, Catherine was having a hard time concentrating on the elaborate sermon and the ancient rituals. *Something about Micah, or Michael...* She didn't know. She wasn't interested.

Catherine's mind was drifting toward the evening's feast. Nerve endings tingled as she felt a disconcerting excitement at the very thought of seeing Miles again. Strange butterflies danced in her stomach as she thought about his dark, wavy hair, his intense brown eyes, and his wicked sense of daring. It was Miles who'd made up most of their childhood games. More than once, he'd gambled with their young lives, challenging Catherine and Charles to reckless games; swinging on vines over brooks or balancing on fallen trees that stretched across deep chasms in the woodlands that surrounded the two estates.

"Please rise," commanded Father Jessup. The small gathering took to their feet.

They'd even kissed once. She was just twelve when he'd caught her up tight in his grasp after a long game of chase through the forest. A soft rain dripped from heavy pine boughs in the deepening shadows and she remembered how his lips felt at once soft and hard, and altogether forceful. He'd caught her by the arms and pressed her up against a massive chestnut tree. The bark felt rough and it scratched against the back of her neck as she let him touch her in places she knew she shouldn't. Unfamiliar, exquisite sensations pulsed through her as he thrust himself against her again and again. She was so ashamed and confused long afterward, but he was older and she trusted him. He was brave, foolhardy, and absolutely beautiful. Oh, how she'd missed him.

"Let us pray," said Father Jessup, raising his palms reverently toward the heavens.

She felt a pinch from Charles, and quickly bowed her head, crossing herself a tick behind the rest. After an agonizing length, final blessings were bestowed and, at very long last, the family headed back up the icy garden path toward the Abbey.

CHAPTER 4

"SEE HOW A GOOD DINNER AND FEASTING
RECONCILES EVERYBODY. NEVER LAUGHED SO IN ALL MY LIFE.
I LAUGHED TILL MY HEAD ACHED"
-SAMUEL PEPYS

By mid-morning, fast-moving clouds billowing from across the Irish Sea began to break apart, creating weak shafts of sunlight that played across the snow-covered grounds of the estate. Lord Abbott gathered his family in the drawing room to open the extravagant pile of gifts under a massive spruce that he and Charles had cut from the forest behind the abbey. Lord Abbott watched as Charles, squirming with excitement and unable to wait, thrust his arm deep under the tree that was hung with festive strings of fruits, nuts and berries and illuminated by small beeswax candles suspended in scrolled iron holders.

"This is for you, Catherine!" exclaimed Charles, withdrawing a small present that was wrapped in bits of lace and tied with a pink satin ribbon from under the bottommost branches. He handed it to Catherine.

"I bought it myself," he said, his ruddy cheeks flushed with excitement and the small glass of mead he'd been permitted to indulge in.

Catherine smiled at her brother and unwrapped the little gift. She held the contents up, not entirely assured of what she was looking at. It was a tear-dropped shaped bit of glass cut with many sides, about as big as a quail egg that was suspended from a delicate black silk cord with an intricately carved silver clasp. The little glass egg turned slowly on the cord.

"Oh, Charles, it's a necklace!" Charles laughed and jumped to his feet.

"It's called a prism! Hold it up to the window!" he cried, barely able to contain his excitement.

Curious, Catherine crossed to the bay window and held the prism up to the leaded-glass panes that were bedecked for the season with heavily laden boughs of greenery. At that moment, the sun broke through a scudding cloud and to everyone's delight; the room was suddenly awash in glorious, spiraling coronas. Every color imaginable was dancing on the walls of the gathering room. Even the servants were drawn from their duties to marvel at the wondrous sight.

"Oh, Charles, it's beautiful!" she breathed. "Where did you get it?"

"I bought it from the instrument maker, Thomas Sutton, when Father and I went up to London to buy a quadrant for the voyage to India. I knew when I saw it, you would like it!"

Sir Abbott beamed with delight. At sixteen, Charles was the very image of himself at that age. Possessed of a quick and curious mind much like his sister, Charles loved maps, sextants, and all manner of navigational instruments. He was even beginning to show the same strong head for business that Lord Abbott had as one of the directors of the East India Company.

All summer long and late into the crisp autumn nights, Lord Abbott had looked on as Charles studied the navigational charts that were laid out over his massive mahogany desk, helping to plot ever more economical routes for the sea captains of the East India Company to sail in their quest for cotton, brilliantly colored silks, salt, opium and mostly, tea. By a fortunate turn of events, tea had become all the rage among the British courtiers and aristocrats of London with the marriage of King Charles II to Catherine of Braganza, for the king's bride had an unending taste for the strong brew and the fickle cream of English society simply could not get enough. The East India Company, and by extension, Lord Abbott, had profited mightily over the last several years from importing thousands and thousands of pounds of tea. Lord Abbott looked at his son with evident pride.

"Well done, Charles, well, done!" exclaimed Lord Abbott, reaching over to hold the necklace up to the light. He examined it from all sides.

"A glass prism made into a neckbob," he mused. "I would not have seen the possibility." He turned the necklace in his hand once again.

"You have a decidedly ingenious turn of mind, my boy. An ability that will be of goodly purpose in but a very few short years."

Lord Abbott gave the prism another twirl, causing the glowing bands of color to dance once more upon the walls. He was amused to see that Viola was positively entranced by the very sight.

"Thank you, Father" said Charles, ducking his head, his red curls bouncing.

Mightily pleased by the attention from his powerful father, Charles gathered his courage.

"Father, I should like to go with you up to London again, if, if I may."

Charles looked troubled, and then words tumbled out of his mouth, thoughts he'd been contemplating for months.

"I...I should like to sign on to a company ship and apprentice myself to learn navigation."

Lord Abbott caught the prism in his fist and looked over in surprise. Charles, who could think of nothing else over the last year, carefully presented his argument.

"Father, I've studied my hornbooks, learnt the algebra and trigonometry for navigational calculations, and how to use the points of the compass on the compass rose."

He took a deep breath and dared a glance at his father. When he realized that he was not to going to be interrupted, Charles continued.

"I know how to use the astrolabe and the tidal charts, I

know the name of every sail and every line in the rigging and how to log a position, and Father, you know that I have worked all year charting navigational routes to India and Canton. I...I should very much like to go to sea, Father."

Lord Abbott drew a pensive breath. His normally expansive and jovial expression turned thoughtful as he turned over his son's wishes in his mind. He gave the proposition serious consideration for, as he fondly remembered, he had spent many a night with his children before a crackling fire spinning exotic tales of far-off worlds. He had watched as the wide-eyed boy, positively enchanted, rested his chin on his hands and devoured every single word of his fanciful stories. Tales of the fierce battles, the intrigues, even the spicy scents of ginger and jasmine floating in the air above the grassy banks of China's Pearl River seemed to come alive for the lad. In his attic suite above the family quarters, Charles had many times drifted off to sleep to the sounds of chirping crickets when the company sailors brought their bamboo and lacquer cages back to his son. Lord Abbott could easily see the enticing lure that distant lands had on the lad.

"Aye," smiled Lord Abbott at the memory. He leaned back in his chair and turned pensive, considering the options aloud. "The *Surat* left port for China nearly a year ago and she'll not return for another two to three years hence."

"I am not afraid, Father."

Lord Abbott chuckled. "No, my boy, I expect that at sixteen years of age, you are not." After several long moments of contemplation, he spoke carefully.

"If you are to join the company at your majority, as has been my profound wish, I can see no reason why you should not begin at sea, as I, myself once did—perhaps not a lengthy voyage to China at first, but mayhaps the colonies?" he smiled.

Viola let out an audible gasp. She could no longer restrain herself. "No! Alvyn, the boy is too young!"

Lord Abbott resolutely turned his back to Viola. Her objections only served to galvanize his decision. He gave Charles his full attention, warming greatly to the idea of his son following in his footsteps.

"Yes, my boy. I give you my full permission…"

Charles shouted in elation, tripping over the presents to hug his father and landing at his feet.

"…in two year's time."

Charles's shoulders fell in disappointment. Lord Abbott saw that Charles was crushed. Viola heaved a sigh in relief. Lord Abbott reached out and ruffled the boy's curls affectionately.

"I will, however, take you with me to London on my next trip to make the necessary introductions."

"Will you, Father?" Charles brightened.

"I think you will find that two years will pass in a jot."

Lord Abbott immediately turned his thoughts toward making the necessary arrangements.

"Yes, my boy, this is a very fine day, indeed."

Charles beamed with excitement. His father grew serious for a moment, tempering that excitement with a caveat.

"Before you commence down this path, however, the board of directors of the East India Company will convene soon, and, Charles, I believe it would be an excellent idea for you to attend. I'm afraid there will be much disagreement among our members over the difficulties in India. These difficulties may significantly affect our trade in the region, and they will certainly have an affect on our board, as well as the path our company will take in the coming years."

He fixed Charles with a serious gaze. "There is a most vexing question that now lies before the company."

"What is that, Father?" asked Charles.

"An extremely complicated political situation at the heart of India, I'm afraid." He paused a moment, trying to find a way to explain.

Lord Abbott took a deep draught of ale, and then wiped the foam from his upper lip, setting the pewter tankard on the plank floor next to his heavily carved armchair. Unexpectedly, he caught a glance at the barley twist spiral turnings on the front leg. He saw a set of tiny indentations where, as an infant, his sturdy son had chewed into the wood when his milk teeth erupted. He wondered wistfully how the years had gone so fast. Even though she'd been gone for fifteen years, unexpected moments like this hit him as hard as the day she died. *How proud Tamesine would be of her two fine children.* She had possessed a lively and quick turn of mind and there had been no one on earth he'd trusted more. *By God, he missed her so.*

Lord Abbott shifted slightly in his chair and collected his thoughts. Catherine often marveled at the way her father was able to explain complicated business concerns in such a manner that she and Charles could easily understand for Lord Abbott was not the sort of English aristocrat who summarily dismissed his family from the room when discussing business as other men of his class customarily did. Though roundly denounced by opinionated men in the clubs he frequented, there was no one he had trusted more than his beloved wife.

He had been a lonesome bachelor of nearly thirty years when she'd unexpectedly captured his aching heart. She was but eighteen years of age when they married in the little stone chapel, and was by turns, both delicately beautiful and fiercely intelligent. Before the children arrived, he had passed many a long winter night holding his lovely Tamesine close in his arms. He would drag a feather pallet before a roaring fire and pile it high with eiderdown coverlets and soft, full pillows then hold her tightly as they talked until only dying embers were left in the grate. Lord Abbott, unlike the other men of Stockbridge, strongly believed in educating both of his children, fully expecting both his son and daughter to use their clever minds. His maiden sister, to the contrary, believed just as strongly in banishing foolish children to either the playroom or nursery, depending on the time of day. Viola further believed that education was quite wasted on girls.

Lord Abbott leaned forward and spoke straight to the heart of the conflict. "Herein lies the very seed of rebellion, my children. King Charles has issued an amendment to our company charter that we are now accorded imprimatur to direct and employ the very strongest of British military force where necessary, in order to establish trading stations throughout the country of India. I am afraid that among the members of the board, there is much support for and great plans to unleash a vengeful jackboot of authority upon the country of India and its peoples for the sole purpose of expanding and controlling our British tea trade."

Aunt Viola was aghast and, laying a palm to her wrinkled forehead, looked very much as though she would faint. Lord Abbott calmly raised his hand to a passing houseboy.

"Boy! A draught of water."

"Aye, sir!"

The boy took one look at the gasping woman beginning to list to one side of the velvet settee, vigorously waving a lacquered Chinese fan at her dampening forehead. He ran for a water pitcher. Lord Abbott was well accustomed to his sister's overly dramatic turns and once satisfied that she would live another day, gave his attention back to his children.

"I am troubled to confess that among the supporters of this vile enterprise is our Lord Mayor, Cecil Hardwicke. Lord Mayor Hardwicke sits with me on the board and he is the gentleman with whom I now find myself in absolute abject opposition to on this plaguesome issue."

Frustration mounting, Lord Abbott began to pound a clenched fist upon his breeches; his impassioned voice began to reverberate through the timbered hall.

"It is unconscionable that we profit from a sword in one hand and a ledger in the other against the good and trusting people of

India! Mark my words; the ruling class of the British Empire will push the natives of India only so far. Sooner rather than later, I fear, they will rise against us in a most venomous fashion!"

At that, Aunt Viola gave a small cry and passed out against the settee. Lord Abbott exhaled and stopped short, looking down at his children who stared up at him with wide-eyed fascination. Instantly chagrined, he apologized.

"Please forgive my outburst, children." He took a deep breath. "This is not a day for expressing troublesome thoughts."

Lord Abbott looked down at his children and smiled, instantly lifting the atmosphere in the festive room. Both Catherine and Charles sat back in awe of the unexpected, passionate display of emotion from their commonly jovial father.

As a handmaid placed a cool cloth on Aunt Viola's forehead, Lord Abbott reached under the tree and sifted through the remaining packages. The cloth did much to revive the older woman and at the sound of rustling papers, Aunt Viola managed to lift one eyebrow, peeking in curiosity at the tantalizing possibility of more gifts. Viola righted herself, working the fan furiously, as Lord Abbott withdrew a very large box tied with a black satin bow. He looked at Catherine.

"Cassie, m'lassie, I do apologize for troubling you with my vexing business matters." He handed her the gift. "This, my dear, is for you."

Catherine pulled the ribbon, lifted the lid and looked inside. She caught her breath. Catherine reached deep into the box and carefully lifted out the most dazzling ball gown she had ever seen. The heavy, shimmering fabric felt cool to the touch. She could not resist the urge to hold it to her cheek. The watered silk taffeta crinkled in her hands as she held it up to the light playing through the window.

"Oh, Father!" she breathed. "It is the most exquisite gown I've ever seen."

It was an iridescent, pale pink and burgundy confection of a frock, with a plunging, rounded neckline edged in a small rufflet. The sleeves were cut just above the wrist and finished with embellished lace ruffles that would hang to her knees. The fitted bodice was dainty and corseted; and the skirts were heavily gathered with layer upon layer of silken slips under the shimmering taffeta overskirt. She was awestruck by the beauty of the gown. Lord Abbott smiled and thought not for the first time what a lovely young woman his daughter was becoming.

Lord Abbott reached under the tree again and handed Charles his own box. Charles unwrapped a custom set of velveteen breeks and a crimson waistcoat and doublet. A white linen shirting with a formal, multi-layered cravat completed the splendid costume. Charles was delighted with his new suit of clothing.

"It would be a very great honor, my children, if you would both stand with me as hosts tonight," pronounced a very proud, if somewhat teary-eyed, Lord Abbott.

CHAPTER 5

Up in her fire-warmed chambers, Catherine was to lay abed for a brief rest after the lively Christmas morning; instead, she sat lingering at her small writing desk, her mind on the long evening ahead. Her eyes fell upon a collection of sketchings that were set to one side of the highly polished escritoire, next to a small silver tray containing a horsehair brush, an ivory comb and two small cut-glass bottles filled with attar of roses and lavender oils. In the collection were nearly fifty pen and ink drawings of butterflies, laboriously hand-drawn and neatly tied with a black silk ribbon.

The elaborately embellished cover was titled, *"Butterfly Observations in The Towne of Stockbridge and The Towne of Wells, In the Southe of England."* At the bottom of the cover, she had signed in her elegant, flowing script: *Writ By, The Honourable Lady Catherine Mary Abbott, 1664."* She slowly leafed through the sketches, remembering the countless hours she'd spent putting her quill to the fine linen papers. Olde World Swallowtail. Chequered Skipper. Woodland Grayling. She remembered them all.

Catherine crossed the room and kneeled down. She opened the lid of her copper trunk and lifted out layer after layer of butterflies carefully mounted to thin strips of wood with small pins. As she spread the displays across the floor, she caught a sudden glimpse of the *Ursa Major* sketchings she'd done years before and not for the first time did she marvel at the extraordinary things one could find in the natural world if one only looked.

Catherine sat on the carpet and gently grazed her fingertips over the fragile, gossamer wings, remembering exactly when and where she'd caught each velvety insect with a small net she'd made of twigs and cheesecloth. *The world is such a wonderment of order and symmetry, and yet, within that order, there are such wild, dazzling variations of beauty to be found.* She carefully unpinned a delicate Chequered Skipper and held it high to the window light, examining it from all sides. She tilted her head, thoughtfully considering the whole of her collection. *Each butterfly possesses exactly the same ordered set of wings, body, and antennae, and yet, within that order, there are an infinite variety of patterns, markings, and colors waiting to be discovered, if one only looked,* she marveled. *Would the girls from town notice these things? Would they care, even if she could try to describe her fascination with science and nature?* She thought not. The Abbey tutor, Master Howell, had been singularly impressed with her work, even telling her once that her collection of butterfly drawings could be published as a book by one of the small London publishing houses. An exasperated Viola had put an immediate stop to such stuff and nonsense. Her sketches had been banished to the trunk after that, she thought wistfully.

When she was young, to her aunt's everlasting vexation, Catherine cared little about the way she looked, daydreaming more about the trees she climbed or the rocks she collected. Unlike the other young maidens of Stockbridge and Wells, Catherine's turn of mind lay in the marvels of the natural world and in the wonderings of how things worked. As she the years went by, she found that she had no time for their idle gossip and silly chatterings. She was surprised then, to find herself day-dreaming once again about the party and the beautiful dress that had been designed by Lisette Chanon, the French dressmaker who owned the little dressmaking shop in Wells. It was Mademoiselle Chanon who had spent weeks designing and sewing the magnificent gown for her *petit chou*.

Catherine leaned quietly against the massive tester bed, her delicate fingertips resting lightly on the intricately woven tapestry mantelet that was tied back at the corners and stared at the gown hanging from the peg in her armoire. She knew the other girls, the petulant Barlowe sisters in particular, would be envious of her betrothal to *the most eligible young man in the two villages*, as her aunt often prattled, but since she'd known him the whole of her life, she could not be troubled by schoolgirl jealousies. She sat on the corner of the bed and drew her knees to her chest. She imagined Miles holding her close as they danced, his strong hands gently enclosing hers, his musky scent enveloping her senses. *Life will certainly never be the same after tonight*, she thought. Catherine glanced down at her butterfly trays with a sudden hope that Miles would look with favor upon her love of science as her father always had. An inexplicable, brief wave of melancholia washed over her. Sighing, she arose and put the trays back into the trunk and closed the lid, then quietly lay down on the bed.

Howling winds swept the clouds from the evening skies and as night fell, the stars began to sparkle above the pastoral countryside. Catherine was awakened from a dreamless sleep by a knock at her bedchamber door.

"Time to dress, Miss," said Jane, as she swept into the cozy timber and brick room carrying a mother-of-pearl handled hairbrush and a selection of jeweled hair bobs into the room on a silver tray. Jane set the tray down on the copper chest. The sparkling clasps belonged to Catherine's mother and Lord Abbott now wished for his only daughter to choose her favorites.

As her maid pulled the rustling gown from the armoire, Catherine's thoughts once again turned to Miles. When he left for Paris, she'd been a thirteen-year-old girl, a child, a playmate; but Catherine had begun to change over the last four years. Though her waist was yet slender, unmistakably lush curves had begun to soften and transform her boyish frame. She arose and began to dress.

"Take a deep breath, Mi'Lady," said Jane, after carefully drawing the gown over Catherine's head. Jane pulled the laces tighter and tighter. Catherine inhaled deeply and steadied herself against the four-poster bed.

As her chambermaid worked to fasten the intricate hooks up the back of the dress, Catherine was startled to see in the looking glass that she now more than generously filled out the deep, plunging neckline of the shimmering gown. She could almost see the rosy coronets of her breasts teasing above the crimped rufflet. She wondered if Miles would notice. Jane caught her contemplating her reflection in the glass.

"Aye, yer' beautiful, Miss," said Jane, smiling.

Catherine laughed and moved to the dressing table. She watched as Jane put the finishing touches on a fashionable updo, and even she had to admit that the elaborate curls of her despised copper-colored hair were fetching. The deep burgundy of the silken gown favored her high coloring and brought out the pink in her cheeks. She squinted and took a long, critical look at a face at once familiar, and yet so different. She could now see that not only had her figure softened and matured, but that her face had also lost its girlish fullness. Prominent cheekbones had slowly emerged beneath wide-set gray eyes and served as a counterbalance to her full lips, giving her face a quiet strength. She seemed a grown woman, yet she neither looked nor felt quite like herself. She knew she should be strong and confident, but she felt terribly unsure and ill at ease and not for the first time, wished her mother could be with her tonight.

Jane lifted Charles's gift from the little box and fastened the black silk ribbon around Catherine's neck. The glass prism fell into her décolletage and she was highly discomfited by the sight. Catherine reached behind, desperate to shorten the ribbon.

Aunt Viola appeared in the doorway, becostumed in a heavily frilled, emerald green gown, and an overwrought peacock feathered headdress tucked into the graying hair piled high upon her head. Viola simply adored peacocks. She thought they were quite regal. In fact, she thought herself quite regal. She stopped short at the threshold and gazed at Catherine standing by the bed, resplendent in the shimmering gown, as though seeing her for the first time.

"My dear, you are simply exquisite," she exclaimed from the doorway.

From an elaborate oil portrait hung above the Abbey staircase, Catherine could see that Viola Abbott had once been a beautiful young maiden, though it was clear that she had long since surrendered to the merciless passage of time. Her unending taste for rich Belgian chocolates, and perhaps an unspoken but deeply broken heart, had added ample creases and considerable rolls of soft, plump flesh to the comely figure of her youth. Practical and proud, however, Viola seemed to thrust aside all memories of the captivating young woman she might have been and strode into the room with a haughty imperiousness, taking charge of the maid's ministrations.

"Do stop fussing, Catherine," said Aunt Viola, firmly removing Catherine's hands from the necklace. Catherine set them reluctantly into her lap. The glass prism nestled deeply into abundant cleavage. Viola raised an eyebrow and looked at her niece critically in the glass.

"You have become a most lovely young woman," she paused to consider her next words, then spoke crisply, looking down as she smoothed her skirts. "Miles, I am certain, will be most gladsome enough to take you into his bed."

Startled, Catherine looked sharply up to her aunt, shocked by her unseemly words. She saw a strange smile play across her aunt's face, and then Viola narrowed her eyes, searing into hers. Her voice took on an unfamiliar, abrupt edge.

"Catherine, it is high time you grew up," she said sharply. "It has been made abundantly clear to you that you have a duty to both your father and to this family." She paused. "And you shall keep to it."

At that, Viola gathered her voluminous skirts and swept from the room, leaving a trace of lavender water floating on the air behind her. Catherine was shaking. She walked out to the landing as the first guests began to draw up to the manor in their finely appointed carriages. Her mind reeled as she tried to make sense of her aunt's unexpected words. Aunt Viola had never before spoken about marriage-bed intimacies and certainly never in that sharp tone of voice. In her confusion, Catherine had to admit to herself that she was terribly unsure how she would react to seeing Miles again.

She nervously wiped her damp palms together, and then set them on the heavy wooden balustrade overlooking the entryway. Catherine looked down into the gathering-room at the swaths of bay laurel, rosemary and holly that surrounded the windows, doorways and rustic beams and thought, not for the first time, how beautiful the abbey was.

The silverlight of the moon shining through the heavy lead glass windowpanes played across the herringbone-patterned English oak planked floor and the timbered barrel ceiling of the finely proportioned gallery. She watched as a manservant kneeled before the towering hearth of golden Cotswold fieldstone stoking the coals in the grate. When he finished, the old man carefully set the forged iron fire screen that carried the Abbott crest of a soaring falcon and thistle before the roaring fire and disappeared quietly belowstairs.

Calming her nerves, Catherine breathed deeply of the exotic fragrances filling the hall. Masses of peonies, roses and fragrant lavender grown out of season in the estate's orangery had been carefully arranged in intricately scrolled copper and brass vases brought by sea-faring merchants in her father's employ from their travels to India as gifts for Lord Abbott.

Catherine took in the exquisite sight of the richly embroidered red and gold Indian silk table runners adorning the hand-hewn trestle tables. The tables were arranged around the perimeter of the gallery and the family silver and pewter had been polished and carefully laid out on the head table by the servants in preparation for the evening ahead.

Footsteps from the gallery caught her attention. She turned to the head of the stairs where her father and Campbell now stood, magnificent in their formal attire. Her father looked every inch the lord of the manor with his crimson waistcoat that set off a pair of finely tailored black breeches. Silver buckles on his velvet brocade slippers echoed the silver grommets of the ribbons that gathered his breeches at the knee. For this most formal occasion, Lord Abbott had donned an impressive white wig, the curls of which tumbled around his shoulders. An ornately engraved silver walking stick completed his fashionable ensemble. Campbell had chosen to forego the hot, heavy wig, but was otherwise dressed much as their father. It was clear that Aunt Viola most certainly had a strong hand in choosing the family's clothes for the Christmas feast.

At her step, Lord Abbott turned. His smile faltered. *Was that a tear she saw in his eyes?* He reached for her and she went into his arms, his kiss brushing against her own cheek.

"My dear, you are an absolute vision. And how like your mother you look," Lord Abbott said, stepping back to take the full measure of both Catherine and Charles. His voice was husky with the unshed tears. "I do wish she could be here to see her children grown."

"I'm sorry, Father," whispered Catherine. She pulled a linen handkerchief from his waistcoat pocket; giving it a smile for the elaborate embroidery was surely Aunt Viola's handiwork, heaven forbid her family carry a plain square of linen. She dried the tears on her father's smooth-shaven cheeks, and then stood on tiptoe to tuck the handkerchief back in his pocket. "Do I really look like her?" She looked down at the daring neckline. "I'm afraid I don't feel much myself in this gown. Perhaps it is more Aunt Viola's liking than my own."

"You do indeed, though I cannot say that it is the gown. I think it has made me see you for the woman grown that you have become."

"And I, Father? Am I a man grown?" Campbell grinned, his eyes wide with hope.

Lord Abbott laughed at his son over Catherine's shoulder.

"That day comes all too soon for my liking, but not yet, son." Lord Abbott offered Catherine his arm. "So, my children, shall we prepare greet our guests?"

At that, Catherine joined hands with her father and brother and turned to greet the first of the many revelers that were beginning to arrive for the party. The old butler, Cedric, swung the door open to the first guests.

"Welcome, Welcome!" cried Lord Abbott, as Lord Mayor Hardwicke entered the Abbey carrying gifts of claret and chocolates for the house. Lord Abbott hurried down the stairs to greet his arriving guests.

"Ahh, Abbott! So good of you to have me," said the Lord Mayor, shaking hands profusely.

Though Catherine knew that Lord Mayor Hardwicke was a wealthy man and a kind benefactor to the people of both Stockbridge and Wells and that he was well known for generously extending credit to local farmers who often struggled to survive through the cold, brutal winters, she also knew that he was a gleefully unrepentant, lecherous old whitebeard who most likely had indulged in a pint or three well before the evening began.

Hardwicke caught sight of Catherine on the landing and giddily laid his blood-shot eyes on the full, voluptuous breasts that threatened to spill from the silken confines of her gown. He lurched his way up the steps toward Catherine and leaned in for a kiss, his hands slyly drifting upward from her waist.

"My dear, you look positively enchanting tonight," he whispered, eagerly grazing her breasts with nimble fingers.

Startled, Catherine drew back sharply and pulled her brother near. Charles scowled at the mayor as Lord Abbott firmly took his arm and pulled him from the stairs.

"This way, Hardwicke," said Lord Abbott, firmly steering him toward the festive gathering hall. Lord Abbott glanced back toward Catherine and gave her a sympathetic wink. *He would have to beat the men back from his only daughter tonight*, he thought with dismay.

Excited guests began to pour into the manor. Charles escorted a large group of villagers into the hall, as Catherine's attention was drawn back to the Abbey doorway. A howling gust of wind blew swirling earthbound snowflakes up through the open portal. A massive figure stood in the arched entryway, his arms heavily laden with Christmas packages, his cloak billowing. Catherine caught her breath. Suddenly, her heart began to pound, the sound of each beat echoing inside her head. She felt a warm, prickly flush begin to rise and held her cool, trembling hands to her reddening cheeks. *Miles.*

She was astonished to see that he was even more striking than she remembered. After nearly four long years on the continent, time had chiseled his soft, young features into a fine-boned jaw with high, aristocratic cheekbones that were offset by his dark hair and long, curling sideburns. Deep dimples brought a roguish countenance to his face that tempered the angular, almost delicate features. Miles shook off his costly woolen doublet in the general direction of the butler who stood by the door.

"Thank you, Cedric," said Miles, his manners impeccable. He turned toward the gathering room.

Out of the corner of his eye, a rustle, the slightest movement of shimmering fabric caught his attention. Miles looked up to the landing and for the first time in years, saw Catherine standing there. He froze. She was stunning. He instantly longed to run to her, to gather her into his arms, but he could not seem to make himself move from the doorway. The sounds in the room drifted away and everyone in it blurred into nothingness.

He could not take his eyes off her, so thrown was he by the beautiful woman she had become.

"Shall I take your packages, sir?" Cedric's voice rang faintly behind him.

Miles stood there staring up at her, marveling. He could not quite reconcile the image in his head of the laughing, teasing childish playmate she was when he left for Paris to the exquisite young maiden who now stood just steps away. She smiled shyly at him and began to make her way down the stairs.

"Your packages, sir?" inquired Cedric, once again.

Without taking his eyes off her, Miles wordlessly handed his gifts to the old butler. A lifetime of aristocratic restraint was abandoned as he ran to the bottom of the stairs and held his hand up to Catherine. She descended to the formal entry hall and stepped softly to the marble floor. Staring into her steady, slate-grey eyes, Miles gently took Catherine's hand into his and raised her wrist gently to his lips.

That hair. Those dimples. The highly polished, sophisticated airs about him. He was no longer the boy Catherine played with in the forests. He was a man, a man who clearly had tasted a very different life in Paris during his years abroad. A man who now had her heart pounding in her head and her muscles tensing with a blistering charge that raced through her. She could feel the eyes of everyone in the room, but disoriented and helpless by the sudden, overwhelming sensations that swirled around her, she could think of nothing else to do but stand there. She watched in utter fascination as he drew her fingers to his lips and softly kissed the back of her hand. She was electrified by his touch.

He held her fingertips for a long moment, looking into her eyes, at her lips, her hair. So unsettled was he by the beautiful creature standing before him that he began to search her face for anything familiar, almost desperately trying to find a trace of the girl he once knew, but he was completely at sea. Then, as they stepped apart, she laughed. Her taunting, teasing peals took him instantly back to those long summer days in the forest behind the Abbey, when he ran through the darkening shadows, chasing the girl he knew so very well. There she was, his Catherine. He looked around the room at the villagers who were staring at him and gathered his wits.

"Shall we join the others?"

He smiled down at her and offered his arm. She tipped her delighted face up to his. She set her hand on the cobalt-colored sleeve of his velvet waistcoat and together, they walked into the party.

The candlelit gathering hall was filled with high-spirited revelers. Exuberant shouts of laughter echoed from the rough farmers and tradesmen of Stockbridge and Wells, as they hoisted pewter tankards brimming with cold, foaming ale on high to toast the lord of the manor and his grand generosity again and again. Sturdy, sensible wives tried, mostly in vain, to muffle drunken husbands all the while indulging in a pint or two themselves in the far corners of the grand hall.

Belowstairs, Gussie bellowed orders to the staff as platter after magnificent platter was hauled up to the banquet tables by every possible set of hands. It was an impressive achievement and Gussie, who had orchestrated every detail of the feast, finally sat alone at the empty worktable in the cookery, and breathed a huge sigh of relief. Exhausted, she reached for an earthenware jug she'd hidden for the occasion behind a stone ledge and poured herself her own tankard of much-needed ale. Gussie wiped her brow once more with the hem of her apron and took a mighty, cooling draught.

CHAPTER 6

"VERY GOOD CHEER WE HAD AND MERRY; MUSIQUE AT AND AFTER DINNER, AND A FELLOW DANCED A JIG"
-SAMUEL PEPYS

Lord Abbott sat at the head of the massive oak planked table that was set before the roaring fire. He occupied an impressive throne-like wainscot armchair that was elaborately carved with the Abbott crest that was designed to magnify his social position as head of the manor. Viola, Charles and Catherine sat with Miles and the Houghton's to his right in smaller chairs of similar design. To Lord Abbott's left sat Lord Mayor Hardwicke and Constable Hawkins in turned back stools that had no armrests. The leading citizens of the village were seated on stools in descending order of importance down both sides of the table.

Halfway down the table, Mademoiselle Chanon was seated next to the shy butcher, Eldrick, who could hardly believe his good fortune at being next to the pretty, young French woman. Catherine had mischievously seen to that. Catherine was terribly fond of Lisette Chanon. She admired her courage in sailing from France, then finally settling in Stockbridge to open a small dressmakers shop, and give French lessons to the children of wealthy families to supplement her modest income. During dinner, Catherine looked over to see that Eldrick was so nervous he could hardly keep his hands from shaking, but after a draught or two of ale, did his best to converse with the petite seamstress. For her part, Lisette looked happier than Catherine had seen in a long while.

In the crowded hall, the guests formed long lines that snaked past heavily-laden tables, filling their plates full of the meats, aspics, greens and gravies that had been cooked throughout the day. Sitting at the center of the main table was the most impressive meat dish of all. A spectacular boar's head, with a perfectly ripe, red pomegranate in its mouth had been decorated with holly and carried ceremoniously by the servants into the dining hall to the raucous cheers of the guests who marveled at the sight. The villagers returned to the feast tables again and again, until not a scrap was left. The servants quickly cleared the empty scuttles, and then hauled up platter after platter of magnificent desserts, as the villagers, who largely scrimped through the year, filled their plates to overflowing once more.

During the banquet, wine and ale flowed generously, the conversation was lively and the assembled guests shouted with laughter from every corner of the room. Amid the riotous din, Miles quietly caught Catherine's eye. He'd been staring at her all evening, still astounded at the exquisite changes that had taken place in her. She was, of course, nothing like the women he'd known in Paris. She was a chaste maiden, he knew, but deeply sensual memories of the women he'd since lain with were crowding his thoughts, making him want her all the more. He could hardly keep his desire in check, longing to hold her, to take her deeply into him. He shook his head and took a deep draught of wine.

"You seem lost in thought," she said, trying to ease the awkwardness between them.

How could he tell her what he was thinking? How could he confess his wild desire for the body that was barely constrained by her silks? How could he tell her that he was desperate to gather her into his arms, to unbind both the stays of that delicious, tantalizing gown and the upswept curls of her hair and carry her straight to his bed? He stared into his glass, his reflection wavering in the ruby-colored liquid. He took another long drink and looked over at her.

"I...I was thinking of Paris. After we marry, I should like to take you there."

And I'd like us to remain there, he thought, recklessly daring to imagine a very different life than the one that threatened to stretch endlessly before him into decrepitude. *That magnificent city had charmed him, seduced him and worked its way into his very soul,* he realized with a sigh. *Paris was so completely different from this God forsaken country village of Stockbridge.* A sudden cloud of melancholy enveloped him. *There were simply no words for the comparison*, he thought. *Cardinal Richelieu had vowed to make Paris the most beautiful city in Europe, and by God, he had accomplished exactly that.*

He twisted the glass in his hand, thinking of the Cardinal's own palatial estate, *Palais-Cardinal,* the crowning glory of his extraordinary vision. Miles looked out at the provincial guests in the Abbey, suddenly remembering one balmy, spring night during a break from the university. He had been invited to one of the many spectacular balls the Cardinal held in King Louis XIII's honor. The guests, becostumed in their finest attire and sparkling jewels, danced from nine-o'clock at night until seven the next morning, interrupted briefly by an extravagant midnight supper. *He'd had a grand time the whole night through.*

Sometime during the small hours before dawn, he had stolen away from the dazzling crowd with a taunting, giggling Vicomtesse, savoring the sheer delights of her tender, royal flesh in the palace's fragrant, rose-filled pleasure garden under a brilliant moon. That night had transformed his life. He had thrown himself into the worldly pleasures of Paris, frequenting the shops, the gambling casinos, the gentlemen's clubs and even the riotous, back-alley brothels with high abandon. His studies became an afterthought. Countless women began to blur in his memory, love long replaced by driftless sensation and caprice. His gambling debts began to mount. Stockbridge became an afterthought. He had been gone too long and seen too much. He also knew in full measure his responsibility, his duty to the Earl of Houghton and to Houghton Hall. *Perhaps he could persuade Catherine to visit. Paris would certainly work its charms on her, he was sure. But then, could she ever really embrace the city he'd come to love so much?* Miles looked over to Catherine. She was studying the candle flame. He shook his head, taking in the sight of her in total concentration of one complicated thought or another. *Dear God, she has not changed in all these years. How could she possibly ever abandon herself to the delights and fancies of Parisian society?*

"Would you like that? Paris, I mean," he said, looking about the provincial half-timbered hall. His mood darkened, briefly.

He lifted his glass to his lips, polished off the rest of the wine in the glass and set the empty glass to the side of his plate. He caught the eye of a passing maid and gestured for a tankard of ale. Catherine watched in dismay. *Perhaps he is distressed by the thought of marrying me?*

"It seems peculiar, does it not," she said softly. "That we should be married, I mean."

He glanced at her, his resolve to return to Paris crumbling. *My God, she is beautiful. I do not deserve…* He could not bring himself to finish the thought. Thoughts of his wasted years at the university were beginning to weigh heavily. *The women. The failed academics. The gambling.* He worked his jaw, loosening his uncomfortably tight cravat.

"Ah, yes. The arranged marriage," he said, slowly. The phrase idly rolled off his tongue. A novel thought was beginning to form through the haze in his head. *Perhaps he would nae' have to confess his considerable debts to the Earl.* Miles played with the rim of his empty glass, drawing his finger around the edge until it hummed. *Perhaps he had been a bit too hasty in his condemnation of Stockbridge and of her.* He turned to face Catherine.

"It's not the worst thing, you know, marrying for companionship. God knows love is illusive at best. Ethereal. Impossible to find, really," he mused. "Lord knows I've tried."

She looked down to her plate, uneasy and unsure of the meaning behind his words. *Companionship.* Miles took the tankard from the maid and drank deeply, then set the tankard down on the table and smiled down at her, wiping the foam from his lips.

"But, here you are. As here you've always been."

Again she was unsettled. *Does he condescend?*

"Pray, what will be your pleasure, my darling, Catherine? Will you come with me to Paris?"

She decided to tread lightly.

"Mademoiselle Chanon speaks often of the city. I should indeed love to see Paris."

"Then it's decided," he smiled. "When shall we be married?"

Catherine paused, startled. "I…I have not given a single thought to the ceremony." She paused a moment. "I wonder why." She gave a small laugh. "I daresay that I assumed Aunt Viola would have made the arrangements with Lady Houghton. I imagine she already has, for I confess that the trappings of society are unknown to me."

Miles groaned under his breath. Catherine glanced up sharply at the sound, a look of concern playing across her fine-boned features.

"Perhaps a midsummer wedding? The roses will be in high flower come June," she said shyly, "but perhaps I care far more about such things than you, sir.

He crinkled his eyes, his dark mood lifting to reveal his playful charm.

"Ah, yes. The midsummer trees, and the flowers and the butterflies and all the woodland creatures shall be in full blossom amid the forests of Buckinghamshire," he grinned.

Catherine furrowed her brow. *Does she think I jest at her expense*, he wondered? She looked as though she could neither praise nor condemn his thoughts, as though he were a complete puzzlement. Miles could see his teasing confounded her. Relenting, he took her hand in his and gently kissed it.

"June it shall be, Mi'Lady." Catherine smiled and for the first time that evening, everything felt right.

Lord Abbott, a witness to the exchange leaned against his high-backed chair. Though he was decidedly unsure as to exactly how it had all come about, he was pleased that the two of them seemed to be finding their way to each other. He stood, then took his knife and tapped on his pewter tankard. The roisterous crowd began to quiet, looking from one to another, then back to Lord Abbott. He tapped again, this time, louder.

"Ladies and Gentlemen," he shouted. "My apologies for the intrusion upon this festive celebration, however, I…" He looked over at the Earl of Houghton, "I beg your pardon, *we*… have an announcement to make."

The Earl stood and linked arms with Lord Abbott. The crowd fell silent. Only the sound of bottles clinking against wine glasses could be heard as houseboys filled the vessels around the head table with the wine Archie had set by earlier in the day. The houseboy handed Lord Abbott and the Earl each a generous glass of burgundy. They raised them high in hand.

"We wish, on this Christmas night, to announce the betrothal of Lady Catherine Mary Abbott to Viscount Miles Lewyyn Houghton!"

There was a stunned silence, and then a mighty roar of approval nearly shook the rafters. The radiant young couple shyly stood hand in hand next to Lord Abbott and Charles, smiling at the enthusiasm the villagers had for their engagement. Miles turned to Catherine and took her face into his hands, then kissed her to wild cheers. *Perhaps this could indeed be a successful enterprise.* Over Catherine's shoulder, Miles watched as Viola cast a sly, sidelong glance toward Lady Barlowe and her sulky, sullen daughters who now stared at Catherine in bitter shock. He nearly laughed as Viola lifted the corners of her mouth in triumph, delicately patting her lips to hide her amusement at the disappointment clouding the faces of the dreary girls.

Midnight fell over the Abbey. The musicians tuned their instruments and began to fill the hall with lively strains of Ravenscroft and Jeffreys. Lord Abbott, Catherine and Charles moved gracefully between knots of rowdy townspeople and aristocrats alike, greeting each guest personally. Through the crowd, Catherine saw Mademoiselle Chanon standing alone, warming her hands by the fire. Catherine excused herself and walked over to her friend. Lisette turned and gave Catherine a warm embrace. Her face brightened as she lovingly tucked up a strand of Catherine's curls that had fallen from the jeweled hair clasp.

"*Ma petit chou!* I am so 'appy for you," she said. You will need new clothes, *non*? A new thought struck the seamstress. *Mon dieu! Un robe mariage!* I will go up to London and select the most beautiful *fabriques.* You will 'ave the finest *trousseau!*"

Catherine laughed at the tiny woman's enthusiasm. She took Lisette by the elbow and leaned in to whisper.

"Are you having a good time?" said Catherine, feeling responsible for introducing Eldrick to the Frenchwoman.

"Monsieur Eldrick is very nice," Lisette giggled.

"I think so, too," whispered Catherine.

Fortified by several bracing tankards of ale, Eldrick strode through the crowd to Lisette and set his palm out. "Will ye' have a dance wiv' me?"

"Oui, Monsieur," grinned Lisette. She took his hand and as they stepped onto the dance floor, she glanced over her shoulder and winked at Catherine.

Catherine shyly walked up to a small knot of girls from town. Sisters Flora and Fauna Barlowe stood with their backs to her, elaborate curls bouncing up and down above their ruffled silken gowns.

"Did you ever think *she* would be the first one of us to marry?" sniped Flora.

"You're just jealous because you wanted to marry him," teased Fauna. "Perhaps we should have spent our days climbing trees in dirty skirts catching those detestable little butterflies!"

"Of course, when it's an arranged marriage, one can wear nearly anything, I suppose," Flora giggled.

"She will never belong at Houghton Hall," sneered Fauna. "Can you just imagine?" The girls standing with her burst into laughter.

Catherine cringed, deeply embarrassed. She searched the crowd for her father, her brother or anyone familiar to escape to, for though she desperately wished to flee, she was frozen to the spot. She felt a tap her on the shoulder. Startled, Catherine wheeled around to see Miles bending in a deep bow, his foot catching on an uneven floorboard, causing his step to falter ever so slightly.

"May I have this dance, Lady Catherine?"

"Oh, indeed, sir. Yes," she smiled, gratefully taking his outstretched hand. Miles looked pointedly at the girls and lifted Catherine's hand to his lips, kissing it gently. Catherine caught her breath, and then, composing herself, defiantly gave the girls a withering glance as they swept past.

The group of young girls giggled, whispering to each other and pointing at Catherine as she passed. To her relief, Miles led her through the crowd to an open area of the highly polished wooden floor. He held her gently, with one hand aloft. They walked, turned and spun in unison with the other guests as they worked their way through the complicated steps of the Playford dances. Concentration was agonizing. Catherine felt weak at the touch of his strong hand over hers and wondered if her legs would hold her up, shaking as they were. Without warning, Miles suddenly guided them away from the crowded dance floor, toward a small, dimly lit hallway.

"Where are you taking me?"

"Shhhh." Miles playfully touched a finger to his lips, his eyes crinkling, his dimples, deepening.

He turned a corner and pulled her into an empty butler's pantry that led down to the cookery, the help having long since retired belowstairs to their own rigadoon. A cacophony of sounds drifting up through the stairwell ebbed and flowed around them. Miles slowly took Catherine's face in his hands, and stared deep into the grey eyes that he had once known so well. She could feel her heart racing, beating so loudly that she was afraid he must hear it. He pulled her close until her lips were teasing softly across his. She ceased thinking, only feeling the strength of his arms around her. Their lips met with undeniable fire. He kissed her gently at first, then hungrily, as though he could not stop, as though he could never stop. She was not sure she wanted him to stop. He abandoned all intelligent thoughts. The extravagant amounts of ale and wine he'd drunk through the long night had begun to go to his head. His thoughts swirled as primal instincts collided forcibly against noble thoughts in his befogged brain. He'd become far to familiar with the *putain* who lingered in the dimly lit side streets of Paris, desperate to throw themselves at the wealthy university students after long nights in the *salons*. He swept Catherine up against the wall. Her eyes flew open, startled.

"Miles! No!" Miles caught her wrists, and pulled her close.

"You are absolutely magnificent!" he gasped. She felt the alcohol on his breath hot against her neck.

Miles dropped his hands to her waist, cosseting each exquisite new curve through the shimmering silk of her gown. He stumbled into her, sliding his hands upward to her breasts, curving his damp palms around their lush fullness. His breath came in jagged gasps as he felt himself grow hard. *Her skin was soft and warm, her copper curls carried the scent of thyme, or was it lavender?* His thoughts were jumbled. The tankards of ale and wine were leaving him off-balanced and confused. Try as he might, he could not place the earthy fragrance. He kissed her with a fervid lust he no longer wished to control.

"Miles, please," she implored, trying to push him away.

His thoughts were jumbled. *Why would she turn from him?* Confused and disoriented, he held her tightly in his arms. Catherine's thoughts raced back to the memory of his chase through the pine forest, but he was so much stronger now. She could no longer push him away. Confused, she twisted from him, crying out.

"No!"

From the cookery below, dim shouts echoed up the stairwell. Frantic sounds began to break through the swirling confusion in his head. The sounds became louder as panicked voices rose and tore through the room. Suddenly, Miles stopped short, the murky clouds beginning to clear. He turned his face from her, ashamed.

"I… I beg your apology," he whispered.

Catherine backed against the wall and stared at him, speechless. From belowstairs, a violent, guttural scream shocked them both to their senses. Miles dropped his hands and took a step back. Catherine pushed him aside, gathered her skirts and raced for the narrow pantry staircase.

CHAPTER 7

"Catherine!" Miles shouted, careening down the steps after her. "Please wait, I… I don't know what I was thinking. I beg your forgiveness," he cried. He reached out for her arm. She wrenched from his grasp.

"Please, do not speak of it, sir!" She recoiled. "How dare you force your attentions?" She turned from him and ran down the staircase. Miles followed, shaking and overcome with guilt. He reached the bottom of the stairs seconds behind her. Another blood-curdling scream ripped through the downstairs chambers. Miles froze and squinted across the dimly lit room, frantically trying to make sense of the chaos that seemed to reverberate throughout the cooking hall. As his eyes began to adjust, he was astounded to see that on the floor in the small cove off the cookery, before the massive stone hearth, a young maid was writhing and twisting upon her knees. To his utter shock, she appeared to be deep into the throes of childbirth.

"Oh, dear God!" he cried, instantly sobering.

The wretched girl was backlit by the roaring, spitting flames of a fire that had been stoked to keep her warm, her fertile contours outlined by an unearthly halo of light. The young maid's shrieking, straining silhouette was the very vision of hell itself, Miles thought in horror. He tried to back away, but he could not tear his eyes from the miserable maid. Gussie was helping to balance the girl on the stone floor of the cove that had been strewn with layers of hay and straw to absorb the birthing fluids. Miles had never before seen a sight that he was now witness to. Repulsed and feeling as though he were about to be sick from both the wine and the harrowing images that lay before him, Miles reeled and pulled Catherine toward the stairs to the main floor.

"This is not a sight for you to see," he cried, desperate for escape. She tried to shake off his grasp, ignoring him as she took a step toward the cove.

"Catherine, I beg of you! Come back upstairs," he pleaded.

"Remove your hand," she hissed. He instantly let go.

Defiant, Catherine turned her back to him and moved closer to the young girl. She stared in fascination as Gussie began to work her hands over Annie's stomach, pushing, twisting and pressing hard at the protruding mound.

"Archie, bring more straw!" Gussie was shouting. "Eliza, Alice, bring all th' linens ye' can lay yer 'ands on! God 'elp me, th' wee bairn is turned tiddly!" Gussie sat back on her heels and grimly steeled herself for what she knew lie ahead.

Miles could hardly believe the primordial scene that lay before him. The young girl had obviously been in heavy labor for some time and was now nearly naked, her crumpled cottons gathered in knotted disarray beneath her heavy breasts. She was beyond all caring, sprawling on her hands and knees over the straw and writhing in what could only be described as utter agony. He was horrified. He stumbled over to confront Gussie, forcing his way through a cluster of kitchen maids.

"Is there not a doctor or a midwife to oversee this?" Miles demanded.

"Closest midwife is over in Gravesleigh, Mi'Lord, and a stable boy has been sent. Nae' that she'll arrive in time, by the looks of it," said Gussie.

Knees creaking, she rose and took him by the shoulders, using her considerable bulk to forcibly trundle him out of the way.

"Forgive me, MiLord, but ye'll have to stand aside."

Miles was taken aback by yet another in a series of surprises. *How dare this upstart cook speak to me in that manner,* he thought, astonished by her impudence as this ungodly night staggered toward morning. Another desperate scream erupted from the wretch. Through the thick fog still swimming in his head, he began to slowly comprehend that he held little power in this situation. Working his way over to the stairs, Miles sank to the bottom step and held his aching head in his hands, trying hard to collect his wits.

Annie collapsed to the floor in sheer exhaustion as Gussie gathered together her supplies and prepared for the imminent birth. Jock, Annie's naïve young husband, had been summoned at the first contraction from his pre-dawn milking duties in the barn. He kneeled at her side, gently kissing her forehead, and mindlessly stroking her damp, tangled curls as she lay panting on the straw. Suddenly, Annie screamed out, convulsing through another torturous contraction. She bore down, grabbing desperately for her husband's hands, ripping at his sleeves.

"What's 'appening?" cried Jock, looking wild-eyed to Gussie, terrified for his wife.

"Dinna' push, Annie!" cried Gussie.

Several maids held lanterns up close as Gussie began working frantically to massage the opening with handfuls of cold butter, desperate to make room for the head that was crowning, but to no avail. With one final piercing scream, Annie convulsed, then arched her spine, and then drew her knees to her chest. With all eyes upon her, she rolled her head backwards and collapsed unconscious back onto the stone floor. The room fell silent as Gussie prayed aloud. The long moments ticked by. Suddenly, dark, matted hair appeared, and then a perfectly formed head came ripping through, tearing the soft flesh and viscera along with it. Miles doubled over and violently retched on the stairs. With intense concentration, Gussie gently hooked her fingers under the baby's armpits as the shoulders worked their way out. Moments later, a tiny baby girl came sliding into the world.

"It's a wee lass," Gussie cried out to the anxious crowd.

Within minutes, the afterbirth issued forth, followed by a silent, ominous pool of dark red blood that began to slowly spread through the straw. The horrifying sight quickly tempered any excitement felt at the birth. Catherine shoved her way to Gussie's side through the small crowd of servants that had gathered to watch.

Jock stared in abject fear at the deathly crimson stain that was spreading ever wider into the straw around his beautiful wife. In the flickering lantern light, his tears fell freely; instinctively knowing that any joy he felt at the birth of his daughter was to come at the unspeakable price of his beloved Annie.

"Can nothing be done? Can no one 'elp her?" he begged, wiping anguished tears with the back of his dirty, calloused hands.

Eliza gently covered Annie with a quilt, while another maid tucked a soft, goose down pillow under her head in a futile attempt at making her comfortable. Someone handed Gussie a pair of kitchen shears and ball of string. After tying the twine in two places around the womb cord, she cut between the strings. When that was done, she worked to warm the baby.

Catherine was transfixed, fascinated by every detail of the birth. Gussie took a cloth and gently cleared the mouth of fluid, then patted gently on the soles of the baby's feet until a weak cry was heard. After swaddling the mewing child in a warm blanket, she gave the baby over to Jock. Holding his newborn child close to his chest, Jock collapsed into heaving sobs against the stone hearth. Catherine turned to Gussie, who sank into a nearby chair, exhausted.

"What is happening? Why is there so much blood?"

"There's been a tear in the flesh, my lamb. Too much of the blood humours will be lost." Gussie wiped her eyes. She'll nae' live through th' morning."

"But surely a tear can be repaired?" asked Catherine.

"I dinna' know how. Perhaps the midwife… I canna' do it, my lamb," confessed the grieving cook. Archie brought his wife a basin of water and a clean towel to wipe her hands. He also brought the tankard of ale, which she gratefully accepted. Catherine pressed further.

"But if nothing is done, she will die?"

"Aye, lovey, she will surely die."

Catherine thought for a desperate moment. Surely something could be done. *As with a tear in a stocking, flesh could be sewn.* She was electrified by the very idea. She had read of such a thing in a book. *Have I the nerve to try?* Catherine wavered. *Could it be as simple as making a decision,* she thought? But Catherine was nothing if not decisive. She remembered Master Howell's lessons. *Trial and error, he taught. Scientific experimentation. Logical thought. It was occurring all around them, he said every day in his lessons, and in many fields of study, including medicine. Trial and error.* She nearly spoke the words aloud. *What is the most grievous consequence?* She considered the possibilities. *The maid could die. But, Gussie says that the maid will surely die, thus if I am wrong, the outcome will be the same*, she thought. *If I'm right, she may live. Decisive. I must be decisive*, she thought to herself, as she watched the frightening, bright red pool of blood spreading ever wider. Her thoughts suddenly came into brilliant clarity.

"Jane!" she shouted to her handmaid. "Fetch my sewing basket and thread the largest needle. Use the best silk thread you can find!

"Aye, Miss," yelled Jane, as she raced up the back steps.

Miles leapt from the stairs and tried to pull Catherine away from the unconscious maid.

"Catherine, you must stop!" he commanded. "You don't belong down here. Let the servants look after their own. You know nothing of this!"

Catherine wrenched free and turned to face him, suddenly furious at his tone.

"I know that she will die if nothing is done! She may die still. I don't know if I may be of any use, but something must be done, and you can either lend your assistance, or...

She took a deep breath, "...or you can get out of my way!"

Miles looked as though he'd been slapped; but he kept his tongue and stepped back, managing a slight, if unsteady bow. He disappeared into the small crowd of servants that were still hovering around the girl.

Catherine turned to Gussie with an anxious look etched upon her face. "Please, will you help?"

Wide-awake now, Gussie was ready for anything. She knew how resourceful Catherine could be, and never once doubted that the girl could do anything she set her clever mind to.

"Aye, I'll help ye', lassie," she replied grimly.

She looked at Catherine in all her finery. A sudden thought struck her.

"Alice!" Gussie called out. "Help Lady Catherine out of tha' gown and give her yours," she commanded.

Alice's eyebrows shot up in surprise, but she instantly complied. The maid led Catherine to a nearby storage closet and quickly helped her change from the taffeta gown into her simple skirts and smock. Apron strings flying untied behind, Catherine raced back to Annie who was lying pale and deathly still before the flickering light of the fire.

Catherine kneeled over the unconscious girl and took stock of the worsening situation. Blood seemed to be pulsing from the wound. She grabbed a cloth and tried to staunch the flow. For a just a moment, she could see the rupture, then just as quickly the wound was obscured again. She could feel a tide of panic rising in her chest, as a tendril of hair fell down into her eyes. She sat back on her heels, took a deep breath and shoved the lock away with the back of her wrist. She glanced over to Gussie, searching her worn and beloved face for even the slightest reassurance. Gussie gave a small, worried nod of encouragement as Jane handed Catherine the needle that she had threaded with a length of black silk. Catherine steadied her nerves.

"Gussie, if you are able, wipe the blood away while I try to sew the tear."

"Aye, m'lass."

Gussie took a fresh towel and dabbed carefully as Catherine bent toward Annie and took a good look. Miles, watching from a distance, sagged against a maid standing next to him. Archie slipped away to find Lord Abbott as Catherine gently took hold of the fissures of flesh. She hesitated for a moment, her resolve wavering. She looked up to see Eliza at the doorway of the cove on her knees, praying fervently. She glanced back to Gussie once more.

"Right to it, then," urged the cook, who quickly rolled her eyes heavenward and crossed herself as well, for good luck.

Catherine decided to begin at the top of the tear. She inhaled deeply, and then held her breath. She pushed gently on the needle. Nothing. She glanced to Gussie, who reached in to wipe the wound once again. Gussie nodded.

"Try it again, lassie."

This time, Catherine bore down much harder and shoved the needle in. The tender flesh held resistant to the pressure, then with a sudden pop, gave way. Catherine shuddered, momentarily overcome with revulsion and panic. She stopped, then took another deep breath to calm herself and slowly pulled on the thread. Annie stirred briefly and screamed out; startling everyone in the room, then the maid fell into a frightening silence. Gussie wiped the skin clean, revealing the tear and the first stitch.

"Aye, you've done it, m'lass," cried Gussie in amazement.

Emboldened, Catherine collected her wits and, banishing all fearsome thoughts from her mind, began to work intently. Stitch after stitch, she plunged the needle through until the separated flesh at last became one. As she hoped, once the tear was bound the blood slowed, and then ceased to flow altogether. Catherine tied off the silken thread and cut the length with a small set of engraved embroidery scissors. Gussie held a vinegar-soaked cloth to the wound and secured it with strips of linen.

"Will she live?" begged Jock, his tears flowing freely.

"Tis' in God's hands, nae," whispered Gussie, shaken to her very core by the sight.

Afraid to move the young mother, Eliza covered Annie once again with a blanket in front of the fire, her head still resting on the feather pillow. She would be attended to through the long morning. Lord Abbott appeared at his daughter's side, thunderstruck at the bravery and wits she displayed. Aunt Viola followed not far behind, and for once, could think of absolutely nothing to say.

Catherine sat back on her heels, and then sank to the floor; by turns both exhilarated and completely shattered. She broke down into tears as Miles rushed to her side.

"That was the most astonishing sight I have ever witnessed," he said, humbled. "Catherine, I beg of you. Please forgive me."

She looked up at Miles as weak shafts of light began to shine through the small, spider-webbed covered windows of the cove. Catherine wiped her tears and collected her thoughts.

"Yes, of course," she said, dully.

Then, turning her back to him, she looked straight into the eyes of her father and spoke with a clarity she had never before felt.

"I should like to go with you up to London."

Priory and by 1664 the now-thriving hospital was presided over by the Vicar of St. Bartholomew-the-Less. It was to this formidable Anglican priest, Father Thomas J. Hardwicke, that Simon had been summoned.

Standing outside the administrative offices of the hospital, Simon swayed from foot to foot. He knew precisely why he'd been sent to speak to Father Hardwicke. Sweat beads began to form down the back of his neck. Simon nervously raked his fingers through the straw-blond hair that fell in waves to his powerful shoulders and brushed his hands over the linen tunic he wore to protect his clothing in a useless attempt to straighten his raiment. He was not looking forward to the discussion that was about to take place. He knocked quietly. For a long moment, the only thing Simon could hear was his own nervous, shallow breaths. A high, thin voice floated through the crack in the door.

"Come," directed Father Hardwicke.

Simon gently eased the wooden door open and walked into the office. Ledgers, papers and books littered the heavily carved desk of the head administrator. Father Hardwicke looked up briefly from his writings, and gestured briefly for Simon to sit in a sagging leather chair opposite him, then returned to his journal. The only sound in the room was a ticking clock. Interminable seconds dragged by. Simon shifted uncomfortably in the chair. Father Hardwicke looked up and tipped his head back as he peered through small wire-framed spectacles that sat perilously on the tip of his aquiline nose.

"Distressing news, I'm afraid, Master McKensie."

Simon shifted uncomfortably. He knew what was coming.

"Right to it, then," said the elder man. "McKensie, I have received several notices from the bankers. Your accounts are overdrawn."

"Sir, I offer my sincere apologies."

The priest looked over his spectacles, his eyebrows raised.

Simon took a deep breath and shifted again in the chair, the leather hide creasing under him. Simon pretended to examine the smudges on his tunic left from the soldier's operating bed. He wondered if he should confess to the priest. Perhaps he could simply allude to his situation and be done with it. He decided to try.

"You see, sir, I've had several large expenses of late. Might I ask if… well, if perhaps the registrar could wait until the spring? Were it possible to wait a month, maybe two, possibly three, I'm quite sure to have the funds necessary for the remainder of my training…"

Father Hardwicke cut Simon off with a laconic wave of an ancient and translucent hand that had not once in his life done a hard days work. Chastened, Simon dropped his eyes to the floor where a shaft of light illuminated a fine layer of dust that had settled over a stack of ledgers. He stifled the urge to sneeze.

"Further, I have received a multitude of complaints from Dr. Clarke about episodes of insubordination," continued the priest, absently rifling through a sheaf of papers.

He directed a piercing gaze from under deeply hooded eyes at Simon. "The two of you do seem to find yourselves in profound discord over many of our patients."

Simon exhaled slowly as he felt his irritation building. He'd spent four very long years at St. Bartholomew's in medical training under Dr. Clarke, and he knew those difficult years would be for naught if he dared challenged the old goat. And yet, the surgeon's filthy habits were a constant source of aggravation to him. If he could just convince Father Hardwicke that the philosophy of medicine was beginning to change from easing the patients out of this world to keeping them in it by healing them; then perhaps, he could find what he had been searching for. Perhaps he could find a voice in this hospital.

Simon was painfully aware that he had spent the whole of his savings and so much more, but the knowledge he'd acquired from long nights of research and study was valuable beyond measure. *And yet, he could not speak of his research to a single soul for the punishment he would face would surely be death by hanging in the public square for all of London to witness.* Simon hesitated, and then decided to throw every caution to the winds. He rose from his chair and stood at the massive desk face to face with Father Hardwicke.

"Sir, I beg of you! If you could please see your way clear to listen to my ideas," said Simon, his heart beating out of his chest, as he dared to give voice to the burning thoughts that had consumed his days and nights of study and experimentation.

The old priest pushed his chair back, folded his hands to his chest and studied the determined young man standing before him for a moment. He nodded.

"Go on."

"Sir, I've devoted nearly the whole of my life to the study of medicine. I've dedicated my days, my nights. I've kept meticulous records of my experimentations. And I have learnt so much. So very much."

Simon put both hands on the desk and leaned in. Father Hardwicke narrowed his eyes at the fervent young man, yet, surprisingly, did not stop the unexpected onslaught of words that came pouring out.

"We must heal our patients, Father, not watch them die," cried Simon, with a desperate intensity bourne of fierce intellect and a deeply held desire to understand the human anatomy. Long-held thoughts tumbled from his lips as he dared challenge the old man to his bold new ideas.

"Sir, I have spent countless hours reading journals of treatment practices from both here in England and from the continent. I wholeheartedly believe we must separate the feverish and dying patients from the patients with broken limbs and sprains, lest they too, become feverish and die. I have personally seen it happen time and again, and yet Dr. Clarke will nae' begin to consider the practice of isolation."

Simon raked his fingers again through his straw-colored waves, intensity etched upon his face.

"Father Hardwicke, we must absolutely come to understand why we, who are surrounded by the sick and dying every hour of every day, do not often become just as ill ourselves." He paced, staring at the floor as though the answer were lying there. "This more than any other is the perplexity that haunts my nights and drives my days of study."

The priest shifted in his chair, losing patience. Simon hesitated a moment, then rubbed his damp palms together, sensing that his moment was now or never. He nervously took a deep breath and pressed forward.

"Sir, I've even taken a detailed account of our operating theater practices. I feel most assuredly that we must use clean surgical tools and dressings, for although I cannot say why, I… I know it to be an ill practice." Simon raked his hand through his hair once more, and then offered his most deeply held belief. "And sir, I feel this is of the utmost most importance. We must not abandon a patient to the ministrations of the clergy the moment we pronounce the inevitability of death; rather we must establish a dissection room in order to open the body to scientific discovery. You see…"

"Enough!" Father Hardwicke slammed his hand on the desk, causing Simon to jump and fall silent. "Enough," he said again, more quietly this time.

For a long moment, the priest considered the determined and fiercely intelligent young man standing before him who pushed harder on the boundaries of medical knowledge than anyone he had ever before seen. Father Hardwicke stood and walked to a leaded glass window. He clasped his hands behind his back. The old man looked out to a threatening sky as thick wafts of black chimney smoke curled and tumbled down over the slate rooftops of the hospital, considering the decision he was about to make. Slowly, he turned toward Simon and spoke.

"My brother, Lord Mayor of the town of Wells in the south, is afflicted and in ill health, due in no small part to the self-indulgent and extravagant lifestyle he leads," sniffed the priest. "I have urged him to retain the services of a personal physician, yet he has thus far stubbornly refused. I fear his health will be permanently compromised should he continue in his excessive ways."

He sighed and sat back down at his desk, once again examining Simon's bank ledgers on his desk. Father Hardwicke lifted his head and looked straight at Simon.

"I will pay you, McKensie. I will pay you to travel to Wells for the remainder of this term and attend to his health."

Father Hardwicke rifled through the papers he held once more, and then tossed them onto the desk. He leaned back in his chair and, looking up at the ceiling, noticed a brackish-colored water stain that dripped down the plastered wall above the window. He sighed, dropped his shoulders and looked over to Simon. For one brief, almost transcendent moment, he very nearly smiled.

"These vexing and interminable disagreements with Dr. Clarke aside, your medical work here has been most admirable. You have attained the top rank in your class all four years of your medical training here at St. Bartholomew's Hospital and I'm quite sure the outcome will be the same in your final year. Further, your examination interview by the College of Physicians resulted in excellent marks."

The corners of Father Hardwicke's lips curled ever so slightly upwards. Simon was utterly fascinated that it took the old man such effort to smile.

"Therefore, I am pleased to inform you that you are now accorded the title of physician," he said, pausing for effect. "*Doctor* McKensie."

Simon's eyes widened and he inhaled to quell his surprise.

The old priest reached out from the depths of his chair and straightened a book on his desk, absently aligning the corners at careful right angles. He spoke slowly, his thin, reedy voice circling the prey.

"Should you decide to accept the position I am now offering, I will absolve you of your current debt, and pay you the sum equivalent to the tuition due when the remaining year of your residency resumes in September."

Simon caught his breath as his heart dropped. He was cornered. Trapped.

Father Hardwicke watched carefully as Simon shifted once more in his chair and looked down at the floor. He could see the resistance, the fight, even the barest trace of fear in the eyes of this intelligent, promising young lad. He also knew the very dangerous game the lad was playing.

There had been veiled whispers from the constabulary during the boy's training. Anonymous notes in the night slipped under the priest's doorway. One more just this last fortnight. *The warning was the final nail in the lad's coffin, as it were*, he thought. *He could not; nae, most vehemently would not, allow neither his hospital nor any soul in association with it to interfere with his own divine destiny. No matter the scientific advances. No matter the medical knowledge to be gained! The Father Thomas J. Hardwicke Pavilion for the Infirmed would be built at St. Bartholomew's during his lifetime, by God!* He would absolutely see to that. *No, the lad had to take his leave for a time.* He leaned across the desk to deliver the final, devastating blow.

"Your journals, Master McKensie." He corrected himself. "*Doctor* McKensie. I shall require that your journals also take leave from London."

He probed even further. "I presume you know the journals to which I refer."

A bolt of white-hot terror ran through Simon. He struggled to remain impassive.

"There are laws, Dr. McKensie," murmured the priest. An ominous silence descended over the darkening chamber.

Father Hardwicke stood, setting his palms flat on the desk. He leaned over his piles of work, drawing himself ever closer to Simon.

"Allow me to explain."

His thin voice became very quiet, almost a whisper. He straightened, then walked around the desk and bent in so close to Simon's face that Simon could see his reflection in the priest's spectacles. Simon gripped the arms of the chair, knuckles white, fingernails digging into flesh, willing himself to keep silent. *How he longed to share his knowledge, to put into practice everything he'd learned over these last four years. How he longed to find someone who would listen.* Simon, avoiding the old man's burning gaze, looked down to the floor.

"I do not wish to know how you came to this information, Dr. McKensie, and I certainly do not wish to know of your associates in your clandestine endeavors. I merely intend to separate the reputation of St. Bartholomew's from certain information that could prove damaging beyond compare to this hospital and, I might add, fatal to your health. Do you understand precisely what I am saying to you?"

Simon nodded. Defeated. He spoke slowly. "I do."

The silence in the room hung heavy, interrupted only by the sound of the ticking clock. Father Hardwicke slowly exhaled and stood, well satisfied that he had solved several problems that had been vexing him for quite some time.

"Very well. I shall write to my brother that you will depart for Wells when the term ends. That should give you time enough to gather together your writings and deliver them to me for safekeeping. If you wish, you may take your research with you. I have no course upon your property, so long as there is nary a single whit of your experimentations left in London that can be traced back to or even remotely associated with you or I or, most especially, this hospital."

Simon felt his entire body collapse in relief. He was not to be expelled from medical school. He would be allowed to return for his final year of surgical training. The heavy weight of secrecy seemed to have lifted from his shoulders, and then just as quickly returned in the form of a shapeless, looming dread as he contemplated the coming months. Any promise of income he could offer, any possible sum of royalties left uncollected at the publishers would now be worthless in pursuit of his freedom. *Every possible glimmer of autonomy over his own destiny will be impossible if he were sent away from London.*

Father Hardwicke strode back to the leather chair behind his desk. He took up a pen and parchment and began to write. He looked up to see Simon still sitting in the chair opposite him, and absently waved his hand toward the door.

"That is all, Doctor."

Simon closed the vicar's door behind him, and stepped into the hallway. He leaned his back against the wall, his heart sinking. He was to be banished. Banished to a life from whence he had come, to the fearsome, lonely, hardscrabble country life that he'd fought tooth and nail to escape. A life he thought he'd left so very far behind.

CHAPTER 9

Abbottsford Abbey
Stockbridge, Buckinghamshire
January 1665

The heavy linen missives had arrived at the Abbey for days. They came slowly at first. Every afternoon, Cedric had unlatched the Abbey door and accepted an elegant, hand-written letter from the Houghton Hall coachman. Cedric handed the notes to Jane, who took them up the stairs to Catherine, who dropped them onto an ever-increasing pile on the floor by her desk, unopened. She had not left her room in a week, choosing instead to take her meals by tray. Lord Abbott was so concerned that he joined Viola in the conservatory one afternoon for tea, a cloying ritual he normally despised. Viola looked up from her needlework in surprise.

"This has gone on far too long," fumed Lord Abbott, abruptly taking a seat beside Viola on a settee near the window. "Have you spoken to her?"

Lord Abbott composed himself. "I fear something unpleasant has occurred with young Miles."

"I have not spoken with the girl. She will see no one, not even Charles," said an exasperated Viola. She set her needlework beside her on the velvet cushion and faced her brother.

"With your permission, Alvyn, I intend to put an immediate stop to this absurd nonsense."

Lord Abbott looked uncomfortable. He had no idea what to do when it came to his only daughter and such intimate matters.

"I cannot decide whether to stave off the journey up to London. Will she go? I should think that a grand shopping expedition for a marriage wardrobe would tempt her from her chambers, but, of course, she has never given much quarter to new clothing before. Perhaps we should postpone…"

Viola crisply cut him off. "We will absolutely do nothing of the sort. I have devoted myself for weeks planning an engagement ball for Catherine and Miles and I will not allow the child to be the ruination of all my hard work. Why, it's taken an entire fortnight just to pare the guest list down to sixty two," said Viola, veering easily off the topic at hand when contemplating the decoration of the London house. "I knew we should have purchased a larger table."

He was truly at a loss. Young girls were confounding to his sensibilities. He sighed. "How I wish Tamesine were here."

Viola absently flicked her lace handkerchief toward the parlour maid standing nearby. The young girl quickly poured a cup of tea from a silver teapot into a delicate china cup and saucer. The teapot was part of an elaborate silver service that was laid out on a table next to Viola. The maid handed the dainty cup and saucer to Lord Abbott, then retreated quietly back to her station behind the table. Viola passed Lord Abbott a plate of her beloved Belgian chocolates. He took one, absently biting into the dark, velvety confection.

"You've done well, Alvyn," Viola said softening. She felt a brief, uncomfortable wave of sympathy knowing how hard he had worked to raise the children without his wife. How very lonesome he had been.

Lord Abbott shook his head in dismay. His thoughts began to roil as agitation and anger began to rise in him. Though he had not been privy to the precise details in his youth, he knew full well why he was not related by marriage to Lord Houghton, for the man had not once in his life directed his attention to the concerns of anyone beyond himself and the next social engagement. He desperately feared that the son now followed firmly down that same path. Privately, Lord Abbott could barely tolerate the thought of being related by marriage to the family now. He pounded the arm of the settee; not quite understanding why he'd ever consented to the coupling.

"By God's thunder, if the lad has...

Viola quickly interrupted, diverting his thoughts. Unbeknownst to her brother, Viola had worked ceaselessly for years to maneuver what she considered to be spectacular match between Catherine and Miles, having laid the plot for a betrothal when they both were but in the nursery. The death of Tamesine had allowed her far more primacy over the children and only served to intensify her efforts. She had many years to make manifest her schemes and now she knew, to her unbridled satisfaction, that she would finally be the envy of all the highborn ladies in the valley. The mere thought of a broken engagement sent a cold shiver of fear coursing through her veins. *No, she vowed, after these many years, she would not allow a single error in judgment to be the ruination of all her plans, and certainly not a trifling, feckless denouement.*

"Cease this tantrum at once!" Viola demanded.

Frustrated, Lord Abbott stopped mid-sentence. He took a sip from the dainty cup. A bit of tea spilled onto his cravat, causing a fresh outburst.

"Damnation!" he thundered. "These pindling vessels are not meant for a grown man's hands."

"You know nothing of the cause to her retreat," said Viola, ignoring his bombastic temper.

She faced him head on. "Alvyn, you must promise me that you'll not intrude upon this union until you know the source of the conflict. Perhaps it is the case that the lad has truly done nothing to warrant your wrath."

Viola had been subjugated once before in her tireless resolve to join the Abbey with Houghton Hall, at least ceremonially. Decades of resentment arose still, like bitter acid in her throat, when she thought of her own devastating engagement to the current Earl of Houghton. Viola could have easily turned a practical eye to his philanderings. *Indeed, the silken gowns, extravagant jewels and grand parties that would befit her, as the Countess of Houghton, would naturally have come at a price. It was to be expected.* It was a price she would have most willingly born. Though she'd sobbed for a fortnight, begging her father to allow the union, the pious and devoted Earl of Abbottsford had first sent a summary missive to the Houghton patriarch terminating the union, then sent Viola on an extended visit to relations up in London.

For two very long years in St. James, the most exciting, the most fashionable district in the growing, cosmopolitan city, Viola was abjectly miserable. Though her relatives surely tried their utmost, the lavish parties, the social visits, and even the country house weekends could do nothing to alleviate her unending misery. Viola spent much of the time in her suite of rooms and returned to Stockbridge a much-changed young woman, resentful, ill-humored and remarkably self-indulgent.

Nevermore was she to be the object of a gentleman's attentions, Viola thought bitterly. She would show them, she avowed upon her return to the Abbey. *She would show them still.* The single-minded attainment of the highest social stature and position were the only remaining pleasures of her life. *By God's oath, she would not allow a spoiled, entitled young man, nor a tiresome, studious young girl to be the ruination of her carefully planned scheme.*

"Alvyn, I will speak to Catherine," said Viola crisply. "I will bring to light the cause of her unhappiness and see to it that she rejoins the family this night for supper. I will also see to it that she is packed and ready for the journey to London."

A heavily relieved Lord Abbott arose and sent the delicate teacup clattering on the sideboard, leaving Viola to her confounding rituals.

As Lord Abbott disappeared into his study, Cedric opened the Abbey door to receive the afternoon's correspondence. There was yet another engraved letter addressed to Catherine. Jane walked the missive up the stairs to her door and knocked, then quietly entered the room. She found Catherine still sitting in her dressing gown before the writing table, working quietly on yet another butterfly sketch.

"I have news, Mi'Lady," said Jane, setting the letter on the escritoire. Without taking her eyes off the drawing, Catherine slid the note unopened across the desk with the side of her hand. It fell onto the pile on the floor. Jane furrowed her brow.

"Nae, Miss. There's news of Annie."

Catherine glanced up at her in alarm.

"Nae', tis good news, Mi'Lady! Annie was able to walk to the barn with Jock this morning," said Jane, as she straightened the room.

Jane hesitated over the pile of unopened letters. She glanced to Catherine, then bent down and gathered them one by one into a tidy stack. She set the stack at the back of the desk. Catherine looked up from her sketch, a sense of pride coursing through her. Seeing a spark of interest for the first time in weeks, Jane went on.

"She'll be allowed to return to the kitchen soon."

"Oh! That is very good news, indeed, Jane," exclaimed Catherine.

"Aye'n she's askin' for you, Miss."

Catherine smiled with delight. Jane rushed to her and kneeled by her side.

"Ye' did it, Mi'Lady, ye' saved 'er life." Jane said, looking at her in awe. "I'll not mind tellin' ye', I'd'uv been far too frightened, m'self, to do what ye' did. Ye've a right to be quite proud. Will ye' go to her, Mi'Lady?

"Of course, Jane. I fear that I have spent too much time alone. I'll go down after I dress. Will you choose a gown?" asked Catherine.

"Certainly, Mi'Lady."

Jane went over to the armoire and selected a day gown of charcoal gray wool with an elaborate lace-ruff collar. Jane helped Catherine out of her dressing robe and began to fasten the fitted costume up the back.

Their conversation was interrupted by a knock at the door, and then the door flew open wide. Aunt Viola briskly charged into the room. She ignored the maid and walked straight toward Catherine, facing her head on. She waved a dismissive hand toward Jane.

"Jane, fetch the trunks from the attic and begin to ready Lady Catherine's wardrobe for London."

Jane stood rooted to the floorboards, her hands over the eyelets, unsure of what to do. Her eyes darted between Catherine and Viola.

Aunt Viola clapped her hands sharply, jolting Jane into action. "This instant!"

Jane nodded, wide-eyed. "Yes, Mi'Lady.

"That will be all," said Viola, shooing her away.

Jane hurriedly fastened the last of the delicate ivory horn buttons of Catherine's gown and skittered out of the room, scared of the ill-humored old woman as she was.

"Sit down, Catherine," said Viola, pulling out the dainty chair before the escritoire. Catherine sat, rearranging her skirts. Viola paced before her.

"This childish behavior must stop, Catherine. You must leave your room and rejoin the family. Your father is most distressed, as am I."

Catherine bowed her head, unwilling to speak of that night in the pantry. Viola reached to the top of the writing desk and took hold of the bundle of letters. She easily recognized the Houghton wax seal on the unopened letters. She turned to face Catherine.

"Have you not opened these?" asked Viola, horrified that Miles's letters had been cast aside. "What can you be thinking, girl!" she exclaimed, furious at Catherine's disregard.

"I have been thinking that I no longer wish hear from him," said Catherine.

"Why ever not," snapped Viola.

"I do not wish to say."

Viola steeled herself. "Did he make advances toward you the night of the Christmas feast?"

Catherine did not look up. Her eyebrows furrowed, her lips tightened. She looked miserable. Viola softened. "Come, girl. Answer me."

Catherine remained still. Viola reached out. She took Catherine's chin in her hand and lifted it. Looking into Catherine's troubled and sad eyes, she came straight to the point. "Did Miles force his attentions upon you?" Viola asked, with surprising gentleness.

Catherine looked down at her skirts and gave an imperceptible nod. Viola took a deep breath, and then slowly exhaled. She took Catherine by the hands. "Catherine, your mother is not here to advise you on these matters, so I fear that the duty falls to me. I must insist that you answer his letters."

Catherine raised her head and eyed her aunt, anger again rising in her chest.

"I know full well what is expected of me. But, Aunt Viola, you could not begin to understand."

"If you think you are the first young women to..."

Catherine cut her off. She faced her aunt, and spoke with unaccustomed clarity.

"It is not that he behaved badly that night. The wine and ale had gone to his head. I understand that he was not himself when he caught me tight in his grasp. I can forgive that. You see, the problem runs far deeper than one single misunderstood moment."

Viola looked confused.

"There is a profound discord between Miles and I, and Aunt Viola, I fear that our differences can never be brought into harmonious accord."

Catherine sat straight and tall, unbending in her resolve. She watched her aunt furrow her brow, as though she, for once, had nothing to say. Viola walked to the window and looked out over the frozen gardens. Catherine went on, speaking aloud the thoughts that had been turning in her head since Christmas.

"I have a desire to become a woman of substance. I wish to learn, to think and to understand the world that surrounds me. I do not wish to spend the rest of my days wandering idly about an estate thinking of ways to amuse myself. I wish to become a woman of science and letters, whereas I fear that he would like nothing more than to marry an empty-headed, frivolous ninny who is incapable of thinking no further than the next social gathering."

Viola stamped her foot in anger. Seeming to gather both her wits and her heavy black satin skirts, she whirled about and faced Catherine with a seething fury.

"Who, in God's name, are you to speak of what you desire, you ungrateful child? Have you any idea of the sacrifices that have been made for you? Have you any idea how much your father has done for the family and for the people of the villages? You have a duty to your family. More importantly, you have a duty to your father. You have no more of a right to chart your own course than I did my own!"

Catherine stared at her in shock. Viola stopped short. She looked as though she'd said too much. She walked to the desk and picked up the stack of letters from Miles. She shook them in Catherine's face.

"Let me make myself absolutely clear, my dear. You *will* see him again and this marriage *will* take place. Furthermore, you are never to make mention of a 'women of letters' again in this house. The very idea," she snapped.

Viola dropped the stack of letters into Catherine's lap, her voice lowering to a frightful whisper.

"You are to respond to him immediately. You will see him before we leave for London. Before we *all* leave for London. Do you understand?"

Catherine exhaled. She suddenly realized that she was completely and utterly overmatched.

"Yes, Aunt Viola, I do.

CHAPTER 10

van de Veld Linnenfabriek
Amsterdam, Holland
January 1665

Gossamer tufts of cotton swirled and bounced through the drafty air, before settling softly to the honey-colored wooden floor. The luminous bits were backlit by a weak sun that refracted through a single row of dingy, ice-covered windowpanes of the *Pieter van de Veld Linnenfabriek*. Sixteen-year-old Geertje de Groot hardly noticed. Though she'd cried and sneezed and coughed for months after she arrived at the factory, aching for the clean air and the vast flower-covered fields that surrounded her tiny village of Arnhem, she'd long since made her peace with the floating fibers.

On her ninth birthday, little Geertje had been called from playing in the tulip fields that sprawled behind the family's tiny, one-room thatched cottage. Leading her out to the dirt road that fronted the cottage, her stern-faced father gathered Geertje into his arms and swung her up onto bench of the old horse cart, then hoisted himself up beside to her. Her mother, Marit, remained inside the tiny cottage, silently watching through the bits of lace that covered a small window next to the brightly painted red front door. A single tear rolled down Marit's careworn cheek as she watched the cart disappear in a cloud of dust beyond the rolling hills of brilliantly colored red and yellow flowers.

Sitting next to her father high up in the cart, its sides painted with faded intertwining tulips, little Geertje squirmed with excitement, thinking they were off to a grand birthday adventure. A silent Klaas de Groot flicked the reins, trundling through the pastoral Dutch countryside toward Amsterdam, reaching the city before nightfall. The teeming crowds bustling in all directions fascinated her, as they worked their way through the narrow cart paths to the *van de Veld Linnenfabriek.* Klaas drew his horse up short before the factory entrance. They clambered down from the cart, the dust rising at their feet. He stood next to Geertje and rang the small bell that hung next to the doorway. The office door was opened and a plump woman Geertje had never seen before smiled down at her, then gently took her by the hand and led her into the small entry room. At the doorstep, her father handed the woman a small bundle, then gave a small nod to Geertje. He paused a moment, staring intently at her face, then Klass turned abruptly and walked back toward the cart. The woman closed the door behind him.

"Pater?" she called. Her voice began to waver. *"Pater?!"* The door stayed shut. She could feel a strange panic rise in her chest. *"Pater!"* She began to scream. *"Pater!!!"*

Geertje raced back to the door and fumbled with the latch, but it was complicated and she couldn't work the lock. She ran to the window and looked through the streaked, cotton-covered panes of glass. She watched, tears streaming down her chubby cheeks, as her father flicked the reins once more, and the horse and cart headed back down the road the way he came. Geertje sank to her knees. She had been left with the van de Velds. She had nothing but a small packet of clothing and a tiny cloth doll her mother had sewn from scraps of fabric to remind her of her life before the factory.

Homesick and terribly lonesome, Geertje begged the van de Veld's each day to be sent back to the cozy village of Arnhem and her little cottage by the tulip fields, but with five younger brothers and sisters that the family could ill afford to feed, it was not to be. Geertje stubbornly sat by the door every day for weeks clutching the little doll, but her father never came back. So, she stayed in the factory and she learned. And she was good. She was very good. In short order, her pudgy, calloused fingers shot the shuttle stick through the fibers of the loom with lightening speed.

As the years went by, she learned to weave the finest grade of linen sheetings for Pieter van de Veld to sell across the great cities of Europe. Pieter fondly called her *Getalenteerde één*, the Talented One, for as kind a man as he was; he was an even shrewder businessman. Her talent at the loom brought him great fortune; for her sheetings were the most fine-spun fabrics his factory had ever produced. He even taught her to weave a thin, ice blue-colored stripe, the exact shade of her unusual eyes, through her work to identify the exquisite cloth. Though she was unaware, her work fetched Pieter twice the amount of *guilders* than the rest of his fabric bolts. To the van de Velds she was known as *Getalenteerde één*, but to the factory workers, Geertje was known as *De Rustige*, the Quiet One, for Geertje rarely spoke. In truth, Geertje rarely looked up from her loom, and as the years slowly faded away, Geertje rarely thought about her family anymore.

Jakob Auckes never once forgot his family. Orphaned by a devastating fire that burned his thatched-roofed cottage to the ground and killed his parents, Jakob had been taken by a kind solicitor to the *linnenfabriek.* Once again, Pieter van de Veld's soft spot for unwanted children and orphans matched his formidable business savvy. Childless, Pieter and his wife, Johanna, gladly took the young lad in. As with Geertje and so many others, they gave him room and board, as well as daily lessons in reading and writing in exchange for the free labor and the hugs they had so desperately longed for from children of their own that never came. To those who showed intelligence, as Jakob and Geertje surely did, Pieter taught them to read and write in Dutch, French and English, for the thriving port city of Amsterdam attracted business from all over Europe and beyond. *Language is commerce and commerce is money in the bank,* Pieter was fond of saying. If he could, he would teach them Chinese. Though the van de Velds were especially kind, Jakob had worked in the factory for years and not a day went by that his heart didn't ache for his mother and father.

Now a strapping seventeen year old, Jakob spent his days heaving rolls of fine linens onto horse carts and delivering them to the local tailoring shops or to the massive Amsterdam harbor for shipping. How Jakob loved being sent to the wharves. He loved feeling the cold ocean breezes whip across his face, tasting the salty air on his tongue and hearing the faint cries of the circling gulls in the dense morning fog. He loved listening to the shouts and curses of the sailors as they loaded cargo into the holds of the massive wooden sailing ships. He loved watching the burly dock workers cast off giant rope lines freeing the ships for passage to exotic ports like Bermuda or even the New World. He longed desperately to be away from Amsterdam and the factory. He dreamed of sailing to England and apprenticing himself to a tailor in London, instead of tossing heavy bolts of cloth around the linen factory like so many matchsticks.

Along with his duties on the factory floor, Jakob was in charge of the boy's *slaapzaal*, the dormitory above the factory workroom, just as Geertje was in charge of the girls. At the age of eighteen, both Geertje and Jakob would be sent out to the worker cottages to live and the next oldest would be put in charge of the *slaapzaal,* but until then, they watched over the younger children at night. They lived in the sleeping quarters that were separated by a small wash station and steam room. Working together in the factory, Jakob had somehow seen through Geertje's quiet ways, and he'd loved her for as many years as he could remember. She was a hard-working, solid peasant girl, with strange, ice blue eyes and a pale, almost translucent complexion. Though she wore the somber black pinafore and white lace cap of a modest factory worker, Jakob, to his sheer delight, discovered quite by accident one bitterly cold November evening, that Geertje had a wonderous appetite for sex as robust as her prodigious appetite for *rookworst, sauerbrauten* and *bier*.

Raging winds were blowing drafts of frigid air through the thin glass windowpanes of the *slaapsaal*. Geertje had finally gotten the little ones to sleep under heavy winter blankets, but she could not calm her own restive thoughts. Though she tossed and turned in her creaking rope bedstead, sleep would not come. Pulling off her nightshift, she had wrapped herself in a soft, woolen quilt, and tiptoed into the little steam room to ease the muscles that were aching from her long day at the loom. From the boy's side of the *slaapzaal*, Jakob had finally finished his last delivery of the night and desperately wished to warm his own frozen flesh. Unaware that he was not alone, he had stripped his clothes off and thrown them into a heap on the cold tile floor. Naked and shivering in the raw night air, Jakob grabbed a ladle of boiling water from a copper kettle that sat above a small fire chamber and poured it onto a stone reservoir. He stepped gingerly into the steaming wooden chamber to warm his bones.

"Damn, het is koud!" he swore, blowing warm air from his lungs into his clamped fists as he hopped from foot to foot. When his eyes adjusted to the dim light, he suddenly saw Geertje sitting on the boards in front of him. He jumped back, banging his head against the wall.

"Aaaaahhhh!" he yelled, and then froze to the spot, speechless.

Geertje didn't even blink. She simply sat on the hard, slatted bench and tilted her head to one side, thoughtfully considering the glorious, broad-shouldered lad with an unruly mop of blond hair and earnest brown eyes standing bare-naked before her. Jakob tried desperately tried to cover himself with one hand, while searching the wall behind him for a cloth with the other. In the glow of the moon shining through a small crack in the wallboards, he stared at her in wide-eyed shock. Then, to his amazement, she'd let the quilt slip slowly to the ground, revealing every last inch of her luxurious body. Jakob nearly fainted. He came right then and there in a miraculous, dazzling, mind-numbing explosion. He was deeply embarrassed, but she'd only laughed and when he at last recovered his wits, they found themselves in each other's arms, rolling around the steam room floor until a hazy winter sun rose in the morning. Jakob fell wildly in love with her lush body, her thick, blond hair that fell in waves to her waist and her extraordinary ice blue eyes. He could not get her out of his mind. He knew could not live without her.

The very next day, Jakob snuck into the *slaapzaal* and dragged a mattress and several quilts up to an unused storage room above the sleeping quarters. After the younger children fell asleep each night, he and Geertje would sneak upstairs and hold each other tight until the morning light woke them up again. He loved her more than he thought possible. He loved even more throwing her onto the makeshift bed he'd fashioned to wrap his arms around her lavish curves, burying his face in the tender warmth of her soft, splendid bosoms, making love again and again through the bitterly cold winter nights. In the workroom, he could not take his eyes off her. He managed to linger at her loom as often as he dared, working his fingers through the warp and weft of the raw fibers until they touched hers. Geertje would demurely drop her hands to her lap, keeping her head down and never once letting on that she even knew Jakob. Life was easier that way.

On the very last day of February, before the blustery winds of a long Dutch winter gave way to the soft, pale sun of early spring, Jakob awoke to his eighteenth birthday. He had dreamed of this day for years. While Geertje slept, Jakob dressed quickly, then left the *linnenfabriek* and walked across town to the solicitor's office. Though he hadn't seen the man since the fire, he knew the solicitor would be there waiting, for

Jakob held in his pocket a faded and well-worn letter from the old man containing instructions for this very day.

"*Gefeliciteerd, mijn jongen,*" said Alfers Konigsgaart, unlocking the office door. He heartily embraced the boy.

The gray-haired solicitor had delivered Jakob to the linen factory ten years before and though he was even grayer and more stooped then Jakob remembered, he easily recognized the kind soul who had once cared for him on the worst day of his life.

Alfers had indeed been waiting for Jakob. An open ledger sat on the desk in front of him. Alfers reached deep into his pocket and pulled out a small, well-worn iron key, then unlocked the drawer of his desk and pulled out a soft leather pouch. He tipped the contents onto the desktop with a clatter. Alfers carefully counted out five *guldens*, then placed the coins back into the pouch and set it on the desk in front of Jakob. The *guldens* had been held in safekeeping by the solicitor since the death of his parents. In accordance with Dutch law, Jakob was entitled to inherit the money on his eighteenth birthday. Alfers came around the desk and placed his hands on Jakob's shoulders, facing him with fatherly concern.

"Have you a plan for your life, young Jakob?"

"*Ja*!" exclaimed Jakob, his bright eyes brimming with excitement. Jakob reached for the leather pouch, then tossed it into the air, deftly catching it again and dropping it into a small *rucksack* he carried with him. He wrapped his arms around the old man in a massive hug for a long moment.

"*Dank je, Mijnheer Konigsgaart.*"

Jakob walked to the door, then turned back to give Alfers one last smile, before closing the door behind him. Jakob stood for a moment outside the solicitor's office and took a deep breath of the fresh air that now seemed filled with endless possibilities. He stepped into the road and stopped unexpectedly at a street vendor's stall. After a moment's hesitation, he bought a jaunty, red leather Dutch cap. He took his change from the vendor, slapped the cap on his head, and then turned, heading straight for the docks that punctuated the town's boundaries. Alfers watched him push into the rabble that was beginning to fill the narrow lane, eagerly charging headlong toward a life unknown.

"*Veilig, jonge Jakob*," whispered Alfers, wishing him a good life.

He watched as the young man disappeared into the crowd. Alfers turned away from the window, walked behind his desk and quietly closed the ledger on Jakob Auckes.

Late that night, up in the little storage room, Jakob pulled Geertje close. She lay cradled in his arms, savoring the touch of his warm skin against hers. She silently reached for the lacings of her nightshift. Jakob took her hands into his own, soft and sure, and then quietly set them aside. He pulled slowly at the laces until at last they were free. Her fine-spun cottons fell away in folds laying bare her soft, luminous flesh. Jakob gently stroked her shoulders, tracing a finger down the curve of her neck and across her chest. Her pale skin smelled of a delicious warmth he couldn't quite place. He reached his arms around her and felt the muscles in her back curve toward him as he drew her close. He kissed her, slowly at first, here, there—the tender press of flesh against flesh, thigh against thigh, lips touching, parting, touching again, soft and gentle. Then, an explosion. An exhilarating rush of passion met with dazzling passion. Rhythmic thrust soaring into delicious pull as two bodies melted into one. Jagged breaths, slowly spent, exhilarated, exhausted. He clung to her and she to him. Earthy shudderings gave way to a luminous stillness. Jakob felt a tear dampen his shoulder. He knew he was home. He knew he belonged with her. He knew he would take care of her the rest of his life. Jakob gathered his courage.

"I've bought a ticket, Geertje," he whispered. "I've bought a ticket on the *Beschermer* to England."

Geertje's blood ran cold. Jakob felt her body stiffen in his arms as a wave of nausea overwhelmed her. She fought the urge to be sick. She turned her back to him, drawing her knees to her chest. She was breathing so hard, that he thought she might faint. Jakob instantly realized she didn't understand.

"*Damn! Ik ben een idioot,"* said Jakob, cursing himself for his awkward ways. He crawled over top of Geertje so he could lie facing her and reached to pull the blankets around them both. He took her face gently into his hands and kissed her tenderly. She closed her eyes and tried to turn from him, but he resisted, holding her close. His heart melted when he saw tears glistening.

"*Niet! Niet!* Geertje, I want for us to both go to England!" He faltered, searching for the words to explain. "I only had five *guldens*, you see, and the ticket cost three. I... I'm only sorry I could not buy two tickets." He was profoundly miserable.

She slowly opened her eyes and searched his desperate face, questioning. "Both of us?

"*Ja*, Geertje, what I want is for us both to go to London. What I mean to say... What I meant was..."

Jakob looked down at his hands and noticed dirt under his fingernails. Embarrassed, he quickly hid his hands under the blanket as he fumbled to explain what he felt in his deeply inexperienced heart. He took a long, slow breath calm his nerves and began again.

"When I get to London, I'll find work. I'll send for you as soon as I earn the money," he promised. She was very quiet. He was sorely unnerved.

"What will you do there?" said Geertje, finally.

"My father was a tailor, Geertje. Before the fire, he taught me to use the needle and thread. It's not much, but it's better than throwing bolts of cloth in the *linnenfabriek* for the rest of my life, and it's what I want to do."

"The van de Velds have always been good to me. And they have been good to you, too. I like it here," she whispered. "They would always take care of us." *No matter what,* she thought to herself. *No matter what.*

He knitted his brow at her words, knowing how kindly he'd been treated. He also knew he could come back if he failed and they would welcome him once again, asking no questions. *How could he make her understand that it was because of the van de Veld's that he now had the courage to forge his own future?*

Why can you not stay in Amsterdam and be a tailor?" she asked, quietly.

Jakob face clouded over. He had thought of the idea many times before, but no matter how he looked at his situation, he always came to the same immutable conclusion.

"I am known to the shopkeepers in Amsterdam as just a *fabrieksarbeider*, a…a lowly factory worker. To them, I'll never be anything more than a delivery boy." He rolled over and faced her. His voice began to rise with fresh possibilities.

"But, Geertje, I've made a friend down at the docks," he said, his eyes alight. "He works on the ships that sail to England. He has told me that London is growing. He says that there are now over a hundred thousand people right in the city, with more coming every day. He says it's a…a place where one can start over and be anything they like. People are pouring into the city, he tells me. And, Geertje, they will all need clothing."

Geertje stared at him. She could hear the rush of excitement rising in his voice. She was overcome with a familiar, aching sadness. Absently smoothing the blankets, she sat up and looked at him.

"When do you leave?" she asked, coiling her hair into a loose knot. He watched as golden curls fell about her face. He had become so comfortable, so enthralled with her ordinary, familiar ways.

"Soon. They are making repairs to the ship and when it is ready to sail, I will tell the van de Velds that I am leaving, and make my last delivery. Geertje, I'm to sleep down with the cargo, in a hammock made of rope. Can you imagine that? I will sleep swinging from side to side like a little baby in the cradle," he laughed, trying to cheer her up.

A little baby in the cradle. A curious choice of words. *A little baby in the cradle.* The words echoed round and round in her head, like a *kinderliedje*, a nursery rhyme. For Geertje was late. Or so she thought. She was not so naïve that she did not know that something could happen up in the little storage room, but Geertje could not be altogether sure, either. She had no one to ask. One day, she might have to confide in van de Veld's. Or perhaps not. But either way, she would not tell him. *No matter the outcome*, she thought, she would not hold Jakob from his dreams.

Geertje searched his face, trying hard to memorize the features she'd grown to love. The wild mop of sandy-colored hair, the nose that was the tiniest bit too big for his face, the errant gap in the front teeth of his irrepressible grin. Try as she might, the tears just kept springing to her eyes. He grabbed her and held her tightly in his arms.

"I'll send for you, Geertje, just as soon as I can. It won't take long, I promise," he said, eager, desperate, to see her smile again. "Then you can come to London and we'll be married. Would you like that, Geertje?"

The idea just slipped out. He suddenly became very quiet.

"Would… would you like to marry me?"

Her eyes widened in surprise. "Marry you?"

He never thought he would have the courage to ask such a monumental question, but, to his surprise, the words fell out of his mouth as easily as asking for another bowl of *soep* at supper. He was shocked at how natural it felt.

"Yes," she whispered.

And for the very first time in her entire life, Geertje allowed herself one single, transcendent moment of happiness.

"Yes, Jakob. I would. I very much would."

One week later, Geertje awoke to a strange dread rising in her chest. She threw her blankets off thinking she had overslept and raced from the storage room down the back stairs to the girl's side of the *slaapzaal*. To her relief, the little ones were still asleep.

She stopped a moment, and then realized that the dread she felt was far too familiar. Geertje dressed quickly and descended to the factory floor where she saw that the door to the van de Veld's office was closed. Outside the office door she saw a *rucksack,* a leather valise and the quirky red leather cap piled next to the office door. Her heart stopped. Jakob was leaving.

A sudden, clanging bell shattered the morning quiet. Collecting her wits, Geertje ran back upstairs to shepherd the younger girls down to the breakfast tables laden with the morning *meel,* her attentions wavering between the sleepy little ones and the closed office door. *Would he ever come out,* she wondered? The kitchen girls came to collect the empty tin breakfast plates as the factory workers filed into the workroom and took their places at the massive looms for the long day ahead.

Geertje walked over and sat at a small, vacant loom. She threaded the shuttle stick with her ice-blue thread and, working quickly, wove a small pocket square about the size of a small handkerchief. After tying it off, she looked around the room to make sure no one was watching, then Geertje hid the square in her apron pocket and returned to her own loom. Jakob finally came out of the office with the van de Veld's following close behind. Jakob gave them each a final, heartfelt hug, then doffed his new cap and looked around the factory for Geertje. He quietly motioned toward the loading dock. Making a pretext to visit the privy Geertje slipped away from her loom and met Jakob behind several wide boards that leaned upright against the back wall. Jakob drew her close, stroking her hair, kissing her lips, and hugging her tight. Tears falling freely, she clung to him.

"*Ik kom voor u,*" he whispered, promising to come back for her. He held her, afraid to ever let go. For a brief moment, even he questioned himself, but Jakob quickly pushed the unwelcome thoughts away. He knew his future lay beyond the shores of Amsterdam.

Fearing that her absence would be noticed, Geertje

reluctantly pulled from his arms. She straightened her hair and smoothed her apron skirts. She gave Jakob one last kiss, then reached into her apron pocket and slipped the blue pocket square into his hand before walking back toward her loom, head bent down to obscure her red, swollen eyes.

Geertje settled back on her stool as she worked to finish another fabric length. It was flaxen in color and she'd worked hard to make it perfect. There were no slubs, no knots and no loose threads. She removed the ivory-colored thread and exchanged it for the thread of ice blue, then wove the final strands into her signature stripe and expertly tied it off. She looked out across the room and gestured to the floor boy. Jakob collected his things, and then went out to the back dock to check the load on the delivery wagon.

The floor boy made his way through the maze of massive looms toward her station. Geertje set the shuttle stick across her lap. As the boy came to collect her roll, she took a corner of the fabric in her hand and lifted it to her lips. She looked toward the loading dock and caught Jakob's eye, then quietly kissed the blue threads of the fabric before the boy took hold of the roll. The boy he heaved her bolt onto his cart and steered it out to the back loading dock. Jakob stuck his head back through the back doors.

"Ik ben terug, Geertje!" he yelled, promising to see her soon.

All heads turned toward Geertje, shocked, for no one had ever spoken to her with such familiarity. She never saw them. From under her simple lace cap, Geertje's pale, ice blue eyes filled with quiet tears as she watched him toss her bolt onto the top of the wagon.

Out on the bustling lane behind the factory, Jakob waved to her one last time, then blew into his gloves and drew his cloak tight. Sitting next to the young floor boy who would bring the cart back to the factory, Jakob gave the reins a solid flick. The horse drawn wagon clopped away as the massive wooden doors to the factory slowly rolled shut. *De Rustig* merely looked down and threaded her loom once more, for she knew Jakob would not come back. No one ever came back.

CHAPTER 11

Village of Wells
Buckinghamshire, England
1 April 1665

Catherine sat on the deep imperial purple bench of the Abbey's finely appointed carriage as it jounced its way toward the pretty little country village of Wells, feeling the soft, velvet-tufted fabric under her fingertips. Early morning sun streaming through the carriage window bathed the handcrafted mahogany veneers in a soft, glowing light. Catherine closed her eyes. She tilted her face toward the glass and reveled in the early spring warmth after the long snows of winter. Though heavy snows, much to Aunt Viola's ever increasing frustration and Catherine's relief had delayed the trip to London, to her surprise she now found herself looking forward to the journey. Catherine and Aunt Viola were traveling alone in the formal carriage. Lord Abbott and Charles were following behind in a separate wagon packed with the extra baggage they would need for their month-long visit to London. The household staff had preceded them by a day to open the house and prepare for their arrival.

Wells, with its hilly, winding lanes of thatched, flintstone cottages clustered around a quaint village square of tidy shops, was the bigger of the two villages in the snug valley and was to be the first stop on the daylong journey. On the north side of the square sat the Royal George Coaching Inn, a lively gathering place for the people of the valley. Supplies, correspondence, and anything else the villagers of both Wells and Stockbridge might need were first delivered to the coaching inn that over time became the social center of the bucolic little valley.

The Royal George was but one in a long line of coaching inns that provided spacious stables and fresh horses every seven miles in all directions between London and the rest of the English countryside. A champion of exceptional horseflesh, Lord Abbott had invested heavily in the property, insisting that the stables be as well constructed as the inn itself. They were a point of pride for the entire town. At his request, stables to shelter fifty horses were built down in the rich pasturelands that stretched below the inn, with five separate rows of stalls. Each stall had ingenious wooden floorings rather than the customary dirt floors that became wet and muddy in winter and were swept, cleaned and laid down with fresh hay each day by the stable boys. Next to the stable rows themselves, nestled under a grove of billowing London plane trees, accommodations were built for the stable master and his family, as well as a spare but comfortable bunkroom for the stable boys. Fenced-in corrals for nearly one hundred horses lay among the English oaks that dotted the rolling pasturelands.

Though the inn and stables were most impressive for a traveler's inn, Lord Abbott knew that with the construction, London's *Royal Coach Company, Ltd.*, would consider selecting The George as one of its star properties along the coaching route. He also knew that a designated royal coaching inn would attract trade and customers to Wells, thereby insuring a steady income for many of the Stockbridge and Wells villagers.

For the good of the townspeople, Lord Abbott financed the entire construction. His gamble paid off, for the inn was indeed selected by the coaching line. Lord Abbott insisted they use the public coach, as he'd invested heavily in bringing the service to Wells. *If they do not use it, they why should the others*, he was fond of saying. Aunt Viola had long given up protesting, for he would not budge on the subject.

Seated on the bench across from Catherine, Aunt Viola was attempting to thread a needle with crimson-colored embroidery thread. She had begun a new tapestry to keep herself entertained and the needle jumped in her hand each time they splashed through a rough patch in the road. It was to be an exhausting trip and she was already irritable.

"Can't they *ever* sort this road out?" she exclaimed, dropping the needle and thread to her lap in exasperation.

Catherine paid no attention to her aunt. She was thinking about the intimate conversation she'd shared with Miles weeks ago, before the late snows set in and trapped them all at home. Chagrined, she'd taken her aunt's scolding to heart and was trying to do her best to please her family. Catherine had finally replied to his letters, inviting Miles to the Abbey for a quiet supper before they departed for London. Aunt Viola, surprisingly, had arranged for them to dine alone in the conservatory, allowing them private time to speak together. *Not that they were ever truly alone, of course*, thought Catherine, for Aunt Viola had walked past the archway several times during the meal, as if to remind them they were still under her prudent watch.

Gussie had prepared an elaborate meal of boiled lamb and onions, roasted potatoes, and for dessert, Catherine's favorite, cherry trifle. A small table had been placed in the center of the bay window with floor to ceiling leaded glass panes that afforded a stunning view over the rolling hills of the estate. It had been set with the finest silver, an embroidered silken tablecloth and beeswax candles that had been crafted by the estates chandlers and set into fine silver candlesticks. Though the setting was elegant, the evening was uncomfortably quiet for Miles still felt the full weight of Catherine's reproach. Only the hollow sounds of knives scraping and fork tines clinking upon the china plates could be heard. Finally, Miles could take no more. He broke the silence.

"Catherine," he began.

She looked up from her plate and waited. Her silence unnerved him.

"Catherine, can you ever forgive my appalling behavior?

Catherine played with the food on her plate, shoving bits of boiled onion from one side to the other. God's truth, she hated onions, but she loved Gussie so dearly that she would never think of giving full voice to her displeasure. She sighed.

"Miles, I know that you were not yourself that night. You were worse for the drink." She pushed another onion aside.

He laughed ruefully. "To be entirely truthful that might, on the odd occasion of course, happen again from time to time." She raised an eyebrow. Seeing that she did not share his humor, Miles grew serious. "But, Catherine, I pledge my troth. I will never, ever again press my unwanted attentions upon you."

She looked down to her plate, wary of his impassioned appeal. He could not resist the challenge.

"You have my word as a gentleman."

Still, she said nothing.

"Please accept my sincerest apologies, Catherine." He bent down to her height, searching her eyes. "May we please banish this unpleasantness from memory and be friends once again?" He grinned, his dimples crinkling irresistibly.

She tilted her head, considering his earnest appeal and his merry grin. *Those dimples.* He truly was like an errant schoolboy one could not stay angry with for long. *Would life with him be as terribly purposeless as she feared? She could certainly try to set her ambitions aside and rise to her family's expectations, could she not? But what of her own interests? Would he truly expect her to hide her intellect, her interests, her ambition for a seemingly frivolous life of inconsequence?* Long seconds ticked by. A faint, scratching noise broke the tension. A tiny, frightened mouse skittered across the stone floor in front of the table. Miles jumped back in surprise, his knees knocking the underside of the table and clattering the dishes. The young serving maid screamed and, clutching her skirts high, bolted in terror for the cookery. They both laughed until tears streamed down their cheeks, and with that, the ice was broken. Catherine's resolve crumpled.

"Yes, Miles, I accept your apology," smiled Catherine, at once fully understanding that she was resigning herself not only to his charms, but to, exactly as her aunt had designed it, her fate.

The carriage hit another rut in the road, jarring Catherine from her thoughts. She looked through the glass and knew they would soon be in Wells. Mud and water from an early morning shower splashed out to the sides. Viola glanced through the back glass.

"Goodness!" exclaimed Viola. "I hope the mud does not ruin our baggage," she complained. She put her head out the window.

"Young man!" she yelled up to liveryman. "See to it that you mind the uneven road! Our trunks are back there!"

"Yes, mum," replied the driver, instantly drawing back on the reins. He silently rolled his eyes heavenward, then, glancing back toward the carriage, leaned over and spit on the side of the road.

Just on the outskirts of Wells, at the y-shaped crossing of the roads that led toward Wells, Stockbridge or London, the coach passed a large, flat limestone rock outcropping. The villagers of both towns affectionately called it the boundary stone that marked the boundary between Stockbridge and Wells. In good weather, coachmen from London often left packages bound for Stockbridge at the boundary stone, shortening the delivery route in order to retire early to the Royal George for an extra pint or two. Stockbridge villagers passing by would take the packages the rest of the way into the town.

On warm summer days when Catherine, Miles and Charles were young, they often rode their ponies out to the boundary stone, sharing picnics that had been packed in a woven carry-sack by Gussie. If they found packages, the trio would tear at full gallop back to Stockbridge, racing each other to see who could deliver them first. Once they were lucky enough to find two boxes of Aunt Viola's chocolates tucked under the shade of the rock and brought them home to her. For their trouble, she gave them each their first taste of Belgian chocolate. Catherine laid her head back on the velvet bolster and closed her eyes, remembering how the delicious confection tasted soft and sweet as it melted slowly on her tongue.

The coach swerved to avoid a rock. "Good Lord!" snapped Viola, righting herself. She shook her head in surrender and wedged the embroidery cloth back into her bag that had slid across the livery floor. Catherine reached down to touch the leather traveling case she'd placed at her feet. Feeling its cool, hard leather sides, she reassured herself that the case was still there, for although she had reluctantly surrendered to her aunt's wishes and consented to marry Miles as planned, Catherine bore a deep ambition that would never cease to burn. Nestled at the bottom of the case, buried deep under her traveling kit, were a bundle of papers tied neatly with black silk ribbon. The butterfly sketches. Catherine did not know exactly how or when, but before she married, she was absolutely determined to accomplish something in this world for herself alone.

CHAPTER 12

Village of Wells
Buckinghamshire, England
1 April 1665

Simon McKensie slumped alone in the coach rattling its way southward into the countryside from London, thinking bitterly of his misfortune. He stared miserably out the glass at the passing wooded landscape, carrying him ever closer to the hinterlands. He clenched his fists, his shoulders rising in tense anticipation. His thoughts wandered back to the rocky fields carved out of the cold, desolate forests of the north he knew so very well. Laying his head back against the coach, Simon closed his eyes, and resigned himself to the memories that now flooded over him. *Memories that drove his days and nights of ceaseless study. Memories that tortured his soul...*

Savage winds from a storm off the Atlantic blew through the cracks in the wooden cottage, wavering the feeble light from the wet sod smoldering in the grate. Slashing rain drove water through the thatch on the roof and dripped into chipped pots placed about the dim, smoky chamber. Ten-year-old Simon sat by the straw pallet pressing a damp cloth to his mother's forehead as she bore down through the long hours of fevered, agonizing contractions of her fourth child, desperately wishing his father would come home. The eldest, Simon was born to Angus McKensie, a burly, red-headed Scotsman with a strong taste for the lowland whiskey he kept hidden in his crumbling thatched-roof cowshed, and his English wife, Bess, who when not heavily pregnant, kept the little ploughshare a scant half-step beyond the reach of the solicitors.

The little ones had fallen fast asleep in the tiny back room. He was alone and he was scared. *These fearful screams do not sound right.* He truly did not know what to do. A sudden gust blew the candle by the pallet out. His small fingers trembled in the dark as he struggled to catch the flint. Bess cried out in a long, high-pitched, frightening wail. Simon began to shake. *Something is happening.* The latch on the door clattered. The door slammed open wide. His father, Angus, stood in the doorway, his woolens soaked and roaring drunk from the pub. A half-empty whiskey jug dangled from his crooked finger. Simon raced toward Angus.

"Father!"

"Aye! Wha's this, nae?" He clumsily pushed Simon aside, then fumbled in his pocket for the cork while lurching toward the pallet where his wife lay convulsing in pain. "Bessie!" he cried.

Bess suddenly jerked forward and gritted her teeth. She groaned and bore down hard, giving birth to a baby boy with dark swirling curls of hair and a lusty bawl. Simon slowly rose to his feet, transfixed.

"Barnaby," whispered Bess, before she lay back and closed her eyes. Her breathing grew faint. Angus tripped over a chipped pot and fell onto the floor next to the pallet, rainwater collecting in a puddle at his feet. Simon shook his father.

"You have to help her! Wake up!" Simon cried and pounded on his father's shoulder. "Wake up, Father! Wake up! With tears streaming down his face, Simon sat helplessly watching as his mother's life slowly faded away. Angus sobbed next to her lifeless body for hours, draining the whiskey from the jug.

Sometime in the early hours, Simon stirred, awakening to a strange and eerie silence. He had fallen fast asleep next to the smoking grate, holding the swaddled newborn tight in his arms. His mother lay still in the bed, his father was gone. Shaking, Simon placed the sleeping baby in a crudely carved wooden cradle, and then ran outside. Though the rain had ceased, leaden clouds hung over the wet, rocky fields as the cold, miserable night gave way to an early dawn. Simon called out, his voice lost to the mists. He ran the length and breadth of the ploughshare, then, looking down the hill, saw the figure of a man lying on the slick, grassy path. His heart pounding, Simon raced to his father. He had slipped in the dark and struck his head upon a jagged rock. Angus McKensie had died alone in the barren heath.

Left to fend for the hungry children, Simon somehow managed to place the baby with a neighbor, then learned to plow the field, raise a few meager crops and feed the other children, all the while devouring the arithmetic and science books that a generous priest from a neighboring village lent to him. For years, Simon toiled each day from the moment he milked the half-starved cow at dawn until he fell asleep on his books each night, exhausted from studying by candlelight and driven by an intense desire to learn all he could about the human body so that he would never again feel as helpless as he did the unspeakable night his mother and father died.

His first opportunity for escape came when the priest offered Simon passage to London to study in exchange for tutoring services to his wealthy cousins. By then, his younger sisters and brothers were old enough to manage and Simon accepted the offer, vowing to send what he could to help. Simon packed a bag and left for London at seventeen. He was an extraordinarily bright student, and at nineteen, Father Hardwicke accepted Simon into the medical school, a full two years before most other students. His path seemed settled before him; at least so he thought.

The coachman pulled up short at a jagged, flat stone overhanging the side of the road, jarring Simon from his ruminations. Simon watched as the driver disembarked and went around the back. He heard the man climb the ladder to the top of the coach and toss several packages over to the driver's seat. Then, retrieving the packages, the driver curiously left them beneath the stone and re-boarded the coach, urging the horses onward.

Simon sighed. He gazed around at the cartons, packets and boxes crammed into every possible nook and cranny of the coach, the chaff of his ambitious, impassioned life at the bustling city hospital carried ever further south toward the wretched, rural wasteland he despised.

"Wells, in twenty minutes time, Doctor!" yelled the driver.

"Thank you, sir," muttered Simon, over the pounding hoof beats of four horses charging headlong toward the feedbag.

The driver guided the Abbey's elegantly appointed carriage into the coaching inn's bricked courtyard. Restless border collies jumped and encircled the coach, barking incessantly at the clattering rig pulling into the yard. Catherine looked out of the window and easily recognized the smiling figure standing outside the low, black painted doorway to the coaching inn. Despite a lingering, vague sense of disquietude, she found that she was pleased to see Miles standing by his magnificent chestnut-colored mare, braided leather reins in hand. He cut a striking figure in his bottle green, bespoke riding jacket tailored to perfectly accentuate his lean, muscular body. His handcrafted black leather boots gleamed with a fresh polish. As he waited, Miles bent down to brush a spot of dirt off his fawn-colored breeches. A young stable boy of about seven years dressed in rough linens approached Miles and, taking the leather reins in hand, led the horse down the hill to the stables.

Miles shouted after him. "Boy!" The boy turned back, eyes wide, wary that he'd displeased the fine gentleman, for the stable overseer had a very heavy hand.

"See that he gets an extra ration of oats," winked Miles.

The freckle-faced stable boy's face lit up. He grinned and tipped his cap.

"Aye, sir!"

Miles reached into his pocket and tossed the boy a coin.

"Thank you, sir!" cried the boy, jumping to catch the

glittering brass farthing as it tumbled through the air.

The boy stuffed the coin into his pocket and happily led the horse down the hill.

Aunt Viola was visibly excited to see Miles standing outside the inn. She craned her neck to better see him through the window. "He cuts a fine figure, doesn't he?" she cooed, aquiver once again at the thought of the impending marriage. Catherine visibly cringed.

"Oh, stuff and nonsense, girl," sniffed Viola, settling her hands decorously into her ample skirts. "You should be well pleased that he favors you still in his affections."

He should be well pleased that I favor him *still*, thought Catherine, a small streak of rebellion rising. The carriage drew to a stop with a jerk, scattering a clutch of outraged hens in its wake. The team of horses threw their heads in circles, snorting in protest, impatient for the hay awaiting them in the stalls. Miles walked over and stood by the carriage as the coachman opened the door. He held his hand toward Catherine and Viola. They stepped from the carriage and blinked into the bright sun that had begun to play through a canopy of billowing clouds overhead. Catherine held tight to the ivory handle of her leather case. Miles smiled and offered his arm.

"Good morning, my darling."

He nodded to Viola.

"Ma'am. May I escort you ladies inside? I have a table waiting."

Viola could barely contain herself and made a great show of being the object of Miles's elegant attentions, happily taking his arm. Catherine swept by her aunt, ignoring her theatrics. Though Miles was working hard to win back Catherine's attentions, she wasn't so easily persuaded.

Miles led the way into the plaster and timber-framed inn and invited them to tea while they awaited the London coach. Viola demurred, making her excuses, choosing instead to remain with Lord Abbott and Charles in the entrance hall and watch like a hawk as the servants transferred their leather trunks into a transit room to await the coach.

Miles led Catherine down a narrow hallway, past the raucous, crowded public rooms and into the quieter, more refined dining room that was reserved for the wealthy patrons of the inn. Milk-painted paneling in a soft mustard hue lined the walls of the room, creating a warm, welcoming atmosphere. A wide iron candle chandelier hung from the center of the timbered ceiling. Miles ducked beneath the chandelier and led Catherine to a table by the casement window that looked out to the courtyard. He pulled out a wooden stoolback chair. Catherine sat facing him. She smoothed her dark blue traveling skirts. A maid in a clean white apron and ruffled bonnet quickly brought a selection of biscuits and scones on a silver tray and pot of tea for them both, setting the tray down on the highly polished walnut table.

"Catherine," he began, and then stopped short, a curious look upon his face.

Miles began to pat his jacket with both hands, searching anxiously through his pockets as though he'd misplaced something of great value. A foaming tankard slammed against wood, sending ale sloshing across the table, interrupting his thoughts. Startled, they both looked up to see Lord Mayor Hardwicke standing over to them, leaning on mahogany walking stick, elaborately engraved sterling silver hilt in hand.

"Tis a sad day. A sad day, indeed," moaned the mayor, white-whiskered double chins sagging over the top of his oxblood-colored cravat.

Catherine glanced away, remembering with a groan his enthusiastic attentions the night of the Christmas feast.

"Can I possibly help you, Lord Mayor?" asked Miles, unsure of how to respond to the mayor's declarations.

The mayor snapped his fingers across the room toward a serving girl.

"A plank of Stilton and Cheshire cheddar, and a loaf of bread, my girl, and step lively!" he yelled, sliding his considerable girth into the chair next to Miles.

The girl disappeared into the cookery, and within moments reappeared, setting a heavily laden wooden plank before him.

"Nae, lad," grunted the Mayor.

He grabbed hold of a pewter-handled knife set to the side of the plank and cut heartily into the bread, then topped several slices with a thick wedge of cheese. He offered them each a serving. They declined, shaking their heads. The slight went unnoticed. The mayor inhaled deeply of the fragrant crust, gleefully leaning sideways to admire the generous backside of the serving girl as she bid a hasty retreat into the warm cookery.

"I'll be on porridge and water, soon enough," he sighed, biting lustily into the bread. "A doctor, one foot in the grave, no doubt, has been sent down by my brother from London. He'll be arriving on the coach. Nae' that the old bugger'll make the slightest bang o' difference," he howled, happily digging in to the cheese board once again.

Miles was about to make their excuses when a commotion arose outside. He looked through the window to see the London coach as it clattered into the courtyard, a cloud of dust rising in its wake. From the hill above the stables, a small mutt ran across the bricks, heading straight into path of the horses. The little freckle-faced stable boy ran over to collar the dog. The horses jerked sideways at the sight.

"Look sharp, nae!" yelled the driver, struggling for control.

The lead horses spooked. Panicked neighs and terrified snorts filled the courtyard as the horses reared back, causing the rest of the team to buck and paw at the air. The yapping dog turned this way and that, circling the wagon, terrified of the monstrous beasts lunging around him.

"Whoa! Whoa!!!" yelled the driver, yanking hard on the reins, trying to manhandle the massive, frightened beasts.

The horses shimmied and bucked, then reared back against the wooden cowlings, and lunged forward once again. Panicked, the little cur turned tail and ran straight for the coach wheels. The stable boy lunged for the dog, trying to pull it from under the flailing hooves, but his timing was off. The lead horse struck the boy and sent him flying.

Inside the coach, Simon grabbed desperately for the boxes and packets that were falling from every nook and cranny. His cases banged against the floor and burst open, sending papers and clothing flying through the compartment. He heard the dog barking, and the panicked neighs. He felt the wagon buck in every direction. A piercing scream rent the air. He jerked his head toward the glass, helplessly watching the stable boy sail across the courtyard and land with a brutal crack upon the bricks. Jolted into action, Simon burst from the coach and reached the boy just moments after he landed.

The boy lay against the plastered wall of the inn, semi-conscious, blood pouring from a gash on his forehead and his right leg twisted in an unnatural angle below the knee. Simon leaned over him.

"Hold steady, lad," said Simon, reassuring the terrified boy. He quickly scanned the courtyard for help.

Witness to the gruesome accident, Catherine grabbed her leather case and followed Miles and the mayor as they raced out of the public house. Viola, Lord Abbott and Charles were not far behind. Catherine ran to the boy and dropped her traveling case on the ground. Without thinking, she quickly undid the latches and reached inside. She pulled out a fine-spun cotton nightshift and offered it to Simon to bind the head wound. Miles, watching her race headlong into the action, knew better than to pull her away, though he felt queasy to watch the sight of it. *Is it to always be like this?*

"Are there not linens inside?" Miles muttered, mostly to himself. He caught the arm of a maid in the crowd, craning her neck to see what was happening.

"You there! Bring sheets, linens, blankets, anything you can find!"

"Aye, sir." The maid quickly disappeared into the inn.

Simon held the nightshift up, preparing to rip the fabric into strips. Viola ran over and tried to grab the shift from Simon's hands.

"Stop that, young man!" she cried.

Viola grabbed for a piece of the diaphanous gown and held it tight to her bosom.

"This gown is extremely costly!"

Simon kept firm purchase to the fabric. He was well used to a domineering personality and had absolutely no kit for it. Lord Abbott, coming up from behind, quickly evaluated the situation and interjected.

"Viola, step back and give him quarter," commanded Lord Abbott.

Viola turned to him, aghast at the thought of Catherine's nightclothes upon full display before Miles's eyes. Her voice dropped to a roiling whisper.

"Surely you do not give consent to this presumptuous heathen to touch her…her personal belongings!" she hissed. Simon interrupted the rant.

"Madam, this boy is bleeding profusely and unless you are able produce a suitable replacement at this very moment, the gown is precisely what I will use," insisted an irritated Simon.

To Viola's astonishment, he ripped the fabric from her clenched fists and tore the gown into several strips.

"Here now, young man! Who are you to assume charge of this situation?" demanded the Lord Mayor. "There was to be a doctor on this coach," he said, looking around the courtyard for the older man.

"I *am* Dr. McKensie, sir!" retorted Simon, deftly wrapping the strips around the boy's head. "Please step back and allow me to help the boy."

"You? You? My brother sent *you* to be my personal physician?" he howled.

Simon instantly realized that his tormentor was none other than the Lord Mayor. He turned away, deliberately ignoring the old man. Miles took firm hold of the mayor's arm and pulled him back, lest he come to blows.

"Good Lord, the lad's barely off the teat!" the Mayor blustered, indignant at being ordered about.

Though he'd avowed not to, Miles dared another glance at the injured leg. Another sickening wave of nausea washed over him, nearly bringing him to his knees.

The boy's face was a ghostly, translucent shade, but somehow he was still conscious. Tears ran down his cheeks. Had the injury not been so dreadful, Catherine might have laughed at the impudence of the striking newcomer. Sputtering and red-faced, the Lord Mayor retreated with a very pale and nauseated Miles into the dining room to commiserate over another tankard of ale.

"Be brave, little fellow," whispered Simon, leaning into the boy. "They're all watching. Are you able?"

Wide-eyed, the boy wiped his tears and nodded. Simon reached for a nearby stick.

"Good lad." Simon gently patted the boy's head and put the stick into his hand. "Hold this. You'll need to bite on it in a minute." He turned to Catherine.

"Have you anything else to bind his leg?" asked Simon

Catherine tipped the contents of her case onto the bricks, hesitated for a moment, then reached for the matching robe and handed it to him. She had a momentary flush of embarrassment at her personal kit being so openly exposed to the small, murmuring crowd that had gathered around them, but seeing the young boy in such terrible distress banished all superficial vanities.

"I'm going to straighten the leg."

Simon looked out to the crowd, tearing the robe into strips, as well.

"Is there a man among you willing to help?" he shouted, his pulse pounding after witnessing the accident.

Not one soul stepped forward. Even Lord Abbott and Charles retreated, cringing at the prospect of anyone grasping the injured leg. The crowd fell silent. Simon was acutely aware of Catherine's presence still kneeling beside him. In one brief, sidelong glance, he took in her calm, thoughtful manner, and her steady hands. He also took in her red curls, brilliant in the blazing sun, her slate gray eyes and her singularly appealing figure. For one scandalous moment, he realized he was holding her nightclothes. He froze. *Grab hold of your wits, you juggins,* Simon berated himself. He focused his thoughts back on the grievous injury, and the terrified boy staring up at him. He turned and faced Catherine straight on.

"Would you be willing, Miss?"

Catherine nodded, her heart in her throat. "Aye, if you tell me what to do."

"You'll not faint?"

"Blood does not frighten me, sir."

Simon nodded, impressed by her composure. The maid ran back out, carrying several sheets and blankets. The innkeeper, a burly Yorkshireman, stopped her in her tracks, then quickly snatched the bundle from her arms and clutched it to his chest. Standing next to him, the inn's massive pastry cook set her hands to a pair of formidable hips and leveled him with an accusing gaze. Feeling guilty, he dropped his eyes and tried to mollify her, for he had a strong taste for her fruit pies and he was nearly always hungry.

"Ere' now, Maudie, th' sheets is new," he protested, "an' I'll not have 'em ruined by the likes of a stable boy."

"Yer' an 'eartless toadie, aren't ye', Wilfryd Browne," growled Maudie. "Just look at the poor lamb!" she said, her heart aching for the tears.

Maudie shook her head in disapproval at the innkeeper. He instantly crumpled.

"Aw, use the fekkin' blankets then, they're long paid fer" he grumbled. "An' anyways, them Abbott's can buy new riggin's whenever they like."

He grudgingly thrust the blankets back at the maid, but, cocking an eyebrow, Wilfryd looked Maudie straight in the eye and held fast to his new sheets.

Simon took a blanket from the maid and spread it out next to the boy. He again looked around the courtyard and down to the stable area, searching for something. Stacked against the side of a little-used outbuilding was a small pile of planks and kindling. Charles followed his gaze.

"Can I help?" offered Charles.

"Would you ask the stable boys bring that pile of wood over to me?"

"Aye, sir!" Charles shouted to the boys. They quickly brought the entire pile of wood, and then just as fast ran back to the safety of the stables, far away from the fearsome sight. One young boy stayed behind. He bent down at the waist, his hands on his knees, and stared at the twisted leg. He was fascinated.

"Ye'll be all right, Toby," he whispered to his terrified friend, though he wasn't so rightly sure.

Simon looked the wood scraps over, and then selected several of the smaller lengths. He laid the torn strips of the gown on the ground by Toby, then took one of the thinner pieces of wood and placed it next to the fabric. He forced himself to look at Catherine, so unsettled was he by her close, almost intoxicating presence.

"I…I am going to set the bone. When it is in place, we will fashion a splint from these pieces of wood," he explained, collecting himself. "Then we can move him to the blanket. When we have finished, he will need to be carried inside," he instructed.

Simon gave a sidelong glance toward the small crowd of onlookers.

"Perhaps there is a man among you who would offer to help carry the lad inside," he said, with a just the barest trace of sarcasm.

Simon leaned close to Catherine and spoke quietly.

"I am afraid that setting the bone will cause a great deal of pain," he said, looking down at the boy with an encouraging smile, "but the lad here—what did you say your name was?" he asked.

"Toby, sir."

"Have you a mum or da to send for?"

Toby shook his head the tiniest bit. Another tear fell. "Dead, sir."

Simon stroked the boy's hair in complete understanding. "Right, then." Simon looked to Catherine and suddenly saw the depths of compassion and concern in her eyes. Though he was nearly undone by her outward beauty, he saw an unexpected inner beauty, as well. Though his heart was pounding in her presence, he tried desperately to act with all the authority expected of a doctor. He looked at the boy and tried to concentrate on the task ahead. "Toby assures me that he is quite brave."

The boy nodded, trying hard to smile through the tears that were falling steadily.

Simon took the stick from the boy's hand and gave him a wink. He placed the stick carefully between the boy's teeth, and then glanced at Catherine.

"Hold him down," he whispered.

Catherine leaned over the boy and hugged him tight. Viola looked away, as did rest of the onlookers. The boy began to tremble. He began to breathe heavily, his chest rising and falling rapidly. Simon took a deep breath himself and then hesitated.

"Tell me, Toby, do you have a favorite horse here in the stables?"

"Aye, sir"

"What's his name?"

"Dobbins, sir,"

"Very well, then, close your eyes. Imagine you're riding Dobbins in a race and you are winning! Can you imagine that?"

"Aye, sir, I'll try."

The trembling stable boy squeezed his eyes shut, as though picturing the imaginary horse race. Simon gestured to Catherine to hold him down even tighter as he gently took hold of the boy's leg, and then gave it a strong pull, straightening the limb. The boy let out an unholy scream. Viola fainted. The stick fell to the ground, clattering as it rolled onto the bricks. Toby gave out a second agonizing wail, then turned his head toward the wall and began to whimper. Simon stroked Toby's hair, and watched Maudie run to Viola where lay on the bricks. Maudie took hold of Viola's wrist and patted it gently until she came to, grabbing at Maudie's apron.

"By my oath! I've never before laid witness to such a frightening sight, Maudie…" whimpered Viola.

"Ere, now. Let's get you an' me inside, dearie, we'll 'ave a tot of brandy, we will," said a very shaken Maudie, helping the old woman rise. Maudie swatted at Viola's skirts to wipe off the dust.

"…and I'll thank the Good Lord to never see such a thing again," Viola exclaimed vehemently, leaning heavily on Maudie.

Simon watched the unlikely pair clutch each other and make their way on unsteady feet into the inn. He turned to Catherine and exhaled. He leaned into the injured boy.

"Well done, Toby," whispered Simon, examining the straightened leg. "Very well done, indeed. You are quite brave."

Toby tried hard to manage a tiny smile.

"I'm going to slide this board under his leg and then we'll bind it with the strips of cloth," he said to Catherine.

Simon could not believe that she was still there by his side. The first time he straightened a broken limb he had nearly doubled over and retched from the agony he wrought, but there she was, calm and steady, and awaiting his directions. He turned his attention to Toby.

"Just one more small jostle. Can you take it, lad?

Through his tears, Toby gritted his teeth and nodded. "Aye, sir," he whispered.

Simon gently slid the board beneath Toby's leg and set two more on either side of it, forming a protective triangle. He took the strips of Catherine's robe and tied the wood securely around the leg so that it could not bend.

"You'll feel much better, now," said Simon. Toby nodded. "We'll carry you into the inn where you can rest. You'll be up and about soon enough," said Simon smiling. He looked out to the crowd.

"Gentlemen?"

The few men that remained moved forward and gathered around the boy, astounded by what they had just laid witness to. Following Simon's instructions, they very carefully lifted Toby slightly off the ground as Catherine pulled the blanket beneath the boy. Then, setting him back down, the men grasped the edges of the blanket and carried him into the inn where the maids had already prepared a soft, clean feather bed.

Simon and Catherine followed to check on the boy. Maudie left Viola in the care of Lord Abbott and the Lord Mayor and followed the men as they brought Toby inside. After laying him gently onto the feather pallet, the men quickly took leave for the pub. Maudie pulled a wooden stool up next to the rope bedstead. She softly wiped Toby's face with a warm, damp cloth and gave him several long sips of brandy. In Maudie's gentle, soothing care, he soon fell asleep.

Satisfied that the boy was comfortable enough, Simon walked Catherine back to the courtyard to help collect her belongings that had been scattered over the ground. He reached the traveling bag first and picked up the bundle of sketches that had fallen out. Reading the name on the cover, he was curious. He lifted his gaze to her.

"Might you be... The Honorable Lady Catherine Mary Abbott?"

"I am, sir," she said, reaching quickly to retrieve her papers from him.

He turned his back slightly, so that she could not reach them.

"Butterflies?"

"If you please, sir. May I have my sketches back?"

He playfully lifted the bottom corner of the cover and peeked at the first sketch.

"Did you draw these?"

Though she could not say exactly why, she bristled slightly at the insinuation. *Of course she was responsible for the collection!*

"Indeed I did, sir."

Simon grasped the ends of the silk ribbon with his fingertips and looked at her, questioning.

"May I look... *The Honorable Lady Catherine Mary Abbott*, he teased?"

She did not know whether to be vexed, or intrigued that he desired to see her work. *Was he mocking her title?* Something in his tone chafed, for she was merely born to her station. *How could he know that she was no more impressed by her peerage than he?* As she gathered the rest of her belongings Catherine thought to herself, *men are a constant bewilderment and this man, this doctor, however handsome, is certainly no different.*

Despite her vexation, Catherine could not draw her eyes away from the hands that held the ribbon. They looked rough and strong, yet with the injured boy, they had been so tender. Her emotions in tumult, she reached for her drawings and saw closer that his hands, while pale, and freckled, were also heavily calloused. *He was clearly was not a man waited upon by others. Further, he took no quarter from Aunt Viola.* She thought of his quick wit and the retort that put the Lord Mayor firmly in his place. She unexpectedly laughed out loud.

Her laugh startled him. *Was she mocking him? Women were highly confusing,* he swore. Simon hastily handed her the drawings and cursed himself for being far too forward.

Catherine bit her lip and considered him for a moment. Was it the teasing smile that turned up at the corners? Perhaps it was the smattering of freckles across his perfectly straight nose. Or the quiet authority he displayed when challenged. She didn't know, but something in his attentive manner gave her pause. On impulse, she gave the sketches back to him, nodding briefly.

"Please."

Catherine looked away as he untied the ribbon and began to leaf through the pages. For several long minutes, he was silent. Page after page he turned. Her heart began to pound. *What a fool I was to allow him leave to look upon my drawings,* she fretted. She felt the flush of anger return in full measure, watching as he carefully examined each sketch. *Who is he to find fault?* She grew more irate by the moment. Finally, Simon lifted his head, and looked upon her with amazement.

"You have quite a talent for illustration."

He turned the pages and gestured to the woodland grayling illustrations. He took a closer look. She had sketched three altogether different perspectives of the butterflies she'd caught; top, underside and full wing. Each drawing was a singular marvel of sure, flowing lines and soft, delicate shadings. Each illustration was remarkably precise and detailed.

"You also have a very astute eye for scientific observation."

Simon was intrigued to find anyone outside his small circle of colleagues in medical school who expressed even a modicum of intellectual curiosity toward the natural world. That it would be this titled, and he was quite sure, pampered young heiress in a small country village intrigued him even more. Perhaps his time of indentured servitude in this God-forsaken, forested outpost would not be as abominable as he thought.

Catherine was taken aback. She had not expected compliments. Embarrassed, she looked away.

"I am grateful for your kind words, sir."

"They are not meant to be kind," he said with a direct gaze.

She jerked her head toward him in surprise. He looked down to her, taking in her pale, creamy skin, the wide-set gray eyes beneath her modest, plumed traveling hat. *Aye, she is beautiful.* Irrational thoughts were intruding on his normally ordered turn of mind. He worked to compose himself.

"I speak the truth as I see it, Lady Abbott. Feelings… that is to say, your feelings, are of a lesser consequence to me than scientific discoveries and scientific observations."

He handed the book back to her and regarded her thoughtfully.

"You are leaving on the London coach, are you not, and you are carrying this book with you in your traveling bag rather than in your trunks," he mused. "Euclidean algebra states that a, plus b, always equals c." He cocked his head, questioning. "Might I ask if you intend to perhaps do something more than entertain yourself with it?"

She was thrown by the absolute clarity of his observations and reasoning. *Exactly who is this man that unnerves her so?* Her thoughts were jumbled. *He seemed to see so clearly the things she could not. Could she actually entrust him with her intentions?* Before she could speak, he interjected.

"Have you thought of publishing your work?"

Catherine drew back, startled. *It truly was as though he could read her thoughts.* Pleased and embarrassed beyond measure at the compliment, she stumbled over her words to answer.

"I…I had thought of it, sir."

Simon watched as a high flush rose in her cheeks. *That particular shade of red highly compliments her blue traveling suit,* he thought. He grinned, amused by her discomfort.

"I'll thank you not to laugh at me, Doctor," she snapped, her pleasure turning to vexation once again.

Before Simon could offer his apologies, Catherine felt a tap on her shoulder. Startled, she wheeled around. Miles faced her, a questioning look upon his face. Beyond him, across the courtyard, she could see the driver securing the last of their luggage to the top of the coach.

Miles looked from Simon to Catherine, sensing a strange undercurrent of something he did not quite understand. *If he were honest, he did understand.* Catherine and Simon looked down, unsure of exactly what to say. Miles broke the uncomfortable silence. "The driver would like to depart," he said, a bit too harshly. He turned to Simon and nodded curtly. "Thank you, Doctor."

Catherine looked over Charles's shoulder to see that Lord Abbott and Aunt Viola, now fully recovered from the morning's turn of events, had indeed already boarded the coach. She quickly turned to Simon, who, untroubled in the least by Miles's appearance, grinned at her. *Idiotic.* She seized her drawings and packed them carefully into her leather bag with the rest of her things. She secured the brass latches with a resolute snap. *How dare he lead her to a confession and then laugh at her?* She had told no one of her plans for the very fear of it. His inquisitiveness seemed the height of treachery.

"I must go," she said, abruptly turning away. She gathered her skirts and walked with Miles to the coach.

"Maxwell and Company. Publishing House. Number Ten Sloane Street," Simon called out after her. She gave no acknowledgement in return.

Miles stood by as Catherine briefly glanced back toward Simon standing across the courtyard, *still grinning like a fool. That he is a handsome fool does absolutely nothing to ease my foul temper.* Resolutely turning away from Simon, Catherine took hold of the polished brass bar on the outside of the coach, preparing to mount the wooden step. She gave Miles her other hand. He grasped her fingertips and bowed to kiss her gallantly on the wrist.

"Once again, you were very brave, my dear," he said, with a smile that somehow seemed slightly forced. Viola thought she caught a fleeting moment of displeasure and quickly interjected.

"Catherine, of course, knows that in future it would be unseemly, as the Duchess of Houghton, to be in the habit of saving every poor urchin that manages to come across some distressing misfortune or other," she fluttered.

Miles politely laughed and exchanged a brief moment of mutual understanding with Viola. Catherine was again vaguely unsettled by some strange, unwritten code she seemed not to understand. Unable to resist her curiosity, Catherine glanced toward Simon. Viola, following her gaze, seemed to sense a very unwelcome attraction.

"Catherine!"

A high flush mounting at her aunt's rebuke, Catherine quickly turned her attentions back to Miles.

"I will most certainly speak to the Lord Mayor about dismissing that young upstart!" hissed Viola.

Miles assisted Viola into the coach, then stopped and reached inside his riding jacket. He turned to Catherine and smiled.

"With the injury to the young lad, I fear that I nearly forgot!"

From his pocket, he withdrew a long, narrow box and handed it to her. From across the courtyard, Simon watched as she took the box and opened it. She gasped. Inside the box, was a sparkling sapphire pendant suspended from a thick golden chain. She was stunned. Miles withdrew the pendant from the box and fastened it about her neck. He stepped back to admire the dark stone, nodding.

"The stone does bring out the blue in your eyes, as I expected," he smiled, eyes crinkling. "I thought you might like a fair trinket to take with you."

"Miles, no! It is far too much...

Aunt Viola gasped at her protests. She fanned herself and

scowled across the coach at Catherine. Catherine fell quiet, uneasy for the social blunder she had seemingly made once again.

"One of many, my darling. Just one of the many gifts I plan to lavish upon you in our life together." He grinned and whispered in her ear. "I have something even more special planned for our engagement party in London. Perhaps you will wear the sapphire?" He winked at Aunt Viola, who swooned in her seat.

He laughed delightedly, then kissed the top of Catherine's wrist once again, and then lifted her into the coach, securing the door behind them. He gestured for his horse. Catherine shook off her unease. This was the Miles she'd known so very well. Impetuous, generous and full of fun. Perhaps she had judged him in too harsh of a light. Of course he understood far better than she the customs of peerage. But she would do her best learn. In that moment, she vowed that she would do her best to try harder to adapt to the life her family expected her to lead.

From across the courtyard, an unfamiliar melancholy fell over Simon as he watched Catherine smile down from the coach at Miles, touching her fingers to the sapphire. The driver yelled to his team of horses and the carriage began to pull from the courtyard. As the carriage passed, Simon looked into the cabin, trying desperately to catch her eye, but Catherine gave him no quarter. She sat, staring resolutely ahead. Simon walked out to the road and watched until he could no longer see the coach in the distance. *Never before in his life had he met such an intriguing girl.* Behind him, Miles hoisted himself onto the saddle and wheeled his mount toward Houghton Hall. As he galloped past, he cast a small, triumphant smile toward Simon and then touching two fingers to his forehead in salute, left Simon standing alone in the cloud of dust kicked up by his horse.

Simon's luggage sat on the ground by the Lord Mayor's carriage that was now waiting at the door of the inn. The Lord

Mayor shouted over to Simon.

"If you're the new doctor, you'd best come with me, lad."

Simon took his eyes off the now deserted road and sighed.

"Aye, I'd best.

CHAPTER 13

"DO NOTHING HASTILY BUT CATCHING OF FLEAS"
-THOMAS FULLER

Noorderhaaks
The North Sea
1 April 1665

Jakob was terrified beyond all reason. He'd waited weeks to depart for England, and though he felt the sun had surely risen on a new day, Jakob now huddled miserably far below-decks in his rope hammock trying to find some measure of comfort in the dank, pitch-dark cargo hold of the *Berschermer* as it swayed and bucked its way through a massive North Sea squall toward London. The familiar life he knew in Amsterdam seemed but a distant memory as ear-splitting, thunderous explosions and driving rains raged over the merchant ship.

Unholy oaths crackled throughout the hold as the keeling ship threw the steerage passengers erratically in all directions. Swinging hammocks banged hard against crates of cotton bales, stacks of oilcloth-covered fabric bolts and wooden boxes full of the ships haulage that were piled high against the sides of the heaving vessel. Jakob was bruised from head to toe, queasy and homesick. He sorely missed the soft comforts of Geertje's warm embrace. The massive timbers of the ship shrieked and moaned around him, eerie wails rose and fell with each deafening roar of the colossal storm. Foaming bubbles of seawater seeped from every crack into the hold, oozing moisture down the green lichen stains of every blackened plank of the hull. Howling winds drove icy pellets of rain across the deck and down the hatches. Water surged into hold. Though he tried to find a dry crevasse amidst the cargo to stow them, even his *rucksack* and valise were soaking wet.

Worst of all were the rats. *Mijn God,* he cursed in the darkness, how he hated the rats. He shuddered at the miserable sounds the fiendish creatures made scurrying overhead and underfoot overnight; nibbling at anything they could sink their jagged shards into. Between the rats, the sleeplessness and the torturous scratching at bites from the heinous fleas that infested every corner of the galleon, Jakob was utterly miserable. He felt in his pocket for the blue linen handkerchief. He held it to his face and inhaled deeply of Geertje's scent. He missed her even more than he thought possible. He fought the urge to cry. He did not think he would live through four more days.

CHAPTER 14

Village of Wells
Buckinghamshire, England
1 April 1665

Cecil Hardwicke jiggled the iron hilt on the planked front door of the quaint two-story cottage. It was a timber frame snuggery of oak and elm, clad with weatherboards and a newly thatched roof that stood just down the lane from the village green. Standing on the freshly swept pathway, Simon took in the dwelling that was to be his home for the next six months. With whitewashed windowpanes and tidy window boxes filled with budding flowers, the wood and stone residence looked more than habitable. *In truth, it looks quite pleasant,* he grudgingly allowed.

Simon looked around at the garden, still bare from the cold winter snows that had at long last melted. The hedgerows and rose bushes had been neatly trimmed. He bent down and saw that in the warmth of the early spring sunlight, tiny buds on the rose bushes were beginning to form. It looked as though the entire garden would soon burst into color. A sudden thought struck. *It is not the cottage that lowers my spirits,* he realized with dismay. It was that the cottage was but fifty paces from the Lord Mayor's manor. Simon was to live in the gardener's cottage. Where the poor gardener and his wife had been turned out to, he couldn't say. All he knew was that he was to live within shouting distance of his charge, and he could see already that the Lord Mayor was quite fond of shouting.

"Come along, my boy," bellowed the mayor, as he swung the door open, jolting Simon from his misery.

Simon sighed. He picked up his leather travel bag and followed the mayor into the dwelling. He ducked to avoid the low spar and stepped into a cozy gathering room filled with comfortable furniture. Simon looked at where he would spend the next half-year of his life. Lingering scents of fragrant, earthy pipe tobacco and freshly baked bread hung in the air. A welcoming fire had been stoked to take the chill off the room. Faint wisps of smoke curled up the face of the soot-covered stone chimney, casting a burnished shadow on the low, cream-colored plaster and wood-beamed ceiling. A braided rug lay before the open fireplace. Two low-slung, well-worn wood and leather chairs sat to either side of the generous hearth. Several servants clattered up and down the narrow wooden staircase, unpacking Simon's trunks into the larger of the two sleeping chambers. Simon's medical research would be organized into the other one.

Wide pine floorboards snapped and creaked as the Lord Mayor crossed to a simple wooden cabinet in the corner of the downstairs gathering room. He upended two glass snifters and splashed two fingers of whiskey into each of them from a cut-glass decanter. He took a sizeable draught from one while handing Simon the other, then eased himself slowly down into one of the chairs before the fire and heaved an aching leg onto the hearth. He leaned back and closed his eyes, savoring the smoky amber liquid as it burned its way down the back of his throat.

"Ahhh, that's the stuff."

His shoulders visibly relaxed as he exhaled. The mayor took another long sip. With the whiskey he'd been given in one hand, Simon casually reached for the mayor's glass with his other and pulled it straight from his lips. He turned his back to the mayor and without a moment's hesitation, tossed the liquid from both glasses straight into the fire. A brilliant, sizzling flash illuminated the room. The Mayor's eyes' flew open wide, his jaw dropped in shock. The flames quickly died down to flickering coals.

"Here now!" howled the Mayor. "What the devil do you think you're doing? That's fine Haig scotch!"

Simon turned back toward the mayor and crossed his arms. *If I am to be tethered to this self-indulgent windbag for the next sixmonth, I may as well face this straight on,* he thought.

"With all due respect, Lord Mayor. From this day forward, as your personal physician, I am responsible for your health."

The mayor's face was nearly apoplectic. Simon feared he would choke, as the shock of being ordered about slowly registered across his face. Simon went on, almost enjoying the sight.

"It is yet noon and I strongly suspect that this is not your first libation of the day."

"How dare you, sir!" the Mayor sputtered, half wanting to order him out straight of the cottage, and half wanting to lunge for his throat. If his leg weren't in such agony, he would have gladly chosen the latter course.

"I will allow a single dram each evening, and no more."

If he could have, Simon would have laughed at the astounded, almost comical look on the Mayor's face, for the stalemate was almost too much for the old man. A sharp rap on the iron doorknocker saved them both from fisticuffs. Staring daggers toward the outspoken young doctor, the mayor bellowed in the general direction of the doorway.

"Enter!"

A stout cook carrying a cloth-covered tray pushed the door open with her elbow and carried the tray over to a small wooden table near the center of the room. She cast a welcoming smile toward Simon.

"Afternoon, sir. Name's Eliza an' I'll be cooking fer' ya," she said, cheerfully lifting the cloth and folding it over one of the two chairs.

"Breakfast at seven, dinner at noon, supper at six. Nae', if that's not to yer likin', sir, well, you'll soon get used to it, right as not," she chuckled, pulling a bottle of wine from her apron pocket. Simon laid his hand gently on her arm, refraining her from uncorking the wine. She looked at him in surprise.

Simon stepped to the table and took a closer look at the two plates full of gravy-covered meats and potatoes, the loaf of freshly baked bread, the cream cakes and the two wine glasses laid on their sides. He resolutely shook his head. Simon reached for the cloth and flicked it out, then neatly covered the tray again. He grasped the bone-handles and handed it firmly it back to Eliza.

"Take the tray away, Eliza. Bring back any greens you may have at hand and a slice of chicken. A single slice of chicken, if you please. And tea. Very weak tea."

The mayor let out an incomprehensible roar and slammed his walking stick on the floor in outrage. *It was all too much to endure.* He vowed to put an immediate stop to all this nonsense.

"You are discharged, young man!" he roared.

"Chicken. Greens. Weak tea. As you like, sir," the astonished cook nodded, beating a hasty retreat back out the door.

Simon turned to face the mayor with an unearthly calm.

"Allow me to explain once again. You do not employ me, Lord Mayor. Therefore, you cannot discharge me. In fact, I shall not leave your side, not for one moment, for the next six months."

The mayor blustered, but could not even begin to form the necessary words to express his white-hot wrath.

"I answer directly to Father Hardwicke, and as I fully intend to return to my medical residency in London in precisely one half year's time, mark my words, sir, I will do my job to its very fullest for I do not intend to remain in Wells one moment longer than I am required."

Simon walked back over to the old man sitting before the hearth, then leaned down and carefully removed the mayor's shoe.

"Is there no end to your insolence, sir?" the mayor cried.

Simon said nothing. He reached down and took hold of the mayor's foot, gently turning it this way and that. He touched the mayor's swollen big toe. The mayor visibly winced and rose slightly, grasping tight to the leather arms of the chair. Simon raised his head and spoke matter-of-factly.

"Gout."

"What the devil is *that?*" sputtered the mayor.

"Do you wake in the night?"

To Simon's immense satisfaction, the mayor was caught short. Looking to the floor, he considered the question for a moment. The mayor took a deep breath, and then slowly exhaled.

"Aye," the mayor grudgingly allowed. He relaxed his death grip on the chair. "I am often awakened in the night by execrable pains in the great toe, at times in company with chills, shivers and perhaps a fever."

Simon nodded, replacing the shoe. A bit of the fight seemed to go out of the mayor as he confessed to the infirmity that had been plaguing him greatly.

"My nights of late are passed in such torture, sleeplessness and such tossing about for some measure of comfort," he confessed.

Simon sat took a seat on the stone hearth and considered the mayor's predicament. He turned, idly stoking the fire with an iron rod, poking at the cinders until the flames sprung to life again.

"Gout said to be a wealthy man's affliction, and with good reason, for as your brother expressed, it is a dissolute habit as to be brought about by excessive indulgences," said Simon, musing aloud.

"What the devil are you saying, my boy?" demanded the mayor, clearly exasperated again. "Speak plainly!"

"As you wish, Lord Mayor," said Simon. He turned and sat directly facing the old man. Simon placed his hands upon his knees.

"You eat too much. You drink too much. And although I cannot say forsooth, I presume that you indulge greatly in excessive and exhausting passions."

The mayor was furious. He squirmed in his chair, unaccustomed as he was to his daily habits being so roundly laid bare. He sat back and defiantly crossed his arms, saying nothing in return. The two men sat in uncomfortable silence, staring into the crackling fire, each man dreading the very long months that lay ahead. A soft rap on the door broke the stalemate.

"Ahhh, my single slice of chicken. How delightful," brooded the mayor, staring into the fire. "Come in!" he barked.

The door cracked opened. A tousle-haired boy, about the age of twelve, poked his head inside. His wide eyes were swollen and red, his dirty cheeks tear-stained.

"Who the hell are you!" yelled the mayor, plainly exasperated now at his entire day.

The boy was pushed into the cottage from behind. Eliza followed closely, holding one of the lad's hands high in the air, loosely covered with a kitchen towel. Blood ran down the boys arm and dripped to the floor. Simon rose instantly, and reached for the leather bag that sat on the floor next to him.

"What fresh devilment is this!" bellowed the mayor. "Have we not had enough catastrophe for one day!"

As Simon rifled through the contents of his medical bag, Eliza reached into her apron pocket and pulled out embroidery string and a needle.

"Thought ye' might be needin' these, Doctor," said Eliza, laying them on a small table by the front door.

Simon glanced at her, then pulled thread and a curved needle from his bag. He held the needle into the fire for a moment.

"Come here, lad," he said, removing the towel. He looked closer and saw a deep cut to the bone across the boy's finger.

"He was slicing the chicken for me," said Eliza.

"It appears that the lad missed," the mayor dryly observed.

"It's not too terribly frightful," smiled Simon, reassuring the terrified boy. He pulled out one of the dining chairs. "Sit here and close your eyes for me. Count to twenty."

The boy clenched his eyes shut and counted. Simon quickly stitched the wound. The boy held his breath, wincing at each fiery stab. Eliza marveled at the needle.

"How is it that the needle is curved like that, sir?" she marveled.

"I fashioned it after seeing a sail maker's needle. Makes the stitching easier," Simon answered, concentrating on the cut.

Though the boy grimaced in pain he, mercifully thought the Lord Mayor, bore up in stoic silence. The mayor turned his gaze back to the fire, trying desperately not to look at the gruesome wound. Simon finished sewing and bound the finger tight. The boy opened his eyes.

"Not terribly unpleasant, was it, lad?" asked Simon, smiling down at him. The mayor snorted.

"No, sir," lied the boy, bravely blinking back copious tears.

Eliza quickly shuffled the boy to his feet and hauled him toward the door by his good hand.

"I'll be bringing yer' dinner shortly," she said, calling over her shoulder toward the mayor.

"Under the circumstances, perhaps you'd better bring the meat back," cautioned Simon, with a gentle smile. "No gravy, however."

The mayor, still staring into the fire, let out another incomprehensible grunt. Ignoring him, Simon walked the cook over to the door.

"Have the lad keep his arm up. It will hurt less. Put some wintergreen herbs into a cup of tea if the pain becomes intolerable."

The boy looked as though he might cry.

"If that doesn't work, put two shots of brandy in the tea," he winked. "Come find me tomorrow and I will change the dressing."

Simon paused by the door and watched as Eliza put the thread and needle back into her apron pocket.

"How is it that you knew to bring those things with you?" he asked.

"Why, I watched Lady Catherine sew the flesh of Annie Beckett when she nearly died giving birth.

"Lady Catherine?" Simon was taken aback.

"Stitched her up, she did. Right through the flesh. Saved Annie's life, she did!"

"Lady Catherine?" Simon repeated, incredulous at the thought.

"Aye, sir. Over t' Stockbridge at Christmastide. We all help, we do. Nearly two hundred people to cook fer."

He was sorely confused.

"Lord Abbott opens the Abbey every year for a grand Christmas feast. Couldn't do it with the help they've got, so's we all pitch in, we do," she explained proudly.

Simon knitted his brows trying to make sense of her words.

"Anyways, one of th' maids gave birth right there in the cookery the night of the feast. Oh, an' it was an awful birth, y' know. No midwife to be found. The baby..." She hesitated, looked at Simon, and then continued. "well, seeing's how yer' a doctor 'an all, well, the baby tore right through."

The mayor stomped his walking stick hard on the floorboards.

"Enough!" he roared.

Eliza jumped. She took Simon's arm and lowered her voice to a whisper.

"If Lady Catherine hadn't tried to sew the flesh together, Annie'd 'uv died right there on the cookery floor. But she dinna' die y' know. Lived to tell the tale, she did."

"You say Lady Catherine saved the girl's life? By stitching her up?"

"Aye, sir. She did exactly that, she did."

Simon could only let out a small whistle of amazement. Eliza looked down at the miserable boy, then pulled a cloth from her sleeve and wiped his tears. She turned back to Simon.

"Shall I bring yer' luncheon, nae, sir?"

"Yes, that will be fine, Eliza. Thank you."

He took the cook's arm, opening the door to escort her out and saw with a shock that there was a small queue of people standing quietly on the garden path. They looked up at him, expectantly.

"Are ye' the doctor?" called the old man who stood at the head of the line.

"Aye," breathed Simon, his shoulders dropping in surrender. "I am." *This may prove to be a very long summer.*

CHAPTER 15

Bealeton House
St. James Parish, London
5 April 1665

Most unwelcoming, shuddered Catherine, glancing around at the spare, white plastered walls and black and white marble floorings of the breakfast room, as she spooned down the last of her oat porridge. *Even the single hothouse palm tree that stands in the corner does nothing to lend warmth to these formal rooms.* Catherine sipped her tea and stared out the window to the lane lined of newly constructed mansions. She wondered how anyone could possibly prefer to live in the city.

Catherine remembered the years of argument when the relentlessly social-climbing Viola had pestered Lord Abbott to build a grand residence within London proper and marveled at how determined her aunt could be. In the end, Lord Abbott relented and gave Viola free rein with the family purse to build the three-storied residence on a generous parcel of land leased from King Charles II. It sat square and imposing on an elegant tree-lined street directly across from Hyde Park, former site of the royal hunting grounds. Catherine grimaced as she looked through a carved gothic archway to a series of enfilades, a series of adjoining rooms with doorways sited to perfectly frame the grand vista of Viola's formal gardens at the rear of the mansion. *It was all too much.*

Her eyes fell upon the expensive and highly overwrought oil portraits that Viola had commissioned of Lord Abbott, the late Tamesine, Catherine and Charles that were hanging in the expansive entrance hall above the reverently displayed ceramic vases brought back from China by the company sailors. She winced at the expensive French gilded objet d'art that Viola purchased on shopping expeditions to the continent with her overly enthusiastic French decorator, Monsieur Phillipe. *Did she hope that King Charles II himself would visit?* From the formal Palladian red brick exterior to the cold black and white marbled floors, the multi-columned entrance rotunda and the white marble staircase with its carved acanthus leaf scrollwork balustrade, Viola, with Phillipe's rich taste for grandeur taking the lead, had chosen the latest in what she thought was elegance. Catherine knew that Viola thought the effect was breathtaking. Catherine found the home, if one could call it that, remarkably cold and austere. *Not even the engagement party Viola wished to throw at weeks end could lend warmth and life to this dwelling.* She longed for the fresh air of the countryside and the warmth of the brick and timbered Abbey. She wondered how her father stood it. But then, she doubted that he even noticed.

Catherine glanced toward Lord Abbott sitting the end of the breakfast table next to Charles, as he steadily worked his way through the massive stack of journals and pamphlets saved by the staff for each visit. He was especially hard working on this trip, readying his papers for the brewing confrontation that would most undoubtedly occur at the board meeting. Though she knew Lord Abbott was comfortable enough at Bealeton House, Catherine would change every single inch of the stark dwelling if she had half the chance. The breakfast room most especially.

"Come now, Catherine, finish your tea. We meet with the dressmaker in one hour," said Viola, briskly, her empty cup clinking on the saucer. "I take it Charles is to accompany you to the shipyard?" she asked Lord Abbott.

"Yes!" Charles said, shoveling his porridge down in anticipation. "Father's promised!"

Lord Abbott absently looked up from his papers and nodded fondly at a grinning Charles. "Indeed I did." He smiled once more, then put his head down and returned to his work.

Catherine took one last sip of tea, then gratefully rose from the table, happy to depart the stark mansion for the rest of the day.

The afternoon sun rose high above the slate rooftops of Knightsbridge. Catherine stood in the street before Wilcox & Sons Fine Tailoring, Ltd., at Number Two Sloane Street, and looked at the two cream-colored marble columns standing to either side of the well-swept entranceway. *Not one more,* she whispered to herself. This was the fourth appointment of the busy morning and it was yet noon. The hackney carriage Cedric had hired for the day was already heavily laden with boxes and wrapped packages. Although Aunt Viola showed no sign of slowing down, Catherine was not entirely sure she had it in her to even climb the two stone steps to the shop door.

She and Viola had visited every elegant salon in St. James Parish. Viola had ordered tailored clothing for all possible occasions, as well as anything else she thought Catherine could ever need or want for her new life at Houghton Hall. Catherine been prodded, poked and apprised from every angle. She'd been measured and fussed over by tailors and apprentices, her every move scrutinized, her every utterance notated. She stood on tailoring boxes until she thought she would tumble off.

Viola sat like the imperious grand duchess she wished she were in comfortable side chairs, choosing silks, linens, taffetas, threads and rich trims and laces brought for her critical appraisal by one smiling apprentice after another, with the same enthusiasm she threw into the design and decoration of Bealeton House. Outside, the parcels from shop after shop were stacked high, beginning to fill every bit of space in the hackney. *She is positively indefatigable,* admitted Catherine, with grudging admiration. She feared that she, herself, would scream from the tedium.

"I should also like to order a number of those exquisite Holland sheeting sets from van de Velds." Viola was asking the shopkeeper, disrupting Catherine's internal tantrum.

"I'm quite sure you know the ones to which I refer, the ones with the delicate ice blue stripe?"

Old Jonas Wilcox stood behind a large mahogany worktable, wiping his bald pate and the back of his damp neck with a white linen square. He glanced with furious exasperation in the general direction of his stepson Peregrine, who at the ring of the shop bell announcing the appearance of Lady Viola Abbott, had disappeared like a faint wisp of smoke into the back office. Peregrine knew the woman full well from her orders for Bealeton House, and he was terribly anxious to withdraw from any confrontation that would surely arise. *Thirty years, spinsterly and frightened as a piffling dock rat,* Jonas fumed silently.

"Ah, yes. The van de Veld sheetings. I do, of course, know the ones of which you speak."

He cast a loathsome eye toward the rear of the shop. Wilcox & Sons had been but a wishful dream when a young Jonas proudly opened his business. *Alas, I had but one son, not of my own loins, but my wife's child. And quite the shattering failure, he is indeed. No head for business, no talent for the needle and certainly, no social graces whatever. I shall work until I die,* sighed Jonas, *for the twit is singularly unqualified in every possible respect. Thank the good Lord that he has taken a suite at his gentlemen's club, for that simpering, infuriating presence twenty and four hours a day would surely send me to the madhouse. Or, perhaps, the noose.* Jonas straightened his cravat and fussed with his quill pen, absently spinning it in lazy circles on the worktable. Viola watched him diddle with the pen. She arched an eyebrow. He cleared his throat.

"Ahhh, yes. As you know, Lady Abbott, the van de Veld sheets are highly sought after. You, yourself, purchased nearly all of our stock for Bealeton House."

Viola drew her chin high, inhaled deeply and prepared to mount a most vocal protest. Jonas immediately, desperately, desired to silence the woman. He called out.

"Peregrine! The van de Veld bills of lading. Please bring them to me at once!"

Hiding in the back workroom, Peregrine flounced the curls of his elaborate silver wig over his shoulder with a fluttering hand and tried in vain to ignore the old man's frantic bleating. He nervously ran a finger in each direction across his razor-thin mustache and busied himself by tying a crimson ribbon into a most lovely bow upon one of Lady Abbott's packages. He stood back to admire his efforts. *Indeed, it is a most lovely bow.*

"Peregrine!" shouted Jonas, his voice taking on an urgent tone. He tapped his fingers restlessly upon the worktable.

"Oh, dear God," moaned Peregrine, rolling his eyes heavenward.

Exhaling in exasperation, Peregrine finally thought the better of his retreat and reluctantly emerged from the workroom, holding the sheaf of ladings. Viola watched in utter irritation as he delicately worked his way across the shop, Peregrine averted his eyes to deflect Viola's imperious gaze. Exasperated, Jonas grabbed the lot and nervously flicked through the pages. After an anxious moment or two, he gratefully found the entry he was looking for.

"Ah, yes," Jonas nodded, pointing to the paper. He showed Viola. "*The Berschermer.* Scheduled to arrive…"

He adjusted his tiny gold spectacles and looked closer in confusion.

"…three days ago."

Jonas looked up in surprise.

"It appears that there has been a delay in shipping. Peregrine!"

"Yes?"

"Go immediately down to the Blackwall Docks. Inquire after the *Berschemer* and the shipment from the van de Veld Linnenfabriek.

"Yes, Father." Peregrine headed gratefully toward the door.

Jonas drew himself up and looked toward Viola with a dignified air. Perhaps he could divert her attentions.

"Peregrine will sort the matter out, and then I will personally see to it that we deliver… How many sets would you care to order, Lady Abbott?"

"Upon their marriage, Lady Catherine and her husband." she leaned in, preening conspiratorially, "*the future Duke of Houghton*, are to occupy the East Wing of Houghton Hall. They shall require at least three, no, make it four sets," she said, counting on her fingers.

Catherine turned away, blushing at her aunt's craven bid for stature.

"Very well, then, Lady Abbott. I will personally see to it that we deliver four sets to Bealeton House within the month.

"That will be unacceptable, sir," replied Viola, sharply.

He literally feared this detestable woman. *By God's oath! What act of profound devilment did he engage in that wrought her lamentable personage upon his establishment?* He began to whimper, actually stuttering in protest.

"But, Lady Abbott, I… I fear that with the delay in shipping, of course, you see, that we would be unable to tailor the sheeting sets before months end."

Viola was exasperated. She dramatically leaned her considerable bulk toward him, placed her gloved hands carefully upon the counter and spoke very slowly, as though she were scolding an uncomprehending child. Catherine quickly decided to step away from the uncomfortable exchange and busied herself by trying on a feathered hat.

"It is not the timing, sir. I understand full well that these things take time. However, if the delivery is to be at months end…

Jonas clutched his quill to keep from trembling.

"…I shall simply require that the fabric be delivered to the Abbey as soon as the bolts are available. I shall send a letter to my own tailor in Wells to expect the fabric by the end of April so that he may alter the sheets, himself. Can that possibly be arranged, Mr. Wilcox?"

Jonas Wilcox nearly wept with relief. With a shaky hand, he wiped the beads of perspiration from his upper lip.

"Yes, Lady Abbott, we shall be very happy to deliver the van de Veld fabric to the Abbey. Four bolts, I should think." He turned to the waiting Peregrine. "See to it that the warehouse writes a change order to deliver the four bolts directly to Abbottsford Abbey in Stockbridge, Buckinghamshire."

"Yes, Father."

Peregrine most properly doffed his silver-buckled hat. He gave a courtly nod to the ladies, then whirled about in his exquisitely tailored overcloak and stepped out the door to summon a carriage. *Not that he desired to be anywhere near the filthy rabble of the East End. Or even for that matter, sitting in a hired hackney where other people had sat, for God's sake. Nothing of the sort. He was simply grateful to escape the old hag.*

The shop bell jangled, then as the door slammed shut, fell quiet.

Viola exhaled; well satisfied that she had ticked nearly every single item off her list.

"Come along, Catherine. We are quite finished here."

The door closed smartly behind a cloud of silken skirts. Though he had at just that moment added a small fortune to his ledgers and he was extremely grateful for her trade, to be quite honest, Mr. Jonas Wilcox was very glad indeed to see the Lady Abbott depart.

Out on the sun-drenched lane, the harried hackney driver was repacking the carriage with their purchases made earlier in the day. A young stock boy stacked the additional Wilcox & Sons boxes on the marble steps. The driver worked to make room for them, as well as both Viola and Catherine, but to no avail. A small box teetered, and then fell to the ground.

"Be careful, young man!"

While the driver shoved the box into a small opening, Viola counted the remaining boxes to make sure all the rest were accounted for. *One never knew precisely who had sticky fingers.*

Catherine, standing on the side of the lane, stared up at the Wilcox & Sons, Ltd. sign above the door. *Number Two, Sloane Street. Number Two...* She jumped with a sudden recognition. *The publisher! What was it that Dr. McKensie said?* She thought hard, willing his words from memory. *Number Ten, Sloane Street? Yes, Number Ten.* She looked at the driver unsuccessfully stacking the boxes to make room for the both of them and cast a glance down the lane. She saw a second hackney sitting idle, its horse eating heartily from a burlap feedbag.

"Aunt Viola, if it suits you, perhaps you might take this carriage back to Bealeton House. I can easily engage that driver over there to take me back," she said, pointing to the second carriage. "That way, there will be room enough for the rest of our boxes."

Viola considered the propriety of the scheme. She also considered her aching feet and had no wish to remain standing for one moment longer. She clapped her hands sharply toward the second hackney driver, who clopped his horse up the lane to where they were standing. She mounted the step into the forward carriage, and briskly called back.

"You there! See to it that my niece and these purchases are safely delivered to Bealeton House. You may follow us."

Catherine's heart sank. She had every intention of delaying her own departure in order to visit the publishing house. Number Ten was but four shops up the lane. *Would that she ever had a moment to herself?* She stepped out into the lane and looking from the distance, saw the sign above the door at Number Ten. *Would that she had even the courage to enter the Maxwell & Co. Publishing house?*

"Yes, Mum."

The stock boy loaded the remaining packages onto the second cart. The driver helped Catherine into the carriage and off they trundled down the lane behind Aunt Viola. Catherine looked out the glass window as the swaying cart passed by Maxwell & Co. *She would find a way to return.*

CHAPTER 16

"RING-A-RING O' ROSES, A POCKET FULL OF POSIES,
A-TISHOO! A-TISHOO! WE ALL FALL DOWN"
-UNKNOWN

Blackwall Shipyard
St. Giles-in-the-Field Parish, London
5 April 1665

Peregrine Wilcox disembarked from the hackney at the end of Broad Street and contemplated the unending hordes of people swarming in all directions through the Blackwall Shipyard. *"I should like to throw the lot of them straight into the harbor,* he thought with utter disdain. *Perhaps they'd smell better.*

Peregrine covered his nose with a delicate, lavender-scented lace handkerchief, then with great reluctance, gingerly stepped into the tumult, side-stepping his way past the shouting vendors, the beggars, the wayward travelers, the greedy thieves and the clever pickpockets that all collided together in the vast human stew that was London's East End.

He picked his way through the enormous, nearly half mile-long row of brick warehouses that dominated the massive shipyard. He walked past the shipwrights, the ironworkers, the timber cutters, the rigging and sailcloth workers and the vast ship building clutter that served to build the colossal wooden skeletons of the three British galleons that were hoisted high above the dry-docks. Quickly tiring, Peregrine dabbed daintily at his upper lip and despaired of ever finding the head office of the Thames Ironworks and Shipbuilding Company. He also despaired of the ruination that the filthy quay would wreak upon his new high-heeled linen slippers. Peregrine shuddered and kept walking.

Far above the crowds, to Peregrine's vast relief, he at last saw the faintly visible name of a ship spewing filthy passengers down its gangplank. The *Berschemer.* He headed straight toward the dock and the dreary multitudes that clustered near the bottom of the gangplank, looking for the first deckhand he chanced upon. As he prepared to inquire about the cargo in the hold, Peregrine felt a tap on his shoulder. He whirled about at the touch.

"Een vraag, meneer."

Peregrine instantly recoiled. *Oh, dear God, this filthy wretch actually seems to be speaking to me!* Peregrine was incredulous at the sight of a wan and weary-looking young man standing before him in a ridiculous red leather cap, eyes burning bright. Holding the lace cloth tighter to his face, Peregrine took a desperate step in retreat. To his utter horror, the lad suddenly exploded with an unexpected, violent sneeze; then having no handkerchief, *wiped his nose upon the sleeve of his miserable cloak!* Peregrine was beyond repulsed. *He could not direct the shipping of the fabric to Stockbridge and depart this loathsome shipyard fast enough.* The boy ducked his head in embarrassment and quickly switched to heavily accented English.

"Excuse me, sir."

Peregrine was so shaken by the approach of a… *a peasant—a Dutch peasant,* no less—that he stood fast, desperately swiping at his overcloak with the lace handkerchief. When he finished, Peregrine thrust the cloth toward the boy. *God knows I don't want it now!* The boy held his palms up, politely refusing the offering. Peregrine hastily threw it to the boy's feet.

"*Geldwisselaar?*"

Peregrine took another step backward, in a wide-eyed attempt to flee. The boy dug into his pocket and brought forth a fistful of coins. He anxiously held them out for Peregrine to see.

"*Geldwisselaar…* The boy pounded his aching head in frustration, trying to recall the English word. "*Ahh, ja!* Money changer, please?"

Good God, this deplorable wretch still tries to speak to me! Impatient to escape, Peregrine jerked a finger toward a crowded bank kiosk off to the side of the wharf.

"Lloyds. There."

"*Dank u, mijnheer.*" Again, the boy corrected himself. "Thank you, sir."

Rising upon his tiptoes, arms held high, Peregrine ducked and twisted in every direction, desperate to avoid the touch of *even a single one of these execrable savages that were pouring endlessly into his city.* Shoved awkwardly from the side, he stumbled into a toothless old woman begging for change. Peregrine let loose with a high-pitched shriek and tripped on the heel of his new linen mules. As he teetered, still shrieking, the old woman tried to grab for him, but he shook her off and fell hard onto the dock, soiling his prized hand-embroidered overcloak with heavy streaks of mud and dirt. The woman cried out and rushed to his side to help, planting her dirty, bare feet squarely upon his cream-colored slippers. Enraged, Peregrine shoved her away with a string of godless oaths, then leapt to his feet and tore headlong into the crowd to escape. The boy watched the unfolding chaos with great amusement, laughing to himself at the piercing shrieks as the turbulent crowd ebbed and flowed around the fancy dressed man, and then finally swallowed him up whole.

The boy stood near the bottom of the gangplank. He inhaled the bracing, salt air and marveled at the sheer number of people rushing by him, the vibrant energy of the crowd a stark contrast to the dull, brackish water that lapped quietly against the wooden pilings of the dock. He looked up to the second deck and saw an impressive, well-dressed gentleman with his arm set casually around the shoulders of a boy with a bright mop of curly red hair, not much younger than himself. The gentleman was pointing toward the magnificent ships in various stages of construction above the dry dock, seeming to explain each step of the building process. At the far end of the yard, a newly built ship, the *HMS Royal London*, was being lowered into the water, to the wild cheers of exultant deckhands and shipbuilders. The red-haired lad was excitedly taking it all in, clearly reveling in the attentions of the older man. The boy felt a sudden pang, remembering how his own father had lifted him upon his shoulders to explain how things were built when he was very young. He watched the two a few moments longer, wistfully recalling those fading memories, and then reluctantly, turned and threaded his way through the stream of disembarking passengers toward the Lloyds kiosk. He stood patiently in a long line until at last an irascible banker waved him forward.

"Name!" he growled.

"Jakob Auckes."

The banker diligently transcribed the name into an official-looking ledger. Jakob rubbed his hands together, nervously. Without deigning to look, the man continued his interrogation.

"Name o' your ship?"

Jakob pointed toward the massive sailing ship docked across the shipyard. The man reluctantly followed his gaze.

"The *Berschermer?*"

"Ja," Jakob nodded.

"What 'ave you got?"

Jakob looked confused. The man exhaled in irritation.

"Francs? Lira? Guldens?"

Jakob's face lit up.

"Ja, ja! Guldens!"

Jakob eagerly spread his coins out on the table for the banker. The man counted Jakob's guldens, put them into an iron moneybox, and then carefully calculated the equivalent sum in British currency. He slapped the coins on the table. As Jakob reached for the coins, the banker delicately set a fat forefinger on the largest silver one and pulled it back. It fell with a clunk into the moneybox. Jakob furrowed his brow.

"Tax. Welcome to England."

Jakob carefully counted the remaining coins he had been given. The banker, in no mood, waved Jakob off and bellowed to the waiting crowd.

"Next!"

The man in line behind Jakob made his way to the table, roughly shoving Jakob aside.

"Een vraag, meneer," said Jakob, not bothering to translate.

He picked up his leather valise and his *rucksack*, adjusted his red cap and headed out to the street that fronted the shipyard. As he walked across Broad Street, Jakob stopped and turned back to revel in the magnificent sight of the immense shipyard. He felt curiously out of breath. Jakob leaned against a wooden tenement building, wondering what he should do next. The jumble of languages and accents, the people heading with such purpose in every direction, the sights, sounds and smells of the shipyard excited him to no end. Though his head was pounding, he felt utterly alive. He had survived the terrifying ocean crossing and he was completely on his own. *Completely in charge of his own life.* He leaned against the warm planks and closed his eyes. A wondrous cacophony of sounds assaulted his ears and he reveled in it all. Hackney drivers bellowing, bootleg moneychangers beckoning, pamphlet boys screaming political headlines, snorting horses, barking dogs, astrologers casting horoscopes, medicine men hawking all manner of miraculous cures, prostitutes and even an organ grinder with a playful monkey all surrounded the newly landed and mostly bewildered passengers. *It was glorious.*

"S'cuse me, laddie."

Jakob opened his eyes. Standing before him was a small

woman, dressed in widow's blacks. She looked to be the age of *Mevr. van de Veld.* He looked closer and saw that she even bore a slight resemblance to the woman he knew so well. He trusted her immediately.

"Mind ye' lad, 'ave ye a place to rest yer 'head?"

Jakob suddenly realized that the sun was falling lower in the sky and though it had been a warm, early spring day, the evening air was turning cool. He had nowhere to sleep.

"Nee, mevrouw." He caught himself. "Please excuse me. No ma'am."

"I s'pose you'd best come up with me then, dearie." she said, sizing up his *rucksack* and leather valise with great interest.

With evening shadows beginning to crawl across the crowded city, Jakob followed the old woman through the cobbled streets to a ramshackle tenement building a fair distance from the shipyard. Climbing the set of creaking wooden steps, the old woman opened a door into a dim common room. She crossed to the brick fireplace, heavy with layers of black soot from years of smoke, and poked at a few coals smoldering in the grate until a small flame flickered.

"Name's Rebecca Andrews. Mostways' I'm called the Widda' Andrews, but ye' can call me Rebecca, as ye' like. D'ye's have a name?" she asked, lighting the melted ends of the few candles that were scattered about the room.

"Jakob. Jakob Auckes, Missus Rebecca."

"Glad to meet ye', laddie. If ye'll follow me," she said, briskly walking across the common area of the small boardinghouse into a dark, narrow hallway.

Rebecca led Jakob into a small, dingy room with a lumpy, straw-stuffed pallet and a worn, folded woolen blanket. A small porcelain chamber pot sat on the floor in the corner of the room, its edges chipped. A lopsided chair and small, crude table stood next to the pallet, its uneven legs causing a disorienting tilt to the entire enterprise. The wooden slats of the walls were thin to the outside air and ragged cottons barely covered the cracked panes of a small window that looked out across the lane lined with dilapidated wooden shanties. Rebecca took flint in hand and lit the stub end of a candle that sat on the tilted table.

"Threepence a night, supper's included. Will ye' take it, laddie?"

The room looked bleak, but Jakob was beginning to feel the effects of the trip. He swallowed. His throat suddenly felt as though it were filled with shards of glass. He decided to stay the night, and then look for better lodgings in the morning.

"Ja," he smiled, resolving making the best of it.

Jakob set his valise and *rucksack* on the table and sat down heavily in the chair.

"Righty-o," she said, taking a closer look at him. "Aye, ye' look a bit qualmish, ye' do. The trip was a bit much for ye', like as not," she said, plumping the meager pallet as much as it could be plumped. "Most of ye's come t' me the same way."

"Are there more?"

"Aye. There's two other boarders down th' hall. Ye'll make three."

Jakob could only nod. He cast a longing look toward the lumpy pallet.

"Aye, perhaps you'd like a bit of a lie-down before supper?"

"*Ja.*"

He reached into his bag and pulled a square of parchment, a quill pen and a small glass container of ink. He set them neatly on the table.

"I should like to send a letter back to Amsterdam. Perhaps you would help?" he asked in halting English.

"Aye'n, I'll be glad to help ye,' laddie. Write yer' letter, an' tomorrow when I go back t' meet the incomin' ships, I'll scuttle down to the offices and send it on its way."

"*Dank je*, Missus Rebecca."

At that, Rebecca left him alone, closing the door quietly behind her. Jakob took up his quill. He laid his pen to paper, but the ink blurred before his aching eyes. He squinted in the flickering candlelight.

My Dearest Geertje,

I have just arrived in London and already I have made a friend. Her name is Mrs. Rebecca Andrews and she runs a boardinghouse near the Blackwall Docks. I am renting a room from her and tomorrow, I will go out into the city and find work. The ship docked just this afternoon and I cannot believe the things I have seen in just one day. There was a man in the most beautiful suit of clothing that was knocked to the ground and was very mad. He made me laugh. There was a man exchanging money for everyone at a banking table. I have never seen so much money in one place! I even saw an organ grinder and a tiny dancing monkey in a little hat.

You will love London, my sweet Geertje! The sights and sounds and even the smells are nothing like home. I long to show you everything. I miss you so much that my heart aches. How I long for your soft, gentle touch upon my skin. How I wish we were back in our little room holding each other close, but I know we will be together soon. I will write again when I have found work. I only wanted you to know that I am safe and that I will send money for your ticket as soon as I am able. I love you more than you can ever know, my dearest Geertje. I always will.

Forever,

Your Jakob

He folded the paper several times. Then Jakob tied a length of twine around it, knotting it twice. He addressed the back of the parchment:

Missen Geertje de Groot
van de Veld Linnenfabriek
Amsterdam, Holland

Jakob placed the letter on the desk to give to Missus Rebecca in the morning. He removed his shirt and pants and folded them carefully across the back of the chair and blew the candle out. Then, crawling upon the pallet, Jakob fell immediately into a dark, dreamless sleep.

Rebecca looked in on Jakob before she snuffed her candle for the night. He was drenched in sweat and restless. *The boy seems feverish.* Her eyes fell upon his rucksack set with care upon the table. Treading softly, she held her candlestick high and tiptoed across the room. She lifted the flap to look inside the rucksack, and then froze as Jakob groaned and rolled over. She set the flap back in its place and quickly retreated from the room, closing the door silently behind her.

A single, echoing crack of thunder reverberated like cannon shot through the crowded, filthy slums of the East End, rattling thin glass windowpanes and shaking walls. Lightening briefly illuminated the dull, bone-chilling mist that swirled through the narrow lanes of dilapidated tenements. Jakob awoke with a jerk. Disoriented, and near delirious from the incessant pounding in his head, he tried to sit up, only to fall weakly back upon the scratchy, lumpy pallet. He shivered from the window he had opened in the night in a desperate attempt to cool his intolerable fevers. He tried to call out, but his throat scratched so desperately that he could only croak a sorrowful plea. He lay his aching head back down on the pallet, quiet for the moment, and then reached down to scratch the fiendishly itchy bites that covered his legs. An electric jolt of fear shot through his body as Jakob felt several large knots under the flesh at the tops of his thighs. He half-rose on his elbow to take a closer look in the dim morning light, and was struck with sudden, blinding terror. The knots were black. He knew in an instant exactly what it was for although the *linnenfabreik* had been mercifully spared, the horrific, deadly pestilence had just that winter ravaged its way through Holland, killing thousands.

Rebecca knocked on the door, and then walked in carrying a tray of tea and a small plate of hard bread and jam.

"You missed supper last night, laddie, an' I thought ye' might be a bit peckish by now," she said walking towards him. He looked at her in complete terror.

"*Nee, nee!*" He tried again. "No! No!!!" cried Jakob, waving her away.

"Ach, laddie, you 'aven't got a thing I ain't seen before," she said, greatly amused by his youthful modesty. She set the tray on the writing table.

"*U moet vertrekken!*" His head ached beyond endurance. *What are the words? What are the words?* He couldn't think. His mind swirled with panic at the danger she was now in.

"You must leave!" he begged, finally remembering how to say it. His tears fell in misery.

She peered closer at the distraught young man.

"Ik heb de pest!"

He seemed absolutely terrified.

"I don't understand ye', laddie!"

She looked at the boy desperately trying to rise from the pallet, his eyes imploring her, begging her for something, but she couldn't understand his strange language.

"Perhaps ye' should lay back and rest, nae," she said, her voice turning soft and soothing.

"De pest! De pest!!" he croaked, miserably.

Rebecca narrowed her eyes, then walked over and set the tray on the ground near the pallet. She reached out and felt an intense heat radiating from his forehead. Jakob pushed her hand away, gesturing frantically toward the door.

"*U moet vertrekken,* Missus Rebecca! You must leave!" he insisted, tears falling freely.

She could see that her presence was upsetting him beyond all reason. She backed away. *Damn ye' Ronald Andrews, leaving me penniless, an' takin' in boarders. Was the lad completely mad?*

By my oath, you never could tell with these accursed foreigners.

"All right, laddie. Ye' rest, an' I'll come back later," she said, in a soothing voice. She did not wish to upset him further.

Rebecca closed the door softly behind her. Jakob collapsed back onto the pallet. He remembered. He laid his head on the pillow. His voice dropped to an exhausted whisper.

"The plague."

CHAPTER 17

Bealeton House, St. James Parish
London, England
7 April 1665

Catherine could see that Viola was simply exhausted. With but four days until the engagement ball introducing Catherine and Miles to the cream of London society, there was still much to do. Catherine sat opposite Viola at a gleaming mahogany table that stretched through the cavernous dining hall, picking at the remains of a light luncheon of whitefish and broth. She glanced down the length of a magnificent runner had been draped down the entire length of the table. It had been embroidered with brilliantly colored silken threads depicting Viola's cherished peacocks. Their turquoise feathers were a stunning contrast against the deep mustard background. The table runner and the seat pinnings that were intricately embroidered with botanicals scenes of fruits and lush flowers lent the singular touch of color and warmth to the room. Heavily wrought sterling silver candelabras placed down the length of the table numbered nearly four and twenty. When lit, the effect would be nothing short of spectacular. Stretched to its fullest length for the party, the bespoke table would soon be laid out for over sixty very fashionable guests. At that moment, however, the women were two very lonely-looking figures sitting across from each other in the middle of the vast expanse.

"There are still a great many details to attend to," Viola fussed.

Catherine nodded absently. She set her luncheon plate aside and returned to the task of sorting piles of formal reception cards into a complicated seating arrangement. *Not that she would actually attend to those details,* thought Catherine; peevish at the tedious chore she herself was attending to. *It's the poor staff that gets the back end of the stick in her foolish flights of fancy.* Catherine was not remotely interested in a society gathering to announce her engagement. That her father actually seemed to be in favor was the only reason she submitted herself once again to one of Viola's tedious rituals.

Viola rubbed her temples as though her head ached beyond endurance.

"My head is simply pounding, my dear," she moaned to Catherine.

Catherine turned to her with a sudden inspiration. "Aunt Viola, I'm nearly finished with the seating arrangements. Perhaps you would like to retire upstairs and rest a bit this afternoon? Margaret will bring your headache powders."

"Oh, my dear, those make me sleep like the dead."

"As you like, Aunt."

Viola looked at the stack of reception cards in front of Catherine and gave a sigh, as though she quite felt overcome with the tedium.

"By my troth, you may be right, dear. I think some rest would do me good. Perhaps if you would be so kind as to finish the seating arrangements…" Her voice trailed off in anticipation.

"I have only one question. Mr. Samuel Pepys?

Viola's face lit up momentarily.

"Such a delightful man!" Viola squirmed with excitement, and patted the chair next to the one she was sitting in. "Place Mr. Pepys just to the right of me, with the Lord Mayor Hardwicke to my left. Oh, I shall enjoy the evening all the more."

Catherine reluctantly moved his card to the top of the stack, fearing for poor the man. She rang a small bell, then reaching across the table, rang Viola's slightly larger one, as well.

Both Margaret and Jane appeared quickly. A kitchen maid followed close behind to collect the empty luncheon plates and disappeared back into the cookery.

"Lady Abbott would like to rest this afternoon, Margaret. Would you see to it that she is not disturbed? Also, please bring her headache powders, as she is feeling unwell."

"Yes, Mum."

"Jane, would you please help me sort these reception cards?"

"Yes, Miss."

Margaret followed Viola up the stairs.

Jane watched the two of them retreat up to the private quarters, then turned toward Catherine, and reached for the cards.

"Shall I place these upon the table, Mi'Lady?"

Catherine nodded. Jane walked around the quiet room and placed the response cards into the seat positions that Viola and Catherine had agreed upon. On a carved sideboard, a German porcelain clock, its face delicately painted with botanical fruits, chimed the one o'clock hour. Catherine watched the minutes slowly tick by until Margaret came back down the stairs.

"She will sleep th' afternoon away, like as not," said Margaret, her hand on the dining room doorway. She looked back. "Can I get you anything, Mi'Lady?"

"No, thank you, Margaret. I believe Jane and I will go out for a walk." Jane looked surprised, but said nothing.

"Yes, Mi'Lady," said Margaret and disappeared into the kitchen.

Catherine looked at Jane and smiled.

"It's lovely outside, Jane. Would you accompany me?"

"Aye, Miss."

Catherine disappeared upstairs, and then just as quickly came back down, leather bag in hand. The pair descended the formal stone steps of the mansion, then turned toward the Thames, passing the quaint storefronts and small, elegant brick residences of St. James. At the end of the cobblestone lane, they walked past one of the new coffeehouses that were springing up around the city. They turned once more. Catherine's heart began to pound for there she was, standing in front of Number

Ten Sloane Street, Maxwell & Co. Printers, Ltd. She stared into the printing shop window.

"Are we stopping here, Miss?" asked Jane.

Catherine hesitated. "Yes."

Catherine held fast to the ivory handle of her bag with one hand and set a gloved hand upon the door latch with the other. She began to breathe faster. *Dare I enter? Perhaps I should indeed take the easier path and simply marry as Aunt Viola and Father expect of me.* She looked back to Jane who gave her an encouraging nod. She berated herself. *What is the most grievous consequence? Perhaps they might laugh at me? I have certainly been made sport of before. They could say my sketches are not skillful enough and ask me to leave. Is that reason enough to surrender my courage? Reason enough to not try and prove that I am capable of far more than everyone expects?*

"Are ye' nae going in, Miss?" asked Jane, jarring her thoughts. That was enough.

"Yes, Jane. I am."

Catherine lifted the latch and pushed on the door. It creaked and became stuck on a plank that rose slightly higher than the rest of the floorboards. She peeked through the crack, curious. A man in a formal suit of clothing standing behind the scarred and ink-stained wooden counter smiled and waved her in. She nodded and shoved the door harder. It swung open wide and Catherine stepped into the publishing house. To her surprise, the only patron in the shop was a woman leaning upon the far end of the counter reading aloud from a manuscript to an old man in a heavy leather apron. The man held a quill pen and was taking careful notes. He did not look up at Catherine's entrance, so intent was he upon the woman's quiet words.

The woman was an astonishing sight to behold. Taller by far than both men, she appeared an impressive and commanding presence, dressed as she was in a most unusual and bold frock of dark purple velvet with heavily gathered sleeves and several layers of luminous skirts. The whole of the gown's waistcoat was embroidered in an intricate, swirling paisley design of shimmering gold and red silken threads. A cloak that trailed on the floor behind her nearly six feet in length was embroidered in the same exotic, swirling design. The extraordinary costume looked as though it had been magically transported to London by Panchatantra's faeries from the dark and mystical reaches of the Indian sub-continent. A deep green headpiece nearly as wide as the doorway with several dark purple-feathered plumes completed the wondrous ensemble.

Catherine was truly mesmerized, feeling as though an entirely new world was slowly revealing itself to her. She closed her eyes and stood in the middle of the shop, inhaling the thick, heady scent of printer's ink. She reveled in the atmosphere of intellectual promise. *Everything here seems so foreign, yet at once so very familiar.* She could hear the shouts of the workers over heavy metal clanking rhythmically against metal from the printing machines in a back workroom. *I have never felt as though I belonged anywhere more than I belong right here.*

"May I help you, Miss?" asked the man.

She opened her eyes. To her relief, he welcomed her with a warmth she did not expect.

"Ambrose Maxwell. Publisher," he said, by way of introduction.

"I…I'm Catherine Abbott." She took a deep breath and collected herself. "I have some illustrations, sir. I was told you might consider them for publication."

"Have you now?" said Ambrose. "Let's have a look, then, my dear."

He watched as she set her bag down and unhooked the brass clasps. He could see her hands were shaking. She glanced at him with an embarrassed smile, then reached in and pulled out several illustrations.

"Ah, yes. 'Ere we go, Miss," he said, taking the stack from her outstretched arms. He set the pages on the counter and looked with interest at her elaborately drawn signature on the cover. *Lady Catherine Abbott.*

"My apologies, Lady Abbott," he said, correcting himself.

He carefully examined the pages, one by one.

"Ah, yes," he exclaimed, looking at length at the checquered skipper sketches. "Magnificent. Magnificent creature, indeed!"

He turned the pages, growing more excited with each new drawing.

"Ye' drew these, y' say?

"I did. Would you perhaps like to see the rest?"

"Indeed I would."

She pulled out the rest of her drawings, placing them one by one on the countertop. The shop bell jangled. Catherine was so completely intent upon showing her work that neither she nor the publisher paid scant attention to the man who walked in, though he seemed to take up a great deal of space in the small reception area of the shop. After a moment, the man walked over and stood next to Catherine. Without looking up from the collection, she sensed a powerful masculine presence standing next to her and instinctively stepped to the side to make room for him. She inhaled. *What is that? Leather. Yes, a warm, delicious scent of leather and smoke. And soap. The clean scent of soap.* The earthy scent was delicious. She closed her eyes and breathed deeply again. *What a remarkable establishment.* The man leaned in to examine the drawings that were spread across the counter, accidentally brushing her arm with his shoulder, his muscles rock hard against her own. So distracted was she by his unsettling presence, that she had to force herself to remain attentive to Mr. Maxwell. Catherine took another step to the side.

"I recommend that you look at the woodland grayling, Ambrose."

At that, Catherine jerked her head toward the voice, and with a shock saw Simon McKensie standing at her side, grinning, eyes crinkling. She was instantly undone by his presence, as close as he was to her.

"Dr. Mc…!"

Simon quickly put a hand on her arm. A lightening bolt of excitement ran through her, a shiver she had never before felt. *Not even with Miles. Not once.* Shocked by her reaction, Catherine fell silent. The publisher looked up at the sound of Simon's voice and then broke into a broad smile.

"Ah, Marlowe!" he shouted, reaching across the counter to vigorously shake hands with the man.

Marlowe? She stared at Simon. Her confusion was evident. As were her instantly reddening cheeks. *What is it about this man that causes such befuddlement in my mind?*

"Glad to see you, Marlowe! It's been far too long," he exclaimed.

Hearing the name, a gray-haired woman in a simple black linen frock poked her head around the wall from the printing room. She walked to the counter, pulled out a drawer and rifled through several compartments. She removed a small leather pouch and set it on the counter next to a ledger and quill pen. She looked up and smiled.

"Good afternoon, Dr. Marlowe. We've missed seein' ye 'round." She opened the ledger to a blank page, and then spun the ledger towards him. She held out the quill pen. "I've been savin' yer' royalties for ye'. If ye'll just sign, sir."

The man quickly glanced around the room, then dipped the quill into the bottle of ink and scrawled his name into the ledger and closed it with a snap. He reached over the counter for the pouch, then turned his back and stuffed it quickly inside his vestment.

Catherine took note of his curious actions. "My apologies," she broke in, questioning. "Dr. Marlowe, is it?"

Simon turned to face her.

"Yes." He spoke carefully. "Dr. Robert Marlowe." Something in his eyes stopped her from further inquisition. An instant mistrust rose in her. *Just who was this man?* Stung still from the seeming jests at her expense, the vague slight to her title in the courtyard of the coaching inn, she eyed him warily. *What game does he play? I will not be made mockery of again.*

"I see," she challenged. "May I ask, how is it that you are in London?" She narrowed her eyes. "In fact, may I ask how is it that you are in this very shop, Doctor...," she hesitated, "Marlowe?"

Caught off balance, Simon could see both the doubt and fire in her eyes. He had not collected his royalties in months, daring not to make himself conspicuous and give cause to anyone who might still wish to report his nocturnal research to the constabulary. He hesitated. *Would she even begin to believe his appearance today was but a coincidence? Would she believe anything he said?*

He tried to explain. "I am employed by the Lord Mayor who is this fortnight in London on business." Feeling foolish at the defense of his actions, Simon began to take umbrage at her tone of inquiry. He drew himself up. "I do, however, have my own personal business to attend to, Lady Abbott."

Chagrined, she instantly fell silent.

They stood in the shop for several awkward moments, neither quite sure of what to say next. Ambrose glanced from one to the other, and then quickly deciding discretion a far better course, turned his attentions back to the butterflies. He leafed through the thick linen pages until he found the wooded grayling illustrations. He leaned in close to examine the delicately detailed work through a wooden handled magnifying glass.

"Excellent. Just excellent," he murmured.

The woman in the velvet gown completed her business and turned toward the door, handing her belongings to a formally dressed footman who stood attentively by to arrange her train. Catherine was in awe of her quiet, commanding presence as the woman walked past. She paused for a moment at the counter in front of Ambrose.

"May I look?" she asked in a very quiet, unexpectedly shy voice, pointing to Catherine's work.

"As you wish, Mi'Lady." He turned the page toward her.

The woman leaned over and peered closely at the illustration, then set her fingers atop the page and brushed lightly over the ink strokes. She touched her thumb and middle fingers together, rubbing slightly, then turned to face Catherine. She spoke softly, her succinct words barely audible above the din of the workroom.

"You have a special talent for scientific illustration. Use it."

She turned back to her footman, gesturing softly to her embroidered carrying case and then pointed to both Simon and Catherine with a small, elegant wave of her impeccably manicured fingertips. The footman pulled out a stack of papers, and set them upon the counter. He took two leaflets from the top of the stack and handed one to Simon, the other to Catherine. He put the papers back into the case and stepped away. The woman spoke softly again, nodding toward the leaflets.

"I would be honored by your presence."

The plumes of her headpiece quivered in a slight breeze from the door that had been opened by her footman. She demurely cast her eyes downward, then turned and floated out of the publishing house to a waiting carriage. The footman quietly closed the door behind her. Catherine stared, mesmerized.

"If I may ask, who that was?" she asked, incredulous at the very sight of her.

"Lady Margaret Lucas Cavendish, the Duchess of Newcastle," answered Ambrose. "The first woman ever invited to speak before the Royal Society. We've published several of her books," he said proudly.

Catherine looked down at the paper she was holding in her hand. It read, *"A Sociable and Pleasant Afternoons Meeting of "Philosophical Letters and Observations Upon Experimental Philosophy."*

"An invitation to a philosophical lecture!" exclaimed Catherine.

Simon also looked at the paper, then folded it and placed it carefully in the pocket of his cloak, a sudden inspiration overtaking his normally sensible thoughts. Ambrose turned and faced a wall lined with bookshelves, searching through the titles. At great length, he pulled one down from the shelf and handed it to Catherine.

"Ere, Mi'Lady, 'ave a look."

"*CCXI Sociable Letters,* written by *The Thrice Noble, Illustrious, and Excellent Princesse, The Duchess of Newcastle.*" Catherine looked up. "Lady Cavendish wrote this?" she asked, intrigued by the very thought.

"Indeed, she did!" said Ambrose, proudly. "I've published many a book by Lady Cavendish. Plays and poetry, too, Mi'Lady." He tapped his finger on the leaflet. "The lecture on Friday is to be an advance discussion of her next book."

Catherine felt a chill up her spine. *Master Howell was right. It is possible for a woman to publish a book. Lady Cavendish had done it several times over!*

"You might enjoy attending, Lady Abbott," asked Simon, trying to lift the mood.

She had forgotten he was standing there. All manner of questions were filling her mind. She looked at the bottom of the leaflet.

At the home of the Honourable
And Most Gracious
Sir Charles Cavendish
27 St. James Place
Friday, 17 April 1665
2:00pm
Service of Tea Following

Catherine was stunned, for 27 St. James Place was just opposite the park from Bealeton House; no more than ten minutes walk. She thought she recognized the name of Charles Cavendish. She pointed to the paper.

"Is Sir Cavendish her husband?"

"Her husband's brother," corrected Ambrose. "Both he and her husband champion the interests of Lady Cavendish."

Catherine could hardly believe his words. *There were two men, two very powerful and influential men who not only shared, but also actually encouraged the interests of a woman writer.* Unexpected tears sprang to her eyes. *She was not alone.* Catherine always knew that her father was quite unusual in the way that he, as a learned man, had supported her interest in acquiring scientific knowledge, but now she knew for a fact that there were others like her. The relief she felt was enormous.

"Lady Abbott?"

She jerked her head toward the publisher. He held her illustrations in both hands.

"Yes, Mr. Maxwell?"

"Your drawings are excellent. Technical, precise, and beautifully drawn and I do believe that they would make a most interesting book." He paused a moment. "If you would allow me, I would be quite pleased to publish it."

Catherine felt weak. Her knees began to sag, the clanking sounds of the printing presses faded, her mind fogged. She grasped at the counter for support. Within moments, she felt a very strong hand at her elbow guiding her to a nearby bench. Someone pressed a vessel of water into her fingers. She sat on the wooden slats and tried to clear her racing mind.

"Excuse me, Mr. Maxwell. What did you say?"

He kneeled down to her level and spoke gently. "If you would kindly give your permission, my dear, Maxwell and Company would very much like to publish your book."

CHAPTER 18

Catherine and Jane walked along the Thames quay toward home. "An' ye' say they'll pay ye'?" exclaimed Jane. "Coo-ee!"

The fading sunlight sparkled off the dark waters, casting a golden glow against the heavy gray thunderclouds that gathered in the skies above the West End. Catherine could hardly keep her excitement in check. *Was that a fiction or did it most verily occur?* A dizzying kaleidoscope of emotions clouded her recollection of Mr. Maxwell's precise words, but crystalline sharp in her memory was the strong, sure hand at her back guiding her to the bench when his intentions became clear. Momentarily overcome by the offer, much to her embarrassment, she had nearly fainted. Simon instantly took charge. His quiet authority had been on full display, and although after the sip of water she'd regained her wits enough to speak with Mr. Maxwell, she was nonetheless intrigued by the doctor's ministrations.

"They will! Can you imagine it, Jane? Of course, Mr. Maxwell will keep everything until the costs of printing are paid back, but then we're to halve the profits on every book sold thereafter. Jane, I'm to be a published author!"

"I'm 'appy fer' ye' Mi'Lady," said Jane, with a sincere smile. She jolted Catherine back to reality with another thought. "Aye, then, can ye' imagine what yer' aunt will have to say about it?"

Catherine stopped short. She turned and faced Jane with an anxious look.

"Oh, please, Jane—we musn't say anything to either of them. You mustn't say anything until I tell Father. You are my most trusted confidante. May I have your word?"

"Of course, Mi'Lady. I'll nae' say a thing. Ye' have my word."

They fell silent, each deep in thought as they turned away

from the river and walked past the shops and the elegant row houses that lined the cobblestone lanes. The sky darkened with the late afternoon hour. In the windows, the soft, warm glow of candlelight began to appear as a light drizzle fell from the gathering thunderclouds. Catherine lifted the hood of her cloak over her head, muffling the hollow, echoing clops of a horse drawn carriage conveying its weary passengers homeward for the night. She could hear the sound of heavy footfalls behind them. She glanced over her shoulder and turned onto a quiet street. The footsteps drew closer. She and Jane began to hasten their steps, turning once more. Still, the footsteps followed. Catherine stopped and whirled about.

"Why do you follow us, sir?" she demanded.

"Lady Abbott!"

In an instant, she saw that they were face to face with Simon. She exhaled in relief.

"You frightened us!"

"I…I only wished to again offer my congratulations and to see to it you that you arrive safely home."

She considered his proposal, confused yet again by his contradictions. *No, his deceptions.*

"Thank you, but we have no need for an escort, Dr. McKensie…or Dr. Marlowe, or whomever you choose be at this moment."

Catherine and Jane turned to continue their walk. Simon stopped her, putting a light touch on her arm. She looked down to his hand on her arm and felt once again a sudden shiver of excitement. He quickly retracted his hand. Startled, she stopped and stared up at him.

"Please, Lady Abbott, might I explain?"

They stood before a quiet butcher shop, empty of customers at the end of the day. The feathered carcasses of several geese, a fat hen and two brown hares hung from fearsome iron hooks in the front windowpanes. Inside, a stout butcher in a bloodstained apron stood behind the counter plucking feathers from a goose. Catherine considered the strikingly handsome man standing before her. *Dare I give him leave to make plain his deception?* Jane looked from one to the other, and sensing an unfamiliar, yet not unwelcome attraction.

"Perhaps Charles would like a collops of bacon for his breakfast," murmured Jane, artfully disappearing inside the shop.

The butcher leaned over the counter toward the maid, seemingly eager for company. Catherine turned to face Simon. She looked up at him with a mixture of fascination and confusion and followed his gaze to the coffeehouse in the next building.

"Please, Lady Catherine, might you join me for a cup of tea?

She hesitated. Coffeehouses were new to the city. They were warm, comfortable meeting places where rich and poor men alike sat side-by-side sipping the strong brew as they whiled away the hours spinning tales or arguing politics. Aunt Viola would be aghast at the mere thought of her entering such an establishment. *In fact, she would probably faint.* At the thought, a trace of a smile played at the corners of her mouth. She collected herself.

"I fear that it is not proper for a woman…" she began, and then stopped, tempted now beyond all measure for one more daring feat before returning to Bealeton House and Viola's suffocating presence once again. Through the windowpanes, Catherine could hear shouts of passionately exchanged argument and debate from the men who gathered at the tables. *What an extraordinary day.* She hesitated. Simon stood before her, his eyes searching for some small measure of absolution. How she longed to take part in passionate debates and ideas. *And why should I not? Are not women just as intelligent?* Taking sudden umbrage at the injustice, an invigorating, even thrilling boldness began to manifest. *He was inviting her in.* Catherine looked back to see that Jane was deeply engaged in a conversation with the butcher. Catherine turned to Simon and smiled.

"Yes. I would like that."

Simon offered his arm and together they walked into the warm, richly fragrant coffeehouse. *But, which was more the thrill, daring to walk into a coffeehouse, or daring to walk in with this man?* At the sight of a woman entering their masculine retreat, a strange silence began to spread throughout the room. Chairs scraped as the men turned to watch them walk to a vacant table near the window. She held her head high, gracefully taking a seat in the chair that Simon proffered. Catherine began to lose her nerve. Completely unaware of the spectacle they were making, Simon sat down across the table and gestured to the serving girl who herself seemed momentarily taken aback by Catherine's presence. The men watched for a moment, fascinated by the very sight of a woman in the coffeehouse.

"What may I bring you, sir?" asked the girl, regaining her composure.

"Two coffees and a plate of biscuits, if you please," requested Simon. As Simon rose to hang their over cloaks on a peg, Catherine fully expected the serving girl to ask her to leave. The men in the coffeehouse seemed to expect the same. When no drama unfolded, the men turned back in their chairs, gradually resuming their arguments. Catherine felt emboldened.

The girl brought a tray and set the dishes before them. Catherine took a tentative sip of the hot brew. It was bitter and burned her lips. Instantly setting her dish on the table, Catherine stared at the young man who sat across from her. She could see the intelligence in his kind eyes and the confidence in his bearing, but unexpectedly; there was an endearing humbleness in his manner. He was friendly to those he met, although he could certainly display his strength and authority when necessary. He was an intriguing presence, and yet Catherine clearly saw something in him that he could not or would not share. *Why does he unsettle me so?* She swirled her dish, dislodging the scant coffee grounds that had settled to the bottom. She watched them tumble round, then sink back down once again. *And yet, I fear it is far more troubling that Miles unsettles me not.* She looked up from her coffee. He was watching her with such open, honest concern that her reserve began to thaw. Though she could feel the weight of disapproval upon her from the men sitting at a nearby table, Catherine closed her eyes and slowly inhaled the scent of both coffee and heady freedom.

Catherine leaned back slightly in her chair, listening to two old men bemoaning tax increases on one side of her and three young men arguing about the newly declared war with the Dutch on the other. Within moments, she laughed delightedly as they all began shouting at one another, increases in taxes to wage war being very similar subjects, evidently. "Is this not most exciting?" she asked, opening her eyes wide.

"Taxes? Or war?" he grinned.

She tried another sip of the bitter coffee, then set the dish back on the scarred, stained table. She regarded Simon, thoughtfully. *There is something more to this man than is evident to my eyes.* She leaned over the table.

"Who are you," Catherine asked simply.

He hesitated a moment. "I am Simon McKensie."

"Are you a doctor, or is that a fiction, as well?"

"I am, Lady Catherine. That is to say, I am in medical school. I have one year remaining."

Catherine fidgeted with her skirts. She could suddenly feel the eyes of the men boring into the back of her and her bravado began to falter, although her curiosity overcame any thoughts of escape.

"Why were you called Dr. Marlowe in the publishing house?"

Simon froze, in obvious distress, remembering all too well Father Hardwicke's ominous warning. *There are laws, Dr. McKensie.* He played with his biscuit, breaking it into small bits. *It could be dangerous for her. It could be even more dangerous for me. How can I possibly explain?*

"I fear that I cannot say." He furrowed his brow in frustration. He looked down to his coffee; his thoughts conflicted.

Catherine stared at him, taking the full measure of his words. *He plays a game still.* Outside, she could see Jane on the corner, looking up and down the lane for her. Catherine could take no more. *Or plays me for a fool.*

"Then I fear that we have nothing else to say. My maid is looking for me. I…I must leave."

"No, Lady Catherine, please do not leave." She hesitated, for he looked miserable. "It is necessary that I…" He stopped, and then fell into a resigned silence, defeated.

She gathered her things together and looked through the window to wave Jane. From across the lane, Jane saw her and nodded. Simon tried once more to turn Catherine's attentions, for although he surely could not say why, he felt compelled to see her again.

"I… I have decided to attend Lady Cavendish's lecture. Might I invite you to accompany me?"

Momentarily intrigued by the tantalizing thought of meeting Lady Cavendish once again, Catherine considered the invitation, and then just as quickly changed her mind.

"I'm afraid it would not be proper, as I am betrothed."

"Perhaps you would invite your maid as an escort. I'm quite sure that Lady Cavendish would welcome…

Catherine cut him off. "Just as important, I fear there is something wrongful behind the falsehood you present, sir, and I'll not be an accomplice to it."

Simon was sorely troubled. He had made a grievous impression upon her, and his necessary fiction was making it worse. He felt a reckless impulse to confide the truth of his illicit research. Never before had such unsettling thoughts as these intruded upon his normally scientific and careful mind. He thought of her bravery with the dying maid. He thought of her strength with Toby when no other could abide the trauma.

Dare I confess my experimentations to this extraordinary creature? By my oath, I gainsay she is a kindred soul. Perhaps she would keep a confidence. His better sense, however, compelled him to remain silent, *for his very life, and hers should he dare to confess, depended upon the absolute secrecy of it.* He bowed his head.

"I will nonetheless be in attendance at the lecture." He looked down. "Perhaps you will change your mind," he said, softly. Simon lifted his head and stood, reaching for the cloaks. "If you will forgive me, Lady Abbott, I apologize for having intruded upon your afternoon."

He left a few coins on the table, and then escorted Catherine out to the lane to meet Jane who was carrying a small, wrapped bundle. Simon smiled gamely at the ladies. He tipped his hat, then turned and walked away. Jane watched him leave with a mixture of appreciation and admiration.

"E's a fine-looking gentleman, is 'e not, Mi'Lady," Jane whispered.

Catherine whispered back. "Yes, Jane. He very much is.

CHAPTER 19

"EVIL THINGS THERE BE A COMET BRINGS, WHEN IT ON HIGH DOTH HORRID RANGE: WIND, FAMINE, PLAGUE, AND DEATH TO KINGS, WAR EARTHQUAKES, FLOODS, AND DIREFUL CHANGE"
-UNKNOWN

St. Giles-in-the-Field Parish
London, England
8 April 1665

On Jakob's third morning in the boardinghouse, Rebecca grew concerned. The boy hadn't taken a single meal since he'd arrived. *A'course them other two boarders ain't complainin',* she thought, buggered by the extra expense. *More in the stewpot for them grubbin' mitts.* Rebecca knocked softly upon Jakob's door. *Perhaps the lad has recovered enough for a bit of tea and biscuits.* There was no answer. *Aye,' an' wouldn't I like a sip, me'self. Me' achin' throat burns like th' very spittin' fires of Hades.* She knocked harder. Alarmed at hearing a weak, muffled cry, she balanced the cup and saucer in one trembling hand and with the other, unlatched the door. She stepped warily into the room.

"Mornin' lad, are ye' perhaps feelin' a mite bet…" She instantly recoiled, for the fetid smell was overwhelming.

Rebecca froze. The cup fell to the ground and shattered as it hit the floorboards, splashing hot tea down the canted, stained walls, onto the plankings and over the toes of her tattered leather boots. She was shocked by the desperate appearance of the boy lying on the pallet, deathly pale, sweating, shivering and struggling to breathe. She rushed to his side.

"Aye, laddie!"

Jakob turned to her, his eyes imploring, his voice the barest trace of a whisper.

"*Ik verontschuldig me.*"

Rebecca leaned in closer to hear him. He tried weakly to push her away.

"*Ik verontschuldig.*"

"I don't understand ye', laddie. I don't understand," she fretted. She grasped the ceramic handles of the chamber pot by the bed and, recoiling from the contents, looked out the open window. Seeing that the way was clear, Rebecca threw the contents down to the lane below. She glanced down with a shudder at the remains, and then threw the chamber pot out the window, as well. It hit the dirt with a thud and rolled in a lazy circle before coming to a rest at the side of the lane near the sagging wooden steps of the boardinghouse. She watched as a matted, stray mutt wandered over and idly sniffed at the pot. He turned around, lifted his leg and added to the mess, then meandered on down the lane in search of any food scraps lying about. Though the morning fog carried a bone-chilling dampness, she left the window open to air the room, and then pulled the chair beside the pallet to sit with him. The wooden legs scraping across the floorboards shattered the unearthly silence in the small room, startling them both.

Jakob closed his eyes; weary from the effort it took to translate. His face contorted in pain as he swallowed. He raised a finger toward the window.

"I'm sorry," he whispered.

Her old heart broke. He lay quiet for a moment, then Jakob rose slightly off the pallet and clutched for her apron, anguish etched upon his face.

"The letter, Missus Rebecca. I beg of you, please send the letter."

Rebecca took his hand and held it tight.

"I will, laddie. I promised ye' and I'll keep to it."

He lay back and fell silent. Through the confusion that swirled in his mind, Jakob had one last moment of clarity.

"Mijn geld..." He swallowed, the pain springing tears to his eyes. "Mijn geld...my money," he croaked. Jakob tried to lift his hand again to point, but the strength was nearly gone. He could only cast his eyes toward the table.

"*Mein rucksack.*"

Rebecca pulled the bag to his side and opened it so that he could see the contents. With shaking hands, he reached in for the small leather pouch. He felt the blue square of cloth. He pulled them both out of the bag and handed Rebecca the leather pouch. She felt the heft of the coins inside between her fingers, then set the pouch on the table next to her. He held the cloth to his face, its soft fibers a cooling touch to his fiery cheeks. He was overcome with tears. *Geertje.*

"Send the money with my letter, please, Missus Rebecca. Send it to Geertje."

"I will."

"Dank je, Missus Rebecca," he whispered.

"Fer' what, laddie?"

Jakob struggled for a breath. "For being with me."

Her old heart aching, Rebecca reached over to push a damp curl off his wet forehead, and then tenderly laced her gnarled, arthritic fingers around his. Jakob fell silent once again, desperately clutching the blue cloth with one hand and Rebecca with the other. His mighty strength began to ebb, as he surrendered to an unseen, relentless and inevitable force. His grip loosened, his tortured, ragged gasps dwindled to feathery, almost imperceptible puffs. As Rebecca sat stroking his hand, Jakob's eyes gradually took on a faraway look, as though he saw the angels themselves hovering above his miserable bed. Slowly fading into an unknown void, he turned slightly toward Rebecca and gave her the softest trace of a smile. Then Jakob let go of the world. His head fell to the side, his eyes staring into a vast, empty nothingness. The blue square slid to the floor. Rebecca dropped his hand. A single, glistening tear trickled down her wrinkled cheek as she crossed herself and whispered a prayer for the dead.

"Aye, laddie."

Rebecca sat quietly beside his body, gazing down at the young man who's future seemed so full of promise three very short days ago. *Life is but one lamentable disappointment after t'other,* she sighed. Rebecca finally reached over and closed his eyes. After another long moment, she wiped her tears and shifted her chair to the table. She picked up the letter he had neatly folded and tied with string, and held it thoughtfully in her hand, wondering about the girl he cried out for. *The poor lass.* She turned the letter over and with the quill pen, scratched a barely-legible note between the strings.

"I regret to informe ye' that yer' Jakob died o' the fevers this on varie day." I am sorrie fore yer' loss. Signed, The Widow Andrews, St.-Giles-in-the-Fields Parish, London. 8 April. In the Year of Our Lord, 1665.

She stood and shifted her apron to the side, sliding the letter into the pocket of her skirts. She wiped her eyes once more, then sighed and turned her practical attentions to his belongings. *They'll do him no good now.* Opening the valise, Rebecca lifted out two course woven linen shirts, a pair of leather breeches, a faded brown linen vest and the red leather cap he wore the day he arrived. His overcloak hung on a peg by the door. She held the breeches up to the light from the window and examined them for wear. *Aye, an' won't these fetch a fine penny down at the docks.* Something caught her eye on the floor. The ice blue square of fabric. She leaned over and picked it up, then having no use for it, tossed it aside.

Her eyes fell upon the leather pouch. She tipped the contents onto the table and glanced toward Jakob lying motionless in the bed. *Aye.' Forgive me, laddie.* One by one, she counted the coins. *Seven shillings an' two p. Enough t' get me through th' spring.* She crossed the hall to her own room and latched the door behind her. She rested her aching head against the back of the door, and then lifted her eyes to the heavens. *Damn ye' t' hell, Ronald Andrews.*

Rebecca kneeled down and, reaching deep under her straw mattress, withdrew a small sack tied with string. One by one, she dropped the coins in, the silver clinking dully against the precious few coins left at the bottom. She hid the sack under the mattress once again, and then rose on creaking knees. Glancing in the broken shard of a looking glass by the door, she caught an expression of guilt and shame upon her old face. She quickly looked away, for Rebecca Andrews was most certainly no longer a woman to think upon life as she wished it to be, but rather one who fully understood that life was unrelentingly cruel and one needs do what one must. She straightened her shoulders and resolutely donned her cloak and bonnet, for now what Rebecca Andrews must do is pay a most lamentable visit to the undertaker.

CHAPTER 20

East India Arms
Fenchurch Street, London
11 April 1665

Simon sat brooding in the common suite between the two rooms that the Lord Mayor had let for the fortnight in advance of the East India Company board meeting. A mighty stack of journals and treatises from the Royal College of Physicians lay at his feet, but he had not the heart to delve into the research with his usual robust curiosity. His life had been jostled more in the last several weeks than it had been in years, and his mind was weary trying to keep abreast of it.

The Fenchurch Arms, a solid brick inn sited just two blocks from the Leadenhall Street headquarters of the East India House, was built to accommodate Company members while in London on business. The rooms were small but comfortable enough, Simon thought, furnished as they were with generous leather chairs, a warm fire crackling in the common room, and a soft, clean bed in his own chamber opposite the Lord Mayor's. A dull, steady rain slapped against the windowpanes as night fell and left dripping, wet streaks that refracted light from the chest-high forged candlestand next to Simon's chair. He held a new copy of *De Anatome Cerebri,* that he had just that day bought from Ambrose Maxwell, but try as he might, he could not concentrate his mind enough to open the book to the astounding research of the nervous system done by Dr. Thomas Willis. His eyes were drawn to the rain beating against the window as he despaired of the terribly wrong course he'd gotten off to with Lady Catherine.

The door to the common room swung wide. Simon jerked his head up at the bang of the wood against the plaster wall and saw the Lord Mayor bursting from his bedchamber, fastening a wide lace collar to his formal shirting. Simon had to admit that he was an impressive, if not slightly comical figure in his most fashionable black velvet Rhingrave breeches that hung wide above his white lace stockings and lavishly beribboned scarlet knee cannons. An intricately patterned velvet coat draped over his arm swung to and fro as he struggled with his slippery silks. *He is quite a sight,* thought Simon, taking in the elaborate costume.

"Ready yourself, lad!" The mayor looked down at an engraved watch hanging about his neck. "It's half-nine. We're late!"

"For what?"

"The engagement ball at Bealeton House!"

"And who, might I ask, is engaged?"

"The Lady Catherine Abbott to the Viscount Houghton."

Simon inhaled sharply, rolling his eyes up to the timbered ceiling. *Lady Catherine engaged to that half-wit. What the devil does she see in the idiotic popinjay?* The Lord Mayor stared into the looking glass and fumbled with his cravat, winding it first one way, then back the other, then forwards again. "Blast and damnation!" he bellowed. He quickly recovered his wits and turned to Simon. "You remember, lad, you made her acquaintance at the coaching inn the day the stable boy was kicked by the horse."

"How well I remember," he muttered, half under his breath.

Simon pulled the candlestand closer to his armchair and hunkered in. *I desire no more to celebrate the Lady Catherine's engagement to that idiotic, calculating cad than I desire to pass the night out in this detestable rain.* Stubbornly ignoring the invitation, Simon opened the book to concentrate his attentions on the treatise and found himself staring at a most magnificent illustration of the brain, rendered in extraordinary detail by Christopher Wren. He was mesmerized. It was the very first of its kind. No one else in the known world had ever been able to illustrate the brain to the exacting, minute detail he was looking at. *They've done it!* He was instantly drawn into the book. He absolutely reveled in the sight of it. He barely managed a civil response to the Lord Mayor's invitation, so intent was he upon examining the miraculous sight.

"Enjoy your evening, Lord Mayor," he mumbled.

"Out of the question, laddie! My brother desires an audience with you this night. I have written him that my afflictions are subsiding and my industry has increased since you have but led me around by the nose." He pulled his waistband away from his shirting and looked sideways into the mirror, grinning merrily. "Good Lord, I shall soon have to visit the tailor, as my very breeks are wont to fall down for the extra inch of it!" He reached over, took the book from Simon's hands and closed it emphatically. "I have hired a carriage, my boy, so be quick about it."

Simon groaned. He retrieved his book from the mayor and set it carefully on the floor beside his chair. Resigning himself to the very difficult evening ahead, he disappeared into his chamber to change. Dressing in what few serviceable garments he owned, Simon presented himself minutes later to the Lord Mayor.

"I fear that I am not overmuch attired for such a festive occasion," he said, hoping for reprieve from what would doubtless be an uncomfortable evening.

"Nonsense! You look completely presentable, lad. If you insist, however, I have a coat in reserve."

The mayor retrieved the coat from his trunks and helped Simon into it. Simon's heart sank. It was far shorter than current fashion would dictate, for the mayor was but a full head shorter than he. Taking a second look, however, even Simon had to admit that the elaborate coat with its heavily decorated ribbons, scarlet twist cording and large silver buttons, was indeed more commodious to the occasion. Although it was a far fancier garment than he would ever in his life wear, it fit well enough and, thought Simon, *certainly looked finer than his plain black, boiled-wool vestments.* He sighed in resignation. The mayor held the door open.

"Shall we, my boy?"

Simon headed for the door, and then hesitated.

"By your leave, sir, may I follow in a moment?"

"Aye, lad."

Simon turned back to his bedchamber. He opened his traveling trunk and lifted a small book from the side pocket. *In Systematis Circulatorii ad Pestem, by Dr. Robert Marlowe, M.DC. LX.VIII.* The book was the accumulation of all his research on the system of blood circulation and disease. He still couldn't quite believe his work was in print, even if under a *calamum nomen.*

At the very core of his intellect, Simon knew there must be a *reason* that one in close proximity to an infected person did not always himself becomes ill, though to his sheer frustration, he could not identify exactly why. That his treatise on the circulation of the blood might somehow contribute to the growing body of knowledge on anatomy and disease both pleased and humbled him most greatly, even if his God-given name was not associated with the science.

Simon held the book in his hand and weighed the fearsome consequences should a linkage be made between him and the fictional Dr. Robert Marlowe. After having spent the whole of a year and the entirety of his savings, not to mention endangering his very life and fledgling medical reputation on his illicit, nocturnal research, he had much to lose should an investigation by the constabulary be made manifest. *So very much to lose.* He took a deep breath, closed the trunk and shoved the book into the inner pocket of the waistcoat, then walked four flights downstairs to the waiting carriage.

The driver drew his hackney to a halt outside the palatial stone steps of Bealeton House. As Simon followed the mayor out of the carriage, Simon reached inside the borrowed coat and felt the book; it's heft a sobering reminder of the dangerous course of action he now contemplated. They ascended to the front door of the mansion, and were welcomed into the sweeping entrance hall. Simon caught his breath. The grand foyer was truly magnificent. Not once in his entire life had he ever seen such splendor. Everywhere he looked, standing iron candelabras effuse with candle flame and sparkling crystals illuminated the mansion, casting a wavering glow upon the colonnades, and reflected off the gleaming, highly polished marble floors. The guests that had gathered in clusters around the generous hall were resplendent in their most elegant attire. Simon looked down at his common woolen breeches and felt embarrassed. He cursed the Lord Mayor under his breath for compelling him to attend the ball. *Thank God the borrowed coat is extravagant enough.*

Simon heard cries of welcome from behind. He turned toward the shouts and saw Miles and Catherine standing together to greet the arriving guests. His heart nearly stopped, for standing before the carved stone arch of the foyer Catherine was a vision in a charcoal gray gown that perfectly complimented her slate-colored eyes, coppery hair and pale skin. The facets of her blue stone necklace sparkled in the candlelight. If he tried, Simon could not possibly describe the cut of the shimmering gown, the pattern of the billowy lace of the sleeves or the weight of the silks, he only knew she was breathtaking. He completely lost his nerve. He turned resolutely toward the door with every intention of slipping away from the mayor and the party, only to be stopped by Miles calling out, waving them over to the archway.

"Lord Mayor!"

His arm caught up by the mayor before he could make his escape, Simon reluctantly turned back toward Catherine and Miles and managed a trace of a smile. He took in the sight of Miles standing so at ease in the spectacular setting and felt even more of a clod, for the fop was turned out in an exquisitely tailored and elaborate costume, replete with scarlet ribbons, sterling silver buttons, a wide, square lace collar, a custom sword in a jeweled hilt and a periwig of dark brown curls cascading down his back. Simon fought back the urge to be sick. *Or to laugh out loud.* Simon walked with the mayor toward the couple.

Catherine glanced toward Simon, and then, reddening, lowered her head and nodded a demure greeting. Miles saw the flush rise in her cheeks and reached for her hand, a possessive gesture meant to sting. *It did.*

"Lord Mayor. Doctor…. Welcome to Bealeton House." She turned her gaze toward the ballroom and dismissed them with a gentle wave of her hand.

"Please, if you would care to join the others."

Simon tried to speak. "Thank you, Lady Cather…"

Catherine cut him off with a polite smile.

"If you would."

"Indeed, we will, Mi'Lady," crowed the mayor. Deflated, Simon was acutely embarrassed by the mayor staring with obvious glee into the glittering ballroom and rubbing his hands together in greedy anticipation at the sight of the dazzling women in tempting, teasing low-cut gowns of richly colored satins. The mayor grabbed Simon's elbow delightedly and dragged him straight into the party.

"This way, laddie!"

The mayor pulling him unceremoniously toward a priest in his most formal vestments on the far side of the room irritated Simon. He stepped to the side as the mayor slapped the priest on the back to gainsay his attention.

"Though I am loathe to admit it, Thomas, I daresay you were right!"

Father Hardwicke turned around in surprise. The mayor grabbed the waistband of his breeches and pulled to its limit, revealing for the first time in years, a hint of space.

"The lad's been with me not yet a fortnight, and in that bit of time, the execrable foot pains have eased, and I have more industry than ever." Simon ducked his head in modesty. "The boyo's even got me tramping through the fields every day, no matter the weather."

Father Hardwicke nodded to Simon. "Well done, lad. Do you think he can keep the course?"

"Aye, he's been a fine, if somewhat reluctant, patient."

"I daresay that should my brother remain the very picture of health in but six months time, we should be very gladsome indeed to welcome you back to St. Bartholomew's, Doctor."

"And I should be very gladsome indeed to return," said Simon, barely concealing his dry wit.

Lord Abbott approached the men and placed his arm convivially around the mayor.

"Am I to understand that the lad has taken complete charge of your constitution, Cecil?"

"Aye'n his ministrations do chaff," the mayor grumbled good-naturedly.

Lord Abbott thought for a moment. "And pray tell me, Cecil, do you not take kindly to someone telling you what to eat, and what to drink and exactly how to parse your time?

"'Tis a trial, indeed," the mayor sighed.

Lord Abbott's eye's twinkled.

"Perhaps you might recall these very words, thence speak of your trials to the board on Friday next. In reference to India, of course."

A liveried servant walked by carrying a tray of sparkling wines. The mayor immediately reached for one, then stopped mid-air and looked to Simon, questioning. Simon laughed and nodded his assent. The mayor handed each man a glass, then raised his own in a toast.

"Surely you do not propose to compare my trifling health concerns to the necessary rule of an entire country, good sir."

He smiled, then tipped his head back and drained the glass, well satisfied that he had subjugated the argument.

"Ahh, I intend nothing of the sort, Mayor. I merely wish to propose that as one alone might naturally chaff upon being ordered about, so might an entire country chaff upon the same governance." Lord Abbott drained his own glass.

"But you see, sir, of my own device, I chose unwisely and thus required the services of a more knowledgeable administrator to make things right." The mayor turned to his brother. "Are you not in agreement, Thomas?"

Simon braced himself for an argument. Father Hardwicke simply raised his palms in protest.

"I most certainly do not wish to be dragged into the divisive board member disputes of the East India Company, thank you all the same," he smiled, his thin lips curling ever so slightly upward. "St. Bartholomew's, and my new wing I might add, are far too dependent upon the company's continuing largess," *A poisonous spider seducing its prey,* thought Simon.

Viola walked up and took the mayor by the arm. She instantly recognized the young doctor from his encounter with Catherine at the coaching inn. She looked Simon over from head to toe, with all the pinched-faced enthusiasm of one who detects the foul odor of yesterday's fish.

"Gentleman, gentlemen. Let us not bore our young guest with the dreary triflings of your workaday affairs."

She turned to the mayor with an unfamiliar, coquettish smile that inexplicably seemed to erase years from her heavily powdered face. Simon laughed to himself that for once, the mayor seemed momentarily taken aback.

"How very pretty you look tonight, my dear," whispered the mayor. Simon watched as the mayor looked down at Viola and smiled gently "There is something comforting indeed, about old friends, don't you think, my dear? No need to hide the interminable aches and pains. No needs for false pretense in the merry pursuit of young flesh, if one could, in fact, call it merry."

Viola seemed to melt at his unexpected declarations. Standing to Viola's side, Simon caught a glimpse of something curious. Despite his natural reserve, Simon impulsively leaned in to take a closer look. *Good Lord, she wears a black patch in the shape of a crescent moon upon her cheek. Never have I seen such vanity, such foolery!* Caught in the act, Simon jumped back as Viola snapped out of her reverie. She drew back and sniffed at him in barely veiled contempt. She turned to the mayor.

"Cecil, would you kindly escort me in." He placed his hand protectively over hers. Viola swung her skirts and threw her chin high. She turned back to give Simon a withering glance.

"I would be honored, my dear," said the mayor. He looked back over his shoulder to Simon. "Shall we?" With no alternate course, Simon reluctantly followed.

The dining room sparkled with flickering candlelight from the seemingly endless string of candelabras placed down the entire expanse of the table, casting a warm glow upon the lively guests. A servant led Simon to a table setting at the furthermost end of the table, as far as Viola could have possibly placed him from Catherine and Miles, who were graciously entertaining guests at the opposite end of the impressive expanse. Viola, herself, was seated between the Lord Mayor on her left side and Samuel Pepys, on her right. Catherine was astonished at the elaborate evening Viola had orchestrated. *With every passing moment the invisible ties of obligation bind ever tighter.*

Catherine was taken aback by the scores of servants entering the room to lay platters of early spring vegetables, roast joints of meat, and puddings, followed by game, fish, custards and sweet creams before the fashionable guests. Catherine gasped and applauded with everyone else as four exotically costumed, turbaned bearers carried in the highlight of the feast with a flourish. On a wooden plank sat a three foot wide by one foot tall Bride's Pie, a massive baked dough vessel containing an extravagant mixture of meats, sweetbreads, veal, oysters and dates, spices of cinnamon, ginger and nutmeg all covered by a sauce of wine, butter and eggs. Catherine knew the servants had spent three days in the making, and now the spectacular creation was ceremoniously transported on the decorated, tasseled plank into the dining hall.

Catherine held her breath as Viola rose and walked over to the assembled servants. *Whatever has she planned now?* With great flourish, Viola helped lift the lid to reveal an unexpected surprise. To Catherine's astonishment, four and twenty live blackbirds flew out, wildly scattering in all directions. Catherine quickly ducked under the table as one terrified bird flew straight toward her, grazing her hair. Exuberant shouts and riotous, piercing screams of delight echoed throughout the cavernous dining hall as servants with nets began to chase the wildly flapping, disoriented birds. Catherine cautiously reappeared to watch the chaos as the servants chased the terrorized creatures. When at last the blackbirds were caught and the guests finally settled down to dine, Catherine watched Viola triumphantly return to her seat, tossing off a sidelong glance of victory toward the regal Lady Houghton along the way. Catherine glanced to the end of the table. Simon was staring at her. *What does he gape at?* Simon slowly raised his hand, pointed toward his head and grinned. Embarrassed, she instantly put her hand to her hair and felt the curls that had fallen askew from the wayward bird. A sudden smile flashed across his face. Catherine lowered her eyes, and yet, she could not keep herself from smiling back. She quickly looked to Miles at her elbow. Busy pouring himself more wine, she exhaled in relief, grateful that he missed the entire exchange.

Lord Abbott stood and raised his glass.

"Ladies and Gentlemen. We welcome you tonight to

celebrate the betrothal of my beautiful Catherine to the Viscount Houghton." He turned to the couple. "My dears, we wish you every happiness."

"Hear, hear!" shouted the guests, clapping wildly.

Miles lurched to his feet, taking his own glass in hand. "If I may, we are most grateful you could all be with us on such a joyous occasion!" He threw back the contents of his glass, then turned to Catherine and removed a small package from his pocket. He held it up, with a wink. "If you all will indulge me but another moment, I should like to present the Lady Catherine with a small gift to mark the occasion."

Catherine glanced toward Simon as Miles handed her the gift. She turned the packet over in her hands. *The ties grow ever tighter.* She unwrapped it and held up a wide, hammered gold ring for all to see. Miles poured himself another glass and took a hefty draught, then took the ring and placed it upon her finger. Her heart caught in her throat, Catherine cast her eyes downward as she accepted his gift. *Trapped.* She dared a glance down the table toward Simon. She ached for the look of sadness that played across his face. The entire table broke out in applause once more. She forced herself to smile. Every female eye turned toward a beaming Viola, who straightened her spine, lifted her chin and seemingly rejoiced in the delicious satisfaction of her instantly elevated social status.

A despondent Simon fiddled with his glass, and watched as Catherine sat with Miles speaking to her elegant dinner companions at the other end of the table. He tried hard to reconcile the intelligent artist, the calm, caring and humble soul he'd met in the country village with this aristocratic young woman so confident and at ease with the landed gentry in these fashionable city surroundings. He, himself, felt terribly out of place.

At the stroke of midnight, the musicians assembled beneath the arched colonnade. The ballroom filled with swirling silks and shouts of laughter around the perimeter of the dance floor at the first notes of the violins. Catherine and Miles walked hand in hand to the center of the polished marble mosaic to the applause of everyone in the room. Catherine curtsied to Miles and they began to dance. They were soon joined on the floor by nearly everyone in the ballroom. Standing off to the side, Simon wandered through the surrounding columns until he found the Lord Mayor, flirting madly with a lovely young lady in pink silks. Simon took his elbow and pulled him aside.

"I believe I will turn in for the night," he whispered.

The mayor was appalled. "No, Laddie! You are not leaving—why, I forbid it! Simon shook his head. "You must at least have once dance. I absolutely insist upon it! You spend far too much time in your books. Life is to be savored, my boy. Savored!"

The girl in the pink gown blinked flirtatiously at the mayor from behind a black Chinese enamel fan she held to her pert nose. Her blond curls, heart-breakers, as they were most fashionably called, bounced merrily at her cheeks. The mayor held out his hand, and led the girl toward the dance floor. He grinned back at Simon. "Savored!"

As Simon turned to leave, he came face to face with Catherine.

"Do you intend to follow me in all quarters of my life?" she challenged.

Simon drew back, instantly embarrassed. Embarrassed to be standing before her in his humble garments. *Embarrassed have even allowed himself to be dragged to this preposterous gathering at all.* He bowed slightly and turned for the doorway. And then, she unexpectedly laughed. He stopped as a sudden relief washed over him. *She was teasing.* They stood for an awkward moment, until the musicians began to play once again. Simon cocked his ear and smiled. On a whim, he held his out hand just as the mayor had. To his utter surprise, Catherine gently took it in her own and together; they stepped onto the dance floor. Catherine curtsied as Simon bowed. They set their palms together, and drew close.

"Once I Loved a Maiden Fair," whispered Simon.

Catherine's eyebrows rose slightly in surprise. "You know of this tune?"

"I do." They stepped back and whirled about, then stepped together once again. Hand in hand, they walked in a circle, and then whirled about once more. Her soft hand gently touching his electrified Simon, as the music swept them across the floor and brought them close once again. He caught her eyes and held them in his own.

"Do you love him?"

Catherine stepped back, then forward into his grasp once again, a troubled look clouding her beautiful features.

"I…I fear that it does not matter. My family has long-since made the arrangements."

"Surely that peacock does not capture your interest, your intelligence." They whirled about once again, following the crowd. Catherine kept her tongue. Something over his shoulder caught her attention. He could feel her muscles tense.

"I…I'm afraid, sir, that I cannot speak of it." From behind, Simon felt a strong hand clasp him upon the shoulder. He wheeled about to see Miles standing before him, in all his dandified glory.

"Please, allow me to step in," said Miles, taking Catherine's hand strongly into his own. "Come, my darling, let us finish this dance, then we will have a glass of champagne." As he passed, Miles once again lifted two fingers to his brow and saluted Simon in a small gesture of triumph. "Good evening, sir," said Miles, with more than a trace of mockery in his voice as he twirled Catherine away.

Simon was left standing alone on the dance floor. Furious, he turned and walked off the floor, heading straight for the mayor.

"The rain has ceased and I am most desirous of my bedchamber. I should like to walk back to the inn, if you have no objections, sir."

The mayor hardly heard Simon's words, for he was concentrating his leering attentions on another charming young enchantress as she nonchalantly lifted her skirt just high enough to offer him a saucy glimpse of her delicate, beribboned slipper.

"Yes, yes, Laddie... I have no objections. I bid you good night."

The mayor quickly waved him off, barely hearing a word of it; so gleefully intent was he upon catching sight of the pretty maiden's scandalous bit of ankle. Simon rolled his eyes.

"Good night, sir."

Simon retrieved his cloak from a servant and stood alone in the grand foyer, savoring one last look at the magnificent dwelling. The manservant unlatched the mansion door and Simon stepped out to the landing. He inhaled deeply of the fresh, cool night air, grateful to be free of the overwhelming, cloying scent of perfume that filled the ballroom.

"Dr. McKensie?"

Simon turned about, and to his surprise, saw Catherine standing at the door before him.

"I wished to bid you a good night," she said directly.

The late hour, her beauty and the sight of the broad gold band upon her finger, brought him to unaccustomed silence. Catherine was beginning to lose her nerve, as well. She spoke quickly.

"I fear I was discourteous to you. You were so very kind to me when I felt unwell at the printers. I...I beg your apology, sir."

Simon was taken aback by her raw display of emotion. His defenses instantly crumpled. With one hand on the stone balustrade, he was compelled to reassure her.

"Nae', the fault was mine, Lady Catherine. By rights, I was not entirely truthful."

He felt in his pocket and withdrew the book. He handed it to her, leaning in close.

"Perhaps after you have read it, you will understand why I could not publish under my own name," he whispered. "I beg of you, please keep to your own counsel for I could, even this day, be hung for what I've done."

He turned and walked down the steps toward the inn. At the end of the lane, he looked back. Shafts of silvery light played through the clouds overhead. He saw her, a stationary figure backlit by the brilliant glow of candles, still standing at the open doorway holding his book close to her chest.

In the quiet hours just before dawn, not long after the last guests had departed, the few servants who could stay awake were quietly tidying the mansion. The remaining servants were belowstairs fast asleep, nicking a precious hour or two before the long day ahead restoring the home back to rights. Through a third floor window of the stately mansion, a single candle glowed. Catherine sat in her bed reading Simon's book. Though her eyes ached from fatigue and the dim, flickering light, she was gripped by his words. She poured over page after page until at last she finished, then, returning the first chapter, she began all over again. Though she could not absorb the entirety of his treatise, she understood enough to realize that he was bravely challenging the very methods by which physicians treat disease. It was clear to her that Simon did not believe disease was caused by an imbalance of the four humors the way most physicians she knew believed, nor did he take for God's truth the most commonly accepted medical knowledge. No, he thought far differently than anyone she had ever met.

Though at times the subject matter of his book was perplexing, Catherine was able to understand that Simon vouchsafed the need for cleanliness in the operating theater, and championed the practice of isolation between patients with fevers and patients with broken bones. The final section was the most fascinating of all. He lent his wholehearted agreement to the theory that had been advanced by Vesalius nearly one hundred years before that the study of anatomy in particular, and the scientific world in general, must be based on observation and experiment and not on hypothesis and conjecture. He soundly supported the new philosophy of promoting knowledge of the natural world through observation and experiment rather than hysteria and hearsay as was common with the healers, barbers, charlatans, swindlers and tricksters of the day.

To bolster his argument, there, in the last few pages, were astonishing illustrations of a series of veins and an oddly circulated figure with several large tubes extending from it. He had carefully labeled the figure, 'The Heart." His drawings were crude, to be sure. He was by far a physician more than he was an artist, though his intent was crystal clear. *The knowledge lies in the observation. But, how did he come upon this knowledge? In medical school? If so, why does he not lay claim to the science by his own name? Why did he say he could be hung? What has he done?* She had so many questions.

Of one thing she was certain, he was singularly the most intelligent man she had ever met. The candle flickered. As she reached over to pull it closer, her fingers brushed the announcement of Lady Cavendish's lecture that lay on the table under the candlestick. She picked it up and stared at it. The candle sputtered as it burned down to the quick, plunging the room into darkness. A thin wisp of fragrant beeswax smoke drifted over her bed, scenting the room with the barest trace of honey. She lay back on her lace-edged pillows. She must find out more about Simon McKensie. *"I will nonetheless be in attendance at the lecture."* Nestling deep under the plump, goose down bedcover, she bit her thumbnail to the quick. She finally came to a decision. She would, by every means possible, attend Lady Cavendish's lecture.

CHAPTER 21

THIS DAY, MUCH AGAINST MY WILL, I DID IN DRURY-LANE SEE TWO OR THREE HOUSES MARKED WITH A RED CROSS UPON THE DOORS, AND "LORD HAVE MERCY UPON US" WRIT THERE—WHICH WAS A SAD SIGHT TO ME, BEING THE FIRST OF THAT KIND THAT TO MY REMEMBRANCE I EVER SAW.
-SAMUEL PEPYS

East India Company Headquarters
Bishopsgate Parish
London, England
17 April 1665

Simon sat next to the mayor and watched Lord Abbott pound his fist on the inlaid mahogany council table amid the shouts and flaring tempers of the nineteen other board members of the East India Company. Sitting on the other side of Lord Abbott, Charles looked astounded by the authority his father held over the members. Simon paid scant attention to the volley of opinions flying about the room, turning first this way, then that to tune out the escalating volume. Simon was in a surly mood, having been dragged to the meeting by the mayor. The hospital is infinitely more desirable than this chamber of palavering windbags. His head pounded from the shouting and eyes stung from the thick tobacco smoke that hung heavy in the air and the sharp scent of boiled onions and eggs from the breakfast plates still scattered about the ornate table. Has she read the book, he wondered? Had he made a mistake?

"Gentlemen!" shouted Lord Abbott, interrupting Simon's thoughts.

Vociferous argument, even impassioned oaths reverberated throughout the dark, heavily paneled room of the East India House in Leadenhall Street. Lord Abbott cried out once more, this time with all the authority he could muster.

"Gentlemen, if you please!"

Startled by his forcefulness, angry shouts began to subside. Fiery tempers reluctantly quelled to a simmer. Attentions were directed toward the normally jovial and even-tempered gentleman standing at the head of the table. He waited until all eyes were finally upon him, then Lord Abbott spoke softly.

"The question before us is not easily addressed, nor will it be easily solved. We would do very well to advance our views one member at a time, rather than all at once."

For one single introspective moment the men were quiet, and then all hell broke loose once again. Lord Mayor Hardwicke leapt to his feet to pound home his point, knocking his chair backward, clattering it onto the honey-colored walnut floorboards. Charles quickly rushed over to right the chair. Simon groaned as the mayor paid the boy no mind, enthralled as he was by the sound of his own voice. The mayor banged on the table for emphasis, shouting over the rest of the impassioned voices.

"I tell you this very day, these heathens have absolutely no comprehension of, nor intelligence for, our complicated business interests! They stand in the way of our trade and will cost this company, and the King's coffers, I might add, millions of pounds every year. We must, by all means necessary, take complete control of this situation before they rise up and destroy all that we have created, even if it means war!" cried the mayor, an emphatic fist raised.

Several men shouted, "Hear, Hear!" Others objected vehemently, raising their own voices in protest.

"No, Sir! Violence against the people of India for the sake of Britain's own monetary gain is sheer blasphemy!" shouted Robert Boyle in heated response.

At the far end of the table Simon recognized London's Lord Mayor, Sir John Lawrence, from the engagement party. While everyone else vied for attention, the man sank deeper into his chair, seemingly in an attempt to remain unnoticed. He diddled with a generous tankard of spiced wine and looked as though he greatly desired to be anywhere but at that table. Simon leaned in to the mayor, pointing to the man.

"Has he no opinion?"

The mayor scoffed. "He has been newly promoted to Master of the Vintner's Company. He has no wish to offer his opinion and risk offence with the other board members, so reliant is he now upon their abundant trade. Waffling is his stock in trade. Lawrence!" bellowed an impassioned Mayor Hardwicke. "Rise to the challenge, sir and voice an intelligent opinion!"

Lawrence looked to the floor, as though he wished could fall through. "I see your point, Hardwicke and, of course, I see yours too, Boyle. I…I should like time to consider."

Lord Mayor Hardwicke shook his head in disgust. He leaned over to Simon. "A very weak man, he seems to be. A zealous soul in the King's concernments to be sure; although certainly willing, I fear he is not very able to do great things." Simon marveled at the complex machinations of those who made decisions for the populace.

The room was soon roiling again with the heated exchange of twenty-one wildly differing and highly contentious beliefs. Lord Abbott sighed, seeming to consign himself to silence as the debate exploded around the massive council table. He raised his hands in defeat. "Let them rage. Sooner or later, they will exhaust themselves. Perhaps then a modicum of order can be extracted," he muttered.

Something. A movement. An imperceptible, even strange, ominous sense of dread sent a shiver through Simon. He glanced through a nearby windowpane and took note of an unusual number of passing carriages loaded high with baggage. *Curious.*

Very curious, indeed. Seated next to Lord Abbott, Charles also noticed the goings-on on outside. Simon leaned far back in his chair, craning his neck to look toward the corner. There, he saw a leaflet boy tacking a public notice to the cornerpost. He caught Lord Abbott's eye and pointed to the window. People shouted and pushed each other as they crowded around, clutching for his papers. Simon could hear the muffled shouts from outside. In the midst of the torrid argument raging around the council table, he leaned over to Lord Abbott.

"Shall I inquire?" whispered Simon, all too happy to escape the din.

"Perhaps you should, indeed."

Simon slipped out of the room. He returned minutes later, a deeply troubled look upon his face and handed Lord Abbott a sheet of paper. Lord Abbott looked down at the pronouncement, exhaled slowly, held the paper aloft and waited until the room noticed and quieted down. Grim-faced, Lord Abbott read the notice aloud:

LONDON'S MOST DREADFUL
VISITATION OF THE PLAGUE

A Collection concerning the Bill of Mortality

Beginning the 1st of April 1665 and ending the 14th of April following

According to the Report made to the King's Most Excellent Majesty

By the Company of the Parish-Clerks of London

Plague Victims of the Parish's of London Most Proper:

Unknown Traveler, St. Giles-in-the-Field Parish, April 8 1665

Andrews, Rebecca, Innkeeper St. Giles-in-the-Field Parish, 12 April 1665

Unknown Traveler, St. Giles-in-the-Field Parish, 12 April 1665

Unknown Traveler, St. Giles-in-the-Field Parish, 12 April 1665

Wilcox, Peregrine, Shopkeeper Aldersgate Parish, 13 April 1665

Black, Josiah, Undertaker St. Giles-in-the-Field Parish, 14 April 1665

The board members looked to one another, and then fell into horrified silence, each mentally charting their own course.

"Dear, God!" cried one horrified man.

Simon turned to Lord Abbott. "As of this hour, it is said that the King remains out at Hampton Court."

The men were instantly rendered to silence for over the last year, they had all read the news that thousands upon thousands had died in Holland alone. Not one man among them had trouble divining the very near future for the overcrowded, teeming city of London.

"Well, that's it, gentlemen," said the Lord Mayor, exhaling heavily. "Aye'n it was but a matter of time 'til the vicious pestilence ravaged our shores. Six wretched souls in as many days. It'll spread, mind ye. It will surely spread." The Lord Mayor stood and donned his cloak and hat. He turned to Simon. "With all good wishes, lad, I propose we take leave of this contentious debate and each to a man do what he must. I, myself, propose to abandon London as soon as possible." He faced the men at the table. "I suggest all and sundry do the same."

"But we have our shops, sir! Our livelihoods!" cried the instrument maker, Thomas Sutton. "Indeed, you cannot possibly advocate for the wholesale abandonment of London! What shall befall the commonwealth with no trade to sustain us in the coming months? Disastrous course, I tell you, Hardwicke. You counsel a disastrous course!"

"The comet!" shouted one man. "Last year! T'was the comet that spelt a portent of evil to come!"

"The devil you say!" cried the mayor.

Each man turned instantly to Lord Mayor Lawrence. His eyes widened, his every nerve ending seemed to be charged electric with the unwanted attention.

"What say you, Lord Mayor? With the King at Hampton Court, you must lead! Do you advocate perseverance or abandonment? What shall you counsel the populace!" shouted Sutton.

The Lord Mayor sincerely had no opinion. He looked as though he had not even the barest speck of knowledge as to what to do. Simon was fascinated. The Lord Mayor seemed to be fumbling in his scattered thoughts. Simon watched as every last pair of eyes fell upon the man, awaiting his decision. Thomas Sutton nearly came across the table in desperate anticipation of his directive, just as Hardwicke crossed his arms in a direct challenge from the other side. The Lord Mayor of London looked around the table at the august assemblage, each to a man committed to their own charge and immediately seemed to crumble in his resolve to stay half on a hedge.

"I say… I say, stay the course. Yes. Yes, that is what I shall recommend." He became fully committed to his decision and pounded on the table. "Yes! For the continued trade and the financial well being of our good city, our citizens shall not run! They will indeed stay the course. I shall post the decree this very day."

The room was plunged into vociferous, angry debate once more.

Cecil Hardwicke quietly turned to Simon. "I protest his charge with every ounce of my being. I intend to hire a carriage for you and I, and take leave for Wells this very day for as the members of the royal court have just proved, the best preparation for the plague is to simply and most decisively *run from it*."

"I do not wish to oppose your wishes, sir, but I will be needed at the hospital."

"Absolutely not, lad. For better or worse, I am responsible for your well-being…"

Simon raised his hands in protest. The mayor decisively cut him off.

"It is my charge to keep you safe, and that, my boy, is precisely what I intend to do."

The mayor stood, then looked to the regents at the council table and bowed slightly. "God bless us all and Godspeed, gentlemen."

At that, Lord Mayor Hardwicke and Simon took their leave from Craven Hall. Amid the shouting voices, Lord Abbott remained at the council table, contemplating the ominous course ahead. He stared at Charles for a moment, and then made up his mind. He spoke slowly to his wide-eyed, and very scared son.

"I confess that in a time of evident crisis such as we now seem to face, I am loath to use my influence to selfish interest, as it seems woefully unfair to others without the same. However, as a responsible father, it is my preemptive charge to keep you safe from harm." Lord Abbott exhaled, and then spoke decisively. "The *HMS Royal London* sails for the colonies in but four days hence. We shall return to Bealeton House, pack your trunks and as soon as may be practical, I shall sign you on as navigator's apprentice. My boy, though not to China as you have so wished, you are going to sea."

Catherine sat with Jane in a hackney on the cobbled street outside Number 27 St. James Place at half-one, waiting in the warmth of the carriage. Jane looked at her expectantly.

"Will ye' attend the lecture, Mi'Lady?"

Lord Abbott and Charles having departed for the board meeting and Aunt Viola retired to a quiet day's rest in her chambers, Catherine had every intention of attending the lecture. Were she honest, however, she would confess to feeling far braver within the safe confines of Bealeton House than she did at this exact moment watching one well dressed gentlemen after another ascend the steps to the Cavendish mansion. *Something is amiss.* She suddenly realized with dismay, *there are no ladies in attendance.* Her confidence wavered.

"I…I may."

I have a personal invitation from Lady Cavendish; she reminded herself in a futile attempt to steady her nerves. She nervously straightened her skirts and wished that as declared, Dr. McKensie would soon arrive. The hollow sounds of clattering hoof beats drew her attention out to the street. Looking through the hackney window, Catherine saw several teams of horses pulling fully loaded wagons racing by. She watched as a packet fell off the top of one of the wagons. She instinctively moved closer to the glass and watched it tumble end over end, finally coming to rest to the side of the cobbled lane. Though the family clustered together on the bench glanced back, the driver did not stop to retrieve the fallen package, but rather urged his horses fervently onward. *Curious.*

As she waited, the arrivals slowed to a trickle before the Cavendish mansion, and then ceased altogether. Then suddenly, the street was empty. Catherine looked down at the silver engraved pendant timepiece hanging about her neck: 2:05pm. *The lecture has begun. The scoundrel has misrepresented himself once again, and once again, I have been made a fool.* She looked out the carriage widow down the empty street, then reached into her claret-colored velvet carrybag and pulled out Lady Cavendish's leaflet. She read it one last time, then ripped it into a multitude of pieces. She put the shredded papers back into her bag and yanked the drawstrings tight. She leaned her head out the window and called up to the driver.

"Bealeton House, please."

At the exact opposite end of St. James Parish, a very frustrated Simon was watching the Lord Mayor loudly supervising the loading of his trunks onto a hired coach outside the East India Arms.

"Put that one over there, good sir!" he shouted, instructing the driver as to precisely how he wished his trunks to be stacked atop of the coach.

Though thoroughly committed to his decision to flee, the mayor regretted the unexpected departure, for he always enjoyed the time he spent in London. He relished wandering through the Knightsbridge shops, adding to his own expansive wardrobe with the very latest in fashions, or tinkering with the new inventions in the instrument maker's shops, even purchasing gifts for the staff. It was all too fascinating and nothing escaped his nimble curiosity. He bought Eliza several new cooking aprons and, on impulse, a soft robin's egg blue feathered hat. The mayor chortled to himself just thinking of her opening the box and seeing the pale feathers. She would wear it too, for despite her sensible skirts and plain cotton bonnets, he knew she would be secretly pleased to step out in a bit of finery. The gifts were stacked high inside the carriage.

"Where in God's creation is the lad," he fretted. "We must depart with all good speed!"

It was to be a clear, star-filled night, and even with the waning moon, the mayor had determined that if they left without delay, there would be lantern light enough to ride straight on through to Wells, even if they arrived several hours after midnight. Hiring the coach for such a distance on short notice cost the mayor a pretty penny, but he was certainly not one to quibble about paltry details. The mayor most assuredly got what he desired at all costs, and what he most desired this day was to run hell for leather from the pestilential scourge that he knew would soon descend upon the city. Simon had protested desperately that he would be needed at St. Bartholomew's if the outbreak worsened, but the mayor would have none of it. Begrudgingly, he had become rather fond of the lad, and the mayor felt the full weight of responsibility for his safety.

Simon packed the last of his things into his trunk and closed the lid, fastening the leather straps and iron latch. Two liveried servants knocked at the door, then entered to haul his trunk down to the waiting coach. Simon donned his cloak and, unexpectedly, felt something in the pocket. He reached in and withdrew Lady Cavendish's leaflet. *Damnation!* With the mayor's braying insistence that they depart immediately for Wells, Simon had completely forgotten the lecture. He cursed himself for not standing up to the mayor. In disgust, he crumpled the leaflet and threw it onto the table by the window. He prayed most fervently that Lady Catherine had not been in attendance.

CHAPTER 22

Blackwall Shipyard
St. Giles-in-the-Field Parish, London
21 April 1665

Though not yet May, the windowless clerk's office of the Thames Ironworks and Shipbuilding Company was famously sweltering. The harassed and overworked head clerk peered through his rimless spectacles at the stack of *Berschermer* lading bills and nearly threw them to a heap on the wooden floor in sheer frustration. He lumbered from the airless room and stood at the iron railing, fanning his apron to cool himself. He looked down from the second floor offices into the cavernous brick warehouse stacked to the rafters with cargo from the accursed ship that had been delayed by the violent storm off the North Sea. Nearly three weeks after it reached the docks, fully half of the *Berschermer's* freightage was still soaking wet and nearly all the cargo that remained in the warehouse had been smashed to bits. The heat rising from a young stock boy shoveling coal into a furnace in an attempt to dry the haulage caused the spectacles of the head clerk to slide down his sweating, bulbous nose. He shoved them upwards and swore at the lad under his breath. Adding to his supreme irritation, the execrable customers were to a man howling for delivery.

"Baaar…naaa…baaas!" he roared down toward the sinister furnace, drawing out the syllables as greatly as possible.

The boy stopped shoveling and quickly looked up to the bellowing clerk.

"Yes, sir!"

The clerk wadded up a sheet of paper and threw it down. "This one next!"

The boy unfolded the paper and quickly read the transit numbers. He hustled to the A4 bay and rifled through the contents until he found an oilcloth sack covering a large number of woven bolts of fabric from the van de Veld *Linnenfabrick* in Amsterdam. He cut the strings that bound the oilcloth and looked inside. *The oilcloth sacking appears to have done its duty*, thought the boy, grateful that the ivory-colored fabric with a thin blue stripe inside appeared to be undamaged, for he despised the wicked tongue-lashings laid upon him by the old goat upstairs. Barnabas quickly pulled four bolts from the sack. He laid them on a worktable to ready for delivery to Wilcox and Son's, Ltd. in Knightsbridge. He knocked away several fleas that hopped from bolt to bolt, then wrapped heavy paper around the fabric and tied the entire enterprise tightly with thick string. As he prepared a delivery scutcheon with name of the tailoring shop on the package, he once again heard heavy footfalls from above. Every muscle in his body seized up in anticipation as the corpulent clerk screeched once more from the upstairs deck.

"Bar…na…bas!"

"Aye, sir!" he called up, anxious for the infernal bellowing to cease.

The clerk wadded up another sheet of paper, and threw it down, hitting Barnabas on the head.

"Change Order!"

"Aye."

Barnabas ran his filthy fingers through his hair, roundly cursing the clerk himself. He picked up the crumpled paper and read it, then turned to worktable and ripped off the first scutcheon. He grabbed another, and then on the new label, carefully scribed:

The Most Honourable, Lady Viola Abbott
Abbottsford Abbey,
Stockbridge, Buckinghamshire

When he finished, Barnabas flagged down a passing warehouse cart. He hoisted the parcel as high as possible, then heaved it onto the top of the cart and gladly sent the fabric on its way, washing his hands of the lot. He turned back toward the remaining cargo and stared upward at the enormous, soggy pile that was stacked two floors high against the brick walls of the warehouse. *It will never cease.*

CHAPTER 23

"THE TOWN GROWS VERY SICKLY, AND PEOPLE TO BE AFEARED OF IT—THERE DYING THIS LAST WEEK OF THE PLAGUE 112, FROM 43 THE WEEK BEFORE..."
-SAMUEL PEPYS

Blackwall Shipyard
St. Giles-in-the-Field Parish, London
25 April 1665

Charles ran his fingers across the freshly hewn Douglas fir railing of *HMS Royal London,* absorbing the sheer enormity of the rough wood timbers on the newly christened Carracks galleon. The spicy, woodland scent mingled deliciously with the salty breezes that blew hard across his face. The heavy cream-colored canvas sails fluttered in the stiff breezes. The hull keened and cracked as the new galleon settled low into the water. Around him, a few hardened sailors worked to ready the ship before casting the lines on its maiden voyage to supply the colonies, their sea-going murmurings a foreign tongue to him. He tried desperately to stay unnoticed for he also saw the grizzled men scowling at his fine clothes and soft hands. A lone seagull soared through the fog above him, and then swooped in low to settle on the galleon's fo'c'sle. The bird left a white stain that dripped down the wooden planks of the captain's headquarters before flapping skyward, taking flight once again. Charles watched as the gull made several lazy circles through the galleons four massive square-rigged oaken masts, then drifted down toward the water to float idly on the falling tide.

Charles laid his hands atop the thick wooden railing and felt the comforting solidity of the wood under his grasp. He knew exactly why his father decided to sign him on as an apprentice a full two years earlier than planned, and he did feel badly for the suffering people of London, for there had been over one hundred deaths in the last fortnight, but Charles had dreamed about going to sea for as long as he could remember and at last the day had arrived. He could hardly contain himself. He could actually taste an intoxicating sense of adventure on the cool, bracing sea air. Charles leaned over the side of the ship and waved toward his father who stood on the dock with the captain. He watched as Lord Abbott looked carefully over a set of parchment papers, then, with a melancholy air of finality, handed them back to the captain. The captain returned the final page. They shook hands once more, and with a smart salute, the captain boarded the ship.

Lord Abbott looked upward and tried to smile as he nodded up to his son. A lingering concern was more than evident upon his face, even from the height of the ship's main deck, for he feared he would not see his son for nearly a year or more. Charles waved one last time. He watched his father turn away quickly wiping his eyes, then Lord Abbott disappeared into the company office, and that was that. Charles now took his place as an official part of the galleon's crew on their yearlong journey to supply the colonies. Charles crossed to the waterside and stared out to the horizon, sheer excitement coursing through his veins. A grizzled, toothless old deckhand shuffled down the deck lugging a huge coil of rope toward the aft end of the ship. He stopped short before Charles and gawked from head to toe at the sight of him.

"Aye, an' yer' a right green jim-lad, ain't ye', boyo," the old jack-tar grunted.

Narrowing his eyes at Charles's costly suit of clothing, the old man leaned sideways over the rail. He spit off the side of the ship and shook his head in bewilderment, then kept to his course, dragging the rope behind him.

Charles looked down at his embellished overcloak and tailored velvet breeches, and at once felt very much the prize gudgeon. Vexed at his aunt for insisting, against his own better judgment, that he make a good impression on the captain by wearing his finest suit of clothing, Charles looked about, and found the deck around him momentarily abandoned. He quickly slipped out of the cloak, untucked his linen shirt, and then gathered the cloak into a bundle. He glanced fore and aft of the deserted deck once more to make certain he was alone, then, with all his might, Charles flung the despised cloak off the side of the ship. He leaned over the railing and watched it pitch and toss, floating first one way then tumbling the other as it plummeted downward through the mist. He grinned broadly as it hit the water in full, billowing furl, then watched with singular satisfaction as the cloak became sodden and slowly sank beneath the tranquil waters.

"Aye, tha's the stuff, scrapper."

Startled, Charles looked to his left and saw the old sailor standing next to him at the rail watching the cloak sink below the surface. The jack-tar winked at him. Charles ducked his head, embarrassed that he had been caught out. The sailor leaned his elbows on the rail and squinted across the harbor. He reached into his pocket and pulled out a small leather flasket. With a nudge, he thrust it toward Charles. Unsure of exactly what to do, Charles took the flasket and gingerly pulled the cork. He looked to the man, questioning. The sailor nodded his encouragement. Charles inhaled, then tipped his head back and took a mighty slug. He eyes shot wide-open, resisting a primal urge to scream. He swallowed, tasting at first pungent anise, then a mixture of extraordinary herbs, and then finally the pure, throat-scorching alcohol of the unholy drink. He coughed and choked and spit over the side of the ship as the jack-tar cackled and banged him hard across the back.

"Aye, laddie…

Gulping hard for air, Charles shoved the bottle back toward the sailor with one hand and grasped desperately for the railing with the other. The sailor grabbed the flasket and took his own deep guzzle, then twisted the cork into the bottle and slipped it back into his pocket. Charles's desperate paroxysms began to subside as he slowly caught his breath. The sailor grinned. He jerked his stubbled chin toward Charles in tacit approval, and then limped away, disappearing below decks. Charles turned toward the sea still gasping for air, and knew in his bones that before him lay the most exciting year of his life.

Lord Abbott left the shipyard feeling very much alone. He wished Catherine were with him, but they had all said tearful goodbyes that morning and she had stayed behind to pack for their unexpected, early return to Wells. Not yet ready to face Viola's unending wrath for sending Charles to sea, he turned and walked across Broad Street. He contemplated the binding contract he had just entered into, consigning his son to the perilous journey across the Atlantic. Though he knew full well there were any number of disasters that could easily befall a treacherous voyage such as the one his son faced, he felt in his heart that at least Charles would be far safer in the colonies than he would be by remaining in England. Of that, he was absolutely sure. Viola on the other hand, was not convinced in the least. He dreaded returning to Bealeton House to her temper and her most vocal recriminations as she begrudgingly supervised the mansion's closure for their early return to the Abbey.

Crossing Broad Street as the thickening fog gave way to a soft drizzle, Lord Abbott passed the Ratcliff Alehouse. The noisy dockside tavern barely registered in his attentions, so distracted was he by his own turbulent and unsettled thoughts. A sharp roar of laughter emanating from the crowded publick house pierced his contemplations. He stopped for a moment and looked through the filthy windowpanes, listening to the familiar, easy taunts and jibes from the sailors at liberty that filled the alehouse. The riotous atmosphere instantly flooded his thoughts with sentimental memories.

Staring through the panes at the rowdy sailors, he suddenly felt very old. Indeed, he felt the heavy weight of every single decision, of the endless responsibilities of his family, his estate and the company business that fell upon his shoulders and he was tired. Very tired. And thirsty. *Aye, he was thirsty indeed. Perhaps a tankard or two would taste lively upon the tongue.* On an uncharacteristic impulse, he swung the door open and entered the rough pub, ducking beneath the low-slung doorway into the crowded, smoky tavern. Though he felt conspicuous dressed as he was in his tailored clothing and hand-crafted leather boots, the dreadful prospect of facing Viola seemed far more palatable after a draught or two. *Or perhaps three, if he bloody well felt like it.* He pulled up a stool and sat alone at an unoccupied wooden keg that served as a table in the dim chamber. The crowded room was packed to the timbers with brawling sailors awaiting their own call to sea, exhausted sailors returning from the sea, and desolate, bitter men who could but only dream of a sea voyage to damn near anywhere.

Flynt Pollard was just such a man. What few coins fell into his hands seemed to forever slip through his fingers, most generally from the ruinous wagers he had the unfortunate habit of making in the dark, clandestine back rooms of the Ratcliff. Finding steady work in life was a course he tried desperately to avoid, rather preferring the odd job, nefarious or otherwise, to support his dreadful gambling talents. He often dreamt of a better life in distant lands, preferably with the magnificent Flossie by his side, though he would, if pressed, reluctantly confess to spending nearly a month retching off the side of a Collier brig hauling coal down from Newcastle Upon Tyne before he slipped away one night into a thick, cloaking Yarmouth fog. A sailor, he was most assuredly not.

Pollard sat alone in the corner, nursing what he knew to be his only pint of the day for the coin in his pocket had just that morning fallen once again to a ruinous bet. He saw Lord Abbott enter the pub and hang his overcloak on a peg by the door. Pollard shifted on his stool and watched morosely as Flossie cut a path straight through the rowdy sailors toward the man in the extravagant suit of clothing as he took a seat by the window. *Life was unbearable.* He raised his tankard and knocked back a large slug of his drink.

"What will ye' 'ave, dearie?"

The serving girl startled Lord Abbott. He turned his head quickly about. He found himself staring up to a warm, welcoming presence and, though he tried to avert his eyes, a lush, tantalizing bosom nearly overflowing from a deeply cut ruffled neckline as she leaned toward him to hear over the riotous bedlam. He collected his wits.

"A tankard of ale, if you please, Miss."

"Aye, sir. Ale!" she called across the room.

While she waited for acknowledgement from the harried pubkeeper, she took closer stock of the gentleman she had never before seen in the Ratcliff. He was a rich man. She could see that straightaway. Possessed of a noble and striking countenance, he was impressively clothed and well fed; yet not given to corpulence like other prosperous men his age. Rather, he cut an imposing figure that gave off the unmistakable air of strength, authority and great wealth.

"If I may, ye' don't look like ye' belong at the Ratcliff, sir."

He momentarily chuckled in spite of his melancholy.

"Aye, Miss. Indeed, I have ne'er traded in your establishment before this very day."

The tankard was laid before him and he gratefully took a long, cooling draught. He set the pewter vessel on the barrelhead, positioning it carefully away from the edge. She looked at him with piercing eyes.

"Aye' an' ye' look like ye's got the troubles of the world sittin' on yer' shoulders, if ye' don't mind my sayin' so."

Lord Abbott did not answer straightaway. He gazed out the window for a moment or two, and watched a multitude of heavily laden carts careening headlong away from the crowded, filthy East End. He looked at her thoughtfully.

"What is your name, Miss?"

"Flossie, sir"

"Well, Flossie," he sighed, "I have signed my son to an apprenticeship on the Royal London sailing this day for the colonies. He is but fifteen years."

Flossie surveyed the dingy pub and, seeing that the unruly patrons were largely in hand, slid softly onto a stool next to him. She folded her hands onto the staves of the rough wooden keg and leaned toward Lord Abbott as though he were the only man in the room. She seemed so sympathetic and kind that his confessions came easily.

"Did ye' nae?"

"Aye. I'll not look upon my son for perhaps more than a year hence and," he hesitated, "in all God's truth, I am unsure as to whether or not I have championed the right course." He took another draught.

Flossie's big heart melted at the lamentations he seemed to be suffering. "Ah, dearie, I'm sure ye' did yer' best. Is yer' wife agreeable t' the scheme?"

Another wave of sadness washed over him. He could not bring himself to answer. It seemed to be a day for inexplicable feelings of loss. He watched as tiny bubbles rose and broke upon the surface of his amber ale. In that moment, he missed Tamesine more than his aching heart could stand. Flossie nodded, intuitively understanding.

"D' ye's have a name?" she asked gently.

Lord Abbott stared into the flames flickering in the open hearth behind her, his thoughts floating through the fragmented memories of his own youth when he, too, savored the exhilarating lure of distant seas. Delicious memories of carefree days when the tantalizing possibilities of life stretched far ahead rather than far behind him, days when the heavy weight of responsibility was but a distant thought to be cast aside for more impulsive pleasures. He could scarcely recall those heady, exhilarating days. He felt a soft touch on the back of his hand. Her tender, cool flesh upon his own electrified his senses and brought his attentions instantly back.

"I apologize, my dear. What did you say?"

"I asked if ye's had a name."

He considered the enormously appealing woman who sat across from him, her hands lightly resting on the marred surface of the keg. She radiated a delicious warmth. From the golden glow of her soft, smooth skin, to the tousled curls the color of nutmeg spice that were caught up in loose topknot, to her broad, welcoming smile, she seemed to draw him in to her very being. She seemed neither old nor young, though perhaps she was younger than he thought. *A comfortable age.* The unexpected flash of her incandescent smile drew him to her lush, wondrous presence. He could but imagine the very touch of her soft flesh, the gentle stroke of her fingertips soothing his troubled brow, even the welcoming warmth of her tender embrace. It had been fifteen very long years. He ached for the press of female flesh. In that very moment, he was so unbearably weary of being looked up to, so weary of making every decision, of bringing order to every confoundment, of deciding every course. To the outside world, he was the refined, aristocratic and noble Lord Abbott. But not to her. Not to this earthy, unpretentious and big-hearted woman who in that moment seemed to see straight through to his soul, straight through to the very real man he was beneath the trappings of his station and he was greatly humbled.

"Alvyn," he whispered. He reached for his ale, and then idly ran his fingers up and down the pewter handle, feeling its cooling dampness. "My name… is Alvyn.

"Aye, Alvyn." She gave it her full consideration. "Tis' a good, strong name," she determined. Her eyes suddenly clouded with worry. "I fear that strength will be of a necessary concern in the days and weeks ahead."

Lord Abbott furrowed his brow as the enormity of the peril they all faced came flooding back into his thoughts. He spoke slowly, fearing for her. "Are you very much afraid, Flossie?"

She leveled her gaze to his. "Aye, Alvyn, I am, indeed. There is now such a terror as I have nae' seen before that sets neighbor against neighbor for even as much as a cough. The face of London is being much altered with sorrow, at the very least in here in the East End. Here, the streets are overmuch filled with tears and lamentations, and I fear there is far worse is to come," she said, her voice trailing.

They fell silent whilst all around them raged high spirits.

"Have you relations outside the city?"

"Aye, in the north. Newcastle-Upon-Tyne." She hesitated, a wistful sadness suddenly dimming her luminous smile. "I have a daughter there. She is but seven years."

"Are you perhaps able to go to her?"

"Nae. Transport away from London now is impossible for the public coaches are fully engaged and a private coach that far north is far too dear for the likes of me." Flossie hesitated, and then she too, felt the sudden freedom of confession. She dropped her head, then raised it again and faced Lord Abbott straight on. "Even if I could tender the fare, I am ashamed to say, Alvyn, that am unwelcome in my sister's house."

This time, it was Lord Abbott who instantly understood. He nodded and smiled gently. He thought how astonishing it was that two very distaff lives could suddenly and unexpectedly collide in the briefest of encounters, and then splinter apart once more, never again to cross paths. He knew full well it was but the sheer accident of birth that either condemns or blesses each to their station and not one single day passed that he didn't labor under the full weight of his capricious and very good fortune.

Many a time he wished his constitution were more akin to Lord Houghton's, for the man seemed to lustily savor each day as it came, never once giving a single, passing care to the troubles of others. In all of his nearly fifty years, Lord Abbott had tried his best to take care of those who were born into less fortunate circumstances. He carried an entire staff on the Stockbridge estate and still more at Bealeton House. He found ways to share what he had with the villagers in the little valley he called home. He brought trade and employment to Wells and Stockbridge through his building projects. *And yet, it wasn't enough. Not once in his life had he ever felt that he had done enough.*

There were now hundreds of people suffering, through sickness or loss, from the effects of the plague in London, with much devastation yet ahead. He certainly had the means to transport his own family to the safety of the countryside, but what about the others who could not flee? How could he possibly help them? In Flossie's soft brown eyes, he could see the sheer, overpowering sadness of a mother's unrequited love. He glanced out the window, contemplating a course of action. *No, he could not help them all. But, he indeed could help one.* He took one last quaff of ale. *He could help Flossie.* He set the tankard in the middle of the barrel, then reached deep into his pocket and drew out several coins. He pressed them into her hand.

"Will you take these coins, Flossie, and go safely from London? Go up north to your daughter."

Flossie opened her hand and there, in the light through the dirt-streaked windowpanes, glittered four gold sovereigns. Not once in her life had she ever seen such a fortune.

"No! I cannot take this from ye', Alvyn" she breathed. He smiled gently at her.

"Aye, indeed you can, Flossie. Take it and go far from London, my dear. Find a wee cottage to let for just you and the girl. Buy a new suit of clothing, perhaps. Take it, my dear and start a new life."

"No. It's too dear." She tried to hand the coins back to him.

Lord Abbott smiled once again. "How dear can it be if a few sovereigns cannot be used to ease the troubles of another?" He closed her fingers around the coins. "Take it, Flossie. Take it and go to your daughter. You'll not regret the days you spend with her, just as I have not regretted a single moment with my own children." He paused a moment, then smiled. "I believe the coaching inn in a little village called Wells will provide employment for widows with children."

In an instant, the light went out of her smile, as though the incandescence of the very sun itself had been consumed by an aching darkness. She lowered her head in shame.

"I... I am not a widow, sir."

"In a new town where one is completely unknown, whatever does it matter, my dear?" he said, softly.

Flossie raised her head in sheer wonderment at this most kind and generous man. She placed her hands upon Lord Abbott's cheeks, unabashed tears of gratitude falling freely. He caught her hands tight in his and held them there. *The press of female flesh.* He closed his eyes. He breathed in, savoring the moment, savoring once again the warm, gentle touch of a woman.

"I have nae' touched a woman in nearly fifteen years," he whispered.

She felt his hands tremble over hers and her heart nearly broke for the kindness in his soul.

"Is it enough, Alvyn?" whispered Flossie, slowly glancing toward the stairs.

Lord Abbott took on a faraway look. He was not entirely unacquainted with the meaning behind her words. Faint memories surfaced of another encounter, one single congress, long before Tamesine. A spectacular, youthful tryst. His first. He slowly removed her hands from his cheeks and held them tenderly. Yet another tear sprang to his eye.

"Thank you," he whispered, a catch in his voice. "For this one brief moment, you have made an old man feel young again." He wiped his eyes with the back of his wrist, then pressed her palms between his own, holding them tightly in his grasp. "And yes, my dear, sweet Flossie," he said, his eyes soft with the memory, "it is more than enough."

Across the room, Flynt Pollard watched bitterly as the courtly gentleman held Flossie's hands in his own. A corrosive, jealous bile rose in his throat. He threw back the last of his ale, then stood, grabbed his overcloak and shoved his way through the crowd of raucous sailors toward the door. As he passed, Pollard banged hard into Lord Abbott's stoolback, startling him greatly. Lord Abbott turned and stared at the man who glowered at down at him. Pollard jerked his chin, and then flung his filthy, ragged cloak over his shoulder. A single flea fell from the cloak. It jumped once, and then nestled softly into the folds of Lord Abbott's woolen doublet hanging on the peg. Lord Abbott watched in bemusement as Flynt Pollard strode out onto the mud-spattered street, slamming the pub door hard behind him.

"It truly seems as if the whole of the city is on edge. Even I am at a loss, Flossie." He focused his attentions back to her. "I shall most certainly send my family back to Stockbridge, but is it right that I should take my trade from the commonwealth? How will our shopkeepers sustain themselves if indeed the citizens abandon the city? Is Sutton correct in his charge that fleeing London would be a disastrous course? What duty do we have to our fellow man?

Flossie tilted her head at him, much confused by his tortured contemplations. She did not know a moral choice from a philosophical perplexity, nor did she much care. She did know, however, that she was a strong and practical woman who worked her way through the trials of life by the simple dictates of her own earthy common sense. Flossie gazed with tender compassion at the troubled man who sat before her grappling with an ethical dilemma far beyond her simple thoughts. She grasped tightly the hands of the man who with a single stroke had just this moment changed the course of her entire life, and then spoke straight from the depths of her very big heart.

"Master, I beg of you, save thyself.

CHAPTER 24

"LORD, HOW SAD A SIGHT IT IS TO SEE THE STREETS EMPTY OF PEOPLE, AND VERY FEW UPON THE EXHANGE JEALOUS OF EVERY DOOR THAT ONE SEES SHUT UP, LEST IT SHOULD BE THE PLAGUE"
-SAMUEL PEPYS

The Boundary Stone
Buckinghamshire, England
27 April 1665

Thundering hoofbeats pounded over a rutted, well-travelled road, the horses spewing dirt and rocks in the wake of the Royal Coach delivery wagon as they tore through the verdant forests and rolling hills southwest of London. Loose cargo to be offloaded in the towns and villages along the route pitched and bounced off the sideboards in the bay of the wagon. At the bottom of the freightage, deep within the silent, impenetrable darkness of the wrapped parcel containing four bolts of flaxen-colored linen fabric, a single, tiny black flea that emerged from an infinitesimal egg was joined by another, and one became two.

The driver cracked a set of well-worn leather reins against the sweaty, foam-covered backs of eight powerful draught horses. He urged the team on faster, for the sun hung low and tantalizing thoughts of a generous tankard and a soft pallet beckoned at the next coaching stop in the little hamlet of Wells. The rumbling hoof beats hammered onward and in the fading light of day, deep inside the tightly wrapped rolls of linen, two tiny black fleas became twelve.

As the driver approached the split in the road, the setting sun splashed a deep orange glow across the horizon. He lifted his eyes high above the dark forest silhouetted against a fallow sky where one single star sparkled. *A clear night.* The driver pulled the team up short at the boundary stone and dismounted. He left several small packages and the cumbersome parcel of four bolts of fabric under the stone ledge, then clambered back aboard the wagon bench, took up the reins and steered the horses down valley toward the warm, welcoming Royal George for a night of hard-earned rest. As the hollow sound of clattering hoof beats faded in the distance, twelve tiny black fleas became seventy.

In the quiet hour just before sunrise, one single, fat raindrop splattered onto the ledge of the boundary stone. Somewhere in the distance, an oriole's trill floated across the meadow. A breeze ruffled through the blooming rye grasses. A second, a third, then a fourth ominous drop hit the rock outcropping, quickly absorbing into the porous limestone. Suddenly, the whole of the sky cracked wide open, drenching the stone, the meadow and the deserted road with clear, soaking rainwater. Within minutes, the slapping rain stopped just as suddenly as it had begun and the gray, billowing clouds that briefly hung across the valley tumbled and rolled their way on northward toward Scotland.

The lone figure of an old, bent man on horseback made his way slowly toward the boundary stone. As he approached, he saw packages stacked beneath the ledge and as was the custom, the old man dismounted and packed the small parcels in his saddlebags. He wiped the rainwater off the bigger parcel and squinted hard to read the dripping ink, then looked up to the clouds sailing northward. He shook his head and heaved the fabric bolts over the front of his saddle. He remounted and turned his horse up valley toward Stockbridge. Not ten paces on, the old man pulled his horse to a halt. He thought for a moment, and then turned the horse around in the opposite direction. He gave the mare a little nudge, and ambled instead down the road toward Wells.

In the warmth of the rising sun, the old man plodded up to a small farm. He dismounted and tied the horse to a post outside a stone cottage, then hoisted the awkward parcel over his aching back and carried the wet fabric bolts inside. The common room was filled with elongated strips of colorful fabrics that lay lengthwise down a long, scarred oaken table covered with tailoring tools. The strips of fabric were connected at one end to an iron ring by rough and uneven stitches, for the old man was now nearly blind from a lifetime of close work. Squinting, he thrust a poker repeatedly into the fireplace to coax the glowing coals to flames, and then jostled an ancient Irish setter out of the way with his foot.

"Git."

The dog raised a languid eyebrow, then heaved a heavy sigh and reluctantly shifted, but stayed his ground on the warm stones. The man moved several wooden stools before the hearth, then untied the strings and unwrapped the paper from the wet fabric. He crumpled the paper and threw it into the fire. It hissed and smoked then burst into flames. With practiced hands, the old man unrolled a bolt of cream-colored fabric across the stools to dry in the warmth of the fire. Though he could not see the workmanship clearly, his old hands felt the luxurious weight of the fabric, the smooth, heavy hand and knew it to be of excellent quality. Squinting, he could see the thin, ice blue stripe woven through the edging and knew it to be fine Holland linen. As he slowly unrolled layer after layer to dry before the flames, a multitude of tiny black specks fell onto the stone floor of the cottage. The infinitesimal specks jumped and scattered across the stones. They hopped onto the sleeves of the old man's tunic. They clung to his pant legs and dropped into his boots. They even fell onto the dog. Over the course of the day, the little cottage was overrun with tiny black fleas. The old man saw nary a one.

CHAPTER 25

"THUS THIS MONTH ENDS WITH GREAT SADNESS UPON THE PUBLICK, THROUGH THE GREATNESS OF THE PLAGUE EVERYWHERE THROUGH THE KINGDOM ALMOST"
-SAMUEL PEPYS

Village of Wells
Buckinghamshire, England
1 May 1665

The spade felt good in his hands. Solid. Comforting, even. The heft of the smooth wooden handle, the sharp slice of the iron blade as it cut into the soft, fragrant earth, even the toss of the rich, crumbling soil brought back memories of the rocky fields near Scotland and the hard, physical labor that chiseled his youthful muscles and allowed his nimble, inquisitive mind to wander through the puzzlements of anatomy and algebra. Simon stopped for a moment to catch his breath. He leaned on the shovel and watched as the Abbey carriage pulled into the courtyard of the inn. A rope tied around the top of a bare tree trunk lying on the ground was thrown toward him. Simon caught the rope, tossed the free end over the branch of an immense sycamore and then looped it around his back while straining sideways to watch the occupants disembark from the carriage. The mayor attempted to direct the placement of the tree trunk.

"Pull it this way!" shouted the mayor.

Simon returned his attention to the tree. He and three young men from the village grunted, working to center the unwieldy, fifteen-foot pine tree in a deep, narrow hole they had just dug in the center of the town square. The tree had been stripped bare of its branches and crowned with a curious six-inch iron spike.

"No! That way!" the mayor yelled, gesturing wildly with both hands.

Amid shouts of laughter, the young men worked to pull the unwieldy trunk straight for the Wells mayday fair. Jonathan Smythe, a nineteen-year-old cobbler's apprentice heaved on the rope entwined through his fists until his forearms bulged. The top of the tree tipped precipitously toward Simon then was righted momentarily, before falling again too far in the opposite direction. Gordon Hardy, a twenty-year old carpenter yanked hard on his rope, pulling the trunk back to rights.

Lord Abbott walked to the square and watched the installation of the maypole with great amusement. The first of May was a day he looked forward to every year, for the children of both Stockbridge and Wells spent weeks practicing the intricate, intertwining dance that braided colorful streamers down the length of the pole. He loved to watch the children dance, then dissolve into giggles as they tried to plait the fabric panels. He could well remember the tallest maypole he had ever seen. Just four years before, Lord Abbott stood with the rest of the curious onlookers in London as a massive maypole standing nearly 143 feet tall was erected on the Strand. His smile faded as he thought about the Strand Maypole that would most likely stand bare, past merriments now in stark contrast to the unfolding tragedy that was, on this soft, spring May Day, beginning to overwhelm the city. The mayor walked up to him, out of breath and patting his damp forehead with a cloth. He looked troubled.

"Is it right that we should make merry this day in Wells when the whole of London is in the grip of such sorrows and grief?" asked the mayor.

"We must carry on as is customary, lest we ourselves succumb to such sorrows," replied Lord Abbott, as the villagers dragged wooden tables and blankets from the cottages that lined the lane to display their wares upon during the fair.

The mayor saw Father Jessup across the green and headed his way. Lord Abbott looked up at the maypole and smiled, remembering the many years that Charles had begged to take part in the contest to be the first to crown it with the iron ring of fabric streamers. At the sweet memory, he felt yet another pang of regret for having so capriciously sent Charles to sea, though he dared not give voice to his trepidations for Viola hadn't spoken to him in nearly a week.

"I could climb it."

Startled out of his musings, Lord Abbott looked down to see the scowling face of Toby, the little stable boy standing next to the pole. He stared up to the top as he balanced himself on rough-hewn crutches. His leg was wrapped tightly with cloth bandages to the knee.

"Ahh, could you, now, lad?" chuckled Lord Abbott.

"I almost made it last year." He looked crestfallen. "I wanted to win the shilling this year."

Lord Abbott took in the frown on the boys face, recognizing the same youthful determination he saw in Charles at the same age. He walked over to the pole that had finally been secured into the ground. Lord Abbott raised his hand high above his head and with a knife from his pocket, made a mark on the trunk. He looked back to the boy.

"Does your leg still hurt, lad?"

"No, sir. Not as much."

"This mark is nearly halfway up the pole. I should say that a lad with a broken leg would indeed make it to the top if, with a wounded leg, he could make it halfway. Are you up to a challenge, my boy?"

Toby dropped his crutches and, balancing on one leg, wrapped his arms and good leg around the tree trunk. He began to climb, sheer determination etched across his face, inching his way higher and higher. Lord Abbott watched until at last, Toby reached the mark. He slapped his hand over the scratch and looked down, smiling in triumph. Lord Abbott reached up, grabbed Toby by the waist and hauled him down.

"Well done, lad! Well done." Lord Abbott smiled and dug into the pocket of his breeches. He handed him the shilling.

"Thank you, sir!" said Toby, with a beaming grin. He happily shoved the coin into his pocket. Lord Abbott watched as he took up his crutches and worked his way back to the stable yard, admiring the grit in the boy. Simon made his way across the green.

"Good morning, sir."

"Good morning, Doctor."

"If I may ask, is Lady Catherine with…" He stopped and looked away. He had been too presumptuous. "I beg your pardon."

Lord Abbott looked at Simon with curiosity.

"She is with her aunt, paying a visit to Madamoiselle Chanon in the dressmaker's shop. Shall I tell her you wish to speak with her?"

"McKensie!" the mayor shouted from the square, waving to Simon. Simon took a step back.

"Yes, please." He stopped. "No." He took another step, and then turned back again. "Yes." He ducked his head, embarrassed. "Thank you sir." *The lad seems smitten.* Simon turned toward the mayor, holding the spade high.

"On my way, mayor." Simon stopped and took a second look. Something seemed amiss. The mayor was hurrying toward him. A stout woman followed close behind, apronstrings flapping. Simon remembered her from a visit she paid him over an aching back. It was Maudie, the baker from the Royal George.

"What is it?" called Simon, for there seemed to be an urgency writ upon her face.

"Why, it's Master Seton, Doctor," replied Maudie, running behind the mayor, red-cheeked and breathing hard. She leaned against a tree to catch her breath. "I went to collect the streamers for the maypole." She looked up at Simon, wide-eyed, as though not quite believing what she had just seen. "Why, e's just lyin' right there in the bed!

She fanned herself with her apron. "He's alone, ye' know, wiv' no wife, an' no children. So's I check in on 'im. Ye' know, take him supper, help with the cleanin', that sort of thing."

"And, and...," urged the mayor.

"Well, he didn't answer the knock, ye' know, 'an I don't enter a dwelling without so much as a by your leave. So's I went 'round back." She looked sheepish. "T' 'ave a peek in, ye' know. Well, 'e weren't movin', sir. So's I poked me 'ead through th' shutters. Ooo, an' he had a right pile of dirty clothes on the table. I 'ad to shove 'em aside just to get a look at 'im lyin' there, still as anythin'."

She stopped for a moment, unwilling to say the words aloud. She took a deep breath, scratching at the angry red bites upon her forearm. "If yer' askin' me, sir" she lowered her voice to a shocked whisper, "I thinks 'e's dead."

Simon dropped his shovel. Lord Abbott looked across the road to the courtyard. His carriage was still in the yard. He shouted to the stable boys.

"Call my driver!"

The horses clattered headlong through the rolling hills toward one of the small farmhouses at the edge of the forest on the southern boundary of Wells. The abbey carriage pulled up to the old man's cottage. Fronted by a small garden of well-tended roses, the humble stone dwelling sat on a patch of dirt that seemed to be enveloped in an unearthly quiet. Even the drooping branches of a graceful willow tree on the bank of a small pond down the hill hung deathly still. The men inside the coach donned their hats and prepared to follow Simon into the cottage. As Simon reached for the door, he turned back to Lord Abbott and the mayor.

"Given the circumstances in London, I believe it to be a wiser course if you gentlemen might allow me to enter the dwelling first."

The mayor was about to protest. Lord Abbott laid a restraining hand upon his shoulder, settling him down at once.

"Indeed. Prudence may certainly prove to be wiser course." He patted the mayor's shoulder. "Cecil, we shall remain in the carriage and allow the doctor his inquiry."

Simon dismounted from the coach, blinking in the bright sunlight. Bits of dirt and gravel crunched beneath his feet as he walked to the door of the cottage and knocked. After a moment, he glanced back to see the mayor and Lord Abbott staring intently at him through the carriage glass. He jiggled the iron latch, but the door had been secured from the inside. The mayor cracked the carriage door open and pointed toward the rear of the dwelling. Simon nodded, and then walked around to the back. He saw a set of pale blue shutters above a prickly rosebush. He pushed the shutters open wide and looked into a simple bedchamber.

An old man indeed lay still upon a hay-stuffed pallet that was spread across a coarse rope bedstead. The old Irish setter curled quietly on the scuffed wooden floorboards next to the bed. Simon knocked on the sill. The dog raised his head and, with pleading eyes, let out a pitiful whimper. The man lay motionless. Simon knocked again, this time louder. The dog rose up and barked, but still the man did not move. Simon stood looking through the window a long moment. He quietly closed the shutters, then walked around to the front of the cottage and faced the coach from a distance. The mayor opened the door with a questioning look upon his face. Simon simply shook his head. Both men dropped their heads in sad concern.

"I shall have to break the door," called Simon, grim-faced.

Simon turned and ran his shoulder against the wooden door, but the door did not move. He stepped back a few paces, then tried again, this time forcibly lunging his entire weight into the wood. The door flew open, shattering the jamb. Simon nearly fell into the cottage. He stumbled, and then quickly regained his balance. He stopped short to survey the room. The strips of colorful cloth that Maudie had come for had been whipstitched to an iron ring and carefully stretched out across a worktable. Cinders lay cold in the grate. A bolt of flaxen colored fabric sat unfurled next to the worktable. It had been spread over several wooden stools before the hearth, as though to dry. Three more bolts leaned against the table. Looking closer, Simon saw hundreds of fleas upon the fabric. Repulsed, he quickly stepped back, then crossed the low-timbered room and entered the tiny bedchamber. The old tailor lay quietly under a plain, boiled-wool coverlet. Simon hesitated. *I fear what I may see upon this man.* Simon exhaled. He gently lifted the corner of the coverlet to look at the man's neck. He stopped cold, for there on the man's neck, just below the collar of his cotton nightdress, were several large black knots. He knew in an instant what had killed the man.

Simon dropped the coverlet and immediately raced from the dwelling. He paced in the garden, his fingers balled into his fists. Simon strode back and forth on the path between the rose bushes in deep concentration.

"Well?" asked the Mayor, climbing out of the carriage.

"No!" cried Simon. The mayor froze halfway out of the coach, one foot on the wooden step, the other inside. "Keep your distance, Lord Mayor!"

How does this wretched disease spread? Simon's mind reeled as he paced with the dire realization that the plague had indeed reached Wells. *There is no time to examine the cause. I must take charge or indeed this vicious pestilence will surely advance.* He turned once again. Another thorn pricked his shoulder, leaving a small tear in his linen shirt. He never felt the scratch, for he was in deep concentration desperately charting a course. *Treat the symptoms,* he thought, as he now recalled his own entreaty to Father Hardwicke. Simon continued to pace, grateful that he had indeed paid such careful attention to the medical journals sent from the continent, for there were many recommendations advanced by the physicians who had already faced the contagion in Amsterdam. From his research to his writings, to every single day of his rigorous training, Simon felt as though he had been preparing for an eventuality such as this his entire life. *And he was ready.* He turned to the men in the coach.

"Vinegar! I must have vinegar!" he shouted.

"What in God's name does the lad call for?" sputtered the mayor to Lord Abbott.

The men stared out the carriage window at him as though he were babbling complete nonsense, and then looked with shock upon Simon as he stood in the pathway and completely disrobed, his clothing falling piece by piece into a heap at his feet.

"What the devil—why, he is as bare as the day he was born! The boy has gone completely mad," cried the mayor, flustered at the sight.

Simon gathered his things into a bundle and, holding them away from his bare body, raced straight to the shattered door of the cottage and tossed the entire lot inside. Lord Abbott and the mayor disembarked and began to walk toward the cottage.

"Stay back, gentlemen!" he shouted. Simon headed around the side of the dwelling and charged down the slope at a dead run.

"And flint," he called out over his shoulder.

"Flint?" cried the mayor. "Whatever for!

The men watched in utter confusion as Simon raced straight into the pond, splashing water in all directions. He dove underwater and stayed there for what seemed an eternity.

He came up flinging his hair backward out of his eyes. Water dripped off his muscular arms and ran down his bare chest. He called out once more.

"And scissors. And the local priest!"

"Good God," bellowed the mayor, as Simon plunged himself under the water once again.

Lord Abbott hurried to the carriage to retrieve a covering. "Vinegar. Curious, indeed," he muttered. He looked for his overcloak, but found the coach bare. He knitted his brows in confusion. *Where did I have it last? Ah, the publick house. I must have left it hanging on the peg. Blast and damnation!* He went around to the back of the carriage and, opening a small compartment, pulled a woolen lap blanket from the bin. He shouted up to the driver.

"Go at once to the inn and gather together vinegar, flint and tinderbox, and find Father Jessup. Bring him back here. Speak directly to the innkeeper, Wilfryd Browne. Tell him that I request these things, then return as soon as possible with a change of clothing for the lad. The Lord Mayor's cook, Eliza, will assist you." Grim-faced, he turned back to the pond. "I fear we are about to be beset by disaster."

Lord Abbott gathered the blanket into his arms and hurried toward the pond. Simon threw out both hands, palms upward, stopping him short on the sloping grass.

"Throw it from there, sir!"

Lord Abbott flung the blanket down the grassy bank. Simon waded out of the water, shivering in the cool morning air. Standing well away from the two men, he wrapped himself in the blanket. The Lord Mayor sputtered as he tried to comprehend what was happening.

"What in the very name of God, himself…"

A look of grave concern upon his face, Simon cut him off. "The plague, sir. The man in that cottage has died of the plague."

The men fell silent as a slow, dreadful comprehension dawned upon them all. Out on the pond, a drifting mallard with a shimmering emerald green neckband broke the silence with a violent flight off the water. The startling flap of its wings jolted them all from their troubled thoughts. The mayor spoke first.

"Dear God! That the plague should descend upon London, the city being the very center of commerce, foreign trade and cramped, crowded living, is at the very least comprehensible. But Wells? By my troth, sir! People escape to the countryside to run *from* the plague—not into the very jaws of it! Are you certain, McKensie?"

"Beyond measure, sir."

Lord Abbott heaved a sigh and shook his head in despair at the enormity of what lie ahead. He contemplated the situation. "It appears that we must now face this execrable contagion square on." He turned to Simon standing by the pond, with an air of resigned acceptance.

"What exactly do you propose, Doctor?" he asked.

Simon hesitated but a moment. "Sir, I have read a great deal of the scientific journals from the continent and among other treatments, there has been some success in stemming the spread of the infection with a cleansing of vinegar." He gathered his courage and spoke boldly. "I propose to first douse myself with the vinegar, and then together, we must determine the best course for the town. Isolation. Lord Mayor, we must advocate isolation.

"The devil you say!" He turned to Lord Abbott. "Does he make any sort of sense to you at all?"

"I beg of you, gentlemen, send a man to the boundary stone this very hour. Turn away anyone attempting to enter Wells for the fair and by the same charge, anyone attempting to leave town must be turned back to the village. Simon implored the men. "Lord Mayor, you must isolate the entire town."

The mayor was shocked. "That is impossible, sir! We cannot imprison an entire village!"

"It is not an imprisonment, sir. It is a quarantine." Simon faced the mayor, his voice trembling with desperation. "I beg of you once again, sir. By your authority, gather together everyone in the village this day, and impose an official decree of quarantine upon the town of Wells."

CHAPTER 26

"I SAW A DEAD CORPSE IN A COFFIN LIE IN THE CLOSE UNBURYED AND A WATCH IS CONSTANTLY KEPT THERE, NIGHT AND DAY, TO KEEP PEOPLE IN THE PLAGUE MAKING US CRUEL AS DOGS ONE TO ANOTHER."
-SAMUEL PEPYS

"I expect you realize that the course you propose will condemn this entire village?" demanded the mayor. He slapped his hands together. "I will not do it. I refuse beyond measure to issue a decree that will exact an unconditional death sentence upon the people of Wells. No, sir! I simply will not do it!"

Simon countered, his eyes pleading, his entire body now shaking with conviction.

"Sir, I beseech you to listen! The whole of the East End is now consumed upon itself with disease. They this day bury victims in mass graves in London, in such numbers as cannot be comprehended. Hundreds if not thousands of citizens! But, Mi'Lord, you must also understand that in London, a quarantine of the entire family inside an afflicted house is required by royal decree whether all and sundry are ill or not. I fervently believe this course belies a sure and swift death sentence for all within the dwelling." He looked from Lord Abbott to the mayor, his fervor rising. "Gentlemen, I beseech you to at least give some consideration to my proposal, for I further believe there is a secondary course we may attempt that might offer an additional defense.

"And what, pray tell, might that be?" challenged the mayor.

"I propose that we separate the well from the unwell."

The mayor, shocked by the sheer number of dead in London,

began to listen. "And how exactly do you intend to carry out this scheme?"

Simon took a deep breath. "The stables, sir."

"The what?" Even Lord Abbott was perplexed by the proposal.

"You are an insane fool, McKensie!" shouted the mayor. 'I refuse to consider the plan! Housing desperately ill people in stalls meant for animals is simply out of the question."

Lord Abbott restrained him. "Let the lad speak, Cecil!"

"I propose that we use the stables as a hospital. I have seen the stalls. They were built separate, one from another. I understand that it will not be entirely pleasant, however, we can begin this day to make the stalls habitable enough. At first evidence of affliction, the ill must be isolated from their families and brought into the stables to be cared for, in hopes that the remaining family members may be spared.

"Exactly who the devil do you expect to care for them?"

"I offer myself, sir." Simon explained in earnest. "I have spent five years in medical training at St. Bartholomew's in London with the ill and the afflicted, and yet, to this day, have suffered no major maladies. I must possess some sort of protective resistance, and although I cannot identify this resistance, it does prove useful." He faced them. "Gentlemen, I propose that I move into the stable master's quarters. I shall take my books, my research and such possessions as may be necessary and I will care for the ill for the duration of the quarantine."

The Lord Mayor exploded. "Utterly preposterous. Think of it, sir! Would you have mother separated from child? Husband from wife? No! I will not agree to the scheme," he roared.

The Abbey carriage pulled up to the cottage, breaking the tension among the men. Father Jessup, dressed in a formal black cassock for the blessing of the fair, descended from the coach. He stood apart from the men, listening briefly to the contentious debate, and then turned back toward the carriage. He lifted the lid to a small purple velvet-covered box and withdrew several small cut glass vessels of holy oils. He set them on the floor of the carriage, and then opened his Book of Common Prayer in preparation of an entreaty for the dead man. The driver handed down a parcel containing a dark amber glass bottle of vinegar, the tinder and flint box and the change of clothing to Lord Abbott. He walked down the knoll and placed the items on the ground halfway between himself and Simon, who stood on the bank still wrapped in the carriage blanket.

"And the scissors, too, if you would," called up Simon.

The coach driver tossed the scissors toward the embankment. They bounced several times, then landed softly upon the grass at Simon's feet. Simon waited while Lord Abbott and the driver retreated safely up the hill. He took the bottle and doused himself from head to toe with the acrid-smelling fluid. He took special care in pouring the vinegar through his hair, and then took the scissors to hand. Simon secured the blanket around his waist and sat on a rock. He began to cut his shoulder-length hair nearly to the scalp. Thick locks fell to the grass beneath him. When he finished, Simon gathered up the straw-colored lengths and threw them into the pond. He quickly dressed in the fresh clothing, and then walked toward the priest who carefully laid his oils upon a heavily embroidered cloth that was spread across the ground.

"Does this man have family?"

The priest looked up. "Nae, Doctor. He lived a solitary life.

Simon nodded. He took the flint and tinderbox from the mayor and began to walk back to the cottage.

The mayor grabbed Simon's sleeve. "What the devil are you doing now?" Simon turned toward him and removed his hand, stepping deftly to the side.

"My Lord, although there is fresh inquiry into the treatment of the plague, how this pestilence spreads is still very much unknown. Does it blow upon the wind? Does it crawl upon the earth? Does it spread with the spring rains? Every possibility is to be considered, for no one knows. Therefore, and with the utmost respect, I recommend that after a brief prayer from the good Father, this cottage and all its contents, and with the dead man still inside, be burned to the ground."

"Unthinkable!" shouted the mayor. He felt as though he might be compelled to blows from the white-hot anger that rose inside. "You cannot counsel such a course!"

Possessed of a more rational turn of mind, Lord Abbott laid a calming hand upon the mayor's shoulder, and then turned to the priest. "What say you, Father?"

"Blasphemy. I say it is sheer blasphemy!" he hissed, his eyes narrowing with intensity. The priest stared at Simon, aghast, as though he were in league with the very devil, himself. "There are holy rites to perform upon a death." He held up the prayer book and shook it toward Simon. "The first of which is a solemn prayer over the body and the laying on of holy oils. This man's soul must be saved!" He turned and walked with determined strides toward the cottage.

Simon ran in front of Father Jessup to restrain him, grabbing the priest by both arms. "I beg of you, stop!" Father Jessup hesitated. "I must remind you, this man died from a highly contagious and extremely perilous disease. I do not intend to interfere with your religious obligations, however, sir, if you choose to enter the dead man's dwelling, I cannot avouch for your safety," implored Simon.

The priest began to waver. Unfamiliar, troubling doubts began to cloud his countenance. He took Simon aside. "Is my solemn charge before God that I expose myself to this foul pestilence? And what precisely is my moral obligation to the people of the village, for I neither wish to abandon my ministerial duty, yet neither do I wish to perish from its execution. I confess, sir, that this is a perplexity beyond my reasoning." He looked to Simon, anguished in his thoughts. "What do you counsel, Doctor?"

Before Simon could respond, the sound of low, murmuring voices from the road caught their attentions. He looked beyond the coach out to the lane. There, led by Maudie, were more than twenty villagers, some on foot, some on horseback quietly approaching the cottage. They stopped across the lane and waited under a craggy, ancient oak tree just leafing out, its bright halo of spring green a startling contrast to the somber assemblage below. Some clutched hands; others murmured soft prayers. Men held their hats to their chests. They all kept a respectful distance from the men who stood before the cottage. Simon faced the mayor straight on.

"You must decide now, Lord Mayor. You must speak to them," said Simon, his voice, his manner, his very physical presence commanded an urgency such as he had never before felt. The Lord Mayor was at a loss.

"I do not wish to cause a panic in the village!" he hissed.

Maudie called out from across the lane. "Has Master Seton indeed passed, Mi'Lord?"

"He has."

"Aye, then. He were a good man, sir, an' we've come t' pay our respects." The villagers nodded and began to walk toward the cottage.

"Decide, sir!"

The mayor brooded over the impossible scheme advanced by the young doctor who paced before him.

"If I am wrong, this course will ravage the village. It will cleave neighbor from neighbor and condemn us all," worried the mayor.

"But if I am right, sir, we will isolate the pestilence, contain the infection and save the lives of many who will otherwise perish!"

The mayor looked from one anxious face to another. He shook his head in disbelief at the course he was about to take. He slowly raised his palms and called out to the assembly advancing toward them.

"Stand your ground!"

The villagers halted where they stood. They looked to one other in confusion.

The mayor spoke out once again. "Master Seton has died of the plague."

A palpable, white-hot bolt of fear shot through the villagers. They instantly, instinctively backed away, turning to flee from the infected cottage.

"Stop!" the mayor shouted.

The villagers hesitated, waiting for him to speak. The mayor looked to Lord Abbott and Simon. They nodded their encouragement. The mayor's booming voice rang out.

"I…" He stopped, and then spoke once again. "I…" The mayor fell silent, seemingly unable to give utterance to a confidence he did not possess in the face of the dire situation. Simon watched, as the mayor looked first toward the cottage, and then back to the villagers who stood on the lane, anxious to run away. His shoulders dropped in truthful admission. "Under the circumstances, I, in all honesty, do not profess to the know the right course for our village," he stopped a moment and drew his chest high, "however, as your Lord Mayor, I have been appointed to lead, and lead I shall, indeed." He pointed toward Simon. "This young doctor has far more experience than I with the peril we now face, and so with the best of intentions, I shall defer to his authority."

The mayor looked out over the crowd and pointed. "Eldrick Hadley and Thomas Woollsey!" Startled at hearing their names, the butcher and the blacksmith pushed through the little crowd and stepped forward, caps in hand.

"Aye, sir?" questioned Eldrick. Thomas and Eldrick glanced first toward the mayor, then to each other with brows furrowed, acutely fearful of his next words.

"The doctor requires your services. Are you willing?"

Again, the men looked to one another, then slowly nodded toward the mayor, apprehensive at what was to come. The mayor stepped back in deference to Simon.

"Eldrick, if you would, please take a man with you. Ride at once to the boundary stone. Turn away anyone attempting to enter for the fair or for any other reason, and equally to the task, turn back anyone attempting to flee, as the entire village of Wells is, as of this very moment, under quarantine." A horrified murmur rippled through the knot of villagers, as they began to comprehend their direful plight."

"Aye, sir," replied Eldrick. He turned to Nathan Treadwell, his young apprentice. "Ye'll come?" Nathan nodded, grimly. The two men mounted their horses and wheeled away from the cottage. The villagers watched as they tore down the road toward the boundary crossing, a cloud of dust roiling in their wake. Gordon Jameson headed out in the other direction.

"I volunteer to guard the other side of the village," he said, urging his horse in the opposite direction.

"Thomas, return at once to town. Find the constable. Gather everyone together in the village square. We will take matters in hand here, and when we are finished, we will join you, for there are many decisions to make."

"Aye, sir." Thomas tapped several young men on the shoulder and nodded. They, too, mounted their horses and departed with all haste toward the village. The mayor turned back to those who remained standing under the oak tree.

"As to the rest of you…" The mayor hesitated, and then spoke bluntly. "…the doctor proposes to burn the cottage and all contained therein, including the deceased, Master Seton." An audible gasp rose from the crowd. The mayor faced Father Jessup.

"Are you in agreement, Father?"

Before the priest could respond, a deep voice from the small knot of terrified villagers left standing on the lane rang out loud and clear.

"God save us all… Burn it to the ground!"

The remaining villagers shouted their assents. The mayor turned to Simon and gave a reluctant nod. Simon walked to the knoll and gathered together the supplies that had been brought from town. He carried the tinderbox and flint to the front of the cottage, and then set them on the ground under a blossoming apple tree. He reached up and broke off a branch.

"Have either of you a handkerchief?" he asked the men. Lord Abbott pulled an embroidered square from his pocket and handed it to Simon.

Father Jessup at last gave in to the fear and apprehension he felt. He gave his reluctant approval. Standing well away from the cottage, he turned and solemnly faced the small crowd. He raised his hands, palms outward.

"Let us pray…"

The villagers standing under the oak tree bowed their heads. Simon wound the handkerchief around one end of the stick and secured the end tightly.

Father Jessup raised his voice and eyes to the heavens.

"…*I am the resurrection and the life, saith the Lord: he that believeth in me, though he were dead, yet shall he live: and whosoever liveth and believeth in me shall never die…*"

"Hand me your flask," Simon whispered to the mayor. The mayor instantly drew back in feigned innocence. Simon narrowed his eyes. "I am very well aware that to this day you carry one, still."

The mayor stared at him for a moment. He drew a deep breath, considering the request, then exhaled and reluctantly reached into his doublet. He pulled a thin sterling silver flask from the inside pocket and slapped it into Simon's outstretched hand.

"Hear my prayer, O Lord, and with thine ears consider my calling: hold not thy peace at my tears…"

Simon held the stick downward and poured the forbidden whiskey over the top of the handkerchief until it was completely saturated.

"… *We brought nothing into this world, and it is certain we can carry nothing out…*"

"Steady, now! Not the entirety of it!" begged the mayor, restraining Simon's hand. Simon stopped a moment and then, looking the mayor square in the eye, poured the entire contents over the cloth.

"... The Lord giveth, and the Lord hath taken away..."

"Truer words were never spoken," bemoaned the mayor, as he sadly watched his expensive, beloved Haig scotch splatter onto the dirt, splashing over his boots.

"... blessed be the name of the Lord..."

Simon handed the mayor the branch, then put flint to tinder and struck a spark. He raised the flame to the whiskey-soaked handkerchief. The cloth instantly caught fire. The mayor hastily thrust the flaming branch toward Simon, who took it and drew back, taking careful aim, and then flung the torch toward the unhinged, broken front door. The priest fell silent. He watched open-mouthed, mesmerized by the slow, skyward arc of the flame twirling slowly end around end through the open door, coming at last to rest squarely upon the old tailor's worktable. With a momentary, brilliant flash, the colorful Mayday streamers, the flaxen-colored linen sheeting and the bolts of Holland cloth that leaned against the table burst into flames, and within minutes, the little stone and wood cottage at the edge of the forest was entirely consumed by fire. From inside, one single, ungodly howl echoed through the massive inferno. Immersed in holy prayer, the crowd jerked their heads toward the anguished sound and watched as the ancient Irish setter shot through the flames. He charged past the men, racing straight down the road toward Wells. Father Jessup turned back to the astonished villagers.

"Amen."

CHAPTER 27

Catherine stood on a small wooden box before the looking glass in astonishment at the exquisite marriage gown Lisette had fashioned. Sewn from the palest woodland moss-colored watered taffeta, the ethereal frock's delicate Brussels lace bodice, soft cream-colored ruffles falling from the forearms and layers upon layers of lace underskirtings were like nothing Catherine had ever before seen. A shimmering train of featherweight silk that was fastened at the shoulders by clusters of handmade pink roses seemed to float like a trailing cloud several yards behind her. Lisette reached up and set a wreath of rose and pink silk rosebuds atop Catherine's red curls. The entire ensemble was a breathtaking creation. Catherine was enchanted and nearly in tears at the sight, although these days, tears forever seemed at her fingertips. She sighed. Aunt Viola watched closely as Lisette kneeled down to set the hem.

"Lisette, it is positively beautiful," whispered Catherine. With several pins in her mouth, the dressmaker looked up, her merry eyes crinkling with delight.

"Tournez a` droite, s'il vous plait."

Obediently, Catherine turned slightly to the right.

"A bit longer in the back, I should think," offered Aunt Viola, who sat stiffly upon a stool, both hands resting atop her silver-topped walking stick, her sharp eyes scrutinizing even the tiniest details.

"Oui, oui, Madam," muttered Lisette, deftly removing every last pin she had just set in place, stabbing them back into a cloth holder.

Catherine stared at her reflection. Miles would take great pleasure in the gown; that she knew. He always seemed far more acquainted with the current fashions from the continent than anyone else in the valley. She vowed yet again to pay more attention, for the new wife of Viscount Houghton could not look a bumbler. She could not face the very real possibility that the Barlowe sisters might be right, that the newest Lady Houghton might not belong in Houghton Hall at all. She shuddered at the humiliating thought. She ran her hand over the gown, tracing her finger over the intricate patterns of the fine Belgium lace ruffles. The next time she slipped into its soft, gossamer folds would be for the marriage ceremony. *The marriage ceremony. In just one month's time.* A fleeting, ephemeral sense of unease suddenly enveloped her. She shuddered once again. Lisette looked up, sharply.

"*Êtes-vous malade, Mademioselle?*"

"No, I am not ill, Lisette," smiled Catherine.

Shouts from the square captured their attentions. They turned toward the door and heard the shouts once again, this time, louder.

"Fire!"

The honey-colored pecan floorboards cracked as Viola strode across the tiny shop to see what was causing the commotion. She moved the lace curtains aside and saw Miles leading several young men on horseback galloping toward the outskirts of town, wooden milking buckets in hand.

"Dear God!" cried Viola.

"What is it, Aunt Viola?"

"Miles is riding to a fire!"

Viola gathered her skirts and hurried toward the square where an anxious crowd gathered, for although fire was a most feared calamity, it was especially dangerous for the men who fought them. Lisette looked up to Catherine in deep concern.

"*Je suis fini,* Lady Catherine. I will 'elp you dress."

Minutes later, still knotting the lace shawl that hung about her shoulders, Catherine raced across the lane, with Lisette close behind. The foreboding, pungent scent of smoke drifted through the air. On the green, townspeople left their wares unattended as they hurried to a clearing and looked southward toward the forest where an ominous column of black smoke rose steadily into the brilliant blue morning sky.

Riding hard away from the village, Miles and the others suddenly pulled up short, startled to meet Thomas and several young men coming at them from the direction of the cottage. Thick black smoke and bits of ash swirled through the air. The men wiped their eyes with the back of their hands from the irritation.

"What is it?" shouted Miles, his horse snorting, circling impatiently around the men.

"The plague, Mi'Lord! The doctor says that Master Seton has died of the plague! The Lord Mayor, Lord Abbott and Father Jessup have burnt his cottage in an attempt to contain the infection."

"Good God!"

"We're to find the constable and assemble in the square every citizen in the town of Wells. There is to be a quarantine of the village to keep the pestilence from spreading across the valley and beyond. We're to meet in the village square in one hours time."

Miles's mind reeled, for as his own impulsive flight from London after the engagement ball attested, he had no desire whatever to remain in the presence of that vicious, murderous scourge, *and yet within the hour, a quarantine would be called. A quarantine of Wells. Dear God—a death sentence to be sure! Nae, I will not do it. I will not stay! Let the people of the valley save themselves, for I have absolutely no desire to imperil myself for the common good. A quarantine be damned!* Thomas pointed to the bucket Miles carried.

"No need for that, Mi'Lord. The cottage will burn to the ground. We have been ordered to return to the village. We could use your assistance in finding the constable, though, if you've a mind to it, sir."

Miles thought fast. "You carry on—I must speak to the Lord Mayor." Without waiting for an answer, he wheeled his horse around sharply and gave the mare a kick to her heaving sides, racing hard toward the burning cottage. Thomas watched him ride off, then he and the others turned toward Wells to roust the constable.

Rounding a bend in the road, Miles suddenly pulled on the reins and slowed his horse to a trot. Obscured by dappled shadows from a thick grove of English oaks, he rose slightly in his saddle and turned to look back. Seeing only a cloud of settling dust left in the wake of the men, he suddenly kicked his horse hard in the ribs once again and shouted.

"Ya!"

The mare reared high and pawed the air, then broke into a full run toward the cottage. As they reached the turning for the Seton farm, Miles unexpectedly veered his mount off the road and crashed headlong through the thicket as though they were being chased by the devil himself. Miles charged through the woodlands at a full run, desperate to leave the cottage, the village and the heinous plague far behind. The horse began to falter. Miles urged the mare onward, kicking even harder at her sides. Her breaths came in ragged gasps. Low-hanging limbs slapped at her sides. She stumbled over rocks and rabbit holes. Miles began to sweat heavily through his riding jacket as the horse scrambled for purchase on the slippery pine needles that lay thick upon the earthen floor. Still they ran, hollow hoofbeats echoing through a strange and eerie silence as horse and rider thundered as one through the dark, primeval forest. Clutching the reins high with one hand and the saddle horn with the other, Miles sailed his horse over rotted, decaying logs. They ducked under pine branches heavy with crystalline rainwater. They splashed across eddying brooks and up moss-covered creek banks. On and on they rode through the deepening shadows, forging an untrodden path toward the safety of Stockbridge and Houghton Hall. Miles never once looked back.

"Look there!" cried Gussie in surprise, pointing down the lane as she stood with Catherine, Viola and a small knot of villagers. Catherine followed her gaze and watched the young men returning to the square, their buckets empty.

"Is Miles with them?" asked Catherine, craning her neck to see over the heads of the villagers who ran toward the men.

Maudie and the villagers followed on foot behind the young men, while Thomas Woollsey and several others on horseback brought up the rear. Each to a man looked pale and bewildered, as though they had seen the very haints, themselves. As the group drew closer, those in the square looked to one another in confusion. Catherine searched for Miles once again. Thomas rode around to the front of the group and called out to the villagers on the square.

"Is Constable Hawkins among ye'?"

"Aye! I am!" shouted the constable from the back of the square. He worked his way through the crowd that had gathered on the expansive green and ran across the lane to meet Thomas, who leaned down from his horse to speak privately. With a fearful look of concern, the constable nodded. He turned to a young boy standing near to him.

"Have the stables ready my horse, lad."

The boy ran quickly to the stable yard. Constable Hawkins turned and faced the villagers who had gathered around him, sensing a precipitous announcement.

"Master Seton has died…," he shouted.

A perceptible sigh of relief ran through the crowd, for although it was not entirely expected, he was an old man and had indeed lived a good life. Though the death was sad, the situation was not dire. Then, the constable took a deep breath and shouted out again.

"…of the plague."

It took but a moment for the realization to set in. Panicked screams and fearful shouts arose anew. Her heart in her throat, Catherine ran to the edge of the square to look for Miles. The constable shouted once more. Catherine pushed her way through the crowd to Viola, a foreboding knot in the pit of her stomach beginning to take hold.

"Have you seen Miles?"

Viola shook her head, distractedly. "No, my dear." She strained to hear the constable over the shrieks of the crowd.

"As of this hour, the mayor, the doctor, Father Jessup and Lord Abbott are out to Master Seton's cottage. They have set fire to it in an attempt to contain the infection."

"Alvyn! No!" shouted Viola, unable to silence her concern. She grabbed for Catherine in a near swoon.

"Lady Abbott, we were all kept well back. The doctor forbade anyone in attendance to approach the cottage," shouted Thomas above the din, in an attempt to calm her fears. Someone found Viola a milking stool to sit upon. A cup of water was thrust into her hands.

The constable raised his palms and waited until the terrified crowd fell silent once again.

"In light of the grievous peril we now face, the Lord Mayor has placed young Doctor McKensie in charge of Wells. The doctor has requested that every single person in town assemble here in the square. The Lord Mayor intends to speak before us all. We are to rouse anyone not yet in attendance for the fair and return here in one hour's time."

A stable boy walked the constable's horse across the square and assisted the mount. The constable held the reins tightly, calling down from the saddle.

"I shall return in one hour and I expect all and sundry do the same." He grimly nodded, then kicked the sides of his horse, and headed down the road toward the boundary stone.

Gathered together under the square's massive plane trees at the appointed hour, the entire town stood in hushed, wary silence. All thoughts of the May Day celebration had been abandoned as they clung together anxiously, husband to wife, mother to child. The villagers watched intently as the mayor stepped up to the ceremony platform at the north end of the green. Catherine, Viola, and Gussie stood together watching, their eyes fixed upon Lord Abbott who stood between the mayor and Simon. The constable remained on his horse circling the crowd.

"Is it true?" shouted a man from the crowd. "We've a right to know!" Several men loudly echoed the sentiment.

"What is 'appening?" whispered Lisette. Catherine shook her head, unsure of what was to come. She reached for Lisette's hand and held it tight.

"Aye. It's true. Master Seton has indeed perished of the plague," admitted the mayor.

Several villagers began to back away from the crowd.

"Stop!" shouted Simon, as he watched them turn and hasten from the square. "Constable!" Constable Hawkins rode around the green and drew his horse up before the fleeing villagers, herding them back to the village green.

The mayor called out once again. "As a town, we must come to one accord. The doctor has recommended that we quarantine the village." He took a deep breath. "That means that no one as of this hour may leave Wells—and by the same charge, no one may enter."

A tumult of voices arose from the crowd, some angry, most terrified.

"You cannot hold us captive!" shouted a man holding a small child. "We've only come for the fair!"

"We can, and by God, we will!" shouted the mayor. "The town of Wells is now officially quarantined! Any who chooses to run shall be placed in the stocks!"

Gussie stood rooted to the spot. Catherine quickly glanced

over and saw fear in the cook's eyes, something she had never once in her life seen. "Aye, Archie," Gussie whispered. She reached for Catherine's hand. "E's still at the Abbey." Catherine saw a tear trickle down her wrinkled cheek as the realization dawned over both of them that Gussie would face the quarantine without him. Catherine hugged her tightly. "You'll not be alone," she said, with a confidence she did not entirely possess as she searched over the crowd once again for Miles.

Father Jessup joined the mayor on the platform. His presence did little to calm the terrified villagers. He held his hands aloft and waited until there was silence.

"If it be God's will that we are to suffer this pestilence, then we shall suffer together, obediently and reverently. If we are to be quarantined, we shall do so with the knowledge that in our suffering, we will not endanger the towns around our own for the common good of England herself, and in that knowledge, our sacrifices shall not go unnoticed by God."

The crowd worked to absorb the priest's words. Several women fell upon their knees in prayer. Then, a rising swell of panic threatened to erupt once again, as families clustered together, the women mostly in tears, deep concern evident upon the faces of the men. Simon saw the devastation that the news wrought upon the villagers and was troubled. He turned to the mayor.

"May I speak, sir?"

"Indeed," he nodded.

Simon turned to the villagers and raised his voice for all to hear.

"I may be unknown to some of you. I am Simon McKensie. Doctor Simon McKensie. I have had five years of medical training at St. Bartholomew's The Less in London. As the mayor has proclaimed, with the death of Master Seton, the plague has indeed come to Wells." He produced a bill of announcement he had retrieved from his cottage and held it aloft. "The King has issued a decree for the containment of the plague. By authority of the mayor, I shall oversee the containment here in Wells."

"What do you propose, Doctor?" shouted a man at the front of the crowd.

"I first propose that we turn the stables into a hospital and establish a line around the perimeter where none but the ill can cross. At the very first sign of illness, headache, fever, any sign of infection, the afflicted person, be it man, woman or child, will immediately quarantine themselves to the stables for treatment." He fell silent for a moment, as the villagers struggled to comprehend that they were to be separated from their loved ones, even as they may lay dying.

The mayor spoke again, with unaccustomed compassion. "We understand fully what we ask of you. We understand that what we ask will be our greatest sacrifice, but if the doctor is right, the infection may not spread beyond our borders, and within our town, the majority may be saved."

A soft breeze ruffled through the bright green leaves overhead. The pastoral scene of villagers gathered together on the town square masked the dreadful undercurrent of terror that roiled beneath the surface. A little golden-haired girl in a cotton pinafore broke the silence. Burying her face in her mother's skirts, she began to sob and although she had no understanding of the deadly threat that loomed before them, each to a man assembled felt precisely the same.

Simon stepped to the edge of the speaker's platform. "To convert the stables, I will need a great deal of assistance. Are there any among you who would render assistance?" he called out.

"Aye, Doctor!" yelled Maudie, sensible as ever. Something bumped her skirts. Startled, she looked down to see that the tailor's dog that had found its way across the millstream and into the square. He somehow seemed to recognize the woman who sometimes brought his master food. He shook himself, sending water droplets, mud and fleas flying, and then stood quietly next to her. Lacing her fingers through a rope around the dog's neck, Maudie threaded her way briskly toward the platform. Standing together, the Barlowe sisters cried out and petulantly kicked at the wet dog as they passed. The setter lurched in fear from the girls. He swung his wet tail to and fro, leaving dirt and muddy streaks splashed across their white cotton pinafores. The girls howled at the filthy mess upon their dainty frocks, stamping their feet in fury. The dog recoiled at the noise. Sitting at the edge of the platform, Toby reached out and took hold of the rope. He stroked the shaking dog between its ears until it was calm. Toby scowled at the girls, then looked down and slapped at a flea on his bare arm.

Maudie stepped up to the platform and turned to the crowd. She yelled once again. "Well, nae'. If it's 'appened, it's 'appened, an' there's nae' turnin' back, now. We'll all face this together, will we not?

Craning her neck in every direction to see over the frightened crowd, Catherine again looked around the square for Miles. He was nowhere to be seen.

"Aye' we will, Maudie! What d'ye need, Doctor?" Eliza called out, her steady, direct ways a soothing balm to the fear that gripped the townspeople.

Simon gave them a small, grateful smile, and then looked out to the villagers once again.

"I believe we must start with the elementary figures. Is there a clerk or tax registrar in Wells?"

"Aye, sir!" called a slender, bespectacled man in his twenties. "I am Reginald Larkin, the town clerk.

"Are you able to account for every person who stands on the green this very hour? Are you able to prepare a list of who is missing, and by the same charge, prepare a list of who is quarantined this day from outside the village?"

"If you allow me access to my ledgers, I am, Doctor."

"Indeed, sir. Gather your ledgers and set up a table to your needs. We will wait for your accounting."

Simon thought again. "Is there anyone willing to oversee the cleaning of the stables to make them habitable?"

Eliza grabbed Gussie's hand and moved forward toward the platform. "We will, sir!" Maudie called out, "I'll 'elp, too, Doctor, what d' ye's require?"

"The horses will need to be turned out to pasture. How many stalls are there?"

"Fifty!" shouted John Thayer, from the back of the crowd. Simon nodded in approval to the ladies as they walked across the lane toward the pasturelands and down toward stables.

"Right, then," said Thayer, stoic to the core. He doffed his hat and caught up with the ladies to turn the horses out of their quarters.

Simon had another thought. "How many assembled here are not official residents of the town of Wells?" he called out once again.

Nearly twenty hands shot up. "Thank God the fair has not yet begun," Lord Abbott mused. "Maudie!" he shouted. She stopped in the lane and turned around at the sound of her name.

"Have you room at The George for these people?"

"We 'ave fifteen rooms, sir. But dinna' worry,—we'll fit 'em in."

"Nae, Maudie!" shouted Wilfryd Browne, the innkeeper. "Ye' canna' be fillin' th' rooms—who's going t' pay?

"We'll sort that out in due time, Browne, indeed that is the least of our concerns," reassured Lord Abbott.

"Aye, the least of *yer'* concerns," yelled Browne, "the coaching trade is to be turned back at the boundary stone. How am I to make up the losses? How are we to live?"

Yet another wave of fear and trepidations roiled through the restive crowd. Simon raised his hands and shouted over the din.

"Please. If…if I may speak!" A quiet slowly settled over the troubled villagers. Simon walked to the edge of the platform and spoke more quietly. "It is true that a dreadful visitation has been rendered upon us, however, there is a much to be hopeful for. I have done much research. I have read a great deal about the most successful treatments, and I will offer as much assistance as I possibly can. I propose that we pull together as one and find our way through this." He put his hand on his brow to block the sun and looked out over the crowd. He waved to Lisette. "Mademoiselle Chanon?"

"Oui, Monsieur?"

"Plague masks. Many doctors in Amsterdam were successful in avoiding the infection through the use of plague masks filled with lavender and other herbs. If masks provide protection to the doctors, I propose that we all wear them from this day hence. We will need plague masks for every man, woman and child in the village. If you had an illustration, would you be able to construct such a mask? Perhaps Lady Abbott would draw…" He stopped, realizing that he had said too much.

Lord Abbott looked at him sharply. *How does the lad know that my daughter is an able illustrationist?* He looked out over the crowd and caught Catherine's eye. She quickly bowed her head. *Curious.* Lord Abbott turned back to Simon. The doctor averted his gaze, as well. *Curious, indeed.* Lord Abbott glanced to Viola, who had also caught the accidental exchange. She looked extremely distressed, though he could not say whether it was the doctor's words or the troubling predicament that had befallen the town that caused her consternation.

"Oui, Monsieur. Dans mon jardin, j'en ai tout un tas de lavande." Lisette shook her head in frustration. *"Pardon, monsieur.* I am very distressed." She took a moment to collect herself. "I meant to say that in my garden, I have plenty of lavender. If you are able to collect the other herbs you require, I would be 'appy to sew them all."

"I will give what I have!" shouted someone in the crowd.

"I will, too!" shouted another.

Simon turned to the men standing with him on the platform and nodded. The villagers had begun to turn from their panic to offering useful assistance, for that would help take their minds off the fear they felt.

"D'ye's need anythin' else?" called out yet another.

"Vinegar." Simon turned to the crowd and called out. "I have read that there is a disinfecting property to vinegar. We will need as much as can be collected!"

"We'll give all we've got, Doctor!"

"What else, sir?"

"The afflicted will require fresh air, plenty of rest and liquids. I shall need to be supplied daily with clean water and broth, as well as clean bedding, such sheets, quilts and the like as can be spared, as often as possible. I shall need fires burning constantly, as the infected bedding will be burned; therefore whatever you can spare will be urgently needed, the same with firewood. We will need help to organize these tasks each day. As to the healthy, wipe yourselves down with vinegar as much as possible. Fresh air is better than the tainted air inside a closed dwelling. The night's are now warm enough, I suggest you all take your bedding outside and sleep there."

"Sleep upon the ground? Absolutely not. The very idea...," sniffed Hester Barlow.

Simon had one more thought. "When we run out of food and supplies, I propose that we collect what coins as can be spared and leave them in vinegar at the boundary stone with a list of what we have run short of. Perhaps someone from outside the village would offer assistance in collecting the items we require."

Gussie spoke up. "If I can get word to Archie, 'e'll be 'appy to do it.

Lord Abbott nodded. "Aye, Gussie. I will ride out to Nathan Treadwell at the boundary stone and make the arrangements."

"How long are we to be quarantined, sir?"

"Per the King's decree, when we are five weeks free from infection, the disease shall have been deemed to have run its course."

"We're to be quarantined for five weeks?" shouted a frightened woman from the crowd.

"I'm afraid you misunderstand, Madam. The quarantine will be lifted five weeks after the last soul falls ill. That could be five weeks—or five months, or more, from now." The woman fainted.

Catherine wandered through the square desperately looking for Miles. Simon stepped from the platform and worked his way through the crowd to her side.

"Have you seen Miles? Did he go to Master Seton's cottage?" she asked, desperately worried.

"I am afraid, Lady Catherine, that I am unaware of who was in attendance."

Her spirits sank. "I am in such fear for what lies ahead," she confessed.

He leaned down and took her hands in his grasp, the concern etched deeply in his eyes. She did not shrink from his gentle touch. "I will do my best to keep you and your family safe," he whispered. Tears sprang to her eyes at his kindness. All around her people clung together, trying to grasp the sheer enormity of what lay ahead. She saw Thomas Woollsey pass by. She stopped him.

"Mr. Woollsey! If I may ask, when you were at Master Seton's cottage, did you happen upon Viscount Houghton?"

He doffed his cap. "Aye, M'Lady, I did, indeed."

Catherine nearly wept in relief.

"As we left Master Seton's cottage on our way back t' the village, we came upon him out on the road. I told 'im that the master had died of the plague and that the doctor were about t' call fer' a quarantine. E' said e' were going on out to Master Seton's farm to speak to the Lord Mayor. An' that's the last I seen of 'im, M'Lady."

The gnawing sense of unease that she felt earlier returned with a vengeance. Shaking, Catherine pushed her way through the villagers toward the ceremony platform where Lord Abbott stood with the mayor and Simon.

"Lord Mayor!" she called. The men immediately turned toward Catherine. Hearing an unfamiliar urgency in her voice, Lord Abbott stepped off the platform. Catherine spoke rashly. "I apologize for the intrusion, Lord Mayor, but I…I am unable to find Viscount Houghton. I was told that he rode out to speak with you at Master Seton's cottage—is that true?"

The men looked from one to another, puzzled. Lord Abbott took her hands and spoke gently.

"My dear, Miles never arrived at the cottage."

Catherine went numb with fury. Miles had abandoned her. He had abandoned them all.

CHAPTER 28

"BUT LORD, HOW EMPTY THE STREETS ARE, AND MELANCHOLY, SO MANY POOR SICK PEOPLE IN THE STREETS, FULL OF FEVERS, AND SO MANY SAD STORIES OVERHEARD AS I WALK."
-SAMUEL PEPYS

Village of Wells
Buckinghamshire, England
27 July 1665

A pale nimbus of candle flame threw flickering, otherworldly shadows upon the densely thicketed woodlands encircling the pastures. Lord Abbott held a creaking iron lantern aloft as he picked his way through the brambles and stones that littered the sylvan berm. A faint slash of moon in a flat, inky sky did little to light his way. Damp leaves and detritus from a brief midnight rain clung to his bare feet. He stumbled slightly on a slippery patch of mud, catching the sleeve of a linen nightshirt borrowed from the mayor on a cluster of wild gooseberry nettles. Rustling leaves and sharp twigs scratched at his face as he pushed through the briars, tearing at his cheeks now mercifully freed from the incessant, oversweet aroma of the lavender and bergamot-filled plague mask. He never felt the stings. Wrenching his sleeve from the thorns, Lord Abbott pressed on, his heart heavy from the sheer devastation that had gripped the village in abject fear and aching sadness over the long summer weeks since that first day in May.

Twisting from the nettles, Lord Abbott scuffled headlong into an intricate fretwork of spider webs that glowed in the candlelight between the brambles. He stopped to wipe the webbings from his skin. Pulling the sticky filaments away, he took a moment to collect his bearings. In the warmth of the summer night, his thin cotton nightclothes clung to the dampness on his skin. The chirps from thousands of crickets reverberated through the woodlands, filling the soft air with their raucous sounds. He breathed in deeply, reveling in the languid, sweet scent of honeysuckle. He impulsively plucked a trumpet-shaped blossom from a hanging vine and held the end of the flower to the tip of his tongue. He closed his eyes, savoring the exquisite sweetness of the honeyed droplet. He felt completely at peace. He whispered a quiet prayer of gratitude for his very life itself, and then walked on, offering up a second prayer of gratitude for the doctor whose presence in the village was but a felicitous gift. *The lad had done well. Very well, indeed.* The fearsome outbreak had been a dreadful visitation upon Wells, but the young doctor had proved both a commendable intellect and a calming temperament that had slowly reassured the panicked townspeople enough to concentrate their efforts to holding the contagion at bay.

Poor old Maudie, she had perished after Seton, he thought, sadly, picking his way down the faint, unfamiliar footpath. After rolling up her sleeves and taking charge of the monumental task of converting the stalls to habitable accommodations, she had fallen to the excruciating headaches, fevers and frightful hallucinations. *She was gone in but two days time*, he grieved. *Such was the devastating speed of this merciless, foul pestilence.* Both Barlowe sisters had succumbed soon after. Even young Toby who had suffered such agonies from the horse accident now lay desperately ill upon a pallet. *Aye, though the lad does indeed have a good deal of fight in him,* thought Lord Abbott, praying yet again for the stable boy he'd grown terribly fond of. Desperate prayers and fearful lamentations seemed to enshroud the entire village. In all, seven were this day dead and five more lie grievously ill in the stables. The doctor alone worked day and night in a desperate attempt to cure them all.

One foot in front of t'other, he whispered to himself in the darkness. He stepped on a sharp pebble. He cried out and recoiled, then bent down and cast the pebble into the thicket and absently wiped away the blood that trickled from a gash on the sole of his foot. He continued his way toward the pasturelands, contemplating these last unimaginable weeks. *Aye', but wasn't he proud of the way his Catherine had borne up, though.* She had willingly pitched in with the chores and gratefully clothed herself in the humble garments that had been collected by the townspeople for those visitors caught up in the quarantine; her own gown worn to shreds from nearly three months continuous wear. She had even helped Gussie with the birth of Pricilla Larkin's baby when Nathan Treadwell, who now all but lived in a wagon at the boundary stone, had turned the midwife back to Gravesleigh. *Rose of Sharon, they called her. And a beautifully apt name it was indeed, for she had been but the barest hint of glorious light in this summer of dreadful darkness. Just as Catherine had been his own source of light in these troubled days.* Lord Abbott knew she was highly distressed by Miles's desertion, yet in all these weeks she had spoken nary a word to it. She kept to her own private counsel, preferring instead to immerse herself in communal chores of the village. Viola, he suspected, had something to do with her seemingly loyal silence. The lad's cowardly defection only reinforced his grievous misgivings on the union.

Aye, Miles had deserted, while Viola had immediately taken to the best room at the inn, and had yet to venture forth. Those two had indeed been cut from the same uncharitable cloth. Though he spoke not a word to it, his own sister acutely discomfited him, for not once had she offered aid or assistance, but rather in her retreat, required a tray set before her door each day. *The maids in the inn had quite enough to do, save waiting on a self-serving spinster,* he fretted. To the contrary, Catherine had not once complained of the quarantine or claimed a privilege. They had all worked side by side to survive. *Whatever did peerage and titles mean anymore in the face of the terrifying and cruel ravages of the plague? Peerage and titles mean absolutely nothing for the vicious pestilence knows no rank. This, he knew.*

Breathing heavily, Lord Abbott stumbled once more on the dark, uneven path. Holding the lantern higher, he at last rounded a copse and looked down upon the stables that lay in the distance below the berm. One single, soft light shone from the doorway of an open stall. He limped down the damp, grassy hillock toward the pale glow. Approaching the stable rows, he hesitated at the Heartbreak Line, the rope that had been laid in a wide circle well out from the long, low buildings. Named after the first devastating deaths, the line held back the grief-stricken families that stood sobbing behind the rope, frantically aching to touch, to embrace and comfort their mothers, fathers, children and friends in desperate illness, or to cling to and whisper heartbroken farewells in death.

He exhaled slowly. Then, Lord Abbott took one single, decisive step across the rope. He limped through the stables to the open door and knocked softly upon the jamb. Looking inside, Lord Abbott saw Simon perched upon a milking stool next to the hay-filled pallet where young Toby lay, pale and sweating, tenderly wiping the boy's feverish brow with a damp washing rag. The strong, acrid scent of vinegar permeated the stall. Simon jerked his head toward the doorway in surprise, for none were accorded admittance to the stables lest they, themselves, had taken ill. Lord Abbott weakly held the lantern up to his ashen, feverish face and simply nodded.

CHAPTER 29

Catherine awoke to a strange and vaguely troubling sense of disquietude. From the feather pallet on her rope-strung bedstead, she craned her neck and looked out through the open window to a clear blue dawning sky. A rooster crowed in the courtyard. The sounds of soft snorts and the occasional whinny from the distant pasture drifted in on the slight breeze that briefly ruffled the hem of her cotton window coverings, before falling flat against the plastered wall once again. *Something is terribly wrong,* she thought, though she could not make manifest the exact source of her unease. She cleared her throat. It felt vaguely as though she had swallowed a rasp. Catherine arose and quickly dressed in a plain cotton gown and apron that hung from a wall peg. Something caught her eye. A piece of parchment folded and slipped under the doorway. She instantly recognized her father's distinct, flowing script. She reached down with shaking hands and unfolded the paper and read the missive. The parchment floated to the floor.

Catherine raced across the courtyard and down the hillock to the stables. She stopped just short of the Heartbreak Line and stared down at the rope that lay on the dirt. *One single, ordinary rope, pitiless in its solitary duty, impervious and unyielding to anguished tears and sorrowful keenings, impregnable by all but the ill-fated who one by one stepped across its sad boundary.* She hesitated.

From the stalls, she saw Simon carrying in his heavy leather-gloved hands a soiled clay chamber pot. Though he was sweating from a heavy woolen cape and the woven scarf that he had wrapped around his face, it was the most suitable protective costume he could cobble together. Simon walked to the row of fire pits the stable boys had dug beyond the stables. The fires now burned day and night in an attempt to keep the infection at bay. He made ready to throw the contents of the clay pot into one of the pits. Catherine wavered at the line.

"Stop!" he cried through his mask, the shout muffled.

"My father!" she called out, looking up. "Is he ill? I beg of you, sir, please tell me!"

"Remain where you stand!"

Simon threw the waste upon the fire, turning his head from the foul, fetid odor. Catherine saw him take a deep breath through his herb mask, then bend down and with a small spade, scooped glowing coals into the pot. He swirled them around before throwing them back onto the fire. Simon set the pot into the coals for a few moments, turning the pot on all sides with a pair of iron tongs, then pulled it out and placed it on the ground. He removed the cape and scarf and threw them over a line that had been strung from the stable to a tree above the fires. Smoke and heat from the fire billowed through and around the cape. He strode toward Catherine.

"Where is your mask?" he yelled. "I have not worked day and night these many weeks to spare the village only for you to recant the measures I have set into place," he " he yelled, sounding vexed beyond all measure. With his short, tousled hair tumbling askew and deep circles under his eyes, Simon looked as though he hadn't slept in weeks.

Catherine fumbled through the pocket of her apron and tied the mask in place. "I…I'm sorry, I was not thinking. Please tell me, is my father in one of the stalls?" she cried out once again.

He looked at her determined, fearful eyes behind the mask and softened. *She is as aggravating as she is beautiful.* Through the fog of exhaustion, his compassion returned. He immediately softened. "Yes. In the night."

Catherine turned at the sound of Gussie crying out by the wash barrels the villagers had brought to the stable well just this side of the line. Gussie dropped the sheets she had just washed into a heap on the dirt, then sagged down upon the edge of the stone well and clutched at her apron, picking nervously at the hem. Eliza, pitching in on the wash, reached out to offer a comforting hug.

Tears sprang to Catherine's eyes. She gathered her skirts to cross the rope.

"No! Are you ill?" he demanded quickly.

She hesitated. She looked back to Gussie. More villagers had begun to cluster together at the well to watch the unfolding drama. She could feel all eyes upon her. *How could she expect the others to follow the doctor's measures if she herself renounced them? How could she expect others to bear the sacrifice and heartache of being held far from their loved ones if she were to cross the line for her own selfish needs?* Catherine saw Gussie call out to Eliza's.

"Fetch Lady Abbott!"

Catherine saw a mutinous smirk spread across Eliza's face. She strained to hear. " Aye'n won't I be all the more chuffed to drag tha' old bat from her room. A tray indeed!" Eliza collected her skirts and scuttled up the hill toward the inn.

Gussie began to run toward Catherine.

"Aye, Lassie…"

Catherine stood stock still, looking as though she was desperately weighing the right course from the wrong. She swallowed. There it was. The flinty rasp was still in her throat. She slowly raised both hands and stopped Gussie mid-flight.

"Stay back, Gussie!"

Gussie stopped instantly and cried out. "No! Not ye' both!"

Catherine turned to Simon. "I…I fear that I, too, am unwell."

His spirits sank. *Not her.* He dropped his shoulders in fatigue. He began to pace, his hand raking through his hair, disheveling it further. He stopped and stared at her from head to toe.

She does not seem ill. She appears to have none of the fevers, the tremblings and the direful exhaustion that the others have made manifest. "Do you understand that the very moment you step across this line, I cannot protect you?" he fretted, pacing the other direction. "I have made careful observations of the ill these many weeks and I have made a careful notations as to which treatments were fruitful and which treatments were not, and although I have tried my very best to understand, I yet do not know how this foul pestilence spreads from one person to the next," he confessed. He could see the fear and torment in her eyes. He felt the agonizing torment himself. He was tired. Bone-achingly, desperately, utterly tired. *Should he stand his ground and turn her away? Perhaps the infection is in a nascent phase. Or, perhaps she intends to simply ignore his authority and do as she damn well pleases.* Either way, Simon was no longer in no mood to quarrel. He was desperate for the help. He stopped pacing and stood before her.

"Lady Catherine, I ask again. Do you understand that I cannot guaranty your safety in any way?"

She hesitated once again, and then, nodding, spoke slowly. "I do."

Gussie gasped and held her hands to her heart. Simon looked up to see Eliza leading Viola down the hill toward the others who stood by the well. They all watched, transfixed, as Simon slowly moved aside. He could see Viola clinging desperately to Eliza as Catherine lifted her skirts and with one step, crossed over the heartbreak line.

"Tell me please, where does my father lay?"

Simon pointed down to an open stall at the end of the first row. "At the end."

Catherine glanced back to see Aunt Viola slowly sagging into Eliza's arms. For a moment, she wavered in her resolve, but the sad thought of her beloved father lying alone in the stables served to fortify her nerve. She put her fingers to her lips and blew a soft kiss toward her aunt, and then with her heart in her throat, Catherine turned her back and ran toward the stables. Reaching the last doorway, she set her hands upon the jamb and caught her breath. She hesitated a moment, unsure of what she would see, and then Catherine looked inside.

Lord Abbott lay upon a straw pallet. A brightly patterned quilt was pulled close to his chin. His soft blue eyes were closed to the bright morning light that streamed through the open portal. Highly fastidious in his personal kit, she was shocked to see a hint of white whisker-stubble upon his face. He moaned softly. By turns both shivering and sweating, he lay miserable and spent upon the pallet.

"Father?" she whispered, her tears falling freely.

He slowly turned his head and with a great deal of effort, lifted his eyelids. His eyes burned brightly. His skin, his muscles, the very hair on his head ached beyond all endurance. Catherine stood backlit in the doorway. In the myopic haze of fever, he thought she was an incandescent apparition sent from the angels themselves, until at last she came into focus.

"Cassie, m'lassie," he croaked, his voice faint from exhaustion. He managed a weak smile. She nearly dissolved into tears again. Her heart shattering, Catherine took a deep breath, and then stepped into the small chamber. Though the wooden walls and planked floor had been freshly washed down and swept, the quarters were redolent still of the thick, sweet scent of hay and horseflesh. A clay chamber pot, a small milking stool and a bucket of water had been placed near the pallet. A bale of hay sat on the opposite wall by the door.

Lord Abbott moaned again, and licked his dry, cracked lips. Catherine ran to the bucket and scooped up a ladle of water. She pulled the milking stool next to his pallet and gently lifted his head, touching the ladle to his lips. He took a cooling sip. Small rivulets of water ran down his neck. He tried to wipe them away, but the strength had left his arms. He smiled ruefully, letting the water run, dampening his nightclothes. She held the ladle to his lips once again. He took a second sip. He grimaced as he swallowed, then fell back onto the pallet once more and closed his eyes. She untied the strings of her apron and dipped the hem into the water. She laid the cool, damp cloth gently across his brow and sat quietly until her father fell asleep. She watched his chest rise and fall with faint, shallow breaths, then Catherine leaned her head back against the planked wall and cried as though her heart would break.

Scuffling footfalls outside broke through the descending fog of sadness that threatened to overwhelm her. She collected herself, wiped her eyes and looked toward the doorway. Simon's broad shoulders seemed to fill the opening. He held up a brown glass bottle and several cloths, and then set them upon the ground outside the stall next to a heavy overcloak and woolen scarf.

"Lady Catherine, I much prefer that you remain isolated in your own stall." He faltered. "However, in truth, I… I could use the help.

She readily nodded her assent. "By all means."

"If you will care for your father, I will tend to the rest. Toby seems to be making a recovery, but the others…" He furrowed his brow in weary concern, and then he, too, collected his thoughts. He pointed to the bottle and cloths. "Wash yourself down with the vinegar each time you touch your father. Wipe down even your clothing. I have not yet taken ill, so perhaps there is indeed a disinfecting quality to it." He pointed to the cloak and scarf. "I know the summer air is yet warm, however I have also worn these when tending to the ill. They may offer some protection, so I ask that you to please wear them when you are in the stalls." He looked over at Lord Abbott lying so desperately sick and shook his head, incredulous at the thought of how lively and welcoming his jovial host from Bealeton House had been not so very long ago. "I'll look in later," he said, softly.

Catherine stepped outside and poured the vinegar on the cloth, careful not to spill even a drop of the life-saving liquid. She vigorously wiped her hands and neck, and then, momentarily lifting the mask, her face. She even wiped down the bodice and skirt of her gown. From his pallet, Lord Abbott groaned. She retied her mask tighter, and donned the cloak and scarf, then went back into the stall. Sitting quietly upon the hay bale, Catherine watched him slumber.

Night fell. Smoke from the fire pits wafted through the air. Catherine herself had fallen into a dreamless sleep. She awoke with a start and looked over in fear at her father. He lay sleeping, pale and hollow-eyed, but breathing still. The ache in her stomach seemed not to be only from the uneasy fear that had gripped her earlier. She was hungry. Catherine arose and stepped from the stall into the stable yard in search of food.

Wandering through the stables rows, she quietly marveled at the way the villagers had recovered from the shock at the arrival of the plague and how they had pulled together as one to survive. The Lord Mayor had immediately assumed leadership of the town, capably dividing the tasks to each according to their skills.

The quarantine had indeed been a strain upon them all, but they had made the best of it. Eliza and Gussie took responsibility for cooking meals for the visitors who had been quarantined to the inn from the outlying villages since May Day. They also cooked and delivered broth and warm bread from the baking shed for both Simon and those who lay ill in the stables. Each morning, noon and eventide, freshly made, hot chicken broth was poured from a big copper kitchen pot into a wooden bucket that Simon placed at the rope. Water from the well was poured into a barrel that he could dip from when he needed it. Simon even requested that his meals be portioned onto planks of wood that could be burned in the fire when he finished, so that nothing that had been touched on the stable side of the rope ever crossed back to the villagers.

Stable boys kept the wood supplies stocked for the fires

that burned day and night behind the stables. The woman kept themselves busy stitching and stuffing linen covered hay pallets, desperately praying that no one they knew would need the pallets they sewed, for upon each sad death, Simon required everything in the stalls to be burned to ashes. They all seemed to bathe in the vinegar. *The sharp odor will forever bring back memories of these desperate summer days of the plague.*

Catherine wandered toward the fire pits where she found Simon sitting upon a bench eating the last of a roasted chicken from a wooden plank. His mask hung down from strings about his neck. Flames from the fire cast a warm glow upon his pale, freckled skin and unruly, straw-blond waves that had at last begun to grow out. Not for the first time did she dare to think how handsome he was. He rose, immediately reaching for his mask.

"Good evening, Lady Catherine," he asked, fumbling with the strings. "How is your father?"

"He sleeps this hour."

"Good. Rest is essential." *Rest is essential? You sound like old Dr. Clarke speaking to a child. Grab hold of your wits!* He tied the knots in place, searching for something, anything else to say. "Are…are you perhaps hungry, Lady Catherine?"

"I am, indeed."

He pointed to a second plank of chicken on a worktable that he had dragged over to the fire pits. "I requested a portion for you. I think it best if we not touch each other's food, else I would serve it you."

"That is not necessary, Doctor. Thank you," she said, taking the plank in hand. He watched as she sat on a nearby log, untied her mask and gratefully began to eat. *She is as beautiful in these simple clothes as she was in her magnificent gowns. Perhaps even more so.* She looked up and smiled at him, unselfconsciously eating the chicken with her fingers. Embarrassed to have been caught watching her, he looked down and stared into the fire.

"Perhaps… you would consider calling me Simon?"

She nodded, licking the juices that ran down the back of her hand. "Catherine. Please."

"That does indeed make things simpler." A flaming log suddenly snapped and cracked apart sending a torrent of sparks swirling skyward. The glowing bits of ash lit her face, illuminating the copper curls that fell carelessly over the exquisite angles of her cheekbones. He was unnerved more than he thought possible. *Why does she have this confounding effect upon me?* He reached for a nearby stick and shoved the log back into the center of the pit, causing the flames to flare. His eyes fell to the gold band on her finger that glimmered in the momentary flash, rendering him to silence. He furrowed his brow and stabbed at the fire again.

Catherine felt a disturbing sense of unease in his presence, though she could not say why. *Perhaps he thinks that I am not unwell enough to have crossed the line.* Her temper rose, momentarily. *What proof does he require?* She concentrated on her chicken, stacking the bones carefully to the side of the plank. *And yet, he desires nothing more than to spare the town from unspeakable grief. Perhaps I have once again judged him too harshly.* This time it was Catherine who searched for words to break the discomfiting silence. *His book. She could speak to his scientific enquiries.*

"I read your book, Simon. I…I would have returned it to you had not the quarantine kept me in Wells. I apologize."

"No, no! Please, keep it as a gift, Lady… Catherine." He hesitated a moment, then could not restrain his curiosity. "Did you find it at all interesting?"

"I did!" Her face lit up with genuine interest. "Though I confess that I did not understand the entirety of it, I can certainly see where you have put your ideas to use here in the village."

He looked at her sharply. "It held your attentions?"

She blushed in the firelight. "I found it extraordinary," she said softly. It was his turn to blush. They both stared into the crackling flames that illuminated their faces in the darkness.

"Why did you become a physician?" she asked, softly, afraid of prying.

His mother. The screams haunt me in the night still. So much blood. How could he possibly confess his childhood fears to Catherine? And yet, she may be the only soul who could truly understand.

"Were you afraid?" he asked softly.

"When?"

"The maid's childbirth. Eliza told me you how sewed up the tear."

"Yes. I was. Terribly afraid." She watched as a single spark drifted upwards into the trees, then looked to him with an intensity burning in her eyes. "But, Simon, I confess that I was exhilarated, as well. I was both by turns sickened and afraid, and yet, I felt enormously privileged to have saved her life."

Embarrassed by her outpouring of emotion, she looked down. Her eyes fell upon the wide gold band on her finger. *Miles.* Another wave of melancholia washed over her, at the memory of how he desperately pulled her away from the maid, how he quietly disapproved of her helping Toby and how he had deserted her and the town at the very first opportunity. *Yet, I have given him my troth. I have given a promise to my father, and I shall indeed carry it through.* She sighed. She stared across the flames at the strong and capable man who willingly gave of himself to help the entire town. "In all truth, I was proud that I had even tried to save her life, if that makes any sort of sense."

"It does." He stabbed at the fire. *She was indeed a kindred spirit.* He took a deep breath and opened his heart to memories he tried so hard to forget. Leaves overhead ruffled in a sudden, cooling breeze over the heat of the fire pits. He poked mindlessly at the coals, lost in thought, and then looked up, straight into her eyes. "My mother died in childbirth when I was but ten years old." He paused. "My father died that same night. Of the drink." He shook his head in both sorrow and frustration. "I could do nothing to save my mother. I could do nothing to save either of them. I swore an oath to God himself that I would never be that helpless again."

Tears sprang to her eyes at the thought of a young Simon losing both mother and father the same night. She thought of her own aching loss.

"My mother died giving birth to my brother, Charles," she said, her voice soft with the memory. "I know the sadness."

They sat silently, each lost in memories. A moth flew erratically over Simon's head. Catherine looked at him with curiosity.

"May I ask why you changed your name?"

Simon brushed the moth away. "I did not change my name." My name really is Simon McKensie."

"On the book, then. Why are you called Marlowe?"

Simon drew a breath and held it, thinking of the legal threat that hung heavy over him. *Would it even matter now? In the face of such dreadful calamity as has befallen London, would any of it possibly matter?* He looked at her beautiful face, gazing at him with such interest. He exhaled, finally at peace with confession. "I broke the law."

Confusion clouded her features. These were not the words she expected to hear.

"I…I'm afraid I don't understand."

"There are such perplexities, you see…" Her face contorted with confusion. He tried again. "There…there are such things as I cannot yet comprehend, so I…" He stared into the fire, and then simply gave up. He looked straight at her. She perched forward on the log, her hands clasped under her chin with curiosity. "I paid men in service to the church to exhume the bodies they had just buried, so that I could perform autopsies, you see. For the research in my book." He drew another deep breath. "And that, Catherine, is against the law." *There. He'd said it. Aloud.* The torturous, heavy weight of criminality that he carried these long months seemed to instantly dissipate like the petals of a wildflower in the wind. He felt nothing but relief. He dared a sidelong glance at her. At first, she said nothing. He could see her turning his crimes over in her mind. The crushing weight instantly returned. *She condemns me for my actions. Damnation! I should have kept my own counsel.* She considered him for a moment.

"What is it like?" she asked quietly. He looked up in surprise. "Medical school, I mean. What is it like to operate on someone?"

He was thunderstruck. *She seems not troubled in the least by my crimes.* He thought about it.

"Frightening, at first, if I'm honest. But then, the more you operate, the more you to understand that there are great mysteries to be solved by simple observation.

"I should like to see an operating theater one day, if ever that were possible." *For a woman,* was the phrase she did not voice aloud.

That she was a woman did not even register in his thoughts, so excited was he by her interest. "You would find it fascinating, Catherine, because you see, once one mystery is solved, there are an infinite number more to decipher." He became pensive. "This pestilence, for example. It is confounding beyond measure." Simon stared into the flames, suddenly lost in his own troubled, agitated thoughts. "I cannot decipher this Gordian knot." He balled his fists. "Toby will live, and yet other children have died. Mrs. Farleigh will live, and yet, other elders have died." He pounded his fist on his knees. "I cannot seem to make the connection between who lives and who dies. Am I not intelligent enough to see what must be right before my own eyes?"

She caught his gaze, her voice breaking with an impassioned sincerity. "Simon, you are by far one of the most intelligent men I have ever met."

It was his turn to duck his head in embarrassment. The soft cracklings of the fire hung in the silence. Bits of glowing ash curled upwards toward the massive London plane trees that towered over the stable rows. Simon bowed the stick idly with his thumbs. He furrowed his brow in deep concentration. "There is something I am missing," he brooded, bending the branch. "It lays right here before me, right here in Wells, and yet, I cannot see it, for the cause of the infection and its spread remains unknown to me." He bent the stick as far as it would go until it snapped in half, startling them both. He threw both pieces into the fire in sheer frustration. "It is a damnable puzzlement!" He looked at Catherine, instantly chagrined. "I…

I apologize."

"Please don't apologize, Simon, she said softly. "You have been but a godsend to us!" She thought of something. "You have been quarantined just as the ill have been so you do not yet know, but through the few leaflets that have been left at the boundary stone, we are given to understand that untold thousands have died in London. Yet here in Wells, your measures have limited our sorrows to just seven souls." They sat quietly for a moment, watching the fire burn. She cocked her head at him and spoke softly. "Simon, I have read your book and I have watched you put into practice your ideas of isolation, quarantine, and scientific observation. Those ideas have saved us such sorrows and we are grateful to you, Simon." Her voice dropped to a whisper. "So very grateful." They sat in silence. An idea occurred to her. "Have you kept a journal of your efforts?"

She was singularly the most intriguing woman he had ever before met in his life. "I have, Catherine. Would you perhaps like to see it?"

"I would, indeed." She had another thought. "The rendering at the end of your book… Is that really what the heart looks like?"

"Yes,' he ducked his head, sheepish. "Though I'm not much of an artist."

She laughed, softly. "Nae', not much, indeed," she teased.

An earth-shattering crash from a stall at the end of the row resounded throughout the stables, startling them both. They instantly leapt to their feet. Catherine threw her plank into the fire and reached for her mask and cloak. Simon did the same, grabbing the lantern on the way.

"My father!" she cried.

CHAPTER 30

"EVERY DAY SADDER AND SADDER NEWS OF ITS INCREASE. IN THE CITY DIED THIS WEEK ... 6,102 OF THE PLAGUE. BUT IT IS FEARED JUST THIS WEEK THAT THE TRUE NUMBER ... IS NEARER 10,000"
-SAMUEL PEPYS

They raced through the stablerow until they reached Lord Abbott's stall. Simon held the lantern high and stepped inside. Lord Abbott lay still upon the wooden floorboards, the chamber pot soiled.

"Stay back!" Simon cried to Catherine as he dropped to his knees and set his hands upon Lord Abbott's chest. He looked up. "He lives."

For the second time that day, Catherine broke down in tears. Lord Abbott slowly opened his eyes, much confused as to his whereabouts. Simon held a damp cloth to his forehead. Lord Abbott struggled to rise, but was held back by Simon.

"Rest a moment, then I will help you to bed."

Tears streaming, Catherine sat upon the bale of hay and watched as Simon carefully helped Lord Abbott back to his pallet and covered him with the quilt. He reached over and drew a ladle of water from the bucket. He held it to Lord Abbott's lips. Lord Abbott took the ladle into his trembling hands and spilt nearly all of the water onto his nightshirt. Simon patiently tried again, this time holding the ladle firmly. Lord Abbott took a sip then lay back, violently shaking with fever once again. Catherine was terrified at the sight.

A quiet knock at the doorway interrupted Simon's ministrations. Lisette stood at the door, her eyes anguished above her mask. Time seemed to stand still.

"Excusé moi, s'il vous plait," she whispered. *"Je suis malade."*

"Dear God," breathed Catherine, overcome completely with emotion.

Simon rose and hurried toward Lisette. He pointed to the chamber pot. "Do not go near the effusion. I will return to dispose of it once Miss Chanon is settled." He gestured to Lisette. "Follow me," said Simon, taking the lantern with him.

As the quiet, shuffling footfalls faded and the stall fell dark, Catherine perched upon the stool next to her father. She waited as he lay in a pale shaft of light from the faint sliver of moon until at last he fell asleep, then she rose and walked softly to the doorway to wash herself down with vinegar. She was growing to despise the sharp, tangy smell that now permeated every inch of the stable yard. Even the lavender and sweet hops-scented mask she wore day and night could not temper its acrid vapors. Catherine leaned against the jamb, and stared up to the vast, starry sky in complete wonderment at the inexplicable order of the universe. *What possible manner of sense does this suffering make?* She thought of her father lying so deathly ill on a pallet of straw and was suddenly overcome with aching tears. *How could she possibly carry on without her beloved father, how could she live without the man who in his simple and kind heart tried to do right by every single person he met.* Her only response was the soft, plaintive hooting of an owl echoing across the empty stable yard. She stared at the sky until the moon fell behind the trees. Sighing, she wiped her tears and walked back into the stall. She drew the cloak around her, then quietly lay down upon the hay and finally closed her eyes.

Catherine awoke once again to an overwhelming dread she could not quell. She sat up quickly, jerking her head toward her father. He was sleeping still. Stiff from lying the night on the hard bale of hay, she stood and rubbed her sore shoulders. She swallowed. The strange rasp in her throat still burned, but she felt no other afflictions. Her eyes fell upon the chamber pot. Simon had returned, for it had been emptied. She marveled that she had not awakened when he entered in the night.

Her father stirred, but did not open his eyes. Pulling the stool close, she sat anxiously by his side, horrified by the startling change in his countenance overnight. Rivulets of sweat ran from his forehead, dampening the elegant waves of gray hair at his temples. His ruddy cheeks were now alarmingly pale, almost waxen, the bones in his face stood in sharp relief. He moaned, and ran his tongue across dry, cracked lips. She reached for the water, but the bucket was nearly empty. He turned his head and fell silent once again. Catherine took up the handle and hurried outside to the cistern.

Running toward the water barrel out in front of the stables, she stopped short, for sitting on a chair under a tree just across the heartbreak line, *mending clothes* was Aunt Viola. Catherine was dumbstruck, for not once in her life had she had ever seen her aunt do anything one could call actual labor. Seeing Catherine, Viola stood and dropped the mending into a basket at her feet.

"What news of your father?" she called out, wringing her hands in worry.

Staying well back of the rope, Catherine shook her head, sadly. "He is not at all well, Aunt Viola."

Viola slowly sagged back onto the chair.

Catherine bent down and took hold of the bucket that sat empty upon the grass. She dipped it into the clear water. Her reflection wavered across the cool, dark surface. Watching as the water stilled, she was suddenly struck with the thought that she had very little sympathy for the woman who at every turn seemed determined to put herself above all others. Catherine froze. *Miles was cut from exactly the same cloth*. Her knees felt weak. She grasped at the barrel to steady herself and stared down at her reflection, nearly breathless from the shock of it. *Miles was a coward. He ran from the danger they all faced, while Simon ran straight toward it, willing to sacrifice his own life to try and save them all.* Setting her bucket on the edge of the barrel, Catherine had a most startling realization of her own. Her eyes fell upon the shimmering golden ring on her finger. Slowly at first, then all at once, she felt that singular little seed of rebellion, like the glowing ashes from the fire pit, rising in her once again. *How could she possibly marry Miles?* She took hold of the cistern bucket and resolutely poured the water into her own, filling it to the top. Then, Catherine turned to face her aunt and spoke the words that now held a very different meaning.

"I…I am so very sorry."

Viola reached down for the small pair of breeches she had been mending and wiped her eyes with the coarse linen fabric. She watched Catherine disappear into the stable rows. Eliza walked up behind Viola and, with great satisfaction, dropped another stack of clothes that needed mending into the basket at Viola's feet.

Catherine returned to her father's stall. He had once again fallen asleep, his breathing now shallow and labored. She stood by the pallet in helpless tears at his suffering. Catherine tightened the strings of her mask, then sadly wrapped herself in the cloak and sank onto the hay bale once more, watching the man she adored so very much slowly fade away.

By nightfall, his breathing had become strained. He drifted in and out of consciousness, restless with the fevers that burned hotly within him. She slipped into the stable yard, and pulled her mask down for a gulp of cool night air. She heard him stir, then cry out, his voice weak and tremulous. She raced back into the stall, tying the mask strings tighter. Her father slowly turned his head. He saw Catherine standing over him, wrapped once again in the cloak and scarf. He managed the barest trace of a smile.

"Cassie, m'lassie," he whispered.

"Father," she said, tears springing to her eyes.

He struggled to catch his breath. *He had so much to say.* "I have been so very proud of my children." He gazed up at her with tender pride. He tried again to speak, his words coming slowly. "My dearest girl. Not once in your life have either you or Charles ever troubled my soul." His voice grew faint. Catherine thought again of Miles, the guilt weighing heavily. Lord Abbott cleared his throat and gestured weakly for water. Catherine held the ladle to his lips, and then bowed her head at the rebellious thoughts stirring in her mind.

Simon looked in the doorway. "Would you like some broth, Lord Abbott?" Catherine fumbled with the ladle, splashing water on her father. Lord Abbott shook his head.

"I…I'm sorry, Father," she said, her cheeks flushing red. She looked to Simon with anguished tears falling. Simon nodded, sadly understanding.

"I will return soon," he whispered. He discreetly stepped from the doorway.

Lord Abbott watched them both. *There it was again.* Somehow, through the inexorable fog that was slowly and relentlessly descending over him, *he saw it.* Lord Abbott was now certain beyond measure that he had seen a spark in his daughter. *A spark that comes just once in a lifetime. The selfsame spark he felt for his beloved Tamesine.*

He turned his head and furrowed his brows in grave concern. "Catherine," his voice trailed off. He took a shallow breath and spoke again. "Catherine." He struggled to take another breath. "Find my solicitor in London, Josiah Winthrop. He… has my instructions." He closed his eyes, his words growing faint. "You will be well provided for, as will Viola and Charles." He struggled to breathe.

Catherine sat on the stool trembling with anxiety, her foot jouncing uncontrollably off the wooden floor. She fought the urge to be sick as tears streamed down her face.

"Cassie…"

She straight sat up, fearing what was to come. He gazed at her, his eyes misting over with soft emotion. He lifted his hand toward her. She grasped it tightly, sobbing.

"You must do everything you wish to do in this life."

He turned his head, staring blankly up to the roof boards. "Tamesine," he breathed, falling silent. He closed his eyes. And then, in one very quiet, transcendent moment, Lord Abbott was gone.

Stunned, Catherine stepped back and sagged onto the hay bale. Still wrapped in the cloak and mask, she drew her knees to her chest and began to cry, her heart, her very soul shattered. Walking through the stable row, Simon heard weeping from the last stall. He looked in the doorway and saw Lord Abbott lying still upon the pallet. He looked at Catherine, disconsolate in her grief.

"Catherine," he whispered.

She raised her head. Her mask was soaking wet on her tear-stained cheeks, her eyes, red-rimmed.

"You must leave the stall," he whispered, urgently. He gently held his hand out for her to take. She drew back from his reach, reluctant to leave her father alone. Simon gave her a moment, and then urged her once again. "We must leave."

She nodded and slowly stood. Catherine took one last look at the extraordinary man she adored, and then reluctantly stepped out into the stable row. Simon quickly soaked a cloth in the vinegar. After quickly wiping himself down, he turned and began to stroke her face, her neck, her hair and her clothing with the damp cloth. In her profound sorrow, Catherine stood helpless to his soft ministrations. He reached for her hands. He drew the wet cloth gently across her palms and across her wrists, and then turned her hands over and carefully stroked her fingertips. Her ring glittered in the lantern light. He looked away. Though filled with dread at the thought, he could no longer hold back the question that had simmered in his thoughts since the engagement party. He touched the ring.

"Do you love him?" he whispered.

She hesitated. The full weight of expectation and duty

overcame her, but she was now far too broken-hearted to maintain the fiction. She looked to the ground, unable to speak.

Simon turned away, deeply embarrassed at his ill-timed inquiry. "I… I apologize. 'Tis neither my concern, nor the time to speak of it. Please forgive me, he said, softly"

Catherine was silent for a moment, and then slowly, she lifted her anguished face to his, completely overcome with emotion. "No," she whispered. "I do not love him."

Simon instantly reached for Catherine, gathering her deep into his protective arms, and at last, she collapsed, her heart breaking into his broad-shouldered embrace. In the soft night air, they clung to each other in exhaustion and in sorrow. Simon swept her up and carried her to the bench by the fire. He held her tightly, rocking her back and forth, stroking her copper curls. Then, in the incandescent glow of the fire, he gently removed his mask, and then pulled on the strings of hers, letting them both fall to the ground. He took her face into his hands, and slowly kissed her forehead. She stared into his eyes, unable, unwilling to stop him. He kissed her again, his lips touching softly to her cheek, and then he drew back, wordlessly searching her eyes, entreating her consent. His eyes were filled with such tender concern, that suddenly, every restraint she had melted away. His lips instantly found hers. Catherine wrapped her arms around him, kissing him with a passion that belied her aching grief. As the embers faded into the night, the terribly sad realization that her father was gone once again overcame her and silent tears began anew. Simon held her, letting her cry until at last, exhausted and spent; she fell asleep cradled in the tender warmth of his embrace.

At length, Simon lay the sleeping Catherine on a blanket by the fire and covered her with a quilt, then quietly walked back towards Lord Abbott's stall. He pulled his cloak, scarf and mask tight once more, then donned a pair of leather gloves, and stepped inside. He covered Lord Abbott with extra fabric that had been sewn down the sides of the sheets, and then bound the shroud with several lengths of rope. Looping the ends of the rope over his shoulder, he trudged slowly out to the pasture fence where he had created a makeshift gravesite to quarantine the plague victims, even in death. Only the sounds of the hooting owls in the trees above and the crunching gravel below his feet could be heard on his sad journey. When at last he reached the edge of the pasture, he stopped next to seven freshly covered mounds, each marked by a simple wooden cross. Under the soft glow of the moon, he took spade in hand and shovelful by shovelful, dug one more trough. Then, with a very heavy heart, Simon returned Lord Abbott gently to the earth. When he finished, Simon took two sticks from a pile and with a mallet, nailed them together to form yet another cross. He pounded it gently into the ground. A scuffle of dirt caused him to look up. There, Catherine stood above him wrapped in the blanket, tears streaming down her face. She dropped the blanket and reached for him with both hands. He looked to her, questioning. Her father's words echoed in her mind. *You must do everything you wish to do.* She slowly nodded.

Simon stood, setting the mallet and spade against the wooden railing. Simon wrapped her once again in the blanket, and then gathered her close into his protective embrace. He carried her through a gate out into the pasture. There, on the grass under a billowing oak tree, he spread the blanket wide. Catherine unbuttoned her simple gown and stepped from it, her pale skin illuminated by the soft light of the moon playing through the craggy limbs. Simon cast his clothing to the grass. Taking her hand in his, Simon kissed her gently until all her tears were gone. They fell to the blanket, their lips gently grazing, each giving way to tender passion, skin touching bare skin, reveling in the sheer freedom from the heavy cloaks and sadness, savoring the soft, delicious touch of the other until they, at last, came together as one. The faint slip of moon had long fallen below the horizon when, exhausted and spent, they lay together in the dark. Listening to the soft, soothing night sounds, Catherine and Simon fell asleep, nestled deep in the warmth of their embrace.

Catherine awoke with the sun, the events of the night before a disorienting muddle. She lay quietly under the tree and tried to put together in her mind the fragmented shards of the night before. She looked down. The golden band upon her finger caught her eye. Suddenly, the shattering memories came flooding back, one after another. *Her beloved father was dead and she had found comfort in Simon's arms in the night. Worse, she had betrayed her engagement to Miles, for she had found Simon's embrace pleasurable beyond all measure.* Lying next to her in a languid half-sleep, Simon snuffled and reached out for her. *You must do everything in this life you wish to do.* Catherine lay in the morning light and gazed with wonder at the tousled straw-blond hair, the glint of sun off his pale lashes, the nose so gloriously straight that one could draw a line from bridge to tip and never waver, and slid straight into his waiting arms.

CHAPTER 31

van de Veld Linnenfabriek
Amsterdam, Holland
9 September 1665

Pieter van de Veld paced back and forth along the pathway outside the worker cottages behind the *linnenfabriek,* flinching at every tortured wail of the young woman in heavy labor. A cool, early autumn breeze rustled the leaves along a row of stately Dutch elm trees that hung over the cobbled stone path fronting the cottages. Another agonizing scream ripped through the quiet air. Though Pieter was as anxious as Johanna for the birth of the child, he wasn't entirely sure if he could listen to the panicked shrieks much longer. His knees felt weak at the sound of it.

Inside, Geertje lay on a feather pallet and grasped for Johanna's hand, squeezing hard enough to crush bone. Johanna glanced at the midwife in deep concern, for although she and Pieter had adopted many children through the years, this baby would be the first born by one of them. *Een kleinkind*, a grandchild, of sorts. Geertje screamed out once again. Sweat beads began to form across her forehead.

"Is dit normaal?" Johanna fretted, wincing from the pain.

Geertje howled once more as a sharp, searing pain shot like a knife through her abdomen.

The midwife chuckled. *"Ja, dit is normaal."* She fluffed the pillow beneath Geertje's head. Geertje irritably pushed her hand away and groaned. The midwife chuckled again. *"Ontspannen, Johanna. Zal het niet lang duren, nu.*

Johanna did not know she could possibly relax. She had been sitting with the girl since the first wretched spasm dropped her to her knees, and despite the reassuring words of the midwife that the baby was imminent, the wait felt frighteningly overlong. Poor Geertje had been laboring for nearly twenty-five excruciating hours. Geertje inhaled sharply, then screamed out once more.

"Daar is hij" smiled the midwife. The usually placid Johanna felt strange butterflies of excitement in her stomach. She reached up and re-pinned the loose strands of graying hair that had fallen into her eyes, then moved from the side of the rope-strung bedstead and settled onto a stool to await the imminent birth.

A young boy walked onto the *linnenfabriek* factory floor. He wore a post delivery sash across his tunic. He approached the first person he saw. "*Ik heb hier een brief voor Geertje de Groot.*" He held out a letter carefully wrapped with string.

"Ja, dank u," grunted a passing cart worker. He set the cart down and took the letter into his rough, beefy hands. He walked out to the cottages behind the factory, savouring a rare moment of peace from the clattering looms and the floating fibers that made his eyes itch. He found Pieter van de Veld pacing along the shaded, leafy path. Hearing an endless stream of anguished screams from the cottage, the worker's itchy eyes flew open wide. He quickly thrust the letter into the older man's hands.

"Voor het meisje." He jerked his chin toward the cottage and nearly ran back to the factory, anxious to escape the horrendous racket.

Pieter looked at the letter. It was indeed meant for Geertje. He held it up to the sunlight, and then turned it over. Something had been scrawled on the back. He squinted hard and managed to decipher the nearly incomprehensible scratchings from a Mrs. Rebecca Andrews. He sighed. Heavy hearted, Pieter knocked on the door of the cottage. After a moment, he knocked harder. The door opened a crack.

"Ja, Pieter?" Johanna peered out through the opening, perplexed at his intrusion at such an unsuitable moment. Inside the cottage, Geertje cried out once more. Her screams rose to an endless shriek then descended into a ferocious, guttural growl.

Pieter was beside himself. He pressed the letter into Johanna's hands and quickly retreated down the stone path to the safety of his office in search of *verscheiden biers*.

"Draai het om," he called over his shoulder.

Johanna looked down at the paper so carefully tied with string. As Pieter had instructed, she turned the letter over, curious as to what he thought was so important to have knocked on the cottage door. The rough handwriting on the back caught her attention. She held the letter close to read the words, then looked over to Geertje straining through the yet another excruciating contraction, and furrowed her brow in resigned sadness. With one last howl, Geertje grabbed her knees in desperation and bore down with every ounce of grit she had left. Johanna shoved the letter into her apron pocket and rushed over to the rope bed in time to watch as a screaming baby boy made his entrance into the world.

The midwife efficiently snipped through the birth cord, then swaddled the howling baby into the soft blanket that Geertje had woven in her last quiet days before the birth. The midwife handed the baby to an exhausted Geertje. She cradled the bawling boy in her arms, and then from a memory she thought long forgotten, Geertje quietly began to sing a folk song her mother once sang to her as a child in Arnhem. The boy began to mew softly. He chewed on his fist as he listened to the soothing melody. His eyelids began to droop, and then, in the sweet, gentle refuge of his mother's arms, the *mooie jongen* fell fast asleep. Geertje looked up to Johanna with a quiet radiance, a joy that Johanna had never before seen in her. It suddenly occurred to Johanna that she had never seen the girl smile, not even once. Holding the baby close in her arms, Geertje glowed with an ethereal beauty.

To Johanna's surprise, Geertje suddenly stretched her arms out and handed the sleeping child to her, the woman who had not once condemned her in her shame. Johanna had instead hugged Geertje, holding her close when she tearfully confessed her secret to the gentle woman who had ached for so long to hold a baby of her own. Johanna perched on the side of the bed and tenderly rocked the sleeping baby, the desperate ache she'd carried for so long, slowly melting away at the miraculous sight of a sleeping child in her arms. After a moment, she reached into her pocket and held the letter toward Geertje.

"Het is nieuws van jakob, mijn lieve meisje," she whispered, the tears staining her cheeks. As Geertje eagerly reached for the letter, she saw the sorrow in Johanna's eyes and instantly knew that Johanna's tears were not for the precious baby boy she held in her arms. She looked close and read the unfamiliar writing on the outside of the folded note tied carefully with twine. Geertje's radiant smile slowly faded. She stared at the scrawled message, then, Geertje let the unopened note fall from her fingertips. A single tear traced her cheek. Johanna reached over to wipe the tear.

Geertje reached out to take the baby back from Johanna and nuzzled her cheek to the baby's soft, round jowls. The baby snuffled and kicked in the blanket, and then with a tiny yawn, fell back to sleep. She watched him, mesmerized by his trusting innocence. *I will fight to my very death for this beautiful boy.* Heartbroken as she was, she knew her heart would never again be as full as it was at this very moment.

"Wat is zijn naam?" asked Johanna, as she reached out to stroke the shimmering wisps of his eyebrows.

Geertje looked down at the tiny baby sleeping so peacefully in her arms. She felt his chest rise and fall with each new breath. She inhaled deeply, smelling his sweet baby scent. She softly stroked his tiny fingernails in sheer wonderment. She reveled in the faint wisps and whorls of his blond hair. Jakob's hair. She looked up at Johanna.

"Jakob," she said simply. *"Zijn naam is Jakob,"* and in that single transcendent moment, holding her tiny son so very close in her arms, Geertje De Groot knew that she would never, ever again be alone.

CHAPTER 32

Village of Stockbridge
Buckinghamshire, England
11 September 1665

Catherine sat with Simon and Toby at the fire pit that over the long weeks of quarantine had become a gathering place for the few survivors. In the cool of this early autumn night, only the three of them sat by the fire, the others having gathered by the Heartbreak Line in anticipation of the momentous morning ahead. Toby held one of Charles' small hornbooks that had been brought to the stables in a box of supplies that Catherine had requested from the Abbey.

"Can you read the words?" asked Catherine."

"The b…b..boat f…f…floats…"The boat floats!" said Toby, excitedly.

Simon reached out and ruffled the boy's hair. "Well done, Toby!"

"He has been a very quick study," said Catherine. "When the quarantine is over, Toby has agreed to come to the Abbey to take lessons from Master Howell, haven't you Toby?"

Toby looked up, earnestly. "Aye, I want to be a doctor like Simon!" Unexpected tears sprang to her eyes. Simon gently set his hand upon hers.

"I know your father would approve in full measure, Catherine. He was quite fond of young Toby, here," said Simon. "As am I," he said, well pleased that the boy desired to follow in his footsteps. Catherine stood.

"And now, Toby, set the book aside, for the hour is late and it is time to go bed. Tomorrow will be a very big day." She stood and turned to Simon. "We are all so very grateful to you, Simon." With a tender look, Catherine whispered, "Good night."

Catherine took Toby by the hand and, together, they walked through the stable row to settle him in for the night. The lantern light glinted off the red curls that tumbled carelessly down her back as they walked to the stall. Simon could hardly believe his good fortune. Throughout the quarantine, Catherine had cared for the ill and tutored Toby by day, and in the evenings, she joined him by the fire, organizing his notes and research on the curative measures he took to stem the infection. Though he had desperately wished for another night in the pasture, he knew she was deeply troubled by her loyalties to her father, her aunt, and mostly, to Miles. He had not pressed. He watched the two of them walk together, holding hands. *Would that she were free of that cad.* Before taking Toby to his stall, she turned back and smiled. His heart leapt, for in the midst of such suffering and sorrow, he had never known such happiness.

Simon sat staring into the fire and contemplated everything they had been through since the first of May. In all, thirteen had perished. Lisette had been the last, succumbing just two days after Lord Abbott. Then suddenly, there were no more. With each passing day of each passing week, Simon began to allow himself the barest glimmer of hope. He knew the villagers felt the same, for one night during the fourth week with no new infection; the townspeople began to gather in the square to pray. At first, there were but a few. After that, more and thence more came to the square, until this night, when Simon looked upon the hill and saw that everyone in the village had gathered together, their lanterns held high. Father Jessup led them all in one last candlelight prayer for no new infections.

Dawn finally broke over the little village. There was no need of the cock's crow, for every last villager had gathered together once more at the Heartbreak Line, waiting anxiously for Simon to speak. On their side of the line, Simon stood with Catherine, Toby and five other survivors. Simon stepped up on a milk stool and raised his hands.

"As mysteriously as it arrived in Wells, the plague has officially run its devastating course, and on this, the one hundred and thirty second day, I am overjoyed to say the words we have all so longed to hear." He took a deep breath. "The quarantine is now over," shouted Simon. He stepped to the line, then turned and faced the survivors. Catherine and Toby stood with them, waiting with tears in her eyes.

"At long last, you are free to go."

To resounding cheers, those who had been held for weeks in quarantine grasped hands and together, ceremoniously crossed the line to the desperate embraces of those who anxiously awaited their loved ones return.

At the front of the crowd, the mayor watched with interest as Catherine and Simon stood next to one another. Though they did not converse, *a glance, an attraction passed between them.* Of that he was sure. *There is something there.* Simon swung a jubilant Toby upon his shoulders, his fists punching the air with unbridled joy. In grateful tears, families and friends arriving from the outer villages, embraced for the first time in months. In the midst of the reunions, Simon coiled the dreaded rope. He walked back to the fire pits and flung it triumphantly upon the flames to even more cheers for his extraordinary efforts on their behalf.

With tears in her eyes, Viola ran straight to Catherine and hugged her tightly, unwilling to let go. Catherine was shocked at how much thinner her aunt seemed to be, for her gown hung loose. She looked through the crowd. The privations of the quarantine showed dearly on nearly everyone who had suffered through it. Gussie, Eliza and the mayor stood with Viola, awaiting their turn to hug Catherine and offer their sorrowful condolences for the death of Lord Abbott. The mayor looked much smaller, too.

"I am so very grateful to have you back, my dear," whispered Viola, as she embraced her niece.

"Thank you, Aunt Viola. I'm very grateful to be back." She meant each word as they clung together. Catherine noticed that the mayor stood very close to her aunt. She also noticed that her aunt seemed much comforted by his presence. *Perhaps something good has come from these months of sorrow.*

The mayor stepped forward and reached into the pocket of his waistcoat. "I have received a missive from my brother. It is addressed to you, Doctor." He handed the letter to Simon, who tore through the wax seal and unfolded the parchment.

17 August 1665

Dr. McKensie,

I have been apprised by my brother of your admirable efforts in treating the plague in Wells. I am saddened to tell you that Dr. Clarke has perished this day of the plague and St. Bartholomew's is now overwhelmed with illness that everywhere presents itself, such that we can no longer care for all of the desperate souls that now come to us for mercy. Nearly 30,000 citizens of London have thusly perished.

I have spoken to the local constabulary and any grievances toward you have been summarily dismissed. You are thus free to return to your research, in any manner as you deem necessary, without oversight or imperilment, as your services and treatment methods are desperately needed here in London. You will have complete authority over Dr. Clarke's ward. Please return at the soonest possible hour.

Fr. Thomas J. Hardwicke
Vicar, St. Bartholomew-The-Less
Smithfield Parish
London, England

He had won. Dr. Clarke was one month dead and Simon was to have complete authority over his ward at St. Bartholomew's. He was free from the threat of prosecution and could now freely conduct his research as he saw fit. He exhaled in grateful relief. He looked to Catherine. In an unguarded moment, she was twisting the ring on her finger. Simon folded the note and quietly placed it in his pocket. Archie pulled the Abbey coach up to where Catherine stood in the joyous crowd, Gussie close by his side.

"May I escort you home, Milady?"

Catherine walked into the Abbey for the very first time since the first day in May. Cedric greeted her warmly, and then tactfully retreated, leaving her to her turbulent, unsettled thoughts. She stood alone in the entranceway, staring up at the magnificent oil painting of Lord Abbott that hung over the stair landing. She turned and looked into the gathering hall. The massive stone hearth stood dark and empty. She lifted her eyes to the elaborately timbered ceiling, then looked into the elegant warmth of the family quarters where the Christmas tree had stood in what seemed a lifetime ago. Not one thing seemed familiar. The heels of her shoes clicked across the marble flooring, the hollow echos sounding as peculiar and empty as the house itself felt without the towering presence of her father. *How strange everything seems after these many months away from the Abbey.*

Catherine opened the door and stepped quietly into Lord Abbott's study. She half-expected, half-achingly wished to find him sitting in his carved oak chair, lifting his head from his work and breaking into a delighted smile when he saw her in the doorway. Her heart stopped at the sight of his desk. His beloved white clay Meerschaum pipe sat cold in a wooden ash bowl. His maps, sextants and celestial globe remained right where he left them. His books lay open on the desk, a pair of spectacles set to rights on the pages. *How peculiar it is that objects remain even as their flesh and blood owner perishes. Something is completely mad in God's order.*

"Mi'lady?" came a soft whisper from behind.

Startled, Catherine whirled about. Jane stood behind her, smiling gently.

"I'm so very sorry, Mi'lady." Without thinking, she instinctively stretched her arms out. Catherine broke down and fell into her maid's embrace in tears, aching for the loss of so much in her life—in all their lives.

"Jane…"

Catherine clung desperately to something familiar from the life she once knew. Jane let her cry until she had no more tears to shed. Catherine drew back and collected herself.

"Mi'lady, Viscount Houghton has asked to see ye'."

Catherine caught her breath. *What could she possibly say to him? She could not face him. Aye, she had betrayed her troth. And yet, he had deserted them all for his own selfish gain.* " She paused a moment, then turned decisively to Jane. "Please send word that I will see him tomorrow." *How could she speak to him privately without Aunt Viola intruding?* Her gaze fell thoughtfully upon a woven basket of her father's favorite leather crops. She looked up. "And, tell him that I should like to go riding."

"Aye, Mi'lady," said Jane, tentatively. Catherine could see that the maid was puzzled by the crispness in her voice, yet she had no wish to elaborate. "I've drawn ye' a hot bath, Miss. Why d' ye' not change, then go down an' have a nice, long soak. Perhaps it will make ye' feel better."

Catherine dried her eyes and sighed. "Yes, Jane." She managed a smile at the hopeful look upon the maid's face. "I believe it would."

Catherine climbed the stairs to the family quarters. She grasped the iron latch to the door of her sleeping chamber, somehow gaining strength from its cool solidity, and then, taking a deep breath, pushed the door open. The room was just as she had left it. Everything seemed the same, and yet, she was unsettled by just how much had changed since she last slept in her own bedstead. She sat by the cold hearth. As she stared into the empty grate, her thoughts turned to Simon. She had become so used to working by his side to care for the desperately ill villagers, just as much as she treasured their nights of contemplation and quiet companionship by the fire. She loved his kind, intelligent ways, his nimble curiosity and his genuine interest in her thoughts and ideas. Sitting in the quiet stillness of her chamber, Catherine suddenly realized, *she missed him terribly.*

Shaking her head to clear her troubled thoughts, Catherine rose and changed into a dressing gown. She walked downstairs to the warm washroom off the kitchen and sank blissfully into the marvelous wooden bathing tub, grateful for once that in Aunt Viola's determined bid to outpace the high born ladies of the valley she had copied the bathing tub from the Duchess of Lauderdale's Ham House for the Abbey. She closed her eyes and inhaled the clean, fresh scent of the tallow soap that Jane had set on a small table beside her. As she soaked in the warm water, Jane scrubbed the despised scent of vinegar that permeated her skin and hair. She laid her head back against the oak staves and reveled in the warmth of the clean water against her skin. She drifted off to sleep, recalling every moment of the extraordinary summer they had all been through.

"Ouch!" Catherine jerked awake, splashing water over the side of the tub.

"Cooee! I'm ever so sorry, Mi'lady," apologized Jane, as she untangled a curl from her fingers. Jane reached for a pitcher and rinsed the soap from Catherine's hair. Catherine laughed and made ready to rise. Jane fastened the lacings of the silken dressing gown, and together, they walked back upstairs to Catherine's cozy bedroom. Catherine turned to the maid.

"I believe I will rest a bit this afternoon, Jane."

"Aye' Mi'lady." Jane turned down the coverlet and helped Catherine into the deliciously soft, cool bed. "I'll call ye' for supper." Jane walked to the door, then stopped, her hand on the latch, and turned back. "It's good to have ye' home, Mi'lady." Jane stepped out, closing the door quietly behind her.

Catherine walked barefoot through the trees in a barren apple orchard. Blowing gusts ripped through the branches. Swirling leaves slapped against her skin and caught in her tangled hair. She put her hands against her ears to block the roaring winds that cracked the sturdy trees in half and watched as the billowy crowns toppled to the earth, shriveling to a fine, powdery dust that blew into the gathering cataclysm. She looked for refuge from the storm. An ancient chestnut tree in the distance seemed to beckon to her. She ran to the tree, reaching her bare arms around its massive trunk. She tried to hold on as the bracing winds whipped the dry soil around her into clouds of blinding dust. The wind pressed her harder and harder into the rough chestnut bark that scratched her until she bled. She backed away. A powerful courser charged through the orchard, mane and tail flowing in the wind like eddying water. Catherine reached out for it, but the horse kept running. Violent gusts whipped at her skirts. She looked down in horror to see blood from the scratches slowly staining her moss-colored gown. At her feet, clusters of pink silk rosebuds lay trampled and spent. In the distance, a lone figure stood under the chestnut tree. She squinted her eyes and cried out, for there in the haze stood her father, his arms outstretched. He shouted to her, his faint cries lost to the roaring winds. She tried again to call out, but she could no longer make the sounds. She tried to run to him, but the wind blew her backwards until at last, fading slowly into the swirling dust, he disappeared altogether into the vast nothingness. She turned from the frightening tumult. Suddenly, the howling gales slowed, then ceased altogether. She opened her eyes. All around her the orchard lay in utter destruction. She sank to her knees in tears. Something caught her eye. A woodland grayling fluttered gently about her head. It flitted away, and then flew back again as if beckoning her to follow. In the distance, the chestnut tree split slowly in half, its insides rotted. The tree fell to the ground in a massive, earth-shattering crash. Catherine sat straight up in bed, gasping for air. She had never felt so alone.

Shaking, Catherine arose in the pitch dark and stoked a fire. She sat on a footstool before the hearth and bit her thumbnail watching the embers come to life. Her old habit felt curiously unfamiliar. She suddenly realized that she had worn the herb mask for months. She unexpectedly giggled thinking that Aunt Viola should have tried a mask instead of the useless, vile mustard poultices. She began to calm down. In the dim light of the flames, her eyes fell upon a small package tied with twine sitting on her desk. It was addressed to her. She untied the strings. The wrappings fell away. Her butterfly book. She had completely forgotten. Catherine looked in awe at her name writ large upon the cover. *She had done it. She was published.* She held the book up to the firelight, feeling its weight. She opened the heavy cover. A parchment note slid out and fell onto the floor. Curious, she picked it up, unfolded it and held it to the firelight.

Maxwell & Co. Printers, Ltd.
Number Ten Sloane Street.
St. James Parish, London, England
My Dear Lady Abbott,

Please accept our congratulations upon the publication of your first book. As per our contract, any royalties due (less publication costs) will be held on your account here at Maxwell Printers. You may sign for them at any time. When you are in London next, I would like to offer you employment of an illustration project. If this might be of interest to you, please see me at the earliest.

Most sincerely,
Ambrose Maxwell, Publisher

She thought of her father lying deathly ill upon the pallet. *You must do everything you wish to do in this life.* Suddenly, Catherine knew exactly what it was that she wished to do.

CHAPTER 33

"BUT LORD, TO SEE, AMONG OTHER THINGS, HOW ALL THESE GREAT PEOPLE HERE ARE AFEARED OF LONDON. HOW FEW PEOPLE I SEE, AND THOSE WALKING LIKE PEOPLE WHO HAVE TAKEN LEAVE OF THIS WORLD."
-SAMUEL PEPYS

Village of Stockbridge
Buckinghamshire, England
12 September 1665

Catherine sat before the glass while Jane secured her riding hat. A soft knock interrupted Jane's concentration as she worked to pin the violet plumed topper to Catherine's curls. Jane stepped back; setting the pins on the dressing table, then opened the door to a young maid who handed her a calling card.

"He is early," said Catherine, irritated. She looked at her timepiece necklace. "It is not yet two o'clock."

Jane handed Catherine the card. She mindlessly set it on the dressing table and adjusted the hat a little lower on her brow.

"What shall I tell the gentleman, Mi'Lady?" asked the young maid.

"Please tell him wait in the gallery," said Catherine, pulling once again on the hat. "Tell him I shall come down when Jane is finished."

"Aye, Mi'lady," said the maid, closing the door quietly behind her. Jane took up her pins and set the hat in place. Catherine idly picked up the card. She looked closer. Her heart suddenly stopped, for there in flowing script was the name, *Simon McKensie*. Catherine dropped the card on the table and, pulling the hat from her hair, ran for the door.

Simon stood in the gallery staring out at the elegant, rustic grounds of the Abbey awash in autumnal color, his back to her. "Simon?" she whispered. He turned as she rushed toward him, holding her hands out. He grasped them tight to his chest and brushed her cheek with his lips in greeting. She closed her eyes, slowly savoring his touch, his masculine scent, and the gentle smile she had become so used to seeing each day. *Oh, how she missed him.* Aunt Viola appeared in the doorway and looked askance at him, yet held her tongue. Simon stepped back and bowed slightly.

"I apologize for the intrusion, Lady Abbott, Lady Catherine."

"No, I'm so very glad you're here," she whispered softly, a tear springing unexpectedly. She wiped her eyes and collected herself. She gestured to the settee under the window. "Would you care to sit?" Catherine looked to Viola. "Will you join us?

"No, my dear." Viola quietly withdrew. Catherine gestured to a passing maid. "Perhaps you would like some tea?"

"I…I'm afraid I cannot stay." He walked to the hearth and clasped his hands behind his back. He stared into the fire for a moment. Then he turned and reached into his pocket. He withdrew the letter from Father Hardwicke. "I only wanted to tell you in person that I am returning to London." She stared at him in shock.

"No!" she cried, without thinking.

Flustered by her reaction, Simon unfolded the parchment and handed it to her. Catherine read the letter, then looked up, terrified.

"Oh, Simon…. No! " "You mustn't put yourself into danger once again!" She instantly caught herself. "I'm sorry. I haven't the right." She looked down and read the letter again, and then slowly sank to the settee. A tear trickled down her cheek. He sat down next to her and covered her hands with his own.

"I believe I can help, Catherine," he said softly.

Catherine looked to the ground, embarrassed at her impulsive words. "I apologize, Simon. I spoke for my own selfish gain.

Of course you must go," she said. She looked up to see Simon searching her eyes, tenderly. He began to speak, but was interrupted by Cedric standing at the entrance to the gallery.

"Viscount Houghton, Mi'Lady." From the entrance hall, Miles brushed past Cedric, leaving the old man slightly off-balance. Miles held his hands out in greeting.

"My darling!" he cried, as he strode into the room, startling Catherine. Simon immediately rose to his feet. Miles looked momentarily thrown, himself, but he smiled, then walked over and clapped Simon hard on the back.

"Ah, McKensie. I was about to join Catherine for a ride in the countryside." He stared at Simon, pointedly. "Will you join us?"

Catherine saw the glint of challenge in Miles's eyes. She quickly looked to Simon. He had seen it, too. He shook his head and stepped toward the entrance hall.

"I must go." He turned to Catherine. With Miles's eyes piercing into his back, Simon reached for her hand and kissed it softly. "Thank you, Lady Catherine, for all of your assistance during the quarantine. My condolences once again to you and your family." Miles silently fumed.

Cedric appeared with Simon's cloak. Miles took it firmly into his own grasp and turned to Simon, with a furious flush.

Please. Allow me." Miles roughly tossed the cloak to Simon, then all three walked out of the Abbey to the horses that awaited them in the courtyard. Her heart aching, Catherine watched silently as Simon mounted the mayor's horse and, with a gentle nudge to the ribs, headed straight for Wells. Miles stood next to Catherine's horse, and offered her the reins.

"Shall we?"

"I shall throw you a party!" exclaimed Miles as they trotted along the meandering path behind the Abbey. His horse tossed her head and fought the bridle, longing to break into a run in the crisp autumn air. He held the reins low and tight to control the prancing mare. "We must celebrate your return!" He faced her, growing serious. "We all thought you were so terribly brave, Catherine. I cannot imagine how horrible it must have been for you." The mare snorted, stumbling slightly on a rock. Miles slowed, setting her back to rights. "I offer again my sincere condolences on the loss of your father. Lord Abbott was a kind and generous man."

"Thank you, Miles," she whispered, nearly overcome once again. "It was a terrible experience for everyone."

In the bright late afternoon sun, they rode in silence on the woodland path lined with trees that hung thickly with rich golden yellow, crimson and fiery burnt orange foliage. He turned to her once again, a sympathetic look upon his face.

"And having to wear borrowed cotton frocks the entire time. I should, myself, have been in quite a jigget!" He groaned. "It must have been awful for you, my darling."

Catherine stared at him. She could think of no intelligent response to his unending conceit. *People died! My father died! Thousands upon thousands have died in London—and he thinks only of frocks?* A fire was building inside. They cantered across a small stone bridge arching over a brook that spilled into the Abbey millpond lined with waving cattails and wild irises. An enormous water wheel splashed slowly through the water, rotating the grinding mechanism in the mill house. They stopped in a leafy glen to watch the wheel for a moment, marveling at the ingenuity. Catherine could restrain herself no more. She stared down at her ring, and then turned in her saddle to face Miles. She spoke directly.

"Miles, I must ask. Did you know the village was to be quarantined that day?"

"I did!" he marveled, then quickly seemed to realize how his words sounded. "But I so longed to run to you, my darling Catherine and whisk you away from it all, too." He paused. "Of course, then I would have been caught up in the thick of it, along with everyone else." He shook his head, wide-eyed, incredulous at the thought. "I simply can't imagine."

Miles was a coward. He ran from the danger they all faced, while Simon ran straight toward it, willing to sacrifice his own life to try and save them all. The disloyal thoughts she had toward Miles at the water barrel suddenly rang crystal clear in her memory, for now she knew those thoughts to be true.

She looked down at the band on her finger and wavered a moment. Then, Catherine set her fingertips upon the band and pulled with all her might. Miles watched her slide the ring off. He furrowed his brow in confusion until comprehension set in.

"What the devil…?"

Catherine struggled to keep her temper. "I cannot marry you, Miles." She stared directly at him. "I will not." Though he was not given to anger, she feared his next words. To her surprise, he looked for a moment at the tranquil setting, then faced her with an unaccustomed calm.

"It is not enough, is it? A friendship, I mean. For marriage…" he asked softly. Her temper instantly dissipated.

"No, Miles. It's not enough. Not nearly enough." She sat tall in the saddle, her resolve unwavering, yet she spoke gently. "I cannot possibly be the wife you wish me to be…"

Miles contemplated the loss of the Abbott fortune. "But you would make a…"

She interrupted his protest. "…nor can you possibly be the husband I long for."

He was shocked into silence. The mare snorted, the hollow sounds echoing softly through the damp glen. He worked to counter her thoughts, and yet, *he knew she was right.*

"I'm so very sorry, Miles." She leaned over and handed him the ring. Miles inhaled, absorbing her words, his pride deeply wounded. He contemplated the band for a very long moment, then held it up and twisted it, the hammered gold brilliant against an azure sky. He exhaled. *The gambling debts.* He would indeed have to face his father. *Ahhh, c'est la vie.* Miles tossed the ring into the air, and then deftly caught it. He looked over to her and smiled.

"There is no need. To apologize, I mean" he said, his manners returning, impeccable, as always. "In fact, I've been thinking of returning to Paris." He turned his prancing, restless horse around in glen. And, my darling, now, I believe shall. He flashed his roguish grin.

"Thank you, Miles," she said, softly. "You did not have to ease my path."

He reached for her hand and drew it to his lips. "Ahh, but that is precisely what we gentlemen do." He looked down to the ring he held, and then pressed it into her palm. He winked. "To remember me by." He kissed her hand once more, and then Miles cracked the prancing, restless mare in the ribs and wheeled her around, racing once more down the path towards Houghton Hall. Catherine watched as he disappeared around the bend, her heart growing lighter by the moment.

Catherine walked into her sleeping chamber, greatly unsettled and yet strangely relieved, by the broken engagement. *Whatever had she done?* She was startled to see Aunt Viola sitting at the desk, leafing through her butterfly book. The letter from Ambrose Maxwell sat unfolded on her lap. Catherine froze. *Viola had seen everything.*

"I…I can explain, Aunt Viola."

Viola stared up at her. Her eyes fell upon Catherine's hand to see that she no longer wore Miles's ring. She exhaled, but said nothing. After a moment, Viola closed the book. She set it very gently upon the desk, then rose and walked out of the room, closing the door behind her. Catherine sank against the bed, overwhelmed. She put her hand on the carved post of the bed to steady herself. *You must do everything you wish to do in this life.* Her father's words rang in her head. At once strengthened by his quiet counsel, Catherine mustered her resolve. *She had an offer of employment in London and she was in love, yes, in love with a brave, beautiful man. Gussie always said she could make her way in this world if she had to, and by God's oath, she would, indeed.* Catherine smoothed her skirts, straightened her shoulders and made ready to confront her aunt. Suddenly, the door opened. Viola strode back in carrying with her a large, elaborately tooled leather folio.

"Aunt Viola…" she commanded, holding her chin high, ready to proclaim her independence. Viola brushed past her and took a seat by the hearth.

"Sit down, my dear," she said briskly, pointing to the dressing table stool. "I have something I would like to show you." Catherine watched, entirely unsure of what was about to happen. She held her tongue and moved the stool next to her aunt as Viola slowly opened the folio wide. Catherine's jaw dropped. It was chockfull of meticulously drawn illustrations. Viola began to slowly leaf through the drawings. There were hundreds of them. Botanical illustrations. Peacock illustrations. Even architectural illustrations. Catherine was incredulous. To her shock, Viola tilted her head and smiled a soft, tender smile Catherine had never before seen.

"I suspect you thought it was your father you took after," she said, gently.

Astounded, Catherine reached for the folio and began to leaf through page after page of intricate drawings, each one delicately detailed and beautifully tinted. She looked closely to read the signature. *Lady Viola Eugenia Abbott.* Catherine looked up from the drawings and stared at her aunt. *I understand.* Suddenly, everything fell into place; Viola's lavish use of botanical patterns at Bealeton House, her beloved peacocks, her great love of art, perhaps even her frustration at life in general. Catherine was rendered mute by the unexpected, immeasurable talent of her aunt. Viola broke the silence.

"My dear," she began. "Losing my only brother was singularly the most difficult experience of my life." Her voice dropped to a quivering whisper. "Then, I thought I might lose you, too, Catherine, and that, I did not think I could bear." She paused a moment and gazed out the window. "I had plenty of time to think while I sat at the line mending clothes. When Alvyn died, I slowly came to realize that very little I thought mattered, really matters in this life. Not titles. Not wealth. Not power. Nothing. Except finding happiness, my dear.

Catherine was completely disoriented. Viola took Catherine by the hands and stroked her ring finger, now bereft of the wide gold band. She smiled, then picked up Catherine's book once again and spoke softly as she turned the pages.

"I… I have done you a great disservice by orchestrating a match that was never meant be, my dear, and I apologize. I can only hope that one day, you can forgive me." She looked carefully at one of the illustrations. "You are extremely talented, Catherine. This I know." She pointed to the letter from Ambrose Maxwell. "You must follow your own path, my dear. Wherever it may lead you."

Catherine was in tears. Viola smiled and reached in her pocket. She pulled out a folded parchment. She handed it to Catherine. It was the contract Lord Abbott had signed months ago.

"This was on your father's desk. Charles is to return to port in the next sixmonth. As soon as it is safe, you must return to London to meet the ship and tell him of you father's death. Jane will accompany you to Bealeton House." She pulled at a handful of material on her gown. "I fear that nothing fits me now. I shall have to have a new gown made before I return to London for an entirely new wardrobe. Cecil and I will join you as soon as possible."

"The mayor? And you?" Catherine was completely baffled. Viola smiled once more. In her entire lifetime, Catherine had never seen her aunt so happy.

"Cecil has asked me to marry him, and as I am quite sure that Charles will approve upon his return, Catherine, I have said yes."

CHAPTER 35

"THANKS BE TO GOD, THE PLAGUE IS, AS I HEAR,
ENCREASED BUT TWO THIS WEEK..."
-SAMUEL PEPYS

Village of Wells
Buckinghamshire, England
24 June 1666

The London coach clattered into the Royal George Inn courtyard and pulled to a stop. The driver stepped down, and then set the footstool by the carriage. He opened the door and reached up to take the hand of a disembarking passenger. Eldrick, walking toward the inn to inventory the stores of beef for the autumn, stopped short as a striking woman and a young girl stood by the coach waiting for their bags. The woman wore an exquisitely tailored brown wool traveling suit that perfectly complimented her golden skin and hair the color of nutmeg spice. A wide-eyed little girl stood shyly next to the woman, holding her hand tightly. The woman looked up to the top of the coach where the driver was handing luggage down to a waiting stable hand.

"Excuse me," she called up the driver, "do you know where I might find the owner of the inn? I was told there might be a position available."

"Couldn't say, Miss," he answered, tossing down another bag.

"If you like, I can take you to 'im, Miss," said Eldrick, shyly twisting his cap in his hands. He stepped toward the coach to take her bags in hand. She tipped her head up to him with an incandescent smile and took his arm.

"Yes, please."

Sipping a cup of the in the dining room, Catherine smiled as she watched the gentle exchange between the lonely butcher and the pretty newcomer through panes of glass. The long winter of mourning and seclusion had finally turned spring and a sense of renewal and hope had at last awakened in the townspeople of the valley. A flutter of excitement tingled through her. After months of waiting, the post had finally delivered the news that the plague in London seemed to now be mostly confined to small pockets of the crowded tenements and outlying towns, and people were returning to the city in droves. *Life once again seems so very full of possibilities.* She reached for her traveling bag and pulled out a letter to reassure herself that it was still there. She looked at the address.

Dr. Simon McKensie
St. Bartholomew's Hospital
London, England.

She turned it over. The golden yellow sealing wax was in place. She did not need to break the seal, for she knew the contents by heart. *An invitation to tea at Bealeton House.* She could not wait any longer. She needed to speak to him once more to see if somehow the feelings she had for him were returned in any fashion. She could have used the post, but now fiercely determined to take her fate into her own hands, she would to deliver the note to the hospital herself.

The mayor looked into the room.

"They're ready for you, my dear,"

In the courtyard, Catherine hugged her aunt. With tears in her eyes, Catherine stepped back and grasped Viola's hands, forever grateful for her encouragement.

"Follow your heart, my dear," whispered Viola, glancing toward the mayor. "We shall finish closing the mayor's house and join you in a weeks time."

Catherine and Jane boarded the coach. The driver slammed the door and mounted the bench. Taking up the reins, he slapped them smartly against horseflesh.

"Giddup!"

The team jolted the coach toward the road. Waving through the glass, Catherine watched as Aunt Viola stood arm and arm with the mayor. The coach turned from the courtyard and headed down the road towards London.

CHAPTER 36

St. Bartholomew's Hospital
London, England
5 July 1666

The plump registrar stood behind his massive wooden desk, barking orders like the harried defender of his realm. The day had barely begun and already he was beset with constant vexations. He wiped the ever-present sweat from his balding forehead with the back of his hand, brushing against the strings of the damnable herbal mask he and the staff were still forced by Simon to wear, even though the months-long quarantine had that morning been lifted.

"Damnation!"

A man, carrying a limp child in his arms burst through the door. "Please, I beg of you, 'elp me boy!" The child's head bobbed in his arms.

The registrar stabbed his finger toward the exit. "Turn right 'round and go back out the same door ye' came in!" he roared. "Ye' can't bring 'im in 'ere! We've 'ad no plague sicks for over a month an' we'll nae' 'ave one now!" He banged his fist on his desk. "We have been five weeks free of infection an' I'll nae' serve one day more of this execrable quarantine!"

"It is nae' the plague, sir!" The desperate man looked down to his unconscious son. "My boy fell out the window!" Cracked 'is 'ead on a rock, 'e did!

From the hallway, Simon heard the commotion in the entry and ran to the boy's side. He carefully lifted the boy from his father's arms and headed for the ward he was now in charge of.

"Damn you, McKensie, get back 'ere!" The registrar blocked Simon's path. He craned his neck and looked up to Simon, furiously jerking his head toward the boy's father. "E's got to follow 'ospital procedures! *My* procedures!"

Simon had been working day and night for months, catching sleep when he could. He had just lifted the quarantine from his ward and now, as soon as the boy was settled, he desired nothing more than to fall into his own bed at the cottage. He was in no mood to argue yet again with this vile little man. "You hold no charge over my patients, sir. This boy needs medical attention immediately and he shall indeed receive it!" Simon drew himself up to his full height, towering over the diminutive registrar. "And for the last time, it is *Doctor* McKensie. Now, if you would, please step aside!"

Scowling, the fat little man stormed back to his desk. Simon gently carried the boy through the doorway to an examining bed. The boy's father followed close behind.

"Bastard!" The registrar slammed his ledger down on the edge of the desk. The ledger fell to the shelving below where a collection of paperwork and correspondence had been cached, causing the papers to fall to the ground. Cursing loudly, the registrar bent down to collect the scattered documents. A parchment letter addressed in flowing script with a golden yellow wax seal caught his eye. The letter was addressed to Simon. He had set it there himself and long since forgotten about it, though he damn well remembered with contempt the red headed young woman who delivered it. *A right looker. Respect'ble. Bloody rich. Exactly th' sort th' fekkin' gudgeon would attract.* The registrar spat on the floor in irritation. *How he despised these damnable medical students.* He thought miserably of his own shrew of a wife who bedeviled his very soul from the moment he arose in the morning until the ale blessedly knocked him out at night. *Tis' a singularly wretched life.* The registrar picked the letter up and tapped it idly on the desk. Suddenly seized with a burning jealousy, he cast a poisonous glance in the direction of the sick ward and then, with his big, beefy hands; the registrar slowly ripped the letter into tiny pieces.

He lifted the corner of his mouth in a twisted grin and let the pieces flutter through his fat fingers straight into the dustbin.

Simon stood outside Father Hardwicke's office brooding over why he'd been summoned and he was in a very foul mood. *I have led this hospital through a most troubling peril and that miserable little twit intends to discredit me for not following proper registration procedures.* His normally even temper flared. *Incomprehensible.* In his quiet fury, Simon ripped off his mask and knocked far harder on the door than he intended. There was a moment's hesitation from the other side of the door. Simon instantly composed himself.

"Come."

Simon sheepishly pushed on the door and entered the room, calm, yet fully prepared to defend himself against the surly, spiteful little registrar. The priest looked up from his paperwork. To Simon's utter shock, Father Hardwicke was actually *smiling.* He had never once seen a genuine smile on the old man. The priest gestured to the chair that Simon had sat in nearly one year before when his life had taken a very unexpected turn. Simon warily took a seat with the troubling sense of unease that his life was about to take one more.

"As is my custom, I shall get right to it."

Simon inhaled, sharply, dreading what he was about to hear.

"Doctor McKensie, the Board has been most impressed by what you have accomplished—*I* have been most impressed by what you have accomplished."

Simon tilted his head in confusion. Though still quite wary, his interest was piqued. Father Hardwicke leaned back in his chair, fully enjoying the effect his words seemed to be having on the lad.

"One year ago, I made you an offer of full payment for your final year of medical school if you would attend to my brother's health. Not only have you cured him of his ills, he has married and has settled down to a respectable life." Simon raised his eyebrows in surprise, but said nothing. "You have more than fulfilled your charge with me." Father Hardwicke stood and walked around his desk. He sat on the edge to face Simon. "Further, your efforts to contain the plague by separating the ill from the well, by wearing protective masks and by every other course you have recommended, has wrought nothing short of spectacular results, both in Wells and here at St. Bartholomew's.

Simon looked up, surprised. "Thank you, sir."

"As promised, you are now absolved of your tuition responsibilities for this coming year." He looked out the window, in a forced attempt to remain nonchalant. "Further, we have had an inquiry from Willis at Oxford as to your research. The board has met several times and…"

Simon's eyes flew open in astonishment. *Dr. Thomas Willis? The University of Oxford? Author of De Anatome Cerebri? That Willis? Dr. Willis knew his name?* His heart began to pound so loudly that he could hardly hear the sound of Father Hardwicke's voice. *Oxford University knew of him. The chance to study with Willis was far more than he could fathom. Far more than he could have ever hoped for. Why, the opportunities were boundless.* He forced himself to remain calm so that he could listen.

"…I have been asked to provide further inducement for you to remain here at St. Bartholomew's after your final year of training. Therefore, I…" He corrected himself. "We… should like to offer you the opportunity to set up your own dissection chamber for the study of anatomy here at the hospital."

Simon nearly fell off the chair in shock. The priest was not finished.

"You may kit the chamber out in any manner you desire. You may begin on the morrow to direct the orderlies in moving whatever equipment you will need into your ward. Further, the board will purchase any additional equipment you may require. You will have permission to conduct your research on any focus of interest you may have and you may employ such staff, as you deem necessary. Our only request in exchange for the surgery is that you share your discoveries with the staff and the medical students, and share credit with the hospital in all of your published work."

Simon was truly speechless. *The proposal was everything he could possibly have wished for. And yet... Willis.* He walked to the window and stared at the rooftops of London, thinking how very far he had come from the small village on the border of Scotland. He wiped a smudge of dirt from the glass with the sleeve of his tunic.

"What say you, Doctor?"

He turned toward the old man and took a deep breath. "Sir, beyond all measure, I would be honored to accept your offer."

In the sharp glare of the afternoon sun, Simon walked through the wilting heat towards his little cottage on Hawthorne Lane, contemplating the extraordinary proposal he had just received. So unaware was he of his surroundings that he took a wrong turning and found himself, by force of habit, walking down Sloane Street in Knightsbridge. Passing Number Two, he glanced at the window, still draped in mourning black at Wilcox & Sons, yet another somber reminder of the vile pestilence that had nearly run its course, the odd case now being mostly confined to the crowded slums of the West End. He walked on, the sight of it jolting him from his thoughts. He suddenly felt the summer heat. He looked up to see that he was standing before Number Ten. *Perhaps Ambrose has a cool draught of water.* He pushed the door to the publishing house wide open.

"Ahhh, Marlowe!" shouted Ambrose over the din of the printing machines. "Come in! Come in!"

The name caught Simon short. He smiled, so very grateful that he was no longer encumbered by the necessary deception.

He shook his old friend's hand in greeting. "It's McKensie, Ambrose. "My name is actually Simon McKensie."

Ambrose cocked his head in curiosity. "I s'pose we should have a cup o' tea, then."

He went to the back and came out with the kettle. As he poured them both a cup, Ambrose listened carefully to the explanation of his false name. He nodded, fully understanding the need for the subterfuge.

"Shall we run a reprint with yer' proper name?"

"Nae. I believe that I will soon have more than enough research material for a new book. I shall simply write a forward explaining the necessary deception." He turned to his friend, his eyes wide at the stunning turn of events. "Ambrose, you will nae' believe what has just occurred."

Ambrose listened, fascinated by the new position at St. Bartholomew's. He could see another successful book in the offing. He set his teacup on the workbench. "Do you yet know what ye'll want in your new dissection theater?"

"Aye. I do. I have thought of nothing else since I left the hospital this noon. Plenty of light. An elevated platform for the students to watch." *Not much of an artist.* Catherine's words rang in his head. "A table for an illustrator."

"A what?"

"An illustrator. Someone to draw accurate, scientific illustrations of the human anatomy as the autopsies are conducted. Christopher Wren illustrated the brain for Willis. I will need an artist to produce detailed, scientific drawings. I was once told that I am not much of one," he remembered with a rueful smile.

Ambrose had an inspiration. "D'ye' know of someone for the job, Simon?"

He knew the perfect person. Catherine. She had the strength, the curiosity, and the extraordinary talent. He thought of her beauty and her kind, gentle ways. *How he longed to see her, to talk to her once again.* He thought wistfully of the band on her finger and sighed.

"Nae', I do not."

"Excellent! I have the perfect person. A right talent as I've nae' before seen. Let me set up an introduction. As it is now Tuesday, perhaps Thursday, noontide?"

Simon's mind wandered to the fire pits and the soft, quiet moments he had spent with Catherine. He wasn't paying complete attention. "Aye. Thursday, noontide, indeed."

Catherine sat with Aunt Viola at the game table in the family quarters basking in the gentle afternoon breeze from the open bay windows. The draughts board sat in front of them. Catherine's wooden kings were stacked two-high on the checkerboard squares waiting to be played. She rested her chin on her hand as she watched the shadows from the marble Grecian statues in the formal topiary garden fall across the blossoming roses. To her surprise, the light-colored plaster walls and gleaming floors kept the mansion cool in the early-summer heat. After studying the board for several long minutes, Viola picked up her king and jumped diagonally over three of Catherine's dark-stained mahogany tokens.

"Your turn, my dear," said Viola, as she happily removed Catherine's men from the board.

Catherine turned her head away from the sunny grounds and tried to concentrate on the game. The Lord Mayor walked into the room. He walked over and kissed Viola on her fetching topknot. She reached for his hand. Smiling up at him, she gently kissed the back of it, more content than Catherine had ever before seen her. They had married in a very quiet ceremony at the Abbey on New Year's Eve. Charles would have much to absorb upon his return. The mayor tapped the gazette he carried on the table.

"The quarantine has been lifted at St. Bartholomew's," he announced with a twinkle in his eye. "I believe I shall drop 'round tomorrow and pay a visit to the lad." He looked straight at Catherine. "Shall I give him your regards, my dear?"

She looked at him in surprise. "What do you suggest?

"I suggest nothing more than my own eyes did behold." He laughed. "Is there not an attraction? Do you suggest that my eyes deceive?" He placed his hands tenderly upon Viola's shoulders. "Come now, my dear. I am a man well versed in the games of..." Viola looked up sharply, arching an eyebrow. He instantly retracted. "... nae' the *art* of romance." Viola smiled up at him.

Catherine tried to protest, and then relented. "I am afraid he does not wish to see me. I invited him to tea a fortnight ago. I have not received a reply," she confessed, her mind troubled. *Has he another? Does he play me for a fool, yet again? He was impossible to comprehend.*

Cedric appeared in the gathering room, holding a small silver tray. A note sat upon it. He walked over and held the tray toward Catherine. The mayor chuckled. "Timing is everything, my dear."

Catherine looked at the note, then up to the mayor. "It is not from Simon." She opened it, read its contents, then closed it and set it back on the tray. Cedric returned to his post.

"Ambrose Maxwell, my publisher, would like to see me Thursday, noontide. I have been working on some architectural illustrations for a book he is publishing." She was puzzled. "They are not required until late-September." She shrugged her shoulders. "I suppose he would like to see what I have thus far."

Catherine turned her attention back to the game. She took her king in hand, and jumped over the last two men on Viola's side of the board. She smiled at her aunt.

"I win."

CHAPTER 37

Sloane Street, St. James Parish
London, England
7 July 1666

Catherine carried her folio and walked into Maxwell & Sons, Ltd. at precisely noon. She stopped a moment, listening to the clatter of the printing machines in the back room. She closed her eyes and inhaled deeply of the now familiar sweet scent of ink. *I belong here. I truly belong here.* Ambrose walked out from the back, wiping his stained hands on his apron.

"Good afternoon, my dear Lady Catherine!" cried Ambrose, coming around the counter.

She opened here eyes with a start, and embraced the man she had grown very fond of over the last several months. She set the folio on the wooden counter and opened it. He glanced down at her illustrations and smiling broadly.

"Yes, yes, yes. These are perfect, my dear!"

"I'm sorry that they are not yet finished, Ambrose. I was given to understand that the date of completion was the end of September."

"My dear, these drawings are not why I've asked you here today. I have something else in mind for you. Something quite different. Quite different indeed." He looked at his watch fob.

The door latch rattled. Ambrose nodded. "Right on time." The door opened. A figure seemed to fill the entire room. A very familiar figure.

"Marlowe—Ah, McKensie!" called Ambrose.

Catherine dropped the drawing she held to the counter. She looked up, then turned around and caught her breath. *Simon.*

He saw her in the same moment. He couldn't seem to move for the shock of seeing her standing before him. She stepped to him, taking his outstretched hands into her own. Simon's gaze dropped to her bare fingers. He looked to her, brows furrowed, questioning.

"I am no longer betrothed," she said, anxiously searching his eyes for the least bit of concernment. Simon stared at her, slowly absorbing her words. She began to fret. *He spurned my invitation. God's oath, I will not be made a fool of once again by this man. He is positively infuriating!* She stood, a fire rising within. To her great surprise, Simon suddenly reached out and pulled her straight into his arms, wrapping her in his powerful embrace.

"My darling," he whispered.

Simon and Catherine walked arm in arm through the dappled shade in St. James Park. They stopped to sit on the banks of Duck Island, watching the pelicans cool themselves in the glittering water.

"I have so much to tell you, Simon," said Catherine, reaching into her portfolio. She withdrew her book and handed it to him, her eyes shining. "I have been published!" she exclaimed. "And, Ambrose has hired me to illustrate a book of architecture." Her excitement was contagious.

He laughed at her excitement as he examined the book, and then leafed through her architectural sketches. He turned to her, his eyes serious and sincere. "I am so very proud of you, Catherine. You have accomplished something very few actually do." Tears sprang to her eyes at the compliment. He grew serious. "I must ask. Miles?"

She looked troubled. "I could not marry a man who would desert us at a time of such peril," she said, simply. A pelican flapped its wings, unexpectedly splashing water upon them both. She laughed and wiped the droplets from her cheek. She stared out over the pond. "He has sailed to France," she said with finality. She turned to him, her mood brightening. "And you, sir? What news do you have to tell?"

He smiled. "I have been offered my own dissection room at the hospital to conduct my research…"

"Oh, Simon, I am so happy for you!" she broke in, excitedly.

"…and I am in need of an illustrator. You wouldn't happen to know anyone up to the task?" he teased.

Catherine blushed. "I believe, sir, I would."

Catherine looked up through the leaves of the massive plane trees. Memories of the trees by the fire pits and the nights they shared together flooded her thoughts. She grew silent, and then, as they sat on the grassy banks of the pond, she laid her head on his shoulder. Simon smiled, then gathered her into his arms and tenderly kissed her.

"I shall never let you go again."

CHAPTER 38

"AND ALL ENDED IN LOVE..."
-SAMUEL PEPYS

St. Bartholomew's Hospital
London, England
27 August 1666

Seven eager medical students stood with Father Hardwicke in a clump on a platform in the new dissection room, straining this way and that to watch as Simon carefully set a small, cloth-covered object upon the demonstration table. Catherine sat poised at her drawing desk next to the table. Before her lay several sheets of parchment papers and a selection of finely shaven leads. She took up one of the leads and readied herself to sketch. Simon removed the cloth.

"Gentlemen. The heart," said Simon. He turned his back and discreetly covered the deceased patient with generous linen sheetings. One student gasped, then stood, wavering on the platform in shock. He pulled a cotton cloth from his pocket and dabbed at his forehead. Turning a ghastly shade of green, he awkwardly twisted, then sank to his knees and collapsed to the ground in a sorrowful heap. Father Hardwicke looked down to the student on the floor. He briskly stepped over the young man and turned to his assistant, flicking his hand toward the doorway.

"Remove him."

The assistant nodded. He grasped the fallen student by the arms and dragged him out into the great hall. Simon stepped away from the table so that the rest of the students could all see. Father Hardwicke leaned in and nodded, very well pleased with his work, for he knew the research would further distinguish his hospital and, of course, help raise monies for the new East Wing of St. Bartholomew's, the Fr. Thomas J. Hardwicke Pavilion for the Infirmed. *He was thrilled beyond measure at that.*

Simon, himself, was pleased beyond measure by his dissection theater and even more pleased that Father Hardwicke was as good as his word, having not so much as batted an eye when Catherine's name was advanced as illustrator. Though the subjects were foreign to her at first, she had adapted to the work faster than he thought possible. She had even taken to the autopsies far easier than even he had the first time Simon saw one performed. Squeamish at first, she quickly got used to the peculiar surgical procedure.

During each session, Catherine sat ready at a drawing table lit from the side by a series of windows. Lanterns were kept illuminated upon a shelf above her table. When Simon lectured, the medical students stood on a platform on the opposite side of the room so that he and Catherine had plenty of room to work. And work she did, often late into the night with Simon, making good use of the time before the undertaker came. She willingly sketched anything he placed before her. She was as fascinated as he by the intricate system of veins and arteries that surrounding the heart and illustrated exactly what she saw with scientific precision. Simon had to laugh when he had compared her first finely detailed illustrations to his own clumsy sketches, so impressed by her skills was he.

Catherine laid down a few quick strokes. Next to her, tacked upon the wall, were eight more views of the heart. Simon watched an errant red curl fall loose as she worked intently over her table and smiled. *He could not believe his very good fortune.*

"And what, exactly, are you grinning at, Doctor?" asked Catherine, pausing from her work to tease.

"An extraordinary talent."

Catherine dropped her head, coyly. "I'm grateful for your kind words, sir."

"They're not meant to be kind," he grinned, recalling his words the day they met in the courtyard of the inn. *A lifetime ago.* He stood by her side, watching as her sketch unfolded before him and thought how very much had changed. An orderly approached Catherine and gestured toward the hallway. She set her sketch aside and looked to Simon and the medical students.

"Excuse me, please."

Catherine followed the orderly out of the dissection theater to find young boy with a messenger strap around his arm waiting for her. The boy handed her a note. Simon came into the hallway as she read it.

"Is everything all right?"

"The *HMS London* has docked. Simon, Charles is home."

Catherine stood with her hand nestled in the crook of Simon's arm, as the passengers, the crew and finally the officers and staff began to disembark from the *HMS Royal London,* now secured to its moorings. Simon laughed as she craned her neck over the crowd to get a glimpse of the sailors lining the decks of the massive sailing ship waving down to the cheering crowds anxiously awaiting their return. She playfully tried to wrench her hand away, but he pulled her close and wrapped his arms around her tight, unwilling to ever let go again.

"Have you seen him, yet?" asked an anxious Viola as she and the mayor joined them on the dock.

"He will be here soon enough, my dear," said the mayor, gently patting her hand as it rested in the crook of his elbow. He knew she was worried about how Charles would take the all of the changes that had occurred in his absence.

"He will be fine," he reassured her. "He is a strong lad."

"There he is!" cried Catherine, pointing to a young man waving down from the massive sailing ship, his now-shoulder length red hair glinting in the sunlight. Charles waved and then, squinting, looked down closer. She could see that he knew Lord Abbott was not there to meet the ship. Even from that great height, Catherine could see his shoulders fall. *He knew.* Charles disappeared from the railing. Catherine turned to Simon with tears in her eyes. She leaned her head on his broad chest, knowing how much Charles loved his father and how hard it would be to break the news. Simon tightened his arms around her.

"We will take care of him," he whispered.

As they waited through the endless line of disembarking passengers, Catherine marveled at the astounding changes that had occurred since Charles had been gone. After the death of Lord Abbott, and their broken engagement, Miles had indeed sailed to France. She, herself, had taken up residence in Bealeton House. She had been published and now she was actually being paid to illustrate a book of Simon's medical research. Aunt Viola had married the mayor in a quiet ceremony on New Years Eve. They too resided at Bealeton House and in her blissful, married state, Viola had even let Catherine add some warming touches to the mansion. Though Catherine missed her father terribly, she learned that she was far stronger than she ever thought possible. Catherine glanced down to her left hand, where a new, thin engagement band glittered in the sunlight. She stared at the ring for a moment, smiling softly. It had indeed been a strange, sad, wonderful year.

"Catherine! Over here!" Charles ducked and twisted through the swirling crowds as he ran down the gangplank. He dropped his kit and wrapped her in his arms. She hugged him tightly, then stepped back, astonished at changes in him. He was now taller than Simon, his voice was much lower and he was wearing unfamiliar clothing, having long since grown out of his youthful trappings. Viola reached up to hug him too, finally letting go when the mayor gently pulled her away. Charles turned back to Catherine.

"Father?" he whispered, with the barest trace of hope, though in his heart he knew the answer before she spoke.

Catherine dropped her head then looked up to him, her eyes filled with sorrow. He stood for a moment as the realization of his father's death washed over him. He leaned against a piling for support. Catherine reached for him. He caught her hands in his and saw the ring. Catherine followed his gaze and blushed.

"There is much to tell, she said, softly." Viola stepped between the two of them.

"And tell him everything, we shall, indeed," interceded Viola. "For now, however, I'm quite sure Charles would prefer a hot supper and a good night's sleep." Taking hold of Charles to her left and the mayor to her right, Viola, with her usual briskness, led them straight away from the crowded dockside.

As Catherine turned to follow, she felt a gentle tug on her arm. She hesitated. Simon drew her quietly back to his side, allowing the others to walk ahead toward Broad Street and the waiting carriage. Catherine looked at him, questioning. Smiling, he turned her toward the harbor and the sea that stretched far beyond them. They stood in silence, side-by-side, arm in arm as they watched the seagulls circling in the cool evening breeze that blew the ringlets from her hair clasp. Then, right there, amid the onrushing passengers, the shouting crews, the moneychangers and the charlatans, Simon tipped her chin up in his hands, stared into her steady blue-gray eyes and kissed her with all the tenderness he had kept locked inside for so long. An unexpected tear trickled down Catherine's cheek. He traced his thumb across the tear, his eyes searching with instant concern.

"What is it? Are you troubled?"

Simon's heart leapt to his throat as she turned from him, the pounding in his ears louder than the sails flapping overhead. Catherine stood, staring out at the whitecaps building in the distance. Closing her eyes, she had a sudden vision of the chestnut tree in full, vibrant bloom standing in a vast meadow of wildflowers. Her father stood below its billowing branches, his hand on the solid trunk. He was smiling. She opened her eyes and for the first time in a very long time, she felt utterly at peace. She turned to face the man standing beside her. The strong, dedicated man who, like her father, cared for others above all else. *The man who she knew loved her with all his heart.*

"I have never been happier in my entire life." In that moment, Simon's emotions were entirely laid bare. With sheer relief coursing through him, he swept her up into his arms, holding her tightly. The teeming dockside carnival swirled about them in brilliant explosions of color and sound. He vowed once more that he would never let her go.

Simon felt a tap on his shoulder. He looked down in surprise to see a rumpled young man standing before him, his eyes shining. He set Catherine to the ground as the boy removed his cap with a shy smile.

"Excusez-moi, monsieur. Où est le banquier?"

Simon looked confused. Catherine smiled at the boy and pointed toward the Lloyd's banking agents.

"Le banquier est juste là."

The boy laughed to himself, as he held tight to his battered valise. *"Merci, beaucoup, Madame! Merci!"* he cried. He waved his cap in a grateful salute then turned to make his way through the riotous crush, one more immigrant rushing headlong into a city teeming with infinite possibilities.

As a shimmering, golden glow began to spread across the harbor, Catherine turned back toward the sea to watch the sun fall below the horizon. She shivered in the early evening chill. Simon untied the lacings of his cloak and wrapped it tightly around her shoulders. She tilted her head up to him and smiled, her eyes crinkling with happiness. She laid her head gently upon his shoulder and together they turned toward home.

AUTHOR'S NOTES

The Boundary Stone is a historical fiction romance novel, loosely based upon the real life story of a town in England called Eyam. It is said that in 1665, a tailor carried a bolt of fabric infected with fleas to the village from the St. Bartholomew's Fair in London. When the tailor died two days later, the minister of Eyam convinced the Lord Mayor to quarantine the town in order to contain the infection, thus keeping the plague from spreading further into England. My imagination was captured by the noble intention of the people of Eyam and their incredible sacrifice for the good of others.

While more than 75% of the people of Eyam died of the plague, it is also true that at that same time, people were beginning to figure things out. Science was beginning to evolve from hearsay and myth to observation and logical thought. In 1660, the Royal Society was created at Gresham College in London. Chartered as "The Royal Society of London for Improving Natural Knowledge," the society served as a repository for specimens and observations of the natural world made by scientists and ordinary people alike for the scientific interpretation by the leading experts of the day. Medicine was also evolving from the practice of helping people die to learning how to cure them so they could live. Intelligent, thoughtful men and women helped bring about those evolutions in scientific thought, men and women who dared to push the boundaries of accepted wisdom. What if the right person with the right knowledge and the courage to try something different had been in Eyam during the plague, might the outcome have been different? *The Boundary Stone* is the fictional story of two such people during the plague of 1665. I hope you enjoyed it.

Gail